DETROIT PUBLIC LIBRARY
P9-AZW-010

THE SISTERHOOD OF BLACKBERRY CORNER

THE DIAL PRESS

ALSO BY ANDREA SMITH

FRIDAY NIGHTS AT HONEYBEE'S

THE SISTERHOOD OF BLACKBERRY CORNER

ANDREA SMITH

THE DIAL PRESS

THE SISTERHOOD OF BLACKBERRY CORNER
A Dial Press Book / May 2006

Published by The Dial Press
A Division of Random House, Inc.
New York, New York

Book design by Lynn Newmark

The Dial Press is a registered trademark of Random House, Inc., and the colophon is a trademark of Random House, Inc.

Library of Congress Cataloging-in-Publication Data

Smith, Andrea.
The sisterhood of Blackberry Corner / Andrea Smith.
p. cm.
ISBN-13: 978-0-385-33623-9
ISBN-10: 0-385-33623-3
1. African American women—South Carolina—Fiction. 2. African American churches—South Carolina—Fiction. 3. Foundlings—Fiction. 4. Abandoned children—Fiction. 5. Female Friendship—Fiction.
I. Title.
PS3619.M54 S57 2006
813.'6 22 2006040205

Printed in the United States of America
Published simultaneously in Canada

www.dialpress.com

10 9 8 7 6 5 4 3 2 1
BVG

For Beets & Burn
(Andrew & Barbara Smith)
So glad I'm your child.

PART I

ONE

Canaan Creek, 1985

From the back porch, Bonnie watched Thora Dean in the flowery bramble behind the house. In a wide straw hat, Thora plucked blackberries, each the size of a silver dollar, and set them in her basket. Over the years, the bramble had become one of Thora's favorite places. At the height of the season, the area was peaceful, fragrant, and the prickly shrubs that extended well into the woods were overcome with plump, dark berries.

"Thora," Bonnie called. "I'm fixin' to set breakfast on the table."

"I'll be along," she yelled back.

Bonnie could smell the impending rain. Like most quick showers during a South Carolina summer, the coming storm might be just enough to cool the day off. Bonnie entered the house and the screen door slapped shut behind her. She used a moist paper towel, tucked in the pocket of her housedress, to dab beads of sweat from her face. Sometimes she couldn't tell if it was the actual heat that made her stop and take a breath, or her own "private summer." Perhaps a bit of both. She lifted a platter of pancakes from the stove and laid it on the table set for two. Then Bonnie glanced at the wall clock above the sink. She decided to place an extra plate and coffee cup. Most mornings, Tally, the mailman, stopped in for a quick cup before he ended his run.

"Thora," Bonnie yelled out of the screen door.

"Damn it to hell," Thora hollered as she made her way across the back lawn. "I say I'm on my way, then I'm on my way!" She hooked the basket of berries on her forearm and took the porch steps one at a time. Her large chest, once the highlight of a voluptuous body, now seemed to drag her down, and when she entered the kitchen, she was slightly winded.

"You done made the pancakes already?" she asked.

"That's what I been tryin' to say," Bonnie replied. "I told you that."

"I told you so, I told you so! Girl, you startin' to sound like an old woman."

"That's 'cause I *am* an old woman... and I hate to tell you, dear..." Bonnie let the rest of her sentence dangle conspicuously in the air.

Thora hung her hat on the hook beside the door. A thin black ponytail trailed down her back and a few silvery hairs sprung from her temples. Thora's dark face was misted with sweat but her lipstick remained perfect. Even working in the bramble on a hot summer morning, Thora Dean refused to leave the house without at least applying a subtle coat of Positively Plum.

Thora quickly rinsed the berries in a colander, then dried her purple-stained hands on the dish towel. The two women sat, clasped hands across the table and bowed their heads while Thora said grace. Her mumbled devotion sounded like a familiar song, ending with "... our dear Father, amen."

"Wildflowers 'bout to take over the bushes out there," Thora said, pulling two pancakes onto her plate.

"I can think of worser things growing."

Thora stirred a bit of cream into her coffee. "Weeds, weeds, and mo' weeds," she grumbled. "Them damn Johnny Jump-ups fin to choke the life outta the blackberry roots."

"Why you so contrary this mo'nin'? You up again last night?"

Thora nodded. "Horace come to me."

Bonnie stopped pouring maple syrup and looked at her old friend.

"Somewhere 'round two A.M. there he was a-standing in the bathroom door. Standing there jes' like any other mo'nin'. He was holdin' one them big ole pipe wrenches and wearin' his smock like he was headin' fo' a job. All he said this time was, 'Need to lay that copper pipin', honey. Can't skimp on this one.' Then he left."

Bonnie looked at Thora curiously. "What in the world that mean?"

"Beats me."

Bonnie said, "He was a lot less talkative in this dream."

"Wadn't no damn dream, and you know it."

Bonnie tossed her hand. "You and all that foolishness. All I need right now is to start believin' in haints and things."

They heard a truck pull up outside, then a door slammed shut. Thora's eyes shot up to the wall clock, then she dabbed her mouth with a paper napkin. "Tally late again this mo'nin'," she said.

"Only twenty minutes."

"This time."

"How often do we git our mail late?" Bonnie always defended Tally when he was running behind on his deliveries. "Fo' fact, I cain't remember the man takin' mo' than a day two off in the six years he been deliverin' our mail."

"Five years," Thora corrected. "And Tally took plenty a days off. We jes' ain't got our mail 'til he come back."

"Well, he do alright fo' me."

Blackberry Corner was the last stop on his route and she recognized that Tally was one of only two mail carriers for the Canaan Creek Post Office, so he was responsible for seven miles' worth of mail deliveries every day. Sometimes when Bucky Elworth's arthritis acted up, Tally would take on the additional shift and deliver to the entire tri-county area of Pertwell, Manstone and Canaan Creek, affectionately called the "Three Sisters."

The gate squeaked open in the front yard.

"Hey there, Tally," Thora called out. "Hope you got my check."

"And my Spiegel catalogue," Bonnie put in.

"Seem like I had every catalogue the Lord ever made in my bag today." Tally's sack brushed the foyer walls. He slid it off his thick shoulder and set it by the kitchen door, then placed a bunch of letters into Thora's waiting hands. "It's still summer," he carped, "and here I got all these dern fall catalogues."

In the years that Tally had worked this route, the color of his uniform had changed from navy to light blue to khaki. His hat, once a boller, was now a stiff-rimmed cap. But one thing that never changed was that his uniform had always been too tight, causing his stomach to spill over his belt.

"Set on down and ha' yo'self some breakfast," Bonnie said.

"You know I ain't got no time to sit," Tally said, even as he shifted a couple of pancakes from the platter onto his waiting plate and eased himself into the chair across from Thora. "I'm doin' the Manstone run after this."

"Still takin' on extra shifts?" Bonnie asked.

"Sockin' my pennies away," he said. "Got my eye on a lil' piece a land out there in Taliliga."

"Taliliga," Bonnie said with surprise. She set a cup of hot coffee in front of him.

"Seven acres," Tally added. "Pretty land. And cheap as sin."

"'Course it's cheap," Thora put in. "Ain't nothin' in Taliliga but sticks and mosquitoes . . . and some of the countriest folk God ever made."

"Thora," Bonnie scolded.

"She ain't lyin', Bonnie," Tally said. "But, I'm sho' Columbus men said the same thing when they landed in the New World."

"You mean befo' they commenced to whuppin' on them po' Indians," Thora argued.

"Got to beat some eggs in order to make an omelet," he shot back.

Tally and Thora were always locking horns. And as much as Thora complained about the man, Bonnie was beginning to think that their wrangling was the highlight of Thora's day.

"So you plan on movin' into this new house by yo'self," Thora asked.

"Lessen you got some ideas," Tally said.

As usual, Thora ignored his foolery. She returned to sorting the mail and finally separated a mustard-colored, government-sealed envelope from the rest of the pack. Beneath it was a small white envelope with a handwritten address.

"My mama always said," Tally went on, "that it's bad luck fo' a single man to move into a house by hisself. Say the house swallow 'im up. Say it turn 'im into a man no woman can ever live wit'."

"Why you doin' it, then?" Thora asked.

"'Cause Mama's dead and I'm tired of livin' at Coreen's place. A man of fifty-such-in-such shouldn't be livin' at no roomin' house."

"You mean *sixty*-such-in-such," Thora mumbled. She took a pair of gold-framed glasses from her pocket and slipped them on, then tried to make out the return address on the back of the envelope.

"What you got there?" Bonnie asked.

"Just say, *'Bonnie Wilder, Canaan Creek, South Carolina.'*"

"Meant to mention that one, Bonnie," Tally said. "At the station, we calls it a Christmas letter. Like them letters addressed to *'Santa Claus, North Pole.'*"

Thora handed Bonnie the envelope and her glasses. She opened the seal and unfolded a letter written on plain white paper. Her eyes skimmed it quickly, a smile spreading across her face. "It's from one of our children."

"Gal or boy?" Thora asked.

"Gal named Augusta Randall," Bonnie answered. "She a grown woman now. They's *all* grown now."

"If that don't make me feel old," Thora mumbled.

Tally refilled his coffee cup at the stove. "Them kids must live all over the place."

"One boy," Bonnie started, "or should I say *man,* live right here in the Three Sisters. Work as a porter for the Penn-Eastern Railroad. Outta the blue, he come by one day jes' to say hello."

"And remember the letter we got from that gal live all the way in Barcelona, Spain," Thora said proudly. "Yep, she some kinda translator."

"Must be good to know when the babies grow up and do well," Tally said. "Lotta folk woulda look the other way. Woulda took them babies right on over to the county home."

"I don't know," Bonnie said modestly.

"Heroes," Tally insisted, "all two of you!"

"A few mo' than two," Thora put in.

"And I wouldn't call us no heroes," Bonnie said.

"Bonnie's right," Thora said. "'Cause anybody with the love of Jesus woulda done the same damn thing!"

Tally nodded. "So why'd y'all stop?"

Thora sipped her coffee. Bonnie looked over the top of her glasses. "There's a time fo' things to happen," she said thoughtfully, "and a time fo' things to end."

"What this Augusta Randall have to say?" Thora asked, trying to change the subject.

" '*Dear Miss Wilder,*' " she read, " '*I hope this letter finds you well and in God's favor . . .*' "

"Mean she hope you still alive," Thora said.

Bonnie went on reading. " '*You don't know me, as I've spent most of my life in New Jersey, but I was born in the Three Sisters. My family name was Porter.*' Augusta Porter," Bonnie said. "Y'all recollect any folks named Porter?"

"Maisy Porter," Thora answered. "Lived out by the Main Street. But she was a white woman."

" '*My mama's name was Evelyn and my daddy was called Dorsey. He died when I was just four and that's when Mama and I moved to New Jersey. I work as a schoolteacher now—I teach third grade in a town called Montclair.*' Ain't that nice," Bonnie said. " '*My husband, Joseph, is also a teacher at a college here, and we're about to have our first child.*' Lovely," Bonnie whispered almost to herself. " '*I wanted to thank you, Miss Bonnie. I've had a wonderful life and I know that it was you and the other ladies who started me on my way.*' "

"Heros," Tally insisted. "No, no, *sheros!*"

"You jes' crazy, Tally." Bonnie chuckled. Then she went on reading. " '*The second reason I'm writing is a bit more complicated.*' "

"Ain't it always," Tally grunted.

" '*My mama, Evelyn, went to her glory just a year ago. I can't tell you how painful her passing was for me. Now that she's gone, and now that I'm about to be a mama myself, I'm hoping to find out who my real mother is.*' "

"Lot of folks doin' that now," Tally said, wiping his mouth. "I see on that *Geraldo* show where all these people, young and old, is runnin' 'round tryin' to find out who they is and where they come from."

" '*I miscarried a child two years ago and the doctor says that I should stay off my feet, so I've had a lot of time to sit and wonder. I hope you don't mind if I call you . . . maybe you can tell me what you remember.*' Lord, I cain't recall what my name is sometimes," Bonnie said. "And ne'er a one of us ever kept no records."

"Maybe this gal oughta go on that *Geraldo* show," Tally joked. Thora rolled her eyes. "Geraldo don't play! He find folks whether they wanna be found or not!" Tally finished his coffee in one gulp. "Bonnie," he said, rising, "breakfast was delicious . . . as usual. Hate to eat and run . . ."

"Run?" Thora said. "All them pancakes you scoffed down, man, you be lucky if you can walk."

"Always a pleasure to see you too, Thora Dean," Tally said, lifting his sack. At the kitchen door, he turned back. "Say there, Thora . . ." he began.

"Umm-hmm," she replied without looking up from a Rich's catalogue.

"I hear-tell you like them picture shows . . ."

"I do," she replied.

Tally's sack knocked against the coatrack. "They's got a new one there at the Regal," he said. "*The Color Purple.*"

"Seen it."

He thought a second. "In Manstone, at the Grove is that new *Rocky* . . . *Rocky* number fo' . . . or maybe that's number five . . ."

"Seen it," she said. "And before you go on," she added, "I done seen every movie playin' in all the Three Sisters."

He rubbed the new growth on his chin. "Didn't know you had such an active social life," he said. "Well . . . y'all have a good day, then."

"You too, Tally." Bonnie shot Thora a threatening look, then she set Augusta's letter on the table and followed him out to the porch.

"She a hard nut to crack," Tally said.

"The hardest," Bonnie agreed. "But her shell ain't made a steel."

He nodded. "Hope that Augusta gal find her way."

"I'm sho' she will. Young people get somethin' in they head," Bonnie said, "and most times it's gone after a week or two."

"You right 'bout that," he replied. "Ain't like us old folks. Get somethin' in our head, we see it through. Yep, we see it through, all right."

Tally strode down the steps toward his truck.

"Got some mint jelly settin'," Bonnie called. "Come on by and pick up a couple a jars."

"I'll sho'ly do that. Lamb chops ain't the same wit'out yo' mint jelly."

Bonnie waited on the porch until she saw him drive through the gate. When she returned to the table, Thora was skimming Augusta's letter.

"Why you chop that man off at the knees like that?" Bonnie chided.

"I'm 'bout as interested in seein' Tally Benford as I am in gettin' a new crown on my tooth."

Bonnie piled the dirty cups. "Shame we cain't help that Augusta gal." She took the cups to the sink, then returned and piled the plates. "After all these years I cain't recall what baby went to who and where. I'm jes' surprised she the only somebody who ever ask 'bout her mama." Bonnie noticed that Thora had her lips pursed as she stared at the letter. Thora Dean rarely tucked her lips, for she hated getting lipstick on her teeth. "What is it?" Bonnie asked.

"I think she's the one."

"One what, honey?"

"*The* one."

Bonnie turned with the dishes still in her hands.

"This here girl is Lucinda's chile," Thora said.

Bonnie set the plates on the table and sank into the chair she'd just vacated. "Are you sho'?"

"Mentioned that name Dorsey," Thora said. "You 'member that fella—we thought Dorsey was his last name, but it was his first?"

Bonnie lowered her head.

"This is Lucinda's baby gal." Thora slipped her glasses off.

"Cain't be."

Thora shrugged. "What difference do it make? Lucinda prob'ly dead as a do'nail by now."

"Maybe." Bonnie thought she had moved past the pain. But hearing Lucinda's name still sent a cold shiver through her.

"Gal say she gon' call," Thora said. "You fixin' to tell her?"

"It wouldn't serve nobody to know they mama was somebody like Lucinda." Bonnie took the pile of dishes to the sink and dashed them with pink liquid from the plastic soap bottle, then switched on the tap. Bubbles rose in a thick cloud.

"Ain't it strange, though," Thora began.

Bonnie didn't answer.

"Outta all eleven children that came to us," Thora went on, "this gal, Lucinda's gal, is the *onliest* one who come back and asked."

"That's how life goes," Bonnie said.

"That all you gotta say?"

In the fifty years that they'd known each other, Thora Dean had never been one to hold her tongue, and old age seemed to make her even more direct. "Maybe you should talk to that gal. 'Cause you ain't never come to peace with this thing."

"I come to my own peace, thank you," Bonnie said, dismissing the subject.

Thora stood with her hands on her hips, a look of doubt on her face. "Need to think on what I'm sayin', Bonnie. It might help you as much as it help her." She must've sensed that Bonnie would take the subject no further, for with a final click of her teeth she moved toward the kitchen door. "I ain't studyin' on you neither," Thora said. "Fixin' to take me a nap. Oh, I know it ain't even noon and all that . . . but Horace's visit threw my sleep thang off." Thora paused at the kitchen door. "You hear me, Bonnie," she called.

"Yes."

"I don't think so. Girl, I don't think you hear a word I'm saying."

The kitchen door swung back and forth on its hinges behind Thora until it settled in place. Bonnie stood at the sink with the water running and stared through the short lace curtains and out toward the woods. She understood the need for this woman to find her mama. But there was a place in Bonnie's mind—in her heart—that she had stopped visiting years ago. Occasionally, she let herself drift back to recall the smell of talcum and the taste of sweet Carnation Milk. Such a simple time, yet so complicated. The best and the worst time of her life.

TWO

Canaan Creek, 1957

Naz Wilder reeled in his fishing line, then set down his pole in the mud. The chunk of chicken liver attached to his hook dangled atop the slate gray waters of Canaan Creek. He hoisted himself up from the sandy bank and squinted across the water. A bundle of yellow fluff lay tangled in the rising cattails and blades of swamp grass at least a hundred yards away.

"Scooter," he called, pointing toward the right bank. "You see that?"

"What the hell is it?" Scooter asked.

Naz pushed the brim of his baseball cap away from his forehead.

"Look like a bird done got tangled up in them weeds," Little Jr. offered.

"What kinda yellow bird you ever see in South Ca'lina, boy," said Little Sr. " 'Sides a damn chicken, I mean."

Canaan Creek rose east of Pertwell County. After nine miles, it reached Manstone just past the county of Canaan, then flowed east and emptied into Lake Marion, a tributary to the raging Santee. These waters were the lifeblood for the Three Sisters, known for the flathead catfish and an occasional rush of striped bass.

"Cast yo' girl on out there, Naz," Scooter said. "Maybe you can reel it in."

"Too far," Naz said. "Ain't got the line fo' that." He tilted his head. "Sun be full up soon. We'll check it out when the sun's up." Moments later, the four men had again settled into the task at hand.

"Say, Mr. Naz," Little Jr. started, "my daddy say you had an 11–4 league record. That fo' true?"

The men's eyes focused on Naz. Revisiting his baseball career was a highlight of their regular fishing trips. And this being Little Jr.'s first outting with the men, they could now speak of Naz's career from the beginning.

"Black Crackers went to the pennant that year," Scooter said. "Played the Chicago American Giants."

"Shiiit." Little Jr. smiled.

"Need to watch you' mouth, son," said Little Sr.

"Say you's a triple threat," the boy went on. "Pitcher, outfielder, first base."

"Pitcher mainly," Naz said.

"Hell yeah!" Scooter put in. "Ole Naz had a *stinkin'* sinking fastball."

"Mow you down," Little Sr. declared. "Ain't that right, Naz?"

"That's what they say," Naz said modestly.

"How many pennants?" the boy asked.

"One."

"How many seasons you play?"

"Hurt my leg durin' the third."

The awe in Little Jr.'s eyes melted. "Only three seasons?"

Naz looked out on the water.

"But they's the best seasons any man ever seen," Scooter added.

"Sorry 'bout that, Mr. Naz," Little Jr. said.

"You and me both," Naz mumbled. The conversation about his baseball career always began with triumph, but usually ended with talk of injury and pain. He set his line beside him and stood up on the bank again. The yellow fluff across the water remained hazy. Naz tugged his rubber boots up past his knees, and without another word, he started slowly into the water.

"What you fin to do, man?" Scooter asked.

Naz didn't answer. He simply waded in. The thighs of his denim trousers ballooned with creek water and his flannel shirttails floated behind him.

"You chasin' away all the fish, boy," Little Sr. yelled.

"Might as well call it a day, fellas," Scooter said as they watched the flatheads dart away from the banks.

The men's frustration reverberated through the still morning. In just moments, the cold creek began to warm to Naz's body and the spongy bottom gave way with each step. As a child, Naz used to think the water was so deep. He recalled the feeling of velvet from the creek's bottom against his bare foot before he spread his arms and let his body glide through the waters.

"What you see there, boy?" Scooter called out.

"Don't see no fish," Little Jr. yelled. "That's fo' damn sho'!"

The creek water reached Naz's waist. A slight mist floated toward him as he pushed through thick mesquite shrubs. Fuzzy cattails tickled him under the chin and bristled against the early-morning stubble on his face. The yellow bundle, stained by the creek's brown sediment, now looked like a mass of wet fuzz.

"What is it?" Scooter called.

Naz stopped. A blanket lay tangled in the pickerel weed. He lowered his eyes and felt his lips move in spontaneous prayer. He took a step closer, then reached out and pulled the blanket close to his chest. A lifeless baby girl, so still that she appeared to be asleep, lay in the quilt. Her dark brown body was exposed but almost unseen in the water. He took the bundle in his arms. Naz felt his body begin to shiver from grief and rage growing inside of him. Who was this child? How could this have happened? He suddenly thought that he and the others might have gone possum hunting in the woods, but for the toss of a coin this morning. Did the Lord put him here to find this small girl? Wading back to the opposite bank, he held the baby above his waist like a dismal offering. When he reached the other side, he dropped to his knees, chest heaving, and set the body on the soft bank of the creek.

The men were stricken with disbelief. No one said a word as they looked into the wet coverlet. They had all experienced death in some way. Little Sr. had lost his wife, Little Jr.'s mother, to rheumatic fever when Jr. was only five. Scooter's brother had succumbed to cancer just two years ago and Naz himself had lost his mother on the day he was born. But this was different. This was a baby and the act itself was surely planned and calculated.

Naz sat back on the bank, sucking air through his clenched teeth.

"This is evil," Scooter said. "Pure evil."

"Who in the world . . . ?" Little Jr. whispered.

"Cain't be nobody in the Three Sisters," his father returned. "Don't know nobody wicked enough." None of the men could look directly at the child. Their eyes skimmed her blanket, the grass, the edge of the water.

"How long you think she been out there?" Naz asked.

"Hard to say," Scooter answered. "A day, maybe two."

Little Jr. blurted, "But who in the world coulda done this?"

"That ole boy live down below," his father said soberly, "he an awful busy fella."

After a time, the men clasped hands and said a prayer over the child. Scooter removed his shirt and they wrapped the infant in the warm flannel, then piled into Naz's old pickup. Cold water sloshed in Naz's boots. A fishy stench from the creek water permeated the truck. All were silent as they drove off, bound for the sheriff's office, leaving idle four fishing lines swaying in the agitated waters of Canaan Creek.

Bonnie Wilder had rushed from home to join her husband at the Brethren of Good Faith Hall on Butler Street. Usually when she attended a meeting at the men's club, she was there only to bring a canteen of hot coffee, some sandwiches or a fruit cobbler. With the exception of social functions, like the annual picnic or dance, women weren't allowed. But all the ladies in Canaan Creek would be in the lodge room today. They were outraged that a helpless baby could have come to such an end.

Bonnie sat beside her husband and listened to the confusion swirl around her. She kept thinking how strange the lodge felt in this light of day. A peculiar shadow eclipsed the sunlight and hung over the rows of folding chairs and long maroon drapes covering the side walls. It tilted like a visor over the podium in the front of the room, where a dozen navy fezzes with hanging gold tassels sat like stiff dolls. Of course, the men had dispensed with putting them on since this was an emergency meeting. Even the pictures of each smiling lodge brother that hung above the podium seemed subdued, including a particular photo that the Brethren held dear. It was a shot of Naz in his Black Crackers baseball uniform, his arm around the shoulder of Satchel Paige.

Extra folding chairs were taken from behind the drapes and squeezed between the aisles to accommodate the crowd. There were some new faces, but mostly these were the people that Bonnie had known all her life. Nine of Naz's lodge brothers and their wives were here. Reverend and Mrs. Duncan sat beside Deputy Pine, who appeared even more somber than usual. Of course, most of Bonnie's neighbors had come out, like Bailey Dial and Kitty Wooten. Cal and Tilde Monroe sat up front with two of their four kids. Jenna Dixon and her newborn baby girl arrived with Maggie Kane and the Bell sisters: Birdie Bell, Bessie Bell, and Essie Bell. Most of the folks from the Piney Grove Baptist Church had come. Even Ruby-Pearl Yancy was here, and she rarely ventured out of her house. It seemed the only ones not in attendance were Horace and Thora Dean. They were away in Huntsville tending to Horace's sick mama. Bonnie missed her good friend, but if Thora were here now, she'd be weeping at even the thought of a baby being found like this.

The meeting was finally called to order by Trent Majors, president of the Brethren of Good Faith. Barely five foot and four, he had to whistle to get everyone's attention. Trent wore a white cap tilted backwards. He stood with his hands raised over his head until at last the room had settled down.

"This ain't no easy thing," Trent began. "And I cain't imagine what it was like fo' you fellas," he said, looking at Naz and the other fishermen, "finding that chile in the first place."

"Bad," Scooter called out. "Bad as hell."

"I know that's right," Trent replied. "We understand Sheriff Tucker will do all he can to find out what happened, but y'all know as good as me that this is *our* problem."

Bonnie understood. The Three Sisters, a mostly colored

section, just fifty miles from the city of Charleston, seemed completely separate from the surrounding counties of Hooley and Bostworth. The Three Sisters had its own police department, post office and town hall. With the exception of the sheriff, all of these government offices were run by colored citizens. Whatever problems arose were considered "colored problems." So, though the child was at the moment anonymous, it was everyone's child.

"I guess what I'm tryin' to say," Trent went on, "is that we need to keep our eyes open in our own community, 'cause if it was one of us who did this . . . this evil thing, then they is sho'ly fin to lose they mind."

Deputy Jimmy-Earl Pine stood alongside Trent. He wore an official look that said that although he was *of* the community, because he donned the khaki uniform, in this instance he was also separate from it. His narrow, clean-shaven face gleamed under his uniform cap. He stood with both hands in front of him and his fingers laced together. Deputy Pine rested one foot on top of a folding chair. "Sheriff's men are already out there," he began, "but like Trent say, we need to keep an eye out fo' each other. But y'all got to understand that it ain't fo' n'ere a soul in this room to take the law in they own hands . . . hear me good! If you find somethin', you come to me or the sheriff. You understand?"

A clamor started in the room. Some seemed to agree with Pine, while others looked a bit too disturbed to simply leave this to the authorities.

Tilde Monroe stood up. The beige flesh under her thick arms dangled as she waved them to quiet the room. "I'm fin to talk now," she yelled. The clatter continued. "I said I'm fin to talk!!" The room finally hushed. Tilde took a beat before she spoke, waiting until all eyes were looking her way. "This the saddest thing ever happened in the Three Sisters," she started.

Naz nodded in agreement.

"And we oughta pray fo' that chile."

"Yes," Bonnie said under her breath.

"Oughta pray fo' the chile's family," Tilde added.

"Amen," someone called.

"But you bein' way too kind, Jimmy-Earl," Tilde went on. "Ain't no baby jes' *wind up* floatin' in the creek. Somebody put her there . . . plain and simple!"

"You tell 'im, Tilde," Olive Lockie called.

"And whoever did this," Tilde went on, "oughta be put *under* the jail!"

The room roared their approval. Tilde basked in the attention. She was a large yellow woman and if she hadn't been in the same grade school as Bonnie, it would be impossible to tell how old she was. Bonnie was thirty-one and so was Tilde. But the two women looked to be a generation apart. While Bonnie stood tall and whisper thin, Tilde was short and rotund. Naz once joked that when Bonnie and Tilde stood side by side, the two women looked like the number 10.

"We talkin' 'bout a dead baby," Tilde yelled. "A helpless lil' baby . . ."

"Go 'head, girl," Jenna Dixon called.

She turned to Jimmy-Earl Pine. Her thick chest rose and fell. "I hear what you say 'bout not taking matters in our hands, but when an innocent chile die . . . we regular folk got to stand up and do somethin'." The crowd hollered. Bonnie clapped in agreement. After twelve years of marriage, she and Naz had yet to be blessed with a child. The idea that someone would throw away this precious life . . .

"What kinda woman would leave her baby to die?" Tilde went on.

"How we know it's a woman?" Delphine Peterson asked. "Ain't nothin' say it cain't be a man."

"We all heard 'bout this kinda thing befo'," Tilde snapped back. "Thank the Lord it ain't never happened here in the Three Sisters—but we done read 'bout these things in the papers. And I'm sad to say that it's *always* a woman! And I declare on my soul, this kinda woman gotta be the lowest of the low!" The crowd roared again.

Bonnie clutched her hands in her lap. She agreed with Tilde but couldn't help but wonder about the woman she described. Maybe the baby died at home from some unforeseen circumstance. Like Marva Sunday's child, some years ago, who had just stopped breathing. And Marva was only seventeen. Maybe this child had a young mama who panicked and put her baby in the creek. Somehow, this kind of explanation made the reality bearable. Because otherwise, what would drive a woman to such a thing? Was she sick in the head? Could life be that bad? Bonnie's eyes darted around the room, as if someone could read her thoughts. She suddenly felt guilty even considering the feelings of a person who might've killed their own child.

"When we leave here today," Trent said, "can we simply say we'll keep an eye out fo' each other?"

"And come to *me* if anybody find something," Deputy Pine put in.

"Brethren gon' stay behind this," Trent said to the deputy.

"So will the folks at Piney Grove," Reverend Duncan called.

"And you know the Ladies of the Blessed Harvest'll be on it," Tilde added.

The crowd began to break into small clusters. The Sistren of Financial Affairs drifted toward the window seats, while the Ladies of the Lord's Busy Hands moved to the back of the room. Bonnie looked around for Naz. He was surrounded by his lodge brothers. She could tell that the men were recounting the story again to Jimmy-Earl Pine, for she could see the pain in her husband's face as clear as it was on Scooter's and

Little Sr.'s. Across the room Bonnie could see the Ladies of the Blessed Harvest gathering, and she rose to join them.

At Naz's insistence, Bonnie had begun attending meetings with the Ladies of the Blessed Harvest about a year ago. Made up of the wives of the Brethren of Good Faith, the women mostly organized annual picnics, bake sales and church socials. Bonnie never subscribed to the notion that everyone in town had to be a part of some group or another. She was more than happy to spend her time puttering around the house or visiting with her good friend Thora, but Naz had pushed her to join. He thought she would benefit by getting involved in the community and also thought that she should get out of the house more.

"Jimmy-Earl say we should let the sheriff's office handle this," Delphine said, pushing her cat's-eye glasses on her nose.

"He also said to stay alert," Tilde insisted. "That mean we need to get involved! Need to look out fo' things!"

"But what in the world we lookin' fo'?" Olive Lockie asked.

In all of Tilde's righteous indignation, it seemed she hadn't even considered the question. "Well," she started, "I s'pose we can look fo' gals in the town that give birth and ain't got they babies no mo'."

"And if we find one," Olive inquired, "what we s'posed to do, Tilde? Beat her 'til she bleed?"

An uneasy chuckle erupted. Tilde locked her arms across her chest. "That ain't even funny, Olive."

"I say we leave this business to Pine," Miss Idella said. "That's what he say!"

Still, Tilde wanted to push the case. She had even proposed that the women go door to door, checking on pregnant women in the Three Sisters. It wasn't until the end of the meeting that the Ladies of the Blessed Harvest had convinced Tilde to leave this business to those in authority. And Bonnie was glad. She agreed that such grievous business should be left to Sheriff Tucker, Deputy Jimmy-Earl Pine and the good Lord above.

Insects gathered around the dim porch light. The summer heat had finally lifted and a slight breeze blew in from the creek. Bonnie raised her needlepoint canvas closer to her eyes to make out the design. She had detailed the mesh with colored pencil drawings of roses and lilies. After stitching the green border and most of the phrase in the center, she had only to complete the last few words, "evidence of things unseen."

Godfrey inched closer to her slippered foot. The old hound lifted his head from the floor of the porch and moaned lightly. Seconds later he slumped to the floor again. Even Godfrey had been depleted by the late August heat. His black and tan coat, which had lost its luster years ago, looked even dryer than usual. Now, like Bonnie, the dog enjoyed the tranquillity of a windswept twilight.

Bonnie suddenly heard a car down the road a distance away. Godfrey's eyes snapped open and his head shot up. Bonnie stood on the porch. Naz wouldn't return from his hunting trip until well after midnight. She looked out but didn't see a vehicle, and the sound of the car seemed to trail away. Probably someone who had wandered up too far, she thought. Godfrey's head slumped onto the porch and Bonnie settled back in her chair.

It was calm tonight. Two months after Naz's discovery in the creek, not a single story appeared in the news about the girl he'd found. Time had begun to dull the pain and anger in the Three Sisters. Naz and his lodge brothers had set off for their first hunting trip in over two months. The men had suspended all such sporting activities in respect of the child. And for Naz Wilder, or any of the Brethren, to put off hunting especially at the height of White Tail season was unheard of.

The night had quickly come and Bonnie tucked her needlepoint in the wicker sewing basket. She settled back just in time to catch a breeze. From her front porch, she could look down the road for miles, and now through the tunnel of willows she could see the last of daylight leaving Canaan Creek way off in the distance. Bonnie had always appreciated the remoteness of her home. It had been in her family for over eighty years, having been deeded to her great-great-grandfather, Alton Grayson, by a slave master named Mulcahy. Bonnie gave thanks every night that Alton had had the sense of mind to get everything in writing. More than a few families had lost their houses to the descendants of slave owners. That would never happen to Bonnie Grayson Wilder. This house was more important to her than anything, not only for its historical significance but also for its calm beauty. Large jack oaks spread their branches over the roof, webbing the windows through the morning sun and casting eerily human shadows in the twilight. The pale yellow porch that wrapped around the house like a silk band on a spring hat had been built, Bonnie knew, just for the lady of the house, Edna Mulcahy. On this very porch, Bonnie's daddy once told her, Edna Mulcahy had kept watch over the slave workers that tended the gardens.

Bonnie loved remembering the old stories, good and bad, that her father recounted when she was a child. But Daddy Wilbur, rest his soul, was known to enjoy spinning many a tall tale. He had spoken, for instance, about a small jack oak tree—one he called Edna, that, to this day, still stood close to the blackberry bushes spread out at the edge of the woods behind the house. Daddy Wilbur had said that Edna came alive, resembling a wild woman—hair flying every which way, eyes ablaze and skin the same color and texture as her bark. Supposedly, Edna appeared just to gobble up little bad boys (and boys only!) who tarried too long in the woods. Even at eight years old, Bonnie was suspicious of her daddy's story. It came right on the heels of her being bullied at school by a boy named Joshua Owens who had threatened to follow Bonnie home and beat her up.

Then there was Daddy Wilbur's story about the path in the back of the house that went on for miles and stopped at the waters of Canaan Creek. The clearing was said to have started as a footpath and a tiny part of the Underground Railroad. Like with all of Daddy Wilbur's stories, Bonnie wasn't quite sure of how true it was. But true or not, this one seemed to be a part of Canaan Creek legend. So much so that a tour company from Charleston had asked Bonnie's permission to bring a group out on the weekends to see the path. Having one of the oldest homes in the state of South Carolina and also a husband who was a former Negro League player made it a double attraction. But Bonnie and Naz, being the private people they were, declined the offer.

All at once Bonnie heard a rattling in the bushes just past the porch. Godfrey's growl quickly turned to a bark as he leapt to his feet and dashed down the steps. Bonnie stood at the top of the stairs, her bare arms wrapped across her chest as she scanned the front yard. She would hate to have to fire the shotgun again, but at least it scared off the wild animals. The one and only time she'd ever taken a shot, a coyote had ventured toward the house. The impact had forced her three feet back and flat on her butt.

Godfrey's bark had turned to a howl. Bonnie grabbed a flashlight from the milk bin and stuffed it into her dress pocket, then took the shotgun from inside the screen door. She could hear Godfrey just down the cobblestone walkway and right outside the gate. Bonnie stopped and took a deep breath. She cocked the rifle and aimed out toward the road.

"Who's there?" she called.

No one answered.

"Best show yo'self," she commanded.

"Don't you shoot me!"

Bonnie relaxed her aim. "Thora?"

"And you get on 'way from me, Godfrey," Thora scolded.

Bonnie lowered the gun. She clicked on the flashlight. Thora Dean hobbled up the cobblestone walk on white, spike-heeled shoes. She stopped to kick at Godfrey, who circled her legs. "Git gone, ole dawg," she yelled. "Don'tcha be tearin' my stockin's!" Her blue pillbox hat had fallen toward her face, shaking a few hairs loose from a perfect French twist. A white patent-leather pocketbook was slung over one shoulder.

"What the devil you doing out there?" Bonnie asked.

"Damn blackberries . . ." Thora fussed, ". . . gittin' all over my new pumps." She stopped to scrape the berry pulp from her white heel with a tissue. As she bent over, her heavy breasts threatened to pull her to the ground. "And that Horace," she went on, "say he didn't wanna make that turn on Blackberry Corner. Tole me it was still light enough to git out and walk the rest of the way."

"Well, boo fo' Horace Dean." Bonnie hugged her friend tight, enjoying Thora's favorite scent of fresh gardenias. The woman was a vision in a turquoise dress that cinched her small waist so that it looked even tinier than it was.

Arm in arm, the two women walked toward the house. "You know Horace headed straight fo' the lodge," Thora said.

"I know he did. But he ain't gon' find Naz there. Some of the fellas went hunting this mo'nin'." Bonnie stopped in the middle of the path to embrace her friend again. "I have missed you, Thora," she said. "Ain't had a soul to talk to in weeks... except Tilde and those."

"That mean you ain't had *nobody*!" Thora replied. "And, girl, I missed you too. 'Specially havin' to stay all that time wit' that damn Mama Dean." Thora took a seat in one of the rockers on the porch and hung her purse from the armrest. Bonnie knew that Thora Dean had just begun to talk. And when Thora Dean got to gabbing, there could be no end to the conversation. "I'm so happy to be back... 'cause Lord knows if I'da spent *one* mo' day in the house with Horace mama, I'da had to kill that old woman."

"No!"

"Kill her dead! She a contrary ole bitch."

"Thora!" Bonnie laughed.

"I ain't even lyin'," Thora insisted. "The woman cain't hardly talk since the heart attack, but don't you know, she found a way to cuss me."

"No, she didn't either."

"Went on fo' weeks 'bout how I cain't cook, cain't clean, talk too loud, drink too much, wear too much makeup."

Bonnie had to bow her head on the makeup claim. She had known Thora since they were children and now, both in their thirties, she couldn't recall seeing her friend without her face fully made up. Some folks in church called her "kewpie doll" and said that her makeup looked like "war paint." Those were the people who didn't know her heart.

"Talkin' 'bout how I spend all Horace money on clothes."

"What Horace say?" Bonnie asked.

"Not a *got*damn thing! I love that man, Bonnie, Lord knows I do, but he jes' as weak as water when it come to his mama. She got them apron strings wrapped 'round his damn neck, let me tell ya! Oh, honey," she said on a heavy breath, "I'm so happy to be back!" Thora slipped off her hat and set it on top of Bonnie's sewing basket. "And ha' mercy," Thora's tone quickly changed, "but what's been goin' on 'round here?! I 'clare, I leave town fo' a couple months and things go straight to hell."

"You heard 'bout the chile?" Bonnie asked.

"It made the local paper all the way in Huntsville," she said. "Nearly lost my breakfast when I read that."

The uproar of finding the baby girl had died down in Canaan Creek, but this was still news for Thora.

"That kinda thing *never* happen in the Three Sisters," Thora went on. "Had to be somebody from outta town."

"I thought that too," Bonnie said. "Pine still don't know much. But I did hear, just this past week, that the po' thing did drown there in the water. So that mean..."

"Sweet Lord," Thora said. She sighed deeply. "Such a tragedy. A cryin', cryin' shame." Then she turned to Bonnie. "Befo' we go on with this subject..."

"I know," Bonnie agreed.

"Well, don't jes' sit there," Thora said. "Girl, get to steppin'."

Bonnie dashed into the house and reached under the sink to find a bottle of Naz's homemade blackberry wine. She put it on a wicker tray with two floral-bordered teacups and carried the tray outside.

Thora pulled the stubby cork from the bottle and poured a tiny bit over the porch railing into the grass below. "To the ancestors," Thora said ceremoniously.

"The ancestors indeed," Bonnie repeated. "And by the way, we gon' have to stop po'ing wine over the railin'. A libation is fine and dandy, but them fire ants 'bout to take over the yard."

"I know that's right," Thora said, waving away a fly with her red-tipped fingers.

Bonnie half filled both cups.

"Best po' a lil' mo' in mine," Thora said. "Horace find the club empty, he'll be here soon enough."

The two women settled back, sipping as daintily as if the cups contained hot tea.

"Shoulda been at the meeting they had at the lodge," Bonnie said.

"Sad?"

Bonnie nodded. "Folks come from all over the Three Sisters—a few from as far as Hooley and Taliliga. And, of course, there was yo' friend Tilde Monroe."

"*My* friend." Thora laughed. "Sound like you must be drunk already."

"The woman took charge like she always do," Bonnie said.

Thora slid a pack of cigarettes from her purse. "And of course you agreed wit' her."

"I don't agree wit' everything Tilde say . . ."

"Maybe not," Thora said, lighting her cigarette, "but you sho'ly wouldn't say nothin' 'gainst her. And that go fo' all them Harvest Club biddies."

"I don't like Tilde's ways most times," Bonnie acknowledged, "but I agreed that we need to find out what happened to that chile."

"We all agree 'bout that, Bonnie. But that don't mean that Tilde Monroe got to always have the final say! I 'clare, that woman's mouth is actually outgrowin' her big, fat ass."

The sound of their laughter echoed in the night. Bonnie realized that she hadn't laughed in too long. The Wilder house was usually filled with good spirit, but after finding the child, even Naz seemed more withdrawn than usual. But leave it to Thora Dean to lighten the mood. And the more blackberry wine they drank, the more animated they became.

"Speakin' of babies, Bonnie Wilder . . ." Thora reached over and patted Bonnie's flat stomach. "Anything happenin' down there?"

"Huntsville or no," she said, "I'da called you straightaway if there was news."

"Aw, honey," Thora said sadly.

"'Sides, I ain't even thinkin' 'bout it no mo'."

"You's a lie!"

"I ain't," Bonnie insisted. "A thirty-one-year-old woman ain't s'posed to be thinkin' 'bout havin' no babies."

"Molly Benson had a chile when she was forty," Thora started. "Laura Spence had her *first* at thirty-seven. Not to mention that woman live in Pertwell and still shootin' 'em out at damn near fifty. So don't you start that mess wit' me."

Over the years, the older women in church had said special prayers for Bonnie and Naz. They brought remedies for infertility, like a leather pouch filled with quartz crystal, chrysoprase and adventurine, which Bonnie was to wear around her neck when she and Naz "did it." She was made to sprinkle rosemary under her bed and rub the stomach of every pregnant woman in the Piney Grove church. Bonnie knew these old Southern antidotes didn't mean much, but after a while, she was willing to try anything to get pregnant. Naz wanted no part of the "old lady cures," especially when they suggested that he piss into a red ant's nest for virility. But twelve years into their marriage, the elders were resigned to the fact that this was indeed "the Lord's will." Perhaps not all trees were meant to bear fruit.

"I still say you should at least consider adopting one of them kids from the county home," Thora said, refilling Bonnie's cup and then her own.

"Naz ain't thinkin' 'bout raisin' another man's chile. No way, no how."

"But Naz was adopted himself," Thora countered. "What the hell kinda sense that make?"

Bonnie could feel a headache creeping around her temples. She wasn't sure if it was the wine or the subject matter that had brought it on. Naz had grown up in a home with three other foster brothers. He loved his foster mother, Ida, but his brothers were, as Naz put it, "deviants, all three of 'em." And he insisted that their behavior came right through their blood. Bonnie never did buy into the notion that babies came into the world with evil genes, but Naz was convinced. Though he was open to the idea of having children, they had to be born to him and Bonnie only. He wasn't willing to take a chance with a "state issued" child.

"We ain't got to think about you adoptin' kids no-way," Thora said. "Doctor ain't found ne'er a thing wrong with you, and nuthin' wrong with Naz. So that say to me," Thora reasoned, "that y'all ain't doin' it right."

Bonnie could tell that Thora was already getting a little tipsy from the wine, for her conversation was even more candid than usual. "Y'all need some fire," Thora insisted. "Hot fire! Ever'body know that Naz love you as much as any man could. But you ain't no Virgin Mary and you ain't no damn missionary."

Since they were teenagers, Bonnie and Thora had confided in each other about every aspect of their lives. Times like this, Bonnie often regretted having revealed so many intimate details.

"One thing I can say 'bout my Horace," Thora prattled on, "is that he ain't 'fraid of no heat."

"He afraid of his mama, though," Bonnie threw in.

Thora's eyes squinted. "Now, you ain't had to say that."

"Look," Bonnie said apologetically, "Naz ain't 'fraid of no

passion either. We got passion. It's just that... Naz know I'm from the old school when it come to those kinda things."

"You ain't so old-fashion." Thora smiled.

"Don't start with me, woman."

"I remember the day when you tole me how you would love to mount ole Naz like a racehorse and—"

Bonnie drowned her out with an embarrassed squeal. "I ain't never, *ever* said such a thing in my life."

"Well, you ain't said it exactly like that." Thora chuckled.

"I ain't said *nothin'* like that."

Bonnie could feel her own head beginning to lighten. She loved the sensation of the wind touched by the edge of fall and the scent of Thora Dean's perfume. And though she hated to admit it, she enjoyed talking this freely.

"You know jes' what I'm talkin' 'bout," Thora accused. "We was settin' right here on this porch when you turn to me and say, 'Thora—' "

"Joshua fit the battle of Jericho..." Bonnie sang out loud.

Thora yelled over Bonnie's singing. "Say *you* wanna be the one on top fo' once in yo' life."

"Joshua fit the battle of Jericho and the walls come tumblin' down..."

"You can drown me out if you want to, Bonnie Wilder." Thora laughed.

"Straight up the wall of Jericho..."

"I remember," Thora said, wagging her finger playfully, "and so do you!"

"Well, if I did say it," Bonnie conceded, "then I musta been drunker than I am now."

"Liquor speak the truth," Thora insisted. "And if that's what you want from yo' man... girl, go'n and ask fo' it! Grab Naz and have yo' way."

"I cain't do that."

"Damn sho' can," Thora insisted. "Ain't that why you fell in love with him in the first place? Say you could be yo'self with him. Say he was the most exciting man you ever met."

"He still is."

"All I'm sayin', sweetheart, is that you need to tell Naz what you want! I bet he'd love it! And you never know what might come from that passion."

The wine softened the edges of the trees and the light from distant click beetles looked like tiny flashbulbs in the dark yard. Bonnie and Thora sat in a peaceful silence. Bonnie wondered if her longing to have a baby *did* quench her passion. She loved loving her husband but if the truth be told, she couldn't quite feel him anymore. She could only feel the possibility of a child. Even when Naz touched her in that special place, she reacted more from habit than arousal, so that sex, once so real and uncontrived, had become more of a performance. Still, Naz never complained. His kisses were filled with hunger, his body with longing. But perhaps his performance was as mechanical as hers. Then again, he *did* get to that moment of pleasure, which for Bonnie was the most important part of the act: his pleasure, his seed. She'd never let up from wanting a child, but perhaps, if only for Naz's sake, she would add just a bit more heat.

Thora was pouring the last of the wine between them when a black Lincoln pulled through the gate.

"Damn it to hell," Thora mumbled. "Ain't finished our wine."

Horace Dean got out of the car and walked to the porch. He removed his cap and the top of his balding head was as dark and shiny as an eight ball. Always so neatly groomed, his thin mustache looked like it was drawn above his top lip.

"Hey there, Bonnie." He bent in to kiss her. She detected a hint of Old Spice.

"Welcome back, stranger," Bonnie replied.

"Where that husband of your'n?"

"Went out hunting early this mo'nin'. Him, Coates, Scooter, Little . . ."

"No wonder the club empty," Horace said. He set his cap on Thora's head and she flipped it off quickly.

"Man, you gon' muss my hair," she snapped.

"Come on, woman," he said, picking up his hat. "Let's us get a move-on."

"I need to finish my tea first," Thora said, taking another swallow.

"Tea?" Horace laughed. "I'm gon' tell Naz how the Sistren of the Blackberry Wine been at it again."

"What do you mean to suggest, Horace Dean?" Bonnie was trying to appear sober.

"Y'all ain't doin' all that cacklin' 'cause of no sassafras . . . that I know." He pulled his wife from the rocker and swatted her on the behind. Thora giggled. "That's alright wit' me, though," Horace said. " 'Cause Thora come home all ready fo' her man. Ain't that right, baby?"

"Will you hush yo'self?" Thora whispered. But despite her protest, Bonnie noticed that she headed for the car as quickly as he did. "See you tomorrow, honey-bunny," she called to Bonnie as she slipped into the front seat. "I'll call you befo' we go to the Big Buy."

"Okay, sugar," Bonnie replied. She could hear Horace murmur something and then Thora's laughter as they drove away.

It was past three A.M. when Naz's truck pulled into the yard. Bonnie heard Godfrey's bark and woke instantly. She looked from the bedroom window as Naz pulled around to the back of the house. With the truck lights on, he untied a lifeless deer from the bed of his pickup and dragged it toward the shed. Godfrey rushed out of the dog door, panting excitedly and zigzagged around Naz's large boots as he struggled to haul the dead weight.

"Get on, Godfrey!" he ordered.

Bonnie thought about going out to the shed, but she hated to see the gutted carcass strung up over the center beam and left to bleed into a trough below. She slipped on her robe and went into the kitchen, where she poured a tall glass of ice water, always the first thing Naz wanted when he got home. Bonnie enjoyed tending to her husband after one of his trips. Though she fussed and complained about how bad he smelled, she secretly loved waking early on the morning of his return, helping him bathe and listening to him talk about his trip.

She sat in the kitchen window waiting. After a while he'd appear in the door of the shed, his wide shoulders filling the entire frame. Naz's strength, his stature, had always been exciting to Bonnie. Thirteen years ago, it was this same strong cut of a man that so struck her when he ran out onto the baseball field in Ponce de Leon Park.

Bonnie's father, Wilbur Grayson, had traveled as far west as Texas and had even gone east of Virginia to see teams play in the Southern Negro League. Bonnie never thought much about baseball when her mother, Eleanor, was alive. Wilbur had taken his weekend junkets, while Bonnie and Eleanor spent the days baking, sewing or just talking. As a child Bonnie could talk to Ellie Grayson about most anything. At age ten surely it was nothing more than about school or maybe a boy or two that might've caught her fancy. And her mother always listened with patience and a tiny smile. A smile that Bonnie knew revealed how proud she was of her daughter. But Bonnie's world was suddenly devastated when Ellie Grayson died of influenza. Bonnie was only twelve. Over the years, she struggled to hold on to all that she could remember about her mother. But most of her recollections became like out-of-focus snapshots. Except that Bonnie recalled her mother's laughter, high-pitched and unbridled, the way Ellie smelled, like warm yellow cake, and the way she gently plaited Bonnie's hair in two flat, shiny braids.

After Eleanor's death, Wilbur insisted on taking Bonnie to the ball games when baseball season arrived. Several ladies from the Piney Grove church knew that a ballpark was hardly the place for a young girl, but only occasionally did Wilbur agree to leave his daughter behind to play dolls with Jersa Clayton's girl, Thora, or Minnie Maybry's daughter, Diane. Wilbur wanted to share his passion with his only child. So, Bonnie sat in the ballparks, watching the people watching the game. For her, this was more interesting than baseball itself. She ate peanuts, drank pop and measured the inches between the edge of the bleacher and the tip of one Mary Jane shoe. Every once in a while when her father rose to cheer, she'd pay attention to the game, but all Bonnie saw were men running around the field or sliding toward a burlap sack in a cloud of red dust. On those exciting plays, the thrill of baseball began to get to her. After a while, Bonnie started to understand how the game worked. By the time she was seventeen, she knew the players and their stats as well as any boy her age. But it wasn't until an afternoon at Ponce de Leon Park in Georgia that her real love for the game began.

The Atlanta Black Crackers, one of Wilbur's favorite teams, were being slaughtered by the Birmingham Black Barons. Then the Atlanta team sent out a pitcher that most hadn't seen before.

"That's him, Bonnie," Wilbur said excitedly. "That boy grew up in the next county over from us. Raised right there in the Three Sisters, sho' nuff!"

Bonnie had heard about this Nazareth Wilder, born in

Pertwell, though he had only pitched for the Black Crackers for a season. Bonnie had seen grainy pictures of the young man in the paper more than once, but this was the first time she'd actually get to see him play.

"Strike 'im out, Naz," someone screamed.

"Come on wit' it, boy," her father called.

Six foot and four, Naz Wilder was tall enough to command the blue sky as his backdrop. His chest was like a wall and his shoulders like two strong shelves, but what impressed Bonnie most was that he played an amazing game. Naz Wilder had dominated that season. Sadly, that was the last time. On the first game of his third season, Avery Romell of the Nashville Elite Giants hit a line drive straight at the pitcher's mound. It had all happened so fast. Avery snapped the ball and took off running. It wasn't until he got to second base that Bonnie realized Naz had toppled over and hit the ground. The ball had caught him in the left leg, shattering his kneecap.

Naz finally came out of the shed. He turned off the truck lights and met Bonnie on the back porch.

"What you get?" she asked, handing him the glass of ice water.

"Small buck. Old, though," he said after taking a drink. "Meat prob'ly be tough." Red mud that was crusted around his fingers mixed with the sweat from the glass. Naz offered her a swallow.

"Oh, no," she laughed.

"Why?"

" 'Cause you smell like a polecat." Bonnie grinned.

"You know you love me like this." Naz planted a wet kiss on her lips. Bonnie shrank from the gaminess and the spots of blood on his clothes.

"Now I got to bathe too," she accused.

"We'll do it together."

"I'd rather bathe with that buck in the shed," she laughed.

Naz sat in the porch rocker and Godfrey rushed to sit at his feet. Bonnie moved behind his chair and gently kneaded his shoulders. He welcomed her hands as she smoothed the soft wave that swirled in the crown of his close-cut hair.

"Ain't made no mo' discoveries, I hope," she asked.

"Thank the Lord, no," he said. "And Jimmy-Earl, he come along with us on the hunt."

"Anything new on the chile?"

Naz shook his head no. "Ain't found nothin', ain't found nobody."

"Dear Father," she whispered.

Naz finished the water and held out the glass for Bonnie to refill. "Pine say it's most prob'ly some young gal that left that chile," he called as she went into the kitchen. "And he don't think it was nobody from 'round here."

"Why?"

"Somebody woulda knowed something by now. Sheriff's office think maybe a gal come from another county. Mississippi, Georgia, even."

Bonnie quickly rinsed the glass and refilled it. When she came back out, Naz handed her a tiny brown bag. Whenever he returned from his trip, he always brought Bonnie a gift. Usually something small, but enough to say that he'd been thinking about her. She opened the sack and pulled out a kitchen magnet shaped like a daisy.

"I'm gon' have a whole set of these befo' the year is out," she said, kissing the top of his head. Bonnie was happy to continue rubbing his shoulders, when Naz stood up.

"I know you ain't 'bout to walk into my house with them filthy clothes," she scolded.

"Damn it, Bonnie."

"And you need to take them boots off."

Naz muttered the whole time, but like an obedient child he sat down and unlaced the muddy shoes. She lifted each one like a dead skunk and heaved it over the railing. Then Bonnie went in and ran a hot bath. She threw in eucalyptus soap with a scent so strong it made her eyes water.

He walked into the bathroom buck naked and slowly lowered himself into the sudsy water. His body barely fit into the tub until he propped his feet on either side. Time was, the sight of Naz naked made Bonnie stop and take a breath. Now she could only regard his privates (which used to make her blush) as exactly what God had intended them for: procreation. She sighed in frustration. Why was Thora always right? Bonnie's fixation on having a child had cooled her love life. Twelve years ago when she finally met Naz Wilder, face-to-face, Bonnie thought that he was the most beautiful man that she had ever laid eyes on. But so did every other single woman in the Three Sisters. She recalled when Archie McCoy, pastor from the New Hope Baptist Church in Pertwell, had visited Piney Grove. The congregation looked forward to his arrival, and not just because of Reverend McCoy's enigmatic presence, but because Naz Wilder, a deacon in his church, would surely be one of the entourage accompanying the reverend on his visit.

That morning ladies in the congregation, married or no, were decked out in finery usually reserved for weddings or Easter Sundays. Bonnie, herself, wore her favorite green linen dress with a scoop neck and two ties that gathered on her shoulders. Her hair, modest and short, was swept from her face and flipped in the back. At eighteen, Bonnie liked the way she looked. Surely she wasn't the prettiest girl at Piney Grove—that distinction went to Edris Collins, who everyone claimed looked like Lena Horne. Certainly Bonnie wasn't the most glamorous—hands down that award went to Thora Dean (then Thora Clayton). But Bonnie had confidence in what her father had called a "quiet beauty." When she looked in the mirror, Bonnie saw her mother's dark eyes and fleshy lips. But she also saw her daddy's slightly wide nose and strong square chin. Bonnie had no hopes of actually talking to Naz Wilder... she would be too shy... but perhaps she'd get to see him up close and maybe even shake his hand.

The seats were so packed that Bonnie and her father couldn't sit in their normal pew, second from the front. They inched their way down the aisle as the church quickly filled in the middle and back.

"Ain't seen half these people at service befo'," Wilbur had complained. "Now they show up and take God-fearin' folks' place. Cryin' damn shame."

"Don't cuss in the church, Daddy," Bonnie whispered as she straightened the collar over his tie.

Wilbur's brow remained creased for most of Reverend McCoy's service. She knew that her father was excited at having Naz Wilder at Piney Grove, but he hated sitting so far in the back. Bonnie understood his frustration. Two of the Bell sisters, who only attended church on Christmas, sat right up front. Larney Hayes, who usually made her husband come to church by himself, was sitting right beside him today. Mrs. Simpkins, who complained that her arthritis made her too crippled to walk, looked as strong as ever. And more surprising was that Thora, who always arrived late, got there early and sat all puffed and powdered in the pew right behind Reverend McCoy's contingent.

Bonnie could only glimpse Naz Wilder in the first pew. He set his cane in the aisle and his leg, obviously braced under his pants, remained extended straight out in front of him. Though he looked reserved, Bonnie could feel his power even from the back of the church. Funny that with all the hubbub of his presence, the man appeared calm, almost shy. He didn't seem flamboyant and certainly didn't flaunt his good looks or his stature.

When the service ended, Wilbur was the first to hurry down to the church basement, where the Ladies' Welcoming Committee had set up four long picnic tables with white cloths and paper plates. The scent of buttermilk biscuits and fried chicken would usually make Bonnie ravenous after so long a service, but the thought that Naz Wilder might soon be sitting at her same table gave her a jittery stomach. She could see Wilbur trying to figure at where Naz might sit. The answer was easy: this table had most of the good food on it, including the side of roast beef and Mary Hartland's sought-after potato salad.

Wilbur sat down near the middle of the table and pulled Bonnie over. Moments later, heavy feet rumbled down the basement stairs. Bonnie felt her heartbeat quicken but relaxed a bit when Reverends Duncan and McCoy, their wives, and several deacons flooded the room. Then Naz appeared, flanked by two of the Peterson boys and more than a few ladies from their congregation. Bonnie had to take a breath at the sight of the man this close. His shoulders were wide and he was so tall that he had to bow his head to keep it from brushing the low ceiling.

Thora gestured for Bonnie to save the seat beside her as Naz and the reverend sat at Bonnie's table. But by the time Thora got there, it was already full. Thora simply took a chair from another table and squeezed in beside her friend. After several blessings by every holy man in the room, the meal finally began. And as expected, the men talked baseball while the women listened. Most seemed content just sitting in Naz's presence.

"That boy Edgar Buyers hit 369," Deacon Jenkins said.

"Three *seventy*-nine," Reverend McCoy declared.

"They're both wrong," Bonnie whispered to Thora. "It was 389."

"Lordy, gal," Thora giggled. "How yo' mind hold all that mess?"

Deacon Jenkins went on, "I know it was 369, 'cause that year..."

"Three *seventy*-nine," Reverend McCoy cut in.

Deacon Jenkins said, "I might not know Scriptures like I should, but I know me some baseball. And that there was 369, sho' nuff."

"It was 389," Thora put in.

Reverend Sunday stopped chewing. "What you say, woman?" he asked.

"Bonnie here say it was 389," Thora said.

Naz looked at Thora. She seemed thrilled by the attention.

"Bonnie?" Naz asked.

Thora grabbed Bonnie's arm and raised it up. Bonnie felt so shy with Naz's eyes on her that she wanted to crawl under the table.

"Ain't too many people know it like that," Naz said. "'Specially ladies."

"I guess that's my fault," Wilbur admitted. "I raised Bonnie on my own after her mama passed."

"And you did a fine job," Mrs. Reverend Sunday added.

Wilbur's dark face softened. "Thank you, ma'am," he said. Bonnie nodded at the reverend's wife. "But I have to admit," Wilbur went on, "that I dragged this gal from pillar to post to see all kinds of games."

"Daddy," Bonnie whispered, trying to stop him from talking. She was already as embarrassed as she could be.

"And sometimes," Wilbur went on, "she learn things what only mens should know."

"Sho'ly don't look like a man," Naz said respectfully. He must have sensed how embarrassed Bonnie was, for he felt the need to explain. "Jes' that... well, most ladies that can recite baseball stats..."—he stuttered a bit—"well... they got mo' hair on they arms than me."

The room laughed.

"You a mess, Naz," Thora said, batting her lashes.

"May I ask yo' daughter a question, sir?" Naz said to Wilbur.

"Ask Bonnie whatever you want."

Bonnie felt her heart would burst. She was mortified at the attention, but at the same time, exhilarated.

"Befo' I ask," Naz said to Bonnie, "you got to promise me one thing."

"Sir?" Bonnie said.

"Aw, now, gal," Naz moaned, "please don't call me sir. Yo' daddy... he's a sir... I'm jes plain old Naz."

All at once it hit Bonnie that Naz Wilder was actually talking to her. He was looking at her, smiling that amazing smile that she had seen more than once in the local papers.

"What I got to promise?" she asked softly.

A few men laughed.

"You got to promise to tell me the truth," Naz said.

"Bonnie is honest as the day is long," Wilbur insisted.

"The truth about what?" Bonnie asked.

Naz shifted his body to look directly at her. "I want you to tell me," he started, "who you think was the best pitcher in the league 'tween... say, 1938 and... 1956. But you cain't say me," he put in.

Bonnie held her head down as she thought. When she looked up, every eye in the room was on her. She felt nervous, not only that she had Naz Wilder's attention, but also the interest of the reverends, deacons, wives and ushers. "Well..." she started.

"Cain't say me," Naz repeated.

"I wasn't," she said. The room roared. Naz's laughter was as loud as any. Bonnie finally answered, "Van Eddie."

A collective groan tolled out among the men. The women looked around as if they were all speaking another language. Naz's expression remained thoughtful.

"What about Bobby Spencer," Reverend McCoy asked.

"Boy, ain't nothin' next to Satchell Paige," Deacon Lewis put in. "Satchell the one . . . he the one fo' sho'!"

"Satchell's good alright," Wilbur called out. "Flashy and fast as night!"

Naz quieted the men by simply raising his hand. Then he said to Bonnie, "Gal, why in the world you pick Van Eddie?"

"Van ain't no joke," Horace Dean defended. "Might've picked him myself."

"Excuse me, gentlemen," Mrs. Reverend Sunday cut in. "But there are other ladies present in this room."

"Amen," Tilde Royce called.

"We regret that we don't know nearly as much about baseball as Bonnie," Mrs. Reverend Sunday went on, "but we do have questions of our own for Naz." A wave of feminine voices rose up in agreement.

As the conversation continued, Bonnie sat quietly. Naz graciously answered the women's questions, which mostly concerned when he was going to settle down with a good woman and if he'd stay in the Three Sisters and how many children he wanted to have and if he was looking for a God-fearing girl. But every so often, Bonnie would find Naz's eyes on her. She had never felt so special. She could feel the hum of his laughter still vibrating inside of her. And she had to take a breath at the thought that the questions he had asked had as much intensity as he had offered to any of the men.

Bonnie was suddenly thankful to Wilbur for insisting that she come to all those games. That afternoon she felt herself floating. Above the buttermilk biscuits and sliced roast beef. Above glamorous Thora, pretty Edris Collins, Mrs. Reverend Sunday, the Bell sisters and all the other ladies. Also above Daddy Wilbur, who sat as proud as a big red rooster. This was Bonnie's afternoon. This was her time. And the only day that felt more exciting was the day that she married Naz Wilder.

Bonnie shook her husband awake in the tub. He often fell asleep under her gentle massage and soothing version of "Stormy Weather." The soapy water swirled through the black ringlets of hair on his chest. She ran the washcloth over his legs and past the jagged scar on his knee. Groggy and content, Naz finally pulled himself up, patted himself dry and slipped into his pajama bottoms. He lay down beside her in bed. Just seconds later, his eyes closed. She thought he would fall asleep now and stay asleep until at least noon. Reverend Duncan would send a harsh word home and some would ask if Naz was alright, but most would understand if he didn't make church the next day, for most of the Brethren from the same hunting trip would be likewise absent.

She, herself, was beginning to doze, when he reached out to hold Bonnie. His eyes fluttered open and he pulled her close. Soon his shifting became urgent. Bonnie could suddenly feel his indecision about what he needed more: sleep or her.

"What you think?" he whispered.

His breath on the back of her neck made her body tingle. "Umm-hmm," she replied.

Naz yanked down his pajama bottoms, then slipped her panties off and pulled her cotton gown up above her head. Bonnie felt her breath catch in her chest as her husband lifted himself on top of her. She prayed that as she rocked beneath him, his passion, her prayers, the light of the moon—anything—might lead to a child. It was the wanting of a baby that hurt so bad. The yearning. It was feeling her own flat stomach against her palm and knowing that time was passing. So even now, as Naz moved deeply inside of her, the only desire she felt was that he fill the empty space inside of her womb and her heart. Naz quickened his pace. Just when she felt his body begin to mount toward that place he loved, she gripped him around the waist, rolled over and flipped herself on top.

"Bonita?" he yelled out.

His voice was filled with as much shock as helpless pleasure. The sight of Bonnie on top of him, her hair falling into his face, her body bending so that her nipples brushed his cheek, was all too much. His legs stiffened and his head fell back on the pillow. Naz cried out from the bottom of his soul. Bonnie had never seen her husband react this way. But it was real. There was passion. She had "stirred things up."

Naz lay beneath her, too exhausted to move. Bonnie didn't budge. She dared not disturb the spawning angels, and stayed draped across his body. In the quiet, she could feel Naz wondering about her behavior. Naz lifted her and she slipped into her place beside him. He slowly sat up and swung his legs to the side of the bed and leaned forward with his head in his hands.

"How you think to do somethin' like that?" he asked.

"Jes' . . . come to me, I guess," she said.

"Ain't nuthin' ever come to you like that befo'!"

She sat up and rubbed his back. Naz was quiet for a moment, like he was deep in thought. Then he said, "Don't think I like you like that."

"Seem like you liked it jes' fine." Bonnie felt shy now, but still happy by what had happened between them.

He shook his head no. "It ain't fo' you, Bonita."

"What?"

"That kinda thing . . . it ain't fo' you."

Bonnie felt confused. "Seem like you *really* liked it."

"No."

"Are you . . . sho'?" she asked.

"Yes, ma'am, I *am* sho'. That kinda thing . . . it ain't fo' no decent woman."

Decent woman, Bonnie thought. Thora was a decent woman and surely her and Horace's private life was filled with such intimate moments. Decent woman? Bonnie pulled the sheet over her naked chest. Her husband, the man she loved most in the world, had suddenly made her feel cheap. Common. Naz slid back into bed and turned his back. Bonnie felt hurt and confused. Their lovemaking was different, yes, yet what of the excitement in her husband just moments ago? Naz had reached his moment full of more fire than they'd had in years. Bonnie shut her eyes. Maybe it wasn't her place to change things. Maybe he didn't like it. But *she* did. Whether Naz wanted to admit it or not, there was heat, yet his back faced her like a closed door. Bonnie wasn't quite sure how she should feel right now. But pain and confusion aside, she prayed that the fire might finally fill her womb with life.

THREE

There were never enough pigs-in-a-blanket to go around. The half-dozen women in attendance at the Ladies of the Blessed Harvest meeting might have gotten two each. Not that Bonnie counted, or even cared for pigs-in-a-blanket in the first place. But she did know that the lack of food was avoidable. Especially given that this was Tilde Monroe's house and Tilde was so methodical in her planning. Moreover, Tilde was the first to gossip about anyone's unkempt house or unkempt kids. Bonnie acknowledged that this was just finger food, but when the ladies sat with two doughy cocktail franks wobbling on a spacious paper plate—well . . . it looked strange, cheap. Still, no one ever complained, at least not to Tilde Monroe's face.

Bonnie glanced at the petunia-shaped wall clock above the mantel. The meeting hadn't started yet and already she was checking the time. Bonnie drummed her fingertips on a carnation-spotted doily that covered the armrest of her chair. On one side of her was an end table loaded with Monroe family photos; and on the other, a window that faced out on Tilde's backyard. As they waited for the last lady to arrive, Bonnie settled back into the floral cushion. Sitting in Tilde's house was like being trapped in a garish garden. Flowers of all sizes and textures sprang from every part of the room. The second armchair, where Olive Lockie sat, was dappled with yellow daisies, and the couch where Laretha Bennett and Miss Idella rested was splashed with floating lavender wreaths. The finishing touch, an area rug covered with just about every kind of flower, spread over most of the floor.

"Ladies of the Blessed Harvest," Tilde announced as she rose ceremoniously, "let us start with our thanks to the Lord."

"What about Delphine," Olive called out. "She ain't here yet."

"Delphine come in late all the time," Tilde said. "I'm ready to start this meeting now."

"But the rules say that we supposed to wait 'til everybody get here," Olive protested.

Tilde placed her pudgy hands in her lap. "May I remind you, Olive," she started, "that *I'm* the one who made up them rules. And *I'm* the one who say when we start and when we wait!"

"Well, excuse the hell outta me," Olive mumbled.

Tilde Monroe, self-appointed leader of the Ladies of the Blessed Harvest, was none too shy about reminding folks that the club was *her* idea. The six women met twice a month, each time at a different woman's house. Tilde first convened the ladies three years ago to organize an annual dance. Initially the dance had been handled by the Women's Auxiliary at the Piney Grove Baptist Church. Year after year, attendance waned because the dance became as boring as the senior deacon's church announcements. But worse, the dance never succeeded in bringing in any money. Then Tilde stepped in. She held a separate meeting to plan a separate dance, this time at the lodge. Not only did the affair bring in money, but folks professed to having the best time ever. Bonnie knew it was because the dance was at the lodge instead of the church. Most could party without the sanctity of the altar right above their heads.

"Let us start with our thanks to the Lord," Tilde repeated. All rose and held hands until a circle was formed. Olive bowed her head reluctantly. Bonnie could feel the firm grip of Laretha on one side and Miss Idella on the other.

"You put us here fo' a reason, my Father," Tilde started. "I pray we serve you the best way we can."

Often the prayer circle was quick, but when Tilde led the invocation, it lasted a while.

"We are but jes' women," Tilde went on, "humble wives and mothers. But, Lord, we pray to do yo' service." Tilde's voice rose as it reached for confirmation from the women.

"Amen," Laretha called.

After a few minutes, Bonnie could feel the connection break in the circle. Most had already given their thanks and moved on. But Tilde had the light. Miss Idella shifted from one leg to the other. Laretha's breath was loud and impatient. Tilde's voice reached the last righteous swell before she ended with, "We thank you, O Lord. Humbly, Father, we thank you. Amen."

A silence fell over the room as the five women took their seats. Tilde pounded the coffee table with a meat tenderizer and it bent beneath the blow. Bonnie had often thought that the table would completely collapse. "What's on the agenda first?" she asked.

"Olive Lockie got the flo'," Laretha announced.

Olive slipped on her black half glasses and looked down at her notes. "Clothes drive," she announced.

"Befo' we get to that," Miss Idella said, raising her hand, "I got somethin' to say."

"Miss Idella got the flo'," Laretha called out.

"Lord ha' mercy, Laretha," Tilde whined. "You ain't got to

say that ever' time somebody talk. Jes' go'n, Miss Idella, and speak yo' piece."

Miss Idella stood with her hands on her hips. At sixty-one, she was the elder of the six women and often the voice of reason. The ladies recognized this and respected it. She cleared her throat with a loud "a-hem," then tugged on either side of her unnaturally red wig. "I believe," she began, "that, from now on, whosoever come in late should be charged an extra ten cent dues."

"Great idea," Laretha called out.

Tilde looked straight ahead, her lips pinched thoughtfully.

Bonnie recalled the times when she put in Delphine Peterson's dues because the woman couldn't afford to pay them. Delphine loved attending the meetings of the Ladies of the Blessed Harvest and Bonnie knew she felt proud to be a part of the group. With a bit of shame in her eyes, Delphine would smile wanly, then try to repay Bonnie. Sometimes she'd send her older boy, Davey, to Blackberry Corner to mow Bonnie's lawn or prune the berry bushes. Though Bonnie wouldn't mind putting in the extra ten cents, she knew that Delphine would surely feel even more embarrassed and beholden than she did already.

"I hear what you sayin', Miss Idella," Olive cut in, "but Delphine is the onliest one who come in late."

"So . . ." Tilde said.

"Delphine got six kids," Olive explained. "She cain't hardly afford the fifty cent as it is."

Bonnie was glad that someone had brought up the point. Though if Olive hadn't, she probably wouldn't have had the nerve to say it herself.

"Well, maybe that'll make Delphine git her hind-parts here on time," Tilde snipped. "However, I need to think on it."

"Yes, let's let Tilde think on it," Laretha said.

Olive rolled her eyes at Laretha. It was a known fact that Laretha always took Tilde's side in everything. The result was that Tilde appointed the woman vice president of their little organization.

Tilde pounded the table again. "Clothes drive . . ."

The ladies' agenda usually centered on such things as helping some of the older members in the congregation with their shopping, cooking and cleaning, or organizing the men's lodge to help a church member farm his land. Then, once official business was out of the way, the conversation usually slipped into tittle-tattle and hearsay.

"Olive, I hope you been saving yo' kids' clothes, fast as they grow," Tilde said.

"I put 'em aside. But, girl, Thomas's pants be threadbare befo' he even grow out of 'em."

"I know that's right," Tilde chuckled. "Natalie ain't got ne'er a dress without a hole or some grass or food stain."

Bonnie wore a forced smile as she listened to the women discuss their children. She didn't find it dull but the subject was painful. As the ladies chatted, Bonnie glanced at the end table beside the couch. Photos of Tilde and Cal at community picnics and church socials were spread out among other family snapshots. Most were of their children, four chubby yellow puffs that looked to be plucked from one of Tilde's fat arms. Her three boys—Gary, Cedric and Cal Jr.—and her daughter and oldest child, Natalie, all had the same face: fat cheeks, pug noses and lazy brown eyes. In fact, if it weren't for the pink ribbon that held a chunk of Natalie's short hair, Bonnie wouldn't know one from the other.

"I got two or three bags of old toys from my grands," Miss Idella said.

"How 'bout y'all drop 'em at the church befo' choir rehearsal," Tilde suggested.

Bonnie found it interesting that some of the women felt it necessary to jot this information on the valentine-bordered paper that Tilde had saved from the Loving Hearts dance that she had chaired last February. But Bonnie knew that these meetings, as small as they seemed, made the women of Canaan Creek feel like they were just as important as the men.

"Next time we get together," Tilde went on, "we'll sort out the clothes befo' we take 'em on over to the Red Cross."

"Red Cross?" Miss Idella countered. "Girl, I ain't studyin' 'bout no Red Cross! Plenty a folks right here in the Three Sisters need them clothes."

"That is the truth," Olive chimed in.

Tilde locked her arms across her heavy chest. "Alright," she huffed. "If y'all wanna leave 'em at the church, then go'n leave 'em at the church!"

Whether at the Red Cross or at the church, Bonnie already knew that all *but* Tilde would be sorting clothes. Tilde was good at rallying folks, but come time to step into action, she often disappeared, leaving the grudge work to the other ladies. It was Bonnie who tended to the old folks that couldn't shop for themselves. Miss Idella administered to the sick and shut-ins, and Olive and Bonnie both sat with folks' children when they needed a night out.

Just then the bell rang. Tilde poked her head out into the hall. "Natalie," she called. "Let Miss Delphine in."

With four girls and two boys, ages ranging from three to seventeen, Delphine was always a bit frazzled. Her clothes were hardly ever ironed and she wore her hair in two frizzy braids. Bonnie understood why she often went unkempt. Delphine tended to her kids first. And surely, after plaiting the heads of her four young girls, the woman barely had the energy to do her own.

"Excuse my lateness," she said. "Myra and Sissy both got a devil of a cold and my youngest—"

"Next order of business," Tilde said, ignoring the woman's rambling.

Delphine took a seat on the couch. She waved at Bonnie across the floor and Bonnie gave a tiny wink.

"Ever'body bring they recipes?" Tilde asked.

The light cinnamon scent of Dentyne gum, a Sunday service staple, came from open handbags as the women eagerly removed their recipe cards. Bonnie pulled out her recipe for blackberry cobbler and passed it to Miss Idella, while Olive handed her recipe to Bonnie. Tilde had come up with a new twist for the bake sale this year. Each woman was to prepare another's favorite dessert. Bonnie recognized that this was a recipe for disaster, because if one woman happened to bake a dish better than the original, there would be no end to the grief. But Tilde felt that this was a "very clever" idea, so Bonnie courteously accepted Olive's recipe for Red Velvet Cake.

"I didn't write it in the recipe," Olive whispered to Bonnie, "but fo' the cake batter . . ."

"Yes," Bonnie said, trying to feign interest.

"Instead of the red dye . . . I use a cup a beet juice."

"Shut yo' mouth, girl."

"Gi' the batter a sweeter taste! Don't tell nobody I told you that, Bonnie Wilder."

Bonnie raised her palm toward the heavens. Olive flashed a trusting smile, then turned back to the group. As Tilde went on about pricing for the bake sale, Bonnie's attention drifted out the back window. A pink sheet billowing on the clothesline had caught onto the branch of a camphor tree. Pale pink gloriously tented the yard. About a hundred feet away from the house, Bonnie caught sight of the very edge of the creek. A soft wave rippled in the water. Though Blackberry Corner was nine miles away from here, the creek flowed by both her and Tilde's back doors. Tilde could see it from her porch, but Bonnie had to venture a little ways into the green behind her house. Many folks in the Three Sisters had the waters in common. Bonnie could walk through the woods and find more than a half-dozen dwellings along the twelve-mile path that touched on or near the banks. As a child, she had collected baskets of loganberries, wild grapes or persimmons for her neighbors. She would knock on their back doors and they'd give her a nickel for a basket. Some of the families still lived in these houses, though the generations had changed. Lola Flocker resided in the house closest to Bonnie. She had taken over the deed from her mama. The elder of the Benson boys lived about three miles from Lola, with his wife and two kids. The next house over, once owned by Shirley and Basil Stokes, was now foreclosed and abandoned. The Bell sisters lived about six miles from the Stokes' place. Then there was Tilde.

Bonnie started when Miss Idella shook her arm. The women's voices had become a background hum in the room, their laughter like dry echoes. Bonnie had to adjust her eyes from the bright sunlight outside.

"You with us, Bonnie?" Laretha asked.

"Beg pardon?" Bonnie said.

Tilde sucked her teeth. "I'm sho' we ain't the most fascinating group of folks," she chided, "but I think we a lil' mo' lively than them damn sheets hangin' out there."

"Excuse me," Bonnie said.

"Excuse *us,*" Tilde snipped.

Bonnie felt like a child being reprimanded by the teacher.

"As I was sayin'," Tilde went on, "we'll have Reverend Duncan make an announcement, askin' fo' only baked dishes from every woman in Piney Grove."

"We say that every year," Miss Idella put in, "but folks still bring whatever they wants. Last year Gladys Cointreau walked in with a roast beef."

"Couldn't believe the nerve of that woman," Tilde said. "I mean, here we are with all these lovely desserts and Gladys got a damned roast beef."

"But it sold better than anything," Bonnie put in.

Five sets of eyes turned to her.

Tilde slanted her head. She took a small breath before she said, "It's called a *bake* sale, Bonnie. That mean folks s'posed to bring cakes, pies, cookies and such. When we have us a *meat* sale, then maybe Gladys can bring roast beef."

This was one of the reasons that Bonnie stayed quiet at these meetings. Though her remarks were small, she seemed to always rub the cat from the wrong end. She looked outside again. The sheet on the line had separated from the branch of the camphor tree. The pink glow disappeared and the yard looked pale and normal. Bonnie heard the rattle of Naz's truck, then saw its bumper as it stopped at the side of the house. He was a bit early, yet, to her, he was right on time.

"Will you ladies please excuse me," Bonnie said, hooking the strap of her purse on her forearm. "I need to leave early today."

"Don't forget about the next meetin' at the lodge," Olive called to Bonnie. "Deputy Pine'll be there next week."

"He still don't know nothin'," Laretha said.

"Maybe they'll have found something by next week," Miss Idella said.

"Pine cain't find the nose on his face," Laretha put in.

"In the meantime," Tilde threw in, "don't forgit to bring yo' old clothes." Bonnie quickly strode to the front door. "And tell Thora 'bout the drive," Tilde called. "Maybe she ha' some dresses she care to part wit'."

As Bonnie walked out, she heard Olive Lockie say, "Girl,

Thora wear them tight things." Her voice went up an octave when she added, "And expensive!"

"Honey, hush," Tilde put in. "Hell if I know how Horace can afford to . . ."

That's when Bonnie closed the door behind her.

Bonnie didn't mind shopping for the older members of Piney Grove church. The hard part was making out the chicken scrawl from the women's shopping lists.

"That a number seven or nine?" she asked Thora.

"Look like a fo'." Thora glanced at the paper again. "Got to be a fo' 'cause, Florie Teller cain't eat no nine green tomatoes all by herself. Old lady like that would get the indigestion somethin' bad."

"You prob'ly right."

"I'm gon' leave you wit' yo' old lady writing," Thora said, heading toward the jewelry and makeup section. "And I'll meet you in fabric."

"Flat leaver," Bonnie called out. She usually ended up doing the food shopping alone. Horace and Naz had long since abandoned the women to the bait and tackle section of the store. Bonnie stood at the top of the long produce aisle and marveled at the colors of fresh peaches, oranges and squash. As a child, she loved shopping at the Big Buy with her mother. While most children went wild over Sycamore's Toy Palace just three doors down, Bonnie had always loved the food market. The colors of fresh vegetables and the scent of ground coffee tantalized her. Everyone in the Three Sisters shopped at the Big Buy. Second from church, it was a place to see folks that Bonnie hadn't seen for a while. She rolled her buggy past the produce and down the aisle lined with sweet grass and palmetto leaf baskets. She nodded at an elderly man browsing the short handle and bread baskets. He wore glasses so thick that Bonnie wondered if he could see. She turned to a shelf with large egg baskets. Bonnie ran her hand across the prickly inside of a pine needle pie carrier then spotted a huge white wicker basket, perfect for filling with yarn or clean towels. But alas, at seven dollars, Naz would surely say that the basket was too dear.

"Bonnie," Naz said, approaching his wife. "Me and Horace fin to go on over to the hardware sto'."

"Okay, honey."

"Hey, there," the old man said to Naz. He still held a set of sweet grass coasters in his hand. The man couldn't take his eyes off of Naz. And Bonnie recognized that look. Every once in a while someone still recalled her husband from his baseball days. Naz tended to shy away from folks that recognized him because they always wound up gushing.

"I know who you are," the man said, squinting as he looked up at Naz.

Bonnie smiled as her husband shrunk from the attention.

"You Justice," the old man said.

"Excuse me," Naz said.

"Justice," the old man repeated, "from Lucky's Place."

"I'm sorry, sir," Bonnie said politely, "but you must ha' the wrong person."

The old man peered over the top of his glasses, then pushed them on his nose. After another look, he finally said, "Pardon me, sir."

"That's alright, old-timer," Naz said, patting him on the shoulder.

The man put the coasters back on the shelf. "Well, y'all ha' yo'selves a nice day," he said as he hobbled up the aisle, then joined a middle-aged woman, perhaps his daughter.

"Sweet ole fella," Bonnie said. "Prob'ly recognized you from baseball and jes messed up yo' name."

"I'm sho'," Naz said. "Look, honey, I'll meet you at the car. I'm fin' to join Horace over at the hardware store."

"Okay," she replied. "And don't forget to get them washers to fix the bathroom sink."

Naz kissed her cheek and left. Bonnie glanced at her shopping list again. She managed to make out Anna Frye's half pound of sharp cheddar cheese, sliced slab bacon and . . . it seemed to say "bottle of citric acid." Anna had also given Bonnie a swatch of blue gingham cloth to match in the fabric section. She wheeled her cart toward the reams of material stacked against the wall. Packs of buttons, lace and bric-a-brac were stacked on the shelf.

"What you got there," Kitty Wooten called out. The woman wasn't rude but never quite bothered with niceties like hello or good-bye. Kitty had worked at the Big Buy for as long as Bonnie could remember and most in the Three Sisters had long since gotten over being offended by her brash manner. Her thin brown face spotted with tiny flesh moles always seemed pinched in thought. A pastel cardigan, which she wore in even the hottest weather, had its sleeves rolled up on her skinny arms. Well in her sixties, Kitty had been here when Bonnie had shopped with her mother and daddy years ago. Kitty would often remind Bonnie about how she brought a bin of navel oranges to the house during Eleanor's wake.

"Fo' Anna Frye . . . right?" Kitty asked, raising her silver-framed glasses to look at the swatch.

"You sho'ly know yo' customers," Bonnie said.

"I 'member when Anna first bought that fabric." Kitty pulled out a ream of the same material. "Had to be a hundred and twenty-seven years ago!" Kitty made jokes but never even cracked a smile. "How much she need?"

"Enough fo' mendin'."

"I'll cut her a quarter," Kitty said. "And if she need mo'—"

"Y'all got any linen?" a young woman interrupted.

Kitty pulled her head back. "I'm helpin' a customer here, miss," she snapped.

"It's okay," Bonnie said.

"No, it ain't neither," Kitty huffed. The woman moved away quickly. Kitty called out, "Young gals jes' as rude as they wanna be!"

"Times is changin'," Bonnie acknowledged.

"Ain't changed that much." Kitty unfolded a half foot of the fabric and began to cut with sharp shears. "My mama woulda slapped my ear!" She pointed at Bonnie with the scissors and said, "And yo' daddy woulda done the same thing too. Am I right or wrong?"

"That is the truth," Bonnie chuckled.

Kitty separated the panel of cut fabric from the ream. "And looky there at that one." She pointed her chin at another young woman. The round-faced woman, in a blue blouse and old denim jeans, looked weary. She had a toddler in her arms, a little girl on the floor beside her feet and an older boy of about ten pushing the buggy. Still another small girl sat on the counter beside a mound of white organza.

"Po' thing," Bonnie said. "She seem . . . overwhelmed."

"Seem like she need to cross her legs sometimes," Kitty shot back.

"Lord, Kitty." Bonnie blushed. She watched the woman frantically searching through a purse with one broken shoulder strap.

Thora wandered over. She stood before Bonnie and Kitty wearing her sexiest pout. "What y'all think?"

" 'Bout what?" Bonnie asked.

"This new lipstick."

Bonnie moved closer. "Don't you ha' that color already?" she asked.

"I got Iced Orange," Thora replied. "This here is Iced Tangerine."

The young woman that Bonnie and Kitty had been watching suddenly swatted her daughter on the behind. "Git up from the flo', Elsie," she barked.

"Dear me," Thora said as the child screamed.

The woman yanked the tiny girl's arm until the child was dangling in the air. "Ain't s'posed to be rollin' on the damn flo'," the woman hollered.

"See there," Thora said. "That's why I ain't got no kids."

"It's a different story when you know how to handle 'em," Kitty whispered. "Ain't supposed to let 'em run through the place like hooligans." She folded the cut fabric and stuck it in a small brown bag. "And somethin' else too," she said. Thora and Bonnie leaned in to hear her say, "Jes' a few minutes ago, I asked that gal if she needed any help. You will *never* believe what she said to me."

"What?" Thora asked.

"Just as proud as you please, she tell me that she lookin' to buy some material to make herself..." Kitty raised her hand like she couldn't believe what she was about to say. "Say she wanna make herself a weddin' dress."

"Shut up, Miss Kitty," Thora said.

"All them damn kids and she gon' make a weddin' dress," Kitty went on. "Lord, if that ain't... one, two, three, fo' carts befo' the mule. Am I right or wrong?"

The woman couldn't be older than twenty-five, Bonnie thought. So young and so burdened. The woman set the toddler in the cart, then yanked at the arm of the girl on the floor again. As she reached to pick up the child, the toddler tried to crawl out of the cart. Bonnie was about to approach the woman to help.

"Leave her be, Bonnie," Kitty said. "She made her bed and she need to fend fo' herself."

"She's right," Thora put in.

The woman quickly pulled the plastic wrapper from a green sucker and gave it to the screaming girl she'd just spanked. Then the toddler boy began to cry.

"I ain't got no mo' candy, Bo," the woman said in exasperation.

Bonnie fished a pinwheel mint from her pocketbook, then approached the woman and handed it to the child. He looked up with big watery eyes.

"What you say to the lady?" the mama shouted.

"Thank you," the boy said, sticking the candy in his mouth.

"You welcome, baby," Bonnie said.

"Take Bo out to the bathroom," the woman told her older son, plopping the toddler into the boy's arms.

"Where the bathroom, Mama?"

"Jes' take him out in the bushes behind the sto'."

"Need to find a leash fo' them kids," Kitty whispered. "Make me tired jes' lookin'."

Just then, the girl called Elsie dropped her sucker onto the ream of white organza. Kitty looked at the child like she had personally attacked her.

"You gon' need to pay fo' that!" she said to the mother.

"I *cain't,*" the woman said.

"Don't you see that sign, gal?" Kitty snapped.

Bonnie, Thora and the woman turned to read the sign at the same time. It said, *"Please Handle Fabric with Caution!"*

"That mean there ain't supposed to be no messy kids 'round here."

"I'm sorry but—"

"That's gon' be thirty cents!"

"I ain't got no thirty cents," the woman yelled. The children were quiet as they watched their mother and Kitty argue.

"You come to buy some fabric, didn't you," Kitty quarreled as she yanked the sucker off the material. "Say you makin' yo'self a weddin' dress!" The little girl screamed until Kitty handed the candy back to her.

"I come to *look* at some fabric!"

"What I'm supposed to tell my boss when he see this?"

"I'll pay the thirty cent," Bonnie offered.

"You ain't gotta do that," the woman told her.

"You need to be thankful," Kitty barked.

Bonnie dug into her change purse, ignoring them both. This time the woman didn't protest. She simply nodded her thanks. Moments later the older boy returned with his brother. "Hold yo' sister's hand, 'Lijah," she ordered. "And, Elsie, you keep on cryin' and I'm gon' gi' you somethin' to cry 'bout." The woman left the store, her children following like a row of small ducks.

"Damn shame," Kitty said, shaking her head. "Lil' mama look like she ready to go on down to the creek her damn self."

"Now, Kitty . . ." Thora rebuked.

"Lord forgive me, but y'all know what I mean."

As spiteful as Kitty's remark was, Bonnie understood her point. The woman was overwhelmed. And if she couldn't handle a visit to the market with her four kids, what could her home life be? Bonnie's thoughts came back to blessings. She often wondered about who was blessed with what, and why. This girl, so burdened, with less than a pot to piss in, was blessed, fourfold. And Bonnie, with all the space in her heart and even more room in her home, remained childless. Bonnie stood in the large window of the Big Buy and watched the woman load her children into the open back of an old truck. Who gets what, and why? How were these decisions made? She felt for this mother and her poverty and helplessness. And maybe this was one of Bonnie's blessings. She couldn't do a damn thing for the young woman. But at least she cared.

The second town meeting at the Brethren of Good Faith Hall had half the people that the first one did. But the ones who came still felt the aftershocks of a small life lost nearly three months ago. Several people from Piney Grove returned, along with Reverend Duncan and his wife, and five of Naz's lodge brothers. Thora and Horace Dean were in attendance this time, as were Trent Majors, Bailey Dial, Jess Sinclair and only one of the Bell sisters. Ruby-Pearl Yancy surprised them all by being there again. She sat quietly near the door. One or two faces that Bonnie didn't recognize had come—and of course, all of the ladies from the Blessed Harvest.

Pine stood before them. "About a week ago," he began, "a young gal—live in Manstone—was reported to us by her husband." Pine stuffed his hands in his pockets. "The gal's husband claim she had a baby 'bout fo' months ago..."

The crowd was rapt.

"This husband," Pine went on, "he one a these n'er-do-well kinda fellas... y'all know what I mean. He admit that he drink some and tomcat on the gal..."

"Git to the point," Laretha yelled. "Y'all know who kill this chile or not?"

Pine was unstirred by the emotion in the room. "This gal," he calmly proceeded, "tole her husband that she took the baby to her grandmama, somewhere in Georgia. But this fella come to think that maybe this gal did harm to the chile. Say she never visited the grandmama, never spoke about the chile, and say she was actin' real strange. Walkin' 'round all hours of the night, mumblin' to herself and such. But more, he went to see the grandmama and the grandmama didn't know nuthin' 'bout no chile."

Bonnie could feel her heart pounding. She held Naz's hand on one side and Thora's on the other.

"Was it this gal who drowned her baby or not?" Horace called out.

"She in jail?" Tilde asked.

"Husband say that the gal run off," Pine said. A collective groan sounded through the room. "We cain't find her to ask any questions. Husband say she could be anywhere from here to Michigan."

"You gotta be kiddin'!" Laretha said in disgust.

"Point is," Pine said, jangling his keys, "she was our biggest lead, and now . . . she's gone."

"What is wrong with you people?" Olive hollered.

"Must take stupid pills," Jess Sinclair put in.

"So, what you tryin' to say," Tilde stood up, "is that we may *never* find out who killed this po' chile?"

Pine looked at his hands folded in front of him. "The case'll stay open," he said.

Another groan rippled across the room.

"I'm 'fraid that ain't enough!" Tilde said simply. "And the onliest reason you called us here with a tale 'bout some gal and her grandmama is 'cause ya'll ain't got a damn thing!"

"She was a promisin' lead," Pine argued.

"Promisin', my ass," Tilde spat. "Could be that the woman took her chile and gone."

"Or maybe she wanted to get away from that triflin' man," Delphine yelled. Some of the women nodded their heads in agreement.

"We ladies did what y'all asked," Tilde went on. "We stayed

out of it and left things in the hands of the law. But now it's time fo' the community to get involved."

"You need to *keep* leaving things in the hands of the law," Pine insisted.

"An innocent chile is dead!" Tilde charged. "And y'all ain't found nothin'! Not a goddamn thing!"

"Sound like Tilde 'bout to step up on her soapbox," Thora whispered to Bonnie.

"I think we should all check 'round the Three Sisters," Tilde yelled. "We should find out who been pregnant and who ain't got no baby no mo'. Then we oughta show this woman jes' what it feel like to be left to die."

Tilde's remark brought the room to its feet in support. But Bonnie couldn't share in the fervor of the others. She acknowledged it was deeply unsettling that a child killer was out there, and it was even more disturbing to know that it could be someone who lived in the Three Sisters. Yet she had to wonder just *what* would drive a woman to kill her own infant. And if caught, should she be thrown in jail for the rest of her life, or worse, put to death? Bonnie looked at Tilde Monroe, who, once again, had stepped into the spotlight. She knew that this was where Tilde was happiest, even when she was rousing the town to lynch some woman who might've been desperate enough or just plain crazy out of her mind.

"Ladies and men," Tilde yelled, "we oughta start a committee. And we should canvass the town . . . and I mean *all* a the area, as far no'th as Hooley and as far south as Taliliga."

Bonnie glanced at Delphine. She could see the exhaustion in the woman's body. The enormity of raising six children was present, even in the way she sat, slumped back in her chair. Tilde ranted and Delphine kept her eyes on her four-year-old boy, Lee-Abbot, who sat in the seat next to her. On her other side was her eight-year-old girl, Ree-Ree. Delphine looked up from her lap and caught Bonnie's eye. Again, the shame of her circumstances was evident.

"The Ladies of the Blessed Harvest *and* the Brethren of Good Faith should get out there," Tilde went on, "and we should check the hospitals for any gals that might've give birth in the last few months. We need to find out where these babies are and where they ain't! That'll stir things up! Never know what bad apples might fall from them trees."

Bonnie suddenly thought of the woman in the Big Buy and her desperation, a beleaguered mother's desperation. Certainly, Bonnie could never support a person who drowned her child, but somehow she felt the woman shouldn't be hunted down and slaughtered. Bonnie moved to the edge of her chair. In the middle of Tilde's rant, Bonnie stood up. Tilde looked at her curiously but kept on talking. Even Naz appeared a little taken aback when he saw his wife waiting for the crowd to quiet. Bonnie clutched her hands together to stop them from shaking. She had no idea what she'd say, and when she started, her voice barely rose above a whisper.

"I... agrees with Tilde," she began. "I mean... ain't no excuse fo' what has happened..."

"Damn right," Tilde yelled.

"Whoever did this was wrong... Lord know she was wrong." Bonnie glanced through a sea of distressed faces. "But... what if this woman... what if she felt like she ain't had no choice..."

A thoughtful silence fell over the room.

"What's that s'posed to mean?" Laretha yelled out.

"What the hell you sayin', Bonnie Wilder?" Tilde asked.

"Let Bonnie finish," Miss Idella put in.

"I just mean that the woman who did this," Bonnie went on, "maybe she was in some awful pain..."

"I don't give a damn 'bout how much pain she in," Tilde

yelled. "I'm the mother of fo', and I can tell you that it ain't no easy thing, raisin' kids. And with all due respect, Bonnie, you ain't got no children, so you might not understand."

Bonnie felt her heart sink but she held her head up.

"Bonnie don't need to be no mama to have pity on some crazy woman," Thora yelled out.

"Pity," Tilde said incredulously. "You ain't got no kids neither, Thora Dean . . . so maybe you and Bonnie should both—"

"Aw, now, Tilde," Pine put in.

"Look a h'yere," Tilde went on, "if you don't have no babies, then you don't know! Sometimes you wanna ring they damn necks," Tilde argued, "but hell if I would harm my children for any reason."

"But you have Cal to help you," Bonnie said, "plus family, neighbors and friends. Maybe this woman felt she ain't had nobody . . . no choice!" Bonnie took a breath. "All I'm sayin'," she went on, "is that instead of tryin' to find the person to lynch her up, maybe we need to get help for her."

"You tryin' to defend somebody that done killed a chile, Bonnie Wilder?" Laretha asked.

"You know I ain't!" Bonnie was beginning to wish she'd never stood up in the first place. Still, her conviction gave her strength. "But maybe folks need a place to bring they baby when things get bad. Some safe place so that they won't feel like stickin' 'em in the creek is the answer."

"Like where?" Tilde asked. "Where a mama s'posed to bring a child she don't want?"

"I don't know," Bonnie stuttered. "Maybe the county home . . ."

A murmur of dissent rippled through the crowd. She turned to her husband for support but Naz looked like he wished she would stop talking. Like he wished she would sit her ass down.

"You've seen them kids from the orphanage," Tilde yelled. "They come to our Christmas party two years in a row and act like a pack of wild animals."

"Well, take the chile to the church . . . to a neighbor," Bonnie said helplessly. "Hell, bring the babies to me."

"What?" Tilde said in shock.

"Bonnie," Naz whispered.

"Better than drownin' 'em in the creek!"

"Set on down, girl," Thora said, pulling her arm. "Forgit these people!"

Bonnie was shocked by her own words; she hadn't meant to go this far.

"You done lost yo' ever-lovin' mind, Bonnie Wilder," Tilde called out.

"No lie," Laretha put in.

Naz stood beside his wife. The room went silent. Naz Wilder rarely spoke out, but when he did, he was always dead-on.

"Y'all know what Bonnie tryin' to say," he started. "And y'all know her to be merciful and kind. So don't sit there puttin' evil words in her mouth. I know ever'body excited and upset . . . and we oughta be. But that ain't no reason to turn on each other 'cause somebody might see the situation different than you. We all need to do what we can in our own way." Then he sat back down and tugged his wife's arm until she did the same.

Thora squeezed Bonnie's hand and gave her a sympathetic smile.

"Look, folks," Pine called over the crowd, "ain't nothin' changed. Let me know if you see or hear anythin'."

The crowd began to break up, though many gravitated to the corner where Tilde was holding court. Bonnie and Thora quickly headed toward the door. Some avoided Bonnie's eyes and a few shook her hand but quickly left.

"Jes' a dirty, stinkin' crime to disagree in this town," Thora said.

"How in the world do you do it?" Bonnie asked her.

"Like I give two cent 'bout what these people think of me?" Thora sucked her teeth. "I ain't studyin' 'bout even one." Thora pushed Bonnie's shoulder like she was proud. "You the onliest true and decent soul in this whole room."

"Please."

"Ever'body else set up in church like they's doin' somethin'. Go out and collect clothes and stuff, talk 'bout Jesus this and Jesus that. I like what you said," Thora went on. "You crazy as hell, but yo' heart's in the right place." Thora gave Bonnie a quick hug. "Come on, Sister Sarah, let's wait in the car. I need me a cigarette."

"You go on," Bonnie said. "I'm gon' find Naz first."

The truth was, Bonnie now regretted speaking up. Though no one was outright angry, she sensed there had been a shift in the room against her. It was like she had stepped out of her place. Bonnie had always been respected and well liked in the community, and, unlike Thora, she didn't have the constitution to withstand the town's ill will. She gestured to Naz, who was standing with Pine and Horace, then slipped on her sweater and was about to leave the hall.

"Bonnie?"

She turned to see Ruby-Pearl Yancy standing behind her. Ruby-Pearl was a young woman, no older than twenty-eight, who had lost her husband and daughter in a car accident two years before. Ruby-Pearl was severely hurt herself and her once pretty face still showed scars of the accident. She now had a slow eye and her right cheek drooped. Ruby-Pearl wore a kerchief, obstensibly to keep the sun away, but Bonnie knew that the scarf was more to cover the disfigurement. Even worse than the scars was the guilt that the woman carried with her. Ruby-Pearl had been driving the car that killed her family.

"Good to see you, honey," Bonnie said.

Ruby-Pearl's smile tugged against the taut skin on the side of her face. "Every Sunday," she started, "every Sunday in church I always mean to stop and say hey. But you know me, Bonnie. I like to get right outta there."

"If I didn't have a husband that had to talk 'bout huntin' and fishin' *all* the time, I would leave a lot sooner myself." Bonnie smiled.

Ruby-Pearl tilted her face down when she spoke. "I heard what you said in there. And you weren't jes' talkin' to the wind."

"Thank you, dear," Bonnie whispered.

"Such sins," Ruby-Pearl said, shaking her head. "Folks tho'ing away precious babies, and here me and you would do jes' 'bout anything to have one."

Bonnie was a little taken aback by Ruby-Pearl's candor.

"It ain't no secret," Ruby-Pearl said gently. "My good friend Letty, she live up in Hencil—she trying to have one too. Sometimes it jes' don't happen that way."

Bonnie nodded.

Ruby-Pearl went on, "I want you to know that I heard every word you said. And I agree." She moved closer. "But you know as good as me that the squeakiest wheel gits all the grease."

"Ain't that the truth," Bonnie laughed. She took Ruby-Pearl's hand. Bonnie realized that it was so easy to miss the woman in crowds like this, for Ruby-Pearl tended to fade into the furniture. "Why don't you come a visitin' sometime," Bonnie said. "We'll have us some lemonade."

"I'll do that."

Bonnie knew she wouldn't. The most Ruby-Pearl Yancy did was go to work at the tackle shop, go to church and then go home. It had to be hard to accept, Bonnie thought: to be a young, pretty wife and mama one day, then alone and disfigured the next. Bonnie walked her outside and watched Ruby-Pearl get into her car. She had to wonder how the woman had the courage to drive after all that had happened.

Bonnie peeked in the hall again. Naz and Horace were still standing with Pine and now the lodge brothers. They had clearly moved on to another topic, because the men were examining Lo Baker's new hunting rifle. Tilde Monroe was still in the middle of an animated group. Bonnie took a long breath. As much noise as there was today, and as silly as her remarks were, she knew that, like most everything else in the Three Sisters, people would be in an uproar for a few days and then life would go on.

PART II

FOUR

Canaan Creek, 1985

Bonnie opened her door to a man dressed to the nines. She wasn't used to seeing a gentleman looking so good and smelling so sweet on an early Friday evening... or *any* evening. Bonnie had to look twice at the gray suit and gold-striped tie, shiny black shoes that surely pinched his toes and the cuffed pants that sat a bit too high above his ankles. In the absence of his mail sack, the only thing that looked familiar about Tally Benford was the beer belly protruding way beyond his swank leather belt.

"My, my," Bonnie said.

Tally looked bashfully at his own feet.

"You ain't had to dress up fo' no mint jelly, Tally Benford," she teased.

"Alright now," he mumbled.

She grinned. "You look as good as a fi' dollar piece. Comin' from Friday service?"

"No, ma'am," he replied, then quickly added, "Not that

there's anythin' wrong with the church . . . I mean, the late service and all . . ."

Bonnie had never seen Tally this ill at ease. He glanced over her shoulder.

"Thora in?" he asked.

Tally looked even more uncomfortable when a tiny smile swept across Bonnie's face.

"I . . . come to see if . . . maybe I can set with her this evenin'."

"So you finally got the nerve?"

He shrugged. "Figure I ain't gittin' no younger," he said. Then he whispered, "And neither is Thora."

"You are sho'ly right 'bout that," Bonnie whispered back. "But I'm afraid she ain't here. She went to town to see a movie."

"I knew she ain't seen *every* film." Tally slid his hands in his pockets. "Didn't know Thora was keeping company."

"She ain't," Bonnie assured him. "Thora sit in the cinema house all by herself."

Tally looked relieved.

"Why don't you come on in," Bonnie said. "She be back soon enough." He wiped his shoes on the welcome mat. Tally had been in this house practically every morning for the past five years, but it seemed that his formal clothes and the reason for his visit gave him manners that Bonnie had never seen before.

"She been gone all afternoon," Bonnie said as she led him into the living room, where he took a seat on the sofa. He looked like a stranger without his postal uniform. "Can I get you some sweet tea?"

"That be fine, thank you, ma'am."

Bonnie was about to walk into the kitchen when she noticed that Tally had rested his hat on the couch beside him. "You know better than that, Tally Benford," she scolded.

"'Scuse me," he said, snatching up his hat.

"My house is po' enough," she said, taking it from him and placing it on a coat stand. Bonnie then went into the kitchen. She suddenly wondered how Thora would react to Tally Benford coming to call. Probably not well at all. But Bonnie had to admire the man for even trying.

"What she go to see?" Tally called out.

"That new show started today," she hollered from the kitchen. "That there . . . movie where all them old folks is turning young."

"Cocoon?"

"That's the one." Ice clinked as Bonnie filled two glasses to the rim. "Sometimes I go along," she said, returning to the living room, "but today I wasn't in the mood."

"I know how that be." He took a swig of tea, then reached for a cork coaster from the stack on Bonnie's coffee table. "That gal ever call you?" he asked. "You know, the one from the Christmas letter?"

"Not so far."

"Letter come . . . what, three weeks ago," he said. "Sound like she was chompin' at the bit."

"Jes' as well. Ain't got much to tell the woman." Bonnie hoped that Thora would return soon. If she didn't, Bonnie wondered if Tally planned on waiting the whole time. Good manners prevented her from inquiring.

"I been meanin' to ask you," Tally said. "Thora . . ." he started. "Why she so . . . ?"

"Direct," Bonnie cut in. "Thora Dean always been that way. Tell you 'bout yo'self in no uncertain terms. Tell you 'bout yo' mama too if you push her." Bonnie chuckled. "I've known her since we was gals and I've always 'preciated her ways. I guess her manner got even mo' salty after she lost her husband."

"I've sang that song myself."

"Horace Dean died from a stroke 'bout fifteen years ago," Bonnie went on. "That man treated Thora like a queen . . . and if he didn't, she'd be the first to go upside his head."

"I know that's right," Tally laughed. "Kinda like my wife, Grace. She passed befo' I even moved to the Three Sisters. Had that cancer, you know—cancer in her woman parts. And I 'clare, she was jes' as obstinate as Thora . . . and I mean she was that way befo' the cancer even come along. But, Lord, she was a fascinatin' woman." He shook his head proudly. "Had that same fire as Thora."

"You call it fire?" Bonnie said.

"That's what it is. And at our age, to find someone that make you feel alive, well . . ."

For the first time since he walked through the door, Bonnie took his visit seriously. Thora was her oldest and dearest friend, and Bonnie had assumed that she was the only person who could see warmth in the woman. Clearly, she'd been wrong. Tally Benford wasn't the best-looking man and he didn't have much. But he had driven his old heap of a Bonneville all the way from Manstone to visit a woman who would sooner spit on him than receive him with kindness. He was here to visit with Thora because he liked her heart.

The phone rang, puncturing this brief moment of intimacy. When Bonnie answered, she could hardly make out Thora's panicked words.

"Thora?!" Bonnie said into the receiver. "Wait . . . jes' calm down, honey." Bonnie faced Tally as she spoke. "Say the tire blew?"

Tally stood right up. He took on that look of purpose that Bonnie saw every morning. "Tally is here," Bonnie said. "Oh, I'll explain it to you later," she said, "but I'll have him come and carry you home. No, no . . . jes' set right there in the diner and he'll be along." Bonnie hung up the phone. "She a little nervous, you know."

"I understand." Tally started out the door.

She was about to follow him to the porch when the phone rang again. "Thora. Yes, dahlin'. I know it's gettin' dark, but... jes' stay put. Girl, set on down and ha' yo'self a slice of that apple pie." Bonnie waved Tally out of the door. "He's on his way. Okay... yes, honey... bye-bye."

Bonnie hung up the receiver. She stepped outside just as Tally pulled out of the yard. She watched until his car had disappeared. Bonnie heard the phone ring again. As strong as Thora seemed, it was strange how a small chink in her chain could completely throw the woman off. "Thora, honey, he's on his way..."

"Is this Bonnie Wilder?" a young woman's voice asked.

Bonnie paused.

"Mrs. Wilder?"

Though Bonnie instinctively knew the answer, she steeled herself to ask: "To whom am I speaking?"

"My name is Augusta Randall," the woman said. "I wrote you a letter a few weeks ago. But you might not have gotten it because I didn't have your full address."

"I did get yo' letter, honey," Bonnie said.

The girl sighed happily. "I'm so glad." Bonnie could hear the relief in Augusta Randall's tiny voice. "Sorry I took so long to call, but I wanted to give my letter some time to find you."

"I understand," Bonnie told her.

"It's wonderful to actually talk to you," Augusta said. "How have you been getting along, Mrs. Wilder?"

"I'm in good health. Thank you for asking."

"That's a blessing..."

"Indeed." Bonnie knew that the woman wanted to get right to the point. But she could tell that Augusta had been raised to be polite. Bonnie could feel the woman's breeding—her respect for tradition and formality. "So . . . you're a schoolteacher?" Bonnie asked.

"Yes, ma'am. I teach math to third graders."

"Math?" Bonnie gasped. "Never was good at numbers and figurin'."

"Yes, ma'am," the woman said.

"And yo' husband . . . he's a teacher too?"

"Joe's a professor at Rutgers University," Augusta answered.

"Two such smart people," Bonnie said.

"He teaches social science to incoming freshmen and also a course in pre-law."

Bonnie listened for any sign of Lucinda in the girl's voice. And what would it sound like? Would her words sound loose and uncaring—her voice sensual and hard-bitten? Bonnie suddenly hated herself for trying to find Lucinda in the girl. Of all people, Bonnie knew that these rough traits didn't come through the blood.

"Can you . . . help me, Mrs. Wilder?" Augusta asked. "I would love to, one day, give my own son or daughter a sense of where they came from . . . who their people were."

"It wouldn't serve nobody to know they mama was somebody like Lucinda." And right now, hearing this woman's voice—so excited, so hopeful, Bonnie was convinced of that fact more than ever. She held the receiver with two hands. "I'm afraid I cain't help you, sugar."

"Surely you can tell me something . . ."

Bonnie had always admired people who clung to their convictions. And she could tell that this young woman wouldn't easily give up. Perhaps she was as stubborn as Lucinda once was. Bonnie closed her eyes and offered up a silent apology. She was doing it again. She was assuming traits in this young woman that surely had nothing to do with Lucinda. Then too, stubbornness was a quality that lived in a lot of people, including Bonnie herself. And stubbornness in a woman could often be a strength.

"Is there *anything* you can remember?" the girl pressed.

"You said that yo' mama—yo' adopted mama—was named Evelyn Porter?"

"Yes, ma'am," Augusta replied.

"Small, brown-skinned gal? And yo' daddy, Dorsey... he was a high-toned, good-looking man?"

"Yes, ma'am," Augusta said. "My daddy died about fifteen years ago."

"Nice folks," Bonnie said. "They wanted a child so bad and I was happy when I was finally able to give them a little girl."

"And that child was me?" Augusta's voice brimmed with anticipation.

"Yes, dear, that was you."

It took a while to recall, but Bonnie vaguely remembered. She recalled that Evelyn, petite and soft-spoken, seemed so nervous. When she shook Bonnie's hand, her palm was cool and moist.

"I do remember Evelyn," Bonnie said. "She seemed like a lovely lady."

"Yes, ma'am." Augusta paused. "But can you remember anything about my biological mother?"

Bonnie sat down in the chair beside the phone. "You say Evelyn was a good mama?"

"I loved her dearly."

"How 'bout yo' daddy?" Bonnie asked.

"They were both wonderful parents."

Bonnie shifted uncomfortably in her chair. "Then maybe you should... jes' let things be," she said. For a moment all she could hear was the long-distance static over the phone line.

"Let things be?"

"You are havin' a baby," Bonnie said. "That is such a blessing. And yo' letter say that you need to take it easy. I know many women in my day that had beautiful, healthy babies after months of bed rest. Ain't no need in gettin' yo'self in a state about the past."

"But isn't that for me to decide?" Augusta asked almost desperately. "Isn't that my call?" She took a deep breath. "Mrs. Wilder," she said, "is it that you *can't* help me, or that you *won't*?"

"Oh, gal," Bonnie said wearily. "We didn't see most of the women that dropped these children. They arrived in the night with so many secrets . . . most in a lot of pain. Yo' mama coulda come from a whole 'nother county, a whole 'nother state, even."

"I guess you won't help me, then."

Bonnie could hear the disappointment in the silence that followed.

"Well . . . thank you, ma'am," Augusta said.

"Sound like you got a good life," Bonnie ventured. "A good husband! And you're havin' a baby! Right there . . . right there are three blessings that many women will never have."

"I won't take up any more of your time."

"Just give thanks, gal," Bonnie said. "Relax yo'self and don't be worryin' 'bout all this old nonsense."

"Good night, ma'am."

Bonnie wasn't quite sure how long she sat in the dark room. It wasn't until she heard the insistent drone from the phone that she realized she hadn't even hung up.

FIVE

Canaan Creek, 1957

Mayweather's Diner was right across from the Grove Cinema Playhouse. Bonnie and Thora paused at the corner of Main Street and waited until Canaan Creek's one and only traffic light had turned green. They had just cried through two showings of *From Here to Eternity* and now headed to the diner for dessert. Bonnie closed the tiny pearl button at the top of her white cardigan. She loved this time of year, when the stifling summer had given way to a fresh autumn chill. Most of the shops were decorated with the orange and brown colors of the All Hallows' season. Flickering white lights were strung from telephone pole to telephone pole, through the entire length of the two-block shopping district.

The untroubled mood that had always prevailed in the Three Sisters had finally returned. After four months, questions about the dead child had stopped. Absent of any credible explanation from the Sheriff's office, folks had contrived their own theories, ranging from a band of Gypsies to hoodoo sacrifices. Whatever they had supposed seemed to allow them to sleep, worship peacefully and go on about the business of living.

The light finally clicked to green and Thora took Bonnie's hand as the two friends crossed the street. They were usually delighted to have a bit of time without their husbands. In fact, Bonnie and Thora planned the whole weekend together while the men traveled to see a baseball game in Nashville. And it wasn't *just* a regular game for Naz Wilder. He and Horace were driving Naz's green pickup truck all the way to Tennessee to see Jackie Robinson play. Early that Saturday morning, Bonnie had served her man a breakfast of French toast and honey ham, then Naz grabbed his old Black Crackers cap from the drawer, kissed her on the cheek and bounded out of the house to pick up Horace.

"Is that Ruby-Pearl Yancy?" Thora asked as they stopped in front of the diner.

Bonnie saw the small woman standing at the box office of the movie house.

"Ain't she the saddest thing," Thora said.

The image of Ruby-Pearl, cloaked in a dark chiffon scarf, plucking her own movie fare from her purse, was a sorrowful sight. Ruby-Pearl looked up just in time to notice Bonnie and Thora staring from across the street. Bonnie wanted to let her go on, but they had already seen each other and it would be beyond rude not to speak. Bonnie grabbed Thora's arm and the two dashed back across the street, just as the light was about to change again.

"Why, Ruby-Pearl," Bonnie said, brightening her voice.

"How you doin', honey," Thora said kindly.

Ruby-Pearl nodded at them both. She fiddled with the strap of her purse. "I was gonna call you, Bonnie . . ."

"You got a phone?" Thora blurted.

Bonnie elbowed Thora in her ribs.

"Just a party line," Ruby-Pearl answered. "If you ever need to reach me," she said, "jes' call Ruth and she'll jangle me out there on Route 9."

"That's wonderful," Bonnie said.

"It's jes' a phone," she said modestly. "And it sho'ly took me long enough."

"Folks gotta do things in they own time," Thora said.

Ruby-Pearl closed the cinema ticket in her hand. "I was thinkin'," she said to Bonnie. "Thinkin' that maybe one day I'd come to one of yo' ladies' meetin's . . ."

"Why in the world you wanna do that," Thora put in. "I wouldn't wish any of them Harvest ladies—and especially that damn Tilde Monroe—on my worse enemy."

Ruby-Pearl laughed. "You are a caution, Thora Dean!"

"Ain't she, though," Bonnie said.

"I guess I'm . . . tryin' to get myself out the house a lil'," Ruby-Pearl said.

"That's a fine idea," Bonnie said.

Mrs. Mayfield, the movie usher, was about to close the doors.

"I better get on," Ruby-Pearl said.

Bonnie embraced the woman. "You have yo'self a good time," Bonnie said. "And I will certainly call you befo' our next Harvest meeting."

"Take care of yo'self, girl," Thora said. They were about to walk away. "And you gon' like the movie," Thora called. "Make sho' you got yourself a load o' hankies."

Ruby-Pearl wagged her finger at Thora, then she hurried into the theater.

"Look like she finally comin' along in the world," Bonnie said as they crossed the street.

"About damn time."

"The woman lost her family, Thora! She been to hell and

back." Bonnie suddenly stopped on the sidewalk in front of the diner. "And weren't you the one who jes' said that ever'body got to do things at they own pace. Wadn't that jes' you?"

"Well, yeah . . ."

"I was proud of you . . . bein' so sensitive and all."

"And I meant it," Thora insisted. "But I guess bein' gentle and understandin' jes' don't come natural fo' me."

The glass door at Mayweather's chimed when they entered the diner. A large jukebox by the entrance played "The Woo Woo Train" by the Valentines. "Hey there, Polly," Bonnie called. Thora waved to the slight white woman counting change behind the cash register.

"How do there, Bonnie, Thora," Polly called. "Just set anywhere!" Polly pushed open a door that looked like a pink-wrapped present and went into the kitchen.

Thora chose a booth. She and Bonnie slid in on either side.

"Slow tonight," Thora said, noticing the sparse crowd.

"It's comin' on that time a year when folks like to stay home."

Decorated with pastel pink and blue curtains, Mayweather's was lined with a long brassy counter that practically extended the length of the place. Back in the forties, Polly made the decision to open her door to *all* people, and some of the local white folk decided to frequent Arnold Byer's place instead. Polly didn't much care. She made more than a good living serving the colored folks in the Three Sisters. Bonnie and Naz ate there once in a while, but Thora and Horace were regular customers. It was a little joke around the Wilder and Dean houses that Thora was such a bad cook that Horace knew Mayweather's menu by heart.

Mayweather's *did* have the best desserts. This time of the evening, after a movie or a late church service, dessert is what most people ordered. Bonnie decided on the fried peach pie and coffee. It took only a few minutes for her to gobble it down.

Thora took her time and sat cutting the chocolate swirl from the yellow part of her marble cake.

"Why didn't you jes' order the pound cake?" Bonnie asked.

Thora's attention was focused a couple of booths away. She didn't answer.

"If you gon' cut the dark part out," Bonnie continued, "why not jes' ha' the yellow cake to begin wit'?"

Thora glanced over Bonnie's shoulder. "That's Cal Monroe," she said.

Bonnie turned to look. She could only see the back of a man. A round-faced dark brown woman that Bonnie hadn't seen before was sitting across from him. "No."

"Yeah, it is too."

"You sho' that's Cal?" Bonnie whispered.

"He jes' peeked over his shoulder, lookin' all guilty and everythin'." Thora raised one thin brow. She always raised her brow when she had devilment on her mind. "Think Tilde know her man done skipped out?"

"They only sittin' together, Thora."

"My ass! They's lookin' mighty cozy there."

Bonnie turned again. The woman's hair was swept off her chubby neck and wound on the top of her head like a cinnamon bun. Thora was right. She did appear captivated by Cal's words. And that was saying a lot because Cal Monroe wasn't the most interesting fella in town. Every once in a while, the woman reached across the table and stroked his hand.

"That man love hisself some fat women," Thora said.

"That's fo' sho'." Bonnie giggled. She suddenly felt bad that Cal Monroe might actually be cheating.

"Ole loudmouth Tilde always into somebody else's affairs," Thora went on, "and here her man done gone to town. Now, there's some justice."

Bonnie put her empty coffee cup on top of her dessert

plate. She set a dollar and seven cents on the table before she got up. "I ain't crazy 'bout Tilde's ways," Bonnie said, "but I don't think this has anythin' to do wit' justice. And I know that you don't *really* feel that way either."

"Come on, now," Thora said, batting her lashes. "This don't gi' you jes' a little satisfaction after hearin' that woman's mouth all these years?"

"No," Bonnie said. Then she thought about it. "Well, not much."

"You jes' as bad as me," Thora laughed.

They walked past Cal. Thora, in all her brazenness, couldn't help but slow her pace. Cal's appetite suddenly became so ravenous that he barely looked up. Bonnie could hear his fork nervously tap against the beige glass plate. Thora was about to confront him until Bonnie yanked at her hand and the women left the restaurant. As they walked to the car, Bonnie couldn't help but wonder what made a man go to a woman like that. She wasn't any younger than Tilde, and not even prettier. Yes, Tilde was a loudmouth, but so was Cal. Naz once joked that Cal and Tilde Monroe were a match made in heaven. He said that the only somebody who could tolerate either one was the other.

Thora drove along Baychester Parkway and Bonnie sat silently. After a while, the stores and paved roads turned to thick trees and dry red clay.

"Why you so quiet, Bonnie?"

"Thinkin' of Tilde."

Thora sucked her teeth. "There's a whole lot of other subjects worth considerin'."

"I jes' mean . . . well, why would her husband sneak 'round like that?"

"You *know* Tilde and still gotta ask why?"

"Oh, come on now, Thora. That's not what I mean!"

"He's a *man*, Bonnie."

"They don't all do that."

"Most of 'em . . . at some point."

"How can you say that? Horace never stepped out on you."

Thora's eyes stayed on the road.

"Right?" Bonnie asked. Thora didn't answer. "Right?" Bonnie asked again.

"I 'spect he did," Thora finally said. "Once."

"What?" Bonnie gasped. "When?"

" 'Bout two years ago."

Bonnie was stunned. "And you didn't tell me, Thora?"

"It's embarrassing," she said. " 'Sides, Horace swo' up and down that I was talkin' crazy. But a woman know these things."

"I cain't believe this," Bonnie started. "I tell you all my most inner secrets and you ain't said boo 'bout this! This!"

"It all passed so quick."

"With who? Who was the woman?"

Thora paused. "One of the Bell sisters."

"Shut yo' mouth right now!"

"I ain't lyin'," Thora said.

"Birdie?"

"Bessie."

"Get on away from me!"

"Horace is good wit' people," Thora said. "You know how charmin' he is. But I noticed that they seemed to avoid each other in church. Then he started actin' funny 'round Bessie. Cuttin' his eyes toward her, twirlin' his hat all nervous-like when she come 'round. And the other Bell sisters, they lookin' at him sideways, clickin' they teeth and carryin' on. They all such trollops in the first place."

"I never thought so," Bonnie said.

Thora looked at her friend like she was a traitor.

"Well, I'm sorry, Thora, but I never thought that."

"Come on, Bonnie! Them gals been fast fo' as long as I can remember. And I mean all three—Essie, Bessie and Birdie!"

"But how?" Bonnie asked.

"What you mean, how?"

"How they start carryin' on?" Bonnie asked. "And when?"

Bonnie could see the hurt on Thora's face. "Horace went up to Bessie's house to fix her sink. Before he left home, he tole me it was jes' a routine job and that it wouldn't take mo' than a half hour. Well, Bonnie, the man was gon' three damn hours!"

"Maybe the pipes were all clogged or somethin'. You know how hairy them Bell sisters is."

"That wasn't all. I know he was at her place a few mo' times too."

"How?"

"Mother Carey . . ."

"She a hundred and two, Thora."

"The woman can still see as good as you and me both," Thora argued. "She say them Bells musta had a lot of trouble in they commode, 'cause Horace been in and outta there a lot."

Thora pulled into the gate on Blackberry Corner. She turned off the engine and the two women sat for a moment.

"So . . . one day I asked him," Thora went on. "I say, 'You fuckin' Bessie Bell?' "

Bonnie grabbed her own mouth to stop herself from crying out.

"Yes, I did too," Thora confirmed. " 'Course, he tole me I was nuts. Say my mind was making things up. So I say, 'Well, whether it is or whether it ain't, you fixin' to git up out my house!' "

"And?"

"Ain't had no problem since. You know I don't tolerate that kinda mess. Horace Dean ain't nobody's fool! If there's a choice between Bessie Bell and me . . ." Thora did a double take at Bonnie's front porch. "Who you expectin' this late?"

Bonnie couldn't make out the dark figure standing at her door. Godfrey circled the house, slightly agitated.

"Don't tell me you got yo'self a backdo' man," Thora teased.

"You jes' plain silly." Bonnie got out of the car and walked toward the porch. A young girl, no older than seventeen, was standing at the door. The porch shadows obscured her features. She looked to be carrying a bundle of clothes.

"Hey there," Bonnie called.

The girl didn't answer. She barely attempted to look at Bonnie and Thora as they approached.

"Can we do something fo' you, sugar?" Bonnie asked.

"You mean what you say?" the girl asked.

Bonnie stopped just below the steps. " 'Scuse me?"

"Ain't you Bonnie Wilder?"

"Yes."

"You the woman who want the babies?"

The bundle in her arms suddenly took on a different form. When she shifted the load, Bonnie could see the outline of a head and two little feet. Bonnie felt her heartbeat quicken.

"You *are* the woman that ask fo' the babies, ain't you?" the girl asked again.

"What . . . ?" Bonnie stuttered.

"Stood up at the lodge hall," she said. "I seen you myself."

"I . . . I meant only . . . if somebody 'bout to do harm to a child."

Thora looked as shocked as Bonnie.

"I ain't fixin' to do no harm," the girl answered. "But, I ain't 'bout to take care no chile neither." The girl glanced down into the blanket at the quiet baby. "The onliest reason I didn't go to that nurse live out in Canton and have her . . . well, you know . . . is 'cause a what you said at that meetin'. See, I ain't for killin' no babies, inside me or out."

"I don't . . . understand," Bonnie stammered.

"You said to bring the babies to you," the girl insisted. "That's what you said, right?" Before Bonnie could answer, the girl plopped the child in Bonnie's arms. A slight odor of curdled milk rose from the damp blanket.

"I cain't take yo' baby, miss!"

"Naz will kill you dead," Thora whispered.

"Hush," Bonnie snapped.

"I ain't name 'im or nuthin'," the girl said, picking up what looked like a batch of rags and placing it by Bonnie's feet. "And he only six weeks old, not enough time to know my smell, even." The girl pulled a dark sweater around her shoulders. "I jes' gi' him some milk, so he ain't hungry." She looked directly at Bonnie and said, "I won't ask you no questions 'bout what you plan to do. And I won't be back."

"Look a h'yere," Bonnie cried. "I cain't do this! I cain't be doin' this . . ."

"You look like a nice lady," the girl said as she turned to leave the porch. "You got me and God's blessings both."

"Wait a minute," Bonnie yelled. "Hey, girl!" She had to trot to follow the young woman around to the back of the house. "Wait jes' a damn minute here," she screamed. "Hey you, Mama . . . please . . ."

Seconds later, the girl had disappeared into the woods. The baby cried out as Bonnie labored to run as far as the clearing. Godfrey followed, barking the whole way. Bonnie stopped at the edge of the woods, out of breath, searching the darkness in a panic. "Thora," she hollered toward the house. "Help me here."

"What you want me to do?" Thora called.

"Something!" Bonnie cried.

Thora stepped past the bare blackberry bushes. "You the one stood up and said it, Bonnie Wilder!"

Bonnie rocked the crying baby. "Don't tell me that, damn it!"

"Cain't cuss in front of the chile," Thora teased.

"Don't you dare, Thora Dean. Don't you try me now!"

Bonnie searched the black woods but could see no movement. "Tell me this didn't jes' happen," she said to herself. She peeked into the blanket. The baby's eyes were two slits and his body was shaking from screaming so loud. "Naz is gonna kill me."

"Yep," Thora said, covering her ears against the noise.

"Oh, my Lord," Bonnie whispered when she looked into the blanket again. "That woman jes' left her baby. What in the world am I gon' do with this chile?"

"Don't ask me," Thora said, lighting a cigarette. "I ain't got no kids and don't want no kids."

Bonnie walked warily across the back lawn. She set the batch of clothes at the bottom of the steps, beside her wash bucket, then carried the screaming baby into the house. Godfrey, who usually rushed in, looked content to stay on the back porch. He lay there with his head down, recoiling at the sound of the wailing boy. Bonnie held the child with one arm and clicked on the kitchen light. Her body felt numb and the house seemed almost foreign with the sound of the crying child. She paced the linoleum floor, while Thora opened a bottle of wine. Her expression was one of amusement as she drew on her cigarette.

"This gon' be a two bottle night," Thora called over the wailing.

"None fo' me," Bonnie said. "Gotta keep my wits."

"You been a mama for all of five minutes and already you ain't no damn fun!"

Bonnie took the child into the living room and sat on the soft sofa with the boy in her lap. The child's screaming had begun to calm and his eyes widened. He looked as dazed as Bonnie. Her head spun with questions. Who was this mama and how could she leave this baby? She could tell that the child knew his mama was gone. Surely he could sense the change in body rhythm. Bonnie swayed gently, trying to assure him that everything would be just fine.

Thora walked from the kitchen with a water glass full of wine. The pretense of a dainty cup hardly seemed necessary after the night's events. She sat at the vinyl-covered dining table, just feet away from the couch, and tapped the ashes from her cigarette into an ashtray. "What you gon' tell Naz?"

"Heck if I know." Bonnie lay the baby on the couch and opened his soiled blanket. His clothes were just as filthy and stained. The boy seemed to be watching her as she removed the tiny shirt and the limp saturated diaper. His naked body looked like a chunk of bittersweet chocolate. Bonnie grabbed a dry doily from the armrest of the sofa and draped it over the child's body. She set him in Thora's arms and dashed into the bedroom.

"This chile stink to the heavens," Thora carped, the cigarette clenched between her teeth, "but he jes' as cute as a kitten."

Moments later, Bonnie returned with a damp cloth, one of Naz's old T-shirts and a can of talcum powder. She wiped him down and sprinkled powder over his body. Bonnie used her teeth to bite a tear into the cotton, ripped it and fastened it around the baby's bottom, then secured the makeshift diaper with two safety pins. Funny how she had nothing in the house to take care of a baby, but somehow maternal instinct and imagination took over.

"What the hell are you gon' do, honey?" Thora asked.

"I need to sleep on this one," she said.

"Ain't nobody gettin' no sleep tonight!"

Bonnie's mind clicked away. "I'm gon' tell Naz the truth," she said. "I mean, the chile jes' come to me. Right?"

"You did kinda ask for it."

"I ask for a lotta things," Bonnie snapped.

"So?"

"I don't know!" Bonnie looked around helplessly. "And I ain't gon' think about it no mo', 'cause the mama'll be back. She'll change her mind and she'll be back befo' Naz even come home tomorrow."

"I wouldn't hold my breath," Thora said. "If Mama-gal had the notion to leave this baby, then I'm afraid the chile is jes' plain left." As if on cue, the baby began to whine, then wail. "Damn it, Bonnie. Gi' the boy some milk or somethin'."

"Mama say she jes' fed him."

"Then give him a sip of this," Thora said, holding up her wineglass. "This'll calm his ass down."

Bonnie ignored her friend's trifling remarks. She held the baby's cheek to her own. His little puffs of breath were sweet and his face felt like butter. She couldn't understand how the mother could just leave. And more, Bonnie couldn't believe that someone had actually taken her statement to heart. The infant whimpered, then yawned, then slept on her shoulder. Naz would understand, Bonnie thought. She lay the baby's sleeping body across her chest. Naz would have to understand that the baby had just come to her.

SIX

When Naz left for Nashville that Saturday morning, he'd worn a pair of khaki pants and work boots—he'd been dressed for the park. But when he returned Sunday, he had donned a gray suit, a bold red tie and a fedora with a tiny blue feather. Naz usually felt uncomfortable in anything fancier than leisure slacks and a flannel shirt. One of the reasons he disliked going to church was that he had to dress up. Though he looked magnificent in Sunday clothes, the stiff gabardine annoyed him and the silk of a tie was like a slippery noose around his neck.

Naz stopped in the foyer to skim through the weekend mail. Bonnie looked over at the baby sleeping comfortably in the sewing basket on top of the dining room table. She had to admit that, after Thora had left first thing this morning, it was wonderful puttering around the house, knowing that a baby lay gurgling just feet away. Every once in a while she would talk to him and somehow she felt the baby understood her. At the very least, the child understood love.

Naz walked into the living room and removed his hat. He

didn't seem to notice that the blinds were half closed to the midmorning sun and the room was quiet of the usual TV sounds. Bonnie prayed that the child would give her a few minutes before he woke up and was glad that Baby Wynn slept so soundly. Baby Wynn. Thora had come up with the name. Last night into early morning as the two women sat pondering the fate of the child, the same word kept repeating itself. "*When* the mama comes back, *when* Naz gets home, *when* will that damn baby stop crying..." So Thora started calling him Baby When. Bonnie respectfully changed the spelling.

"Looky there at you, Naz Wilder," she said, running her hand down his lapel. "My man go away fo' a few days and come back sharp as a tack."

"Some of the fellas invited Horace and me to Sunday service," Naz said. Bonnie made sure her body blocked the basket on the dining room table. She followed him into the bedroom. "Jackie 'tend church no matter where the team..."

"You worshipped with Jackie Robinson, sho' nuff?" she asked.

Naz nodded. "Since me and Horace was goin' to Sunday service, we decided to go to the tall man shop there in Nashville and get us a couple of suits. Glad we did, 'cause the evenin' news was makin' pictures of Jackie right there at the church."

"You don't say," Bonnie replied.

Naz slipped the suit jacket onto a wooden hanger and pressed it into the back of his closet behind his flannel shirts. He reached into his bag and handed Bonnie a soft, flat object wrapped in white tissue paper. Most times Naz would bring home a can opener or a pot holder when he returned from a trip. When she opened the tissue, inside was a yellow and green scarf.

Bonnie reached up and hugged him around the neck.

"Got it when I went into town in Nashville," he said proudly. "But I need to warn you, Horace got the same one fo' Thora."

"She'll love it jes' as much as me," Bonnie said, folding the satin square.

"Godfrey," he called.

Bonnie flinched at the loudness of his voice. "I put 'im out back," she said.

"Must mean Thora still 'round."

"She left early this mo'nin'. Say she wanted to roast a duck fo' Horace."

"What you make fo' me?"

"Got a brisket," she answered. Bonnie could feel her heart pounding. She glanced out toward the basket. "Also made some candied yams."

"Sound good," he said, stepping into his overalls. "What you gals been up to this weekend?"

Here was the perfect opportunity to explain what had happened. But she knew that Naz's easy mood would quickly turn to anger. He didn't get irritated too often, but when he did, he would yell at her, then withdraw for hours of silence. "We ain't done much," she said. "You know . . . this and that." Bonnie stayed at his heels when he returned to the living room, where he snapped on the TV. Thankfully it was low. He flicked through the stations until he found a movie with Claude Rains, and took a seat on the couch. Bonnie stood between Naz and the table. She could see that Wynn was still asleep. "You want yo' dinner in here?" she asked.

"If you don't mind. My leg been botherin' me bad and I jes' want the comfort of the couch."

Bonnie thought about taking the basket with her into the kitchen but knew it would only draw Naz's attention to the baby. Also, moving Wynn might cause him to wake. Bonnie prepared a plate of beef and rice. She spooned thick glaze over the yams, then quickly cut a wedge of cornbread.

"Bonnie," he called.

She froze.

"Put some lemon in my tea. You know I like that lemon."

Bonnie took a breath. She placed his dinner plate on a wooden tray, along with a tall glass of sweet tea topped with a lemon slice. When she returned, Naz was standing over the basket.

"Who you sittin' fo'?" he casually asked.

"Sittin'?"

"Don't look like Jenna Dixon's child or any of the babies from church," he said, taking the tray from Bonnie. He crossed back into the living room and set the food on the coffee table. Naz opened a napkin and stuffed it in the top of his shirt.

"It's not Jenna's chile." Bonnie answered. She shut her eyes for a moment and prepared for the worst. But so far, Naz didn't seem bothered or even concerned. His gaze remained on the black and gray figures that darted across the TV screen, even as he leaned over to slice the thick wedge of beef.

"So whose chile, then?" he asked as he stared at the TV.

"I don't rightly know," Bonnie answered.

"Don't rightly know what?"

"I don't know whose chile this is."

Naz turned to her, suddenly focusing on her words. "What you say?"

Bonnie steadied herself before she began. "A gal . . . left the baby with me."

Naz looked at her blankly.

"Thora and me had come from the diner last night," she explained, trying to keep her voice easy and calm. "Went over there to Mayweather's, you know, and we were coming up the drive here and this young gal was standin' at the do'. She was jes' standin' there, Naz." Bonnie could see a strange look slowly etch itself across her husband's face but she couldn't tell if it was anger or disbelief. "Woman say she couldn't take care of the baby . . ."

With the napkin still dangling from his collar, Naz went to the basket again but kept his distance as he looked down at the child, now wide-awake, gurgling contentedly, his limbs thrashing about. "You mean to tell me that some woman come up to this house," he said slowly, "and left a baby wit' you?"

"Yes, sir."

Bonnie braced herself for his anger. She waited for him to tell her how it was all her fault for standing up at the town meeting and making foolish statements. But when she looked up, Naz was bent over, poking at the baby's chin. Wynn's voice pealed like a tiny bell.

"Lord, today," Naz said, his pinky finger caught in the baby's fist.

"You ain't mad?"

"Don't expect you to turn a tiny baby away."

Bonnie was shocked at Naz's response. She suddenly thought that if he were this understanding, maybe he'd let her keep the child.

"But we cain't keep him," Naz went on. "You know that."

That glimmer of hope inside of Bonnie suddenly dimmed.

"Don't mean to piss on the picnic," Naz said, "but you know I cain't abide raisin' nobody else's chile. You know that."

"He's a good baby," Bonnie assured.

"Bonnie . . ."

"Jes' cry when he scared," she said. "And he a good lil' eater—"

"Bonita." Naz's tone had sharpened.

She lifted the gurgling baby and held him close to her chest. "Where am I supposed to take him?"

Naz sat down on the couch and pulled his plate close to him again. "If I know you, Bonnie, you'll figure somethin' out." His focus went back to the TV. The baby began to cry.

"What if I cain't find a place for Wynn?"

"Wynn?" Naz asked. "You done named the boy?"

"Thora named him."

"Ain't no wonder his name is some damn Wynn," Naz blustered.

"S'pose I cain't find a home for him," Bonnie pressed.

"You will."

"But s'pose I cain't," she insisted.

"Then we'll have to take 'im to Pine," Naz said.

"Ain't no way—"

Naz looked over his shoulder. For the first time since finding out about the child, Bonnie saw anger flash in his eyes.

"I'll come to something," she said quickly.

Without another word, Naz's attention went back to the TV. Bonnie lay the screaming Wynn in the basket and carried him to the kitchen. She placed the basket on the counter, then took a can of milk from the back of the fridge, poured it into one of the bottles that the mama had left and set it in a pan of water. Bonnie quickly lit the stove. She had done this more than a few times when she sat for Jenna Dixon and Delphine, but never was she filled with such indecision and uncertainty. Wynn was totally in her care—there would be no mama coming to collect him. After a few minutes, Bonnie saw that tiny bubbles had begun to form at the bottom of the pan. She removed the bottle, tested it on the back of her wrist, then placed the nipple to his mouth. Wynn pulled so furiously that his sucking sounded throughout the quiet kitchen. In just these few hours, she had grown used to his own kind of talk and even his cry. His helplessness was irresistible, his innocence addictive. The thought of taking the baby to anyone made her feel empty. But Bonnie would get over it. She had to.

The Pertwell County Home for Children rested in an old farmhouse on top of Lorden Hill, sixteen miles north of Canaan Creek. Bonnie had only passed the forlorn dwelling a few times, and once she had actually stopped by when the Ladies of the Blessed Harvest had delivered donated clothes around the holidays. She'd never actually gone inside. Tilde Monroe insisted on quickly dropping off the gifts and the woman swooped in like Santa Claus with a box of good cheer while Bonnie and Miss Idella had waited outside.

Over the years, it seemed that no improvements had been made to the house. Shingles on the roof had come loose and the tall splintery beams were covered in chipped green paint. Weeds and dead grass jutted from the crawl space. The porch had a visible dip in the center, where a big woman sat in a rocker reading the paper. About a half-dozen kids played on a tire swing and a small wooden jungle gym in the front yard.

Bonnie pulled her sweater around her shoulders and made her way up the bush-lined path. The woman on the porch lay her paper in her lap.

"Auntie!" a dark brown boy of about nine dashed across the yard and grabbed one of Bonnie hands. He had shiny long hair that brushed his cheeks.

"Hi, Auntie!" A little girl with a chipped tooth and knobby knees tugged at her skirt.

Soon all the children were clamoring around her, excitedly touching her clothes and gripping her hands like a relative they hadn't seen in months. None appeared older than ten and their clothes were ill fitting but appeared to be clean. Two little girls began to fight as they both tried to hug Bonnie around the waist.

The big woman leaned forward in her chair. "Mae-Wanda," she called. "Ya'll stop that mess!"

The smaller of the two girls scuttled up from the dusty ground. The other lay there crying.

"Get up, Molly," the woman went on. "Get up and get on yo' way."

The woman heaved herself up from the chair. She was as large a woman as Bonnie had ever seen. Her bright yellow housedress *had* to be especially made, and the wooden chair that she sat in looked to be reinforced under each armrest with an extra two-by-four. As Bonnie approached, the woman smiled warmly, and her face, the color of chestnuts, appeared open and friendly.

"Y'all go'n 'bout yo' business," the woman said, trying to scatter the kids.

"I wanna talk to Auntie," a boy said, refusing to release Bonnie's hand.

"Me too," one of the taller girls yelled.

"Ain't nobody gon' ha' no oxtails if you don't take yo' lil' asses on 'way from here," the woman scolded.

The children reluctantly returned to the yard.

"Love themselves some oxtails," the big woman said. "'Specially the way Grandmama make it." She trod down the first step. The wood groaned. "I'm Connie Blanton," she said, offering a hand.

"How do," Bonnie returned. She looked back at the kids, now waving from the yard. "Who in the world do they think I am?" Bonnie asked the woman.

"A nice lady," Connie said. "*Any* nice lady."

Connie Blanton led Bonnie to one of the wooden chairs on the porch. A thin red cushion actually made the splintery seat comfortable.

"Can I get you somethin', Auntie?" Connie asked.

Bonnie looked curiously at the woman's huge, dark face. Deep dimples in both cheeks gave her a look of sincerity. "I'm fine," Bonnie replied. "And my name is Bonnie Wilder."

Connie plucked her newspaper from her chair. Without hurrying, she folded it, then settled into the rocker again. Her bare feet looked almost white from the ash. And though she appeared no older than forty, her ankles were as fat as her calves.

"They calls me Big Mama," she said. "And Edie-Grace . . . she the woman who run the place with me, they calls her Lil' Mama—they also calls her Spot sometimes." Connie laughed heartily. "But that's a whole 'nother story. Miss Thompson," Connie went on, "she do the cookin' fo' the kids, and they calls her Grandmama . . . and Sarah Mae, she teach the kids they lessons, they calls her Sister Mama. And whosoever happen to come this way . . . and believe me when I tell you, baby," Connie said, shaking her head, "there ain't many folks wander our way . . . well, the kids call 'em Auntie . . . sometimes Uncle."

"I see."

"We likes to treat folks like family," Connie explained. "Lil' Mama started that years ago. She figure that if you treats folk like family, they cain't stay away too long."

"What about their parents," Bonnie asked. "I mean . . . what do they call them?"

"Call 'em gone," Connie said simply. She sat back and silently rocked. Surprisingly, her chair swayed without a single sound. "What can we do fo' you, Auntie?"

Bonnie placed her handbag flat on her lap. She wasn't sure

what she'd ask here at the county home, or what they'd ask her. "I . . . have a chile," she started. "And I might need to put him up fo' adoption."

"He yo' natural chile?"

Bonnie tucked her lips together. She didn't expect Connie Blanton to be so direct, so soon. And Bonnie knew that if she told the truth, there would be too many other questions. "Yes," she replied.

"And why a nice lady like you wanna gi' up this chile?"

"Circumstances."

She could feel Connie's eyes sweep over her crisp linen dress and brown shoes with a matching purse. She could feel Connie asking, in her mind, "What circumstances?" But the woman only said, "I s'pose that's what brings most of these children to us."

"Ma'am?"

"Circumstances," she said. All at once, Connie lifted herself out of the chair. With the quickness of a woman half her size, she bound down the stairs. "Henry," she shouted. "Don't you stand on that chile's back like that! What in the world's wrong wit' you?"

The boy with long hair threw a handful of dirt at a tall, wiry boy with dusty brown hair.

Connie yelled, "Don't let me tell Lil' Mama that you out here makin' trouble."

Bonnie glanced at the property. She could tell that it had once been a working farm. A chicken coop with tangled wires was now as barren as the small hog pens across from it. Bonnie spied a garden with several patches of collard greens and tiny green squash. She felt relieved to see vegetables growing. In all of this ruin, their presence hinted at life.

Connie made her way back to her chair. Before she sat, she

took a packet of chewing tobacco from the pocket of her housedress. Then she settled in again, leaning her thick arms on the rests.

"May I ask how many children live here?" Bonnie asked.

"We got ten now. Twelve is capacity."

"Do you get . . . a lot of babies," Bonnie asked.

"Hardly never. Mostly older kids," Connie replied. "Rainey," she said, pointing to a small girl of about eight, "she the youngest chile we got. Come to us at two years old."

"And she's still here?" Bonnie couldn't hide the shock and sadness in her voice.

Connie shrugged her heavy shoulders. "The chile got some medical problems. And families 'round here are mostly po'," she explained. "Cain't afford the healthy kids they got already. So there ain't much adoptin' goin' on 'round these parts."

"I see," Bonnie said.

"Don't mean to piss on the picnic, but you know I cain't abide raisin' nobody else's chile. You know that."

"Me and Lil' Mama," Connie went on, "we do what we can." Connie pulled the foil wrapper down the sides of a chunk of tobacco. "But the county cut back on our funds like you wouldn't believe. Sometimes I think they forgets us altogether."

One of the little girls ventured toward the porch. It was the child who had held on to Bonnie's skirt. Two frizzy red braids looked odd against her dark face. When she smiled, she was missing her two front teeth. She slowly eased toward Bonnie to sit on her lap.

"Lisette," Connie said. "You know you ain't s'posed to be up here where grown folks is talkin'."

"I jes' come to say hi," she said.

"Git on yo' way, lil' gal."

She scooted back down the steps.

"We better go on in the house, Auntie," Connie said, standing. "Them kids'll drive you crazy in a minute or two."

Connie opened the screen door and Bonnie followed her into the house. It smelled like chicken soup, mixed with the rural scent of cut green grass and a tinge of backwoods skunk. Connie slipped into a pair of gray loafers that sat by the door. She proceeded to what would be the living room in most houses. Dim and stark, the room, surprisingly, had a fairly new black sofa. It was surrounded by a dozen or so aluminum chairs scattered throughout. One wooden chair sat by the window. Bits and pieces of toys were stacked in a splintery chest pushed off to the side, and an old TV sat in a corner of the room.

"That you, baby?" a woman's voice yelled.

"Company come," Connie yelled back.

"Company! What kinda company?"

"That be Edie-Grace," Connie explained to Bonnie. "She help Grandmama with dinner. She be along directly."

Bonnie nodded.

"Have a seat," Connie said.

Bonnie was about to sit in the wooden chair by the window.

"That be my chair, Auntie," Connie said. "Ain't no offense, but you could sooner take any ole seat. That one made fo' Big Mama . . . if you know what I mean."

Bonnie could see that, like the rocker on the front porch, this chair was a bit larger and also reinforced. And Connie didn't seem the slightest bit embarrassed. She sat down then lifted the dusty rose drape away from the window and peered out at the children. Bonnie sat on the couch.

"Where do the children sleep?" Bonnie asked.

"In the back," Connie answered.

Just then, a short, wiry woman hurried in from the kitchen. She was as brown as Bonnie, but splotches of lighter skin stained her face and neck to the very top of her pink blouse. "Well, dern if we *don't* ha' ourselves a visitor," she said, smoothing down her apron. "I'm Edie-Grace Guy," she said, extending her hand. Her grip was strong and firm. "So glad you can visit, Auntie."

Bonnie nodded politely. She understood why the kids sometimes called Edie-Grace Spot.

"I guess you and Connie already started talkin'?" Edie-Grace went through the room, pushing the chairs neatly against the walls.

"She got a chile . . ." Connie said. "Near as I can tell, a baby boy. That's as far as we got."

"As I mentioned to Mrs. Blanton," Bonnie quickly put in, "I'm *considerin'* . . . I mean to say that I . . . *might* want to . . ."

"How old?" Edie-Grace asked.

"About two months."

Edie-Grace nodded. "When children *do* get adopted from us, it's usually the boys."

"Why?"

"Farmers need boys to help out on the land," Edie-Grace explained. "I guess boys pay off a lil' better than gals."

"She wanna see where the children sleep," Connie said.

Edie-Grace Guy placed a few toys on top of the chest, then gestured for Bonnie to follow. Connie stayed seated, looking out of the window.

Bonnie trailed Edie-Grace through the house. From the outside, the place looked much smaller than it actually was. They walked down a hall, its walls painted a pea green, with about a half-dozen closed doors. Edie-Grace opened the first door, to a room with six identical cot-type beds. Threadbare pink blankets were folded on top of each. Bonnie stepped into the doorway and noticed the top cuff of stained white sheets, neatly folded beneath each blanket.

"This where the girls sleep." Edie-Grace walked ahead and opened the next door as Bonnie followed her. This space had fewer beds. Each was topped with an old blue blanket. "Boys sleep here."

"Girls and boys sleep so close together," Bonnie said.

"Most times we don't ha' no troubles. But I cain't say it ain't *never* happened. Jes' the nature of gals and boys, ain't it?"

"I s'pose," Bonnie said.

She followed Edie-Grace to the next door. "This where Grandmama and Sister sleep," Edie-Grace said, opening the door. Inside, Bonnie spied two full-sized beds. "And this where me and Connie sleep," she said, opening the door to the next room. Bonnie noticed only one king-sized bed. She paused for a moment. Bonnie suddenly recalled when Tilde had referred to the county home women as "a bit peculiar."

"Down there," Edie-Grace said, pointing, "is where the kids do they lessons."

Bonnie was still taken aback by the sight of one bed. She knew that Edie-Grace Guy could sense her apprehension, yet the small woman continued as if she'd allow Bonnie to make her own opinions, as everyone else surely had.

"This last room is the nursery," Edie-Grace said, snapping Bonnie out of her thoughts. She opened the door. The small room, with yellow paint on the walls, contained only one wooden crib. It looked as lonely as everything else in the Pertwell County Home. Bonnie pictured Wynn sleeping in that room, so alone, so bare, and the thought horrified her.

"I ain't gon' lie to you, Auntie," Edie-Grace said as they walked back into the living room. "An adoption is a rare happenin'."

"When was the last?" Bonnie asked.

"Three, maybe fo' years ago. Yes, folks are poor. But also, adoption is so much paper, so many questions, so much time."

"At least... the kids seem happy," Bonnie said, trying to find a silver lining.

"They are happy," Edie-Grace said. "But these kids often come from bad situations. So jes' 'bout anything after their homes would make them happy. That lil' gal, Lisette," Edie-Grace went on, "Lord my God, but the chile probably know mo' 'bout servicin' a man at nine years old then you and me both."

Bonnie didn't want to hear this.

"And the boy Henry," she said, "you wouldn't want to know what his mama put the po' chile through."

"No, I wouldn't," Bonnie whispered.

"We're the last stop, Auntie," Connie added. "That woman who put her chile in the creek..."

"Yes," Bonnie said.

"If she anythin' like some of the parents we done seen," Connie went on, "I 'spect she did that chile a favor."

Bonnie gripped her purse until her hand felt numb. She wanted to run out of here, but of course she couldn't. Though, one thing was clear, she could never bring Wynn here. Her feelings had little to do with the dilapidated house or even where Edie-Grace and Connie chose to sleep. It was the emptiness. The desperation. It was knowing that Wynn *could* possibly be here until it was time for him to go off into the world as a man. There was love here, but how much could these women give to ten or twelve kids, some of whom were so damaged that they surely took up most of the attention. And what about these kids? Would they, in turn, infect Wynn with a darker knowledge of life at such a young age?

"Thank you so much fo' yo' time, Miss Guy, Miss Blanton," Bonnie said, heading for the door.

"When will you bring the chile?" Connie asked.

"I'm . . . still thinkin' things through," Bonnie said.

"Jes' give us a call," Connie said. "Party line three."

"I will," Bonnie said, hurrying out.

"Love to ha' you stay fo' dinner," Edie-Grace offered.

"Thank you, ma'am, no." Bonnie trotted down the steps and started up the path. The kids followed her. Again, they grabbed both her hands and two others yanked at her skirt.

"Y'all go'n back and play," Edie-Grace yelled.

Bonnie got to her car and slipped in. She had to separate small fingers from her forearm before she closed the door.

"Bye, Auntie," the kids called.

"You comin' back?"

"You got any kids?"

Bonnie was so choked up that she couldn't respond. She looked back at the porch of the house. Edie-Grace had gone back inside and Connie had returned to her rocker.

"You kids move 'way from the car," Connie called as Bonnie pulled off. When she looked back, she saw thin brown legs in a fog of red dust. A dozen fluttering palms. Six kids, waiting.

Bonnie's mind was so preoccupied with thoughts of the county home that at first she didn't notice the old blue Dodge parked in her driveway beside Thora's black Lincoln. The Dodge looked familiar but Bonnie couldn't quite place the owner. She suddenly got a tense feeling in her stomach. Maybe leaving Thora at the house to babysit wasn't such a great idea. She ran to the porch, and Wynn's basket sat beside the door, his blanket draped over one of the chairs. Bonnie didn't hear crying. Even when she rushed through the living room to the kitchen, all was quiet, and there was no sign of Thora. Two Carnation

Milk cans had been opened, baby bottles were strewn on the counter and the sterilizing pot was still boiling. She charged toward the bedroom and stopped at the door when she saw Ruby-Pearl, Wynn sleeping in her arms. Thora lay stretched across the bed.

"Demons!" Thora said in a loud whisper. "Babies ain't nothin' but some demons!" Thora's hair was flat in the back and disheveled on the top when she sat up. "That lil' boy... that damn Wynn... cried from the time you left 'til 'bout twenty minutes ago."

Bonnie walked into the bedroom and kissed Ruby-Pearl on the forehead. The woman had never been to her house before and she looked so peaceful holding the baby.

"Yes, I did call her," Thora defended. "I damn sho' did! And I don't care what you say."

"He's fine, Bonnie," Ruby-Pearl said. "Precious as he can be."

"I called Ruby-Pearl on her new party line," Thora went on, "and I begged her... begged this woman on my hands and knees... to come and help me with this hollerin' devil. Lord ha' mercy, Bonnie," Thora rambled, "I didn't know you'd be gone all this time. I had to find *somebody* who knew what the hell they was doin' while you was runnin' all over hell's half acre."

Bonnie had never seen Thora so out of control. On the other hand, she had never seen Ruby-Pearl look so calm. The scarf that usually covered her face rested around her shoulders and there seemed to be life in the slack side of her face.

"I guess Thora told you how Wynn come along," Bonnie whispered.

"You know I did," Thora said, sinking back onto Bonnie's bed. "I'da told ever'body jes' to git some relief from that lil' hollerin' thang!"

Ruby-Pearl said, "Cain't believe a gal jes' left this chile."

"You recall when I stood up in that meeting... when I opened my big mouth 'bout the babies?"

"Wasn't no big mouth," Ruby-Pearl insisted.

"Yeah it was too," Thora put in.

"For out of the abundance of the heart, the mouth speaketh," Ruby-Pearl said gently. "Big heart... that's what it was."

"I don't know," Bonnie said.

"Who is the mama?" Ruby-Pearl asked.

"Never seen her befo' in my life," Bonnie returned.

"It's a miracle," Ruby-Pearl said breathlessly, "and He's working it through you, Bonnie."

"He ain't such a miracle for Naz, though," Bonnie put in.

"But you got the chile you couldn't have," Ruby-Pearl said simply.

Bonnie rarely talked about her personal business, except to Thora. But since Ruby-Pearl was now involved, Bonnie explained the reason.

"Men and their pride," Ruby-Pearl said sadly. She now looked at Bonnie as sorrowfully as Bonnie had looked at her. "I'm so sorry," she said. "But, you know, my Vaughan woulda felt the same way."

"Thank you for sayin'."

The silence that followed was filled with questions.

"What happened at the county home?" Thora asked.

"County home?" Ruby-Pearl asked.

"I cain't take Wynn there," Bonnie said. "I couldn't take any chile there."

"Vaughan used to keep the grounds fo' a boys' home up in Hencil." Ruby-Pearl shifted Wynn on her lap. "He say the ones that grew up there seemed to be missin' somethin'."

"These kids certainly were," Bonnie said. "Part of me wanted to fix 'em all and gi' 'em the love they need. But another part needed to run outta that place as fast as I could."

"Jes' like I want to get the hell outta here," Thora said, pulling herself up from the bed. "I'm fixin' to smoke me a cigarette . . . no, two! One in this hand," she said, raising her pink-tipped fingers, "and one in this hand. Then I'm gon' po' me a glass of that blackberry wine . . . and I mean a big ole water glass full . . . and then I'm gon' take my tired ass home."

Bonnie kissed Thora on her forehead. "Thank you, sweetheart," she said. "We'll figure this all out in the mo'nin'."

"*You'll* figure this out," Thora said, leaving the room.

Ruby-Pearl turned a sleeping Wynn onto his stomach and set him on Bonnie's bed, nestled between two pillows.

"Come back to you easy, huh?" Bonnie asked.

"Like it was yesterday." Wynn was now fast asleep, but Ruby-Pearl continued to pat the boy on his back. She didn't look at Bonnie when she said, "Vaughan's insurance take care of me pretty well, you know."

From the moment that Bonnie had seen Ruby-Pearl with Wynn in her arms, she knew what the answer was. It made perfect sense. Still, Bonnie held on to the idea that maybe, just maybe, if she couldn't find a home for Wynn, Naz might break down and *she* could take the child.

"My house . . . it's so big," Ruby-Pearl said.

"You a woman alone," Bonnie said. "What will folks say?"

"I ain't studyin' 'bout no folks. That's one thing me and Thora Dean have in common."

"Are you sho' 'bout this?" Bonnie asked.

Ruby-Pearl knelt on the floor beside the bed. "You ever wake up in the mornin'," she said, "and somehow the day is jes' different . . . I mean, things smell the same, sound the same, but the color outside . . . the color of the sky tell you that somethin' is comin'. You don't know if it's good or bad. But you know it's fixin' to change yo' life."

"I think I know what you mean."

Ruby-Pearl rubbed circles into Wynn's back. "This feeling only happened twice," she went on. "The first time was when I lost Vaughan and my lil' gal, Glory. That mornin' I made love to my husband, I cooked breakfast, I played with my baby girl, I made lunch, dinner and all the while I noticed how different the day looked . . . the sky was the color of ripe peaches. It was that evenin' that I crashed the car. It was that very strange-looking day that I lost my family and pert near lost my mind." Ruby-Pearl had since gotten past the tears, but the pain was still there. Bonnie could hear it in the catch at the top of the woman's throat. It would surely *always* hurt.

"You say there were two days," Bonnie said.

"Yes," Ruby-Pearl said. "The second one was when I woke up this mo'nin'. The sky had a yellow tone. It like to scare me outta my soul. I wanted to jump back under the covers. Then Thora Dean called." Ruby-Pearl smiled and her scarred face looked so pretty. "I started to tell Thora no. I was fixin' to say, 'No, I cain't make it there today.' I started to hang up on my new party-line phone and have the dern thing disconnected. But something say to me, 'Ruby-Pearl, it don't matter if the day is yellow or gray or purple or white—if you keep hidin', you'll be hidin' fo' the rest of yo' life.' "

Bonnie lowered her head. "This is such short notice . . ."

"I know."

"But . . . if you feel that you can do this . . ."

Ruby-Pearl's voice dropped an octave. "You mean you might actually consider it?"

"If it ain't gon' be me, then I cain't think of nobody better. And if you don't take 'im, he'll jes' wind up at the county—"

"Of course I'll take him," Ruby-Pearl said. "Of course I'll take him!" She raised her arms over her head like she couldn't contain the joy, but quickly drew them back, like if she got too happy, it would all disappear. "When?"

"I . . . I guess . . . I'll pack his things and . . . bring him to you tomorrow."

"Lord Jesus," she called out.

Bonnie had purposely tried to keep an emotional distance from the child. She had bought a few things—necessary things, like diapers, safety pins . . . the ones with yellow ducks on the clasp . . . undershirts and sleepers, just in case it took a few more days to find the baby a home.

The next day, she drove to Ruby-Pearl's house with the baby boy in the wicker basket beside her. These past two weeks had been the happiest time of her life. She looked over at Wynn. The squirming child and the scent of talcum powder in the car became all too much. But she reminded herself that Wynn would now have a wonderful mama. The only thing she regretted, as she placed the child in Ruby-Pearl's arms, was that she didn't have more time. Bonnie only wished that she could have kept the baby at least one more night.

SEVEN

Bonnie woke to the scent of ham and hominy drifting from the kitchen and a glass of freshly squeezed grapefruit juice on her night table. She sat up in bed and smiled. This meant that Naz was in one of his cooking moods. And Bonnie loved being pampered by her husband. She slipped into her white terry-cloth robe, took her glass and headed toward the sound of clanging pots and the sizzle of cured meat. Naz was bent over the stove, coating a skillet with melted butter.

"Mo'nin', baby," he said, without looking up.

Bonnie kissed the closest part of his body that she could reach: the top of his arm. "Fresh-squeezed grapefruit juice," she said. "And on my night table, no less. Toast, grits," she went on as she peeked into the pans. "Even got some ham in there." Bonnie set her glass on the counter. She took a coffee mug from the pantry and filled it at the stove. "All this cookin' goin' on—must mean you 'bout to duck outta goin' to church this mo'nin'."

"Jes' 'cause I'm makin' my sweetheart some breakfast?"

"'Cause you makin' yo' sweetheart some breakfast *on Sunday.*"

"Mrs. Wilder, you cut me to the quick," he said.

"That mean you goin'?"

"No," he replied. "Jes' mean I'm insulted." Naz put his arms around his wife. He placed a light kiss on her forehead, then pecked her lips. Bonnie enjoyed his playful spirit. She loved the firmness of his shoulders when she wrapped her arms around his neck.

"You don't mind if I stay home?" he asked, moving back to the stove.

"You the one paces from the pit, Naz Wilder. But please tell me you ain't fixin' to go fishin' or some such."

"I plan to clean out the shed today, maybe do some yard work." He poured the scrambled eggs into the hot skillet. "And remember you asked me to hang you another clothesline out back?"

"Yes, but why cain't you do these things *after* church?"

"You know I'm much better working in the A.M.," he said. "I come home after settin' in church all mo'nin', and the onliest thing I'm fit to do is listen to the game."

"That is the truth," she admitted.

Naz always appeared childlike in the kitchen... like a boy with a task well over his head. A slapstick mood prevailed as he attempted to use the potato peeler and when he tried to pull the hot bread right from the toaster. The sound of Bobby Darin on WQNB singing "Splish Splash" and the picture of Naz trying to pluck a piece of broken shell from the already set eggs made him look even funnier. The more awkward Naz looked, the more charming and loving Bonnie thought he was. Yet still, he hadn't approached her in that way since the night that she had tried to "heat things up." And Bonnie was much too shy to approach him. Maybe it was too late to try to change things after all these years, she thought. Maybe it *was* a mistake.

"Paper come?" she asked.

"Nope." He slid the eggs onto two plates. "That new boy ain't worth two dead flies. Either the paper git here late, git here soppin' wet or don't git here a'tall." He spooned stiff grits onto both plates. "Yo' Red Velvet Cake lookin' mighty good," he said, gesturing toward the crystal-covered platter on the counter.

"Olive Lockie's recipe." Bonnie took her seat at the table. She flipped through the short stack of mail that Naz had placed beside the napkin holder. "I have to admit that a cup a beet juice do give it a nice texture."

Naz set the plates on the table. "Did you see I got me a card from ole Dewey Bradshaw? Ain't had time to read it yet."

"Dewey Bradshaw?"

"You 'member Dewey," he said. "Played fo' the Birmingham Black Barons."

"Lil' fella? Pitcher too?"

Naz nodded. "Dewey ain't big as a gnat," he said, sprinkling salt on his grits. "But that boy pitch like he was born to it."

Bonnie found the card.

"Go'n and read it fo' me, Bonita," Naz said. "You know my eyes is bad."

It wasn't his sight that made him shy away from reading his mail—the man could see as well as anyone. It was that he could barely read at all. For a proud man like Naz, it was easier to lay the blame on something beyond his control, like his eyesight. At church, he carried his bible just like everyone else. And when asked to read a passage, he'd hold the book at arm's length like the old folks. Once he even cleared his throat like he was about to begin, but spent the next few moments squinting. Reverend Duncan would admonish him about forgetting his reading glasses; even he didn't know the truth. Many times, Bonnie had offered to teach her husband to read, but Naz contended that after thirty-six years, he didn't need to start learning now.

Bonnie reread the first line in the letter twice before she could make out the words. From the chicken-scratch writing, she guessed that Dewey Bradshaw could read and write little better than Naz.

Nazareth,

This here is Dewey. How you been makin out, old boy?

I been good. Don't play no more ball, but we gettin to be old fellas now. Life is like that.

Been a while since I seen you. Last I heard, you was gittin married. Hope you happy. Me, myself, I ain't never got married. But I keeps company wit a fine girl. Maybe one day she be crazy enough to jump the broom . . .

"That Dewey is a madman," Naz laughed. "Crazy as a betsy bug."

Bonnie went on reading.

Speakin of gettin married . . . you member my lil brother Woody? He live in Mississippi. He bout to take the step, and I'm goin down to be a witness. Thought I'd stop in the Three Sisters and say hey . . .

"Dewey comin' here?" Naz asked.

"He left his phone number," Bonnie said. "Say to call him if it's okay."

"Damn right it's okay! Dewey good people." Naz lay another slice of ham onto his plate at the stove. "Usually one team don't get together with another'n, you know? Sometime there be bad blood. But Dewey was different. We hang out at night and be the best of friends, then the next day, when it come time to play each other, Dewey turn into a warrior. And don't git in the way of one of his fastballs. I seen 'im knock ole Kel Smith . . . and he bigger than me . . . knock 'im clean out." Naz beamed at the thought. "He say when he comin'?"

Bonnie skimmed the letter. "Say it won't be until spring."

"Sho'ly don't wanna miss ole Dewey. Whenever it be, I need to cancel my plans."

"Think you could spare it?" she asked sarcastically.

Naz reached across the table and took her hand. "You tryin' to tell me I been away from you too much, Miss Bonita?"

"Ain't said nothin' of the kind," she answered coyly.

"I'm serious," he went on. Three soft knocks sounded on the front screen door. They heard Godfrey howl. "If you think I been gone too much," he said, "I'll stay home more." Naz took his coffee mug and went to answer.

Bonnie stacked the pots and frying pans. Fried egg was spilled on top of the stove and ham grease was spattered everywhere. She wondered if she *had* been missing Naz more than usual. His friends and sports outings were important to his life, and most times, she didn't mind. Lately, the emptiness she felt from being childless was only exacerbated by having to give up Wynn. She had to admit, though, that Ruby-Pearl was the picture of joy. The women decided that the only explanation that could withstand the congregation's scrutiny would be to say that Wynn was a relative . . . Ruby-Pearl's nephew, to be exact. Bonnie hated to lie to the reverend and his wife, and Ruby-Pearl wasn't pleased at the deception either, but Thora suggested it was the only decent way to explain Wynn's sudden presence in Ruby-Pearl's life.

"Bonnie," Naz called from the front yard.

She dried her hands on the dish towel, praying that he hadn't gotten ahold of the paper boy. When she got to the door, Naz was circling the front yard with the morning news tucked under his arm.

"Got you a package," he said, peering up the road.

Bonnie stepped outside and held the screen door open with one hand. There was no box of any kind. Then she heard a tiny mewling. Godfrey sniffed excitedly around her sewing basket, which sat beside one of the porch rockers in front of the door. She released the screen door and bent to look inside. Two tiny sets of eyes stared up at her. Dressed in pink terrycloth jumpers were twin girls no more than two months old. Aside from the syrupy murmurs of contentment, their limbs thrashed so lustily that the basket almost toppled. Patches of brown curly hair dotted their heads.

Naz stood below the steps. "I guess the word is out," he said.

Bonnie could feel a catch in her throat as she gently lifted one of the girls from the basket. A ball of blue yarn rolled into her place.

"Leastwise, the mama had a mind to take yo' knittin' needles out," Naz said, referring to the sharp rods that now lay under the rocker.

Bonnie held the child close. She smelled like caramel and her eyes looked wide and bewildered.

"This is . . . crazy," Bonnie whispered. "It jes' don't make no sense."

"Make perfect sense to me," Naz said.

The twin in the basket began to cry, so Bonnie placed her sister in Naz's reluctant arms, then lifted the child from the basket. Again came the lovely scent of caramel. It was clear that the babies had been well cared for. They were plump and appeared untroubled. Their clothes were new, their bodies shiny from oil and their curly hair clean and tangle free. Bonnie spotted a green hankie tucked in the side of the basket. Inside the tight knot she found seventy-three cents. Bonnie could feel her heart breaking. And not so much for the children—they were safe—but for the mother who had surely summoned all she had to leave her girls.

She sat beside Naz on the steps. Bonnie had to take a deep breath to process it all. She could scarcely believe that not one, but now three babies had actually come to her door. Naz stared at the girls as if they were two aliens, then shifted the child in his arms to hold her head in his palm.

"Where you learn to handle a chile like that," Bonnie asked, quite impressed.

"All us fosters," he said, his voice absent of her same joy, "we older ones had to pitch in."

The girl in Naz's arms began to cry, and her sister immediately joined her. For Bonnie, the sound of babies, *any* babies, gurgling, whining or crying on Blackberry Corner was like a chorus of angels.

"We got to tell somebody," Naz said.

"Blessings," Bonnie said, rocking the child. "They come sometimes. I don't know what's goin' on here but—"

"You know exactly what's goin' on," Naz insisted.

She craned her neck to look at him. "I prayed for a chile . . . that ain't no secret," she said. "But a lot a folks ask fo' a lot a things."

"When this happened the first time," Naz said, "*that* was strange. I know it and you know it too. But twice . . . and now twins!" He shifted the girl in his arms. "Where these babies come from? I mean, we know all the gals in Canaan Creek," Naz went on, "and they raise they own children . . . and that woman Pine been talkin' 'bout—even she cain't spit these children out that fast."

"Maybe God is tryin' to tell me I should be a mama."

"'Scuse me, God," Naz yelled up toward the sky, "I'm *Mister*

Wilder, and I ain't about to keep no babies! So don't send no mo'!"

"You stop yo' blasphemin'!"

"We need to call Pine." He set the whining baby back into the basket, and Bonnie did the same with the other twin. "We shoulda called him in the first place, and that woulda been that."

"I cain't." Bonnie lifted the heavy basket and followed Naz into the house.

"Sheriff's department is lookin' fo' any lil' thing," Naz said. "And this ain't no *lil'* thing."

"I cain't call Pine."

"So . . . you think that you gon' find a home fo' these babies too?"

"If I have to."

Bonnie could see the anger building in her husband.

"Who you know is ready to take even one?"

"Both," Bonnie said.

"Lord above," Naz called out.

"Cain't part 'em," she insisted.

"Who in the world you know ready to take *two* babies?" he asked.

"Ruby-Pearl was talkin' 'bout—"

"You gon' give two mo' children to Ruby-Pearl?" Naz asked.

"If you let me finish," she snapped, "I was gonna say that Ruby-Pearl's friend that live in Hencil . . . she wanted a baby."

"What the hell you know 'bout Ruby-Pearl's friend?" he barked. "What the hell you know 'bout *any* of this?" Bonnie didn't answer.

Naz shook his head in frustration. "Never know to look at you," he went on.

"What?"

"So sweet and kind . . . ever'body love Bonnie. Hell, I love

Bonnie! But folks never would know that you can be selfish as sin."

"Say what?"

"Since day one," he said, holding up his finger, "since the first day I met you, yo' daddy spoil you rotten. Everything had to be Bonnie's way... or no way!"

"If everythin' *was* my way," she argued, "Wynn would be sittin' up on this couch, alongside these gals."

Naz paced the low carpet. "When we got married," he argued, "I wanted to move... wanted to leave the Three Sisters. Go to a bigger city—Charleston, Columbia, even. I coulda worked at one of them colleges or coaching at a ball club..."

"Oh, please, don't start this again, Naz Wilder."

"Hell, I didn't wanna stay in this town, but Bonnie had to be here."

"This is my home," she said. "This is yo' home."

"Don't mean we got to stay here forever! Neither one of us had no family left."

Bonnie shook the basket to calm the screaming children.

"We need to do somethin' 'bout this," Naz said.

"I'm not callin' Pine," she insisted. "He'll take these babies right on to the county home. And no chile need to be there."

"You don't know what you doin' here, Bonita."

"A baby need a mama," she said, "that's all I know."

"But who?"

"I ain't thought that far yet."

"What 'bout yo' church friends?" Naz asked. "Them Harvest ladies."

"They all got kids. Miss Idella got grands."

"I jes' mean that maybe we can open this thing up," Naz said. "Maybe they know some folks wantin' a chile."

"*I* know some folks wantin' a chile," she argued. "Me!"

"Damn it, Bonnie, you ain't hearin' me."

Both girls were screaming. Maybe they were hungry. Or maybe it was because of the tension between her and Naz. Bonnie looked up at her husband. Fire burned in his eyes. "I hear what you sayin'," she said calmly. "I understand that you think we need to tell somebody."

"Good."

"But if we tell the Ladies," Bonnie insisted, "folks like Tilde Monroe'll be on my ass. On my ass," she repeated.

"This ain't 'bout you, Bonnie!"

She felt a stab in her heart. A stab that brought the point home. Perhaps it *was* her own selfishness. If she brought the Ladies of the Blessed Harvest in, she wouldn't have as much time or access to the children. And, of course, Tilde would want to take over everything.

"Look," she said to Naz, "maybe I'll visit with Ruby-Pearl's friend."

"Bonnie..."

"If she take the children, fine," she said desperately. "If not, then... I'll call the Ladies, I promise."

Naz reluctantly agreed. The babies' relentless screams filled the house and Naz took refuge in the shed. She knew that this was the last thing her husband wanted in his life right now, but this was *all* Bonnie *ever* wanted. Suddenly her day was so full. Of course, there would be no church this morning. Her time was, once again, consumed with bottles, feeding, clothing and cuddling, twice over. In a few days, she would visit with Ruby-Pearl's friend up in Hencil. Bonnie prayed that the woman would accept two babies—and more, that she would be even half as loving as Ruby-Pearl. But how would Bonnie know for sure? She pushed those thoughts away for now, knowing that, just like everything else, her heart would guide her through.

Bonnie sat behind the driver's seat of the car, looking at the address that Ruby-Pearl had written on a slip of notebook paper. From the driveway, she and Thora peered at the small white house, its porch strewn with hoes and rakes and rows of empty clay pots stacked on top of each other.

"This it?" Thora asked.

"It say 1515 Jeremy Trail," Bonnie answered. She had asked Thora to come along and was surprised that her friend hadn't fought her about it. Thora wasn't one for being in the company of children, but she seemed to like the idea of helping find a home for them. Thora claimed that visiting prospective parents was like going to their house and telling them that they had hit the number. Bonnie knew it was more. But she didn't embarrass Thora by insisting that she had a heart.

Bonnie rapped lightly with the wooden knocker. Save for the banging of piano keys coming from inside, the house seemed peaceful enough. A water hose lay unraveled on the side of the house, next to a flower bed with a row of dug-up holes. Next to the front door was a planter, shaped like a tuba, crawling with ivy.

"Just remember, Bonnie," Thora said, looking at herself in a compact mirror. "We ain't jes' gon' ask 'em the obvious things, like how long they been married and such. We gotta keep our eyes open fo' the *small* stuff."

"Like?"

"Like . . . if they *look* happy. Like if she *look* like she wanna go upside his head. Don't wanna have them gals 'round folks that fight all the time."

"Anything else?" Bonnie asked sarcastically.

"Don't get all snippy!" Thora pressed her compact closed. "Somebody got to handle the business end of this thing. Not *ever'body's* heart s'posed to be hangin' out they chest." Thora knocked impatiently. "They do know we comin', right?"

"Yes, honey. Ruby-Pearl wrote them two weeks ago."

"And we should prob'ly ask 'bout things that *ain't* so obvious," Thora went on. "We should know if they ever stole something or what grade their mama went to in school and if they ever been in jail . . . you know, stuff like that."

"If they ever been to jail?" Bonnie chuckled.

The door swung open. A tall, lanky man stood inside. His bushy black mustache looked to be glued on the top of his lip and his thin hairline inched back to the middle of his head. "Y'all the baby people?" he shouted.

Thora looked at Bonnie and smiled.

"Yes . . . sir," Bonnie answered.

"Ain't expect two such pretty ladies," he said just as loud. "Lettyyyy," he called.

"That them?" a voice shouted back.

"Yes, ma'am! Baby ladies here, baby!" He laughed at his own play on words.

Letty hurried to the door. She was as tall as her husband. In fact, Bonnie took note of how much the couple resembled each other. Letty put her hands on her cheeks like she had just encountered two movie stars. First she embraced Thora. "Don't know which one of you is Bonnie," she said, "but ya'll both gettin' a big ole hug!"

"Gracious me," Thora mumbled into the woman's chest.

Bonnie introduced herself and Thora Dean, even as the woman hugged her.

Letty Bonton was what the old folks in church would call a handsome woman. Tall, strapping and black as the northern soil, her salt and pepper hair framed her face in a soft puff. She talked loud, gestured big and marched across the wood floor like a small elephant. The piano player Bonnie had heard turned out to be a young girl trying to play "Blue Moon" from some sheet music in front of her.

"Tandy," Letty yelled.

"Ma'am?"

"Go'n home now, dahlin'."

"Yo' company come, Miss Letty?" the young girl asked.

"That's right. And tell Ma Dear it's three dollars come Friday."

"Yes'm," the girl answered. She shut the piano top and hurried out, looking curiously at Bonnie and Thora until she had closed the front door behind her.

Letty led Bonnie and Thora through her house, which was streaming with sunlight and overrun with more junk than Bonnie had ever seen in one place. Chairs of all kinds (and none of them matching!) were stacked on top of each other and pushed into the corners of the small sitting room. Bonnie could only see patches of a threadbare Oriental rug, for most of it was covered by opened cardboard boxes loaded with clothes. Reams of fabric and balls of yarn were strewn here and there, along with chassis of old sewing machines. Paper pockets stuffed with clothes patterns were piled on top of an old piano bench. But most prevalent in all of the junk were trumpets, trombones, clarinets and all kinds of metal and wooden flutes, which sat in boxes against the wall.

"Freddy tune instruments," Letty explained when she saw Bonnie and Thora staring.

"Wind," Freddy put in.

"Say what?" Thora asked.

"Jes' wind instruments!" he explained. "Couldn't tune a string if somebody held a gun to my head."

"And I teaches piano to kids," Letty went on.

"And I mean *all* damn day," Freddy laughed.

"Watch yo' mouth, baby."

"Oh, ya'll jes' be yo'selves," Thora invited.

Bonnie could tell that Thora liked it here. But Bonnie couldn't help but wonder about the safety of small children in such a cluttered environment. The place looked like a death trap. Then too, aside from the music, the Bontons were as loud as sin. Bonnie suddenly remembered that Ruby-Pearl had called the couple "fun."

"That Letty," Ruby-Pearl had said, "she love to laugh . . . her and Freddy both. Letty and Freddy! Names sound like a good chuckle."

Bonnie and Thora sat on a beige checkered sofa that hadn't a hint of a connection to either the brown paisley or red-striped armchairs. And the coffee table, heaped with old newspapers, had just enough space cleared for a couple of bowls: one held potato chips and pretzels; the other had Ritz crackers, Cheez Whiz mounded on them.

"Ya'll ha' some refreshments," Freddy said, taking a handful of chips and piling them into a paper napkin.

Letty dashed him a threatening look. She quickly lost it when she turned to Bonnie. "Tell us 'bout the babies," she said. "Ruby-Pearl ain't said much in her letter. Jes' say they was twins . . . twin gals."

"Well—" Bonnie started.

"Ain't that jes' somethin' else," Freddy interrupted. Crumbs clung to the hairs of his mustache. "Ya'll got babies po'in' down from the heavens like rain."

"That sound so pretty, honey-bear," Letty said to her husband. "Could be one of yo' poems. Freddy write poems, you know."

"Do tell," Thora said.

Freddy set his napkin on the coffee table. He leaned his long-limbed body forward in the chair. "Love come like buds in the spring," he started.

"Go'n baby," Letty said proudly.

"Love come like a church bell ring," he went on.

Thora nodded her head approvingly.

"Love come like a gentle smile," he went on. "Love come, let it stay a while."

Letty clapped for her husband, who beamed appreciatively. Thora also applauded. Of course Bonnie felt obliged to join in.

"Take a tender man to say them kinda words," Letty said, pecking her husband on the cheek. "That's how I know my baby'll make a good daddy. 'Cause he tender."

" 'Scuse me, Miss Bonnie," Freddy said. "But go'n and tell us 'bout the gals."

"Well," Bonnie said, "the twins look to be 'bout two months. And they seem as happy and healthy as they can be."

"Y'all had a doctor to look at 'em?" Letty asked.

Bonnie peered down at her hands folded in her lap. "No."

"Why?" Letty asked.

" 'Cause we wanted to keep this as quiet as possible," Thora explained. "If we brought in a doctor, then chances are, the law would get involved, the kids would wind up at the county home and we wouldn't be sittin' here with you good folks."

"I see," Letty said, satisfied with the reasoning. "And y'all don't have no idea where these gals come from?"

"Not even a clue," Thora said. She looked at Freddy when she said, "They jes' come like rain po'in' down from heaven."

"See how my stuff catch on!" Freddy hollered. "I need to make me a song out of that!"

"So what y'all need to know 'bout us?" Letty asked.

"You seem nice to me," Thora said.

"And you seem nice to me too," Freddy flirted.

"With all due respect," Bonnie started, "this house... it's lovely, but... well, babies need order. Might be a lil' dangerous for a toddler walking 'round all these... well, walkin' 'round all yo'... collectibles."

"Now, that's sweet," Letty said. "I like the way you said that. 'Cause the fact is, Freddy love hisself some junk. The man keep hold to ever'thin'. Still got the first pair of shoes he ever owned."

"She ain't lyin'," Freddy confirmed. "But there's a lot of money in junk. I got three hundred dollars from an old lamp my mama gi' me when I was a boy of seven."

"Shut up!" Thora said in shock.

"If I'm lyin', I'm flyin'," he said.

"But," Letty cut in, "if we knew we was gon' get these babies, we'd throw half this stuff away."

"Be worth it fo' a baby chile," Freddy confirmed.

The couple seemed nice enough, if a bit on the eccentric side. When Bonnie couldn't think of much else to say, she turned to Thora, who was obviously smitten.

"You have any questions?" Bonnie asked her best friend.

Thora pondered a moment. She folded her hands in her lap as she thought. "Ya'll ever been to jail?"

"Thora," Bonnie scolded.

"Never," Freddy said emphatically.

"Just once fo' me," Letty answered.

Bonnie's and Thora's heads whipped around at the same time.

"Ain't nuthin' bad," Letty said. "I mean, Ruby-Pearl can tell you. Just that, when I was a young'un, my daddy ran a still out back. After he died, I kept it goin' 'til I was in my twenties."

"Made her a nice piece a change, and a damn good sour mash too," Freddy said.

"Get outta town," Thora said.

"Letty still make us a batch ever' so often," Freddy added. "Fo' fact, we got some down in the basement. Y'all wanna taste?"

"Maybe this ain't the time, baby," Letty said.

"Perfect time fo' me," Thora said.

"None fo' me," Bonnie put in. "And none fo' Thora either."

Bonnie's words didn't seem to matter, because Freddy dashed down into what looked like the basement.

"As I was sayin'," Letty went on, "the law found me and closed me down. Then they took me in fo' two days."

"In to the jailhouse?" Bonnie asked. She had never known anyone who'd gone to jail, even for a day. And especially not a woman.

"Aw, come on, Bonnie," Thora said. "Ain't no worse than what Naz make out there in *yo'* shed!"

Bonnie was mortified. "Will you hush up," she scolded.

"Ain't nothin' wrong with makin' a lil' somethin'," Letty said. "'Specially fo' yo'selves."

"Did I hear that you brew grapes?" Freddy asked as he clamored back up the steps, carrying three shot glasses and what looked like a mayonnaise jar filled with clear liquid.

"Blackberries," Thora replied.

"Thora . . ." Bonnie gasped.

"Will you relax yo'self, Bonnie," Thora said.

"I hear you, pretty gal." Freddy filled the small glasses with clear liquid.

"Look," Letty said, sensing Bonnie's uneasiness. "Me and Freddy, Lord knows we ain't perfect. But we's good folk. Honest folk. Always wanted us a chile but . . . I cain't have n'an."

"Might be me, baby," Freddy said, putting his arm around his wife's shoulder.

"Who-so-ever it is don't matter," Letty conceded. "Point is, we jes' don't work that way. And when Ruby-Pearl sent us a letter and told us about you . . ." She threw up her hand and shook her head. "I knew our prayers had been answered." Her smile narrowed a bit. "But this is us, Bonnie," she said. "Letty and Freddy. Ain't 'bout to pretend to be nothin' we ain't."

"Amen," Thora said, taking a sip of sour mash. She gasped a bit at the strength.

Bonnie turned to Freddy. "Can I ask you one more question, sir?"

"Anything."

"You . . . don't mind raisin' another man's chile?"

Thora rolled her eyes.

Freddy swirled the liquor in his shot glass. "A chile is a chile," he replied. "And when it comes down to it, all these babies—they's only got *one* Father."

Bonnie hadn't been sure what to search for in the Bontons, or anyone else. What did good parents look like? More importantly, what did bad parents look like? Letty and Freddy certainly weren't perfect. But Bonnie's heart told her they were a loving and honest couple.

"Ya'll wanna pick these gals up tomorrow?" she asked.

"Mean we got 'em?" Letty squealed.

"Far as I'm concerned," Bonnie said.

"Amen," Thora called.

"We'll be there," Freddy shouted. "Be there tomorrow come hell or high water!"

Bonnie had a good feeling about her decision. And, of course, the Bontons were thrilled. Good parents or bad, Letty and Freddy seemed happy and their house was filled with life, albeit slightly disheveled. Bonnie and Thora made their way to the door, once again stepping past old sewing machines and instrument parts. Bonnie waved at the couple as she and Thora let themselves out. She didn't want to disturb their celebration, for Letty was playing the piano and singing "Blue Moon" . . . off-key, while Freddy sat tapping his foot and playing a piccolo.

EIGHT

Naz didn't seem surprised. Nor did he ask the questions he had asked twice before. His eyes were weary, perhaps from having been awakened so suddenly by another child's wailing or maybe from the futility of reprimanding his wife with yet a fourth abandoned infant in her arms. Bonnie could feel his frustration but she keenly felt her own frustration as well. She wondered how such an occurrence could thrill and amaze her and at the same time so thoroughly infuriate Naz. Without a word, he pushed open the screen door and went into the house.

The child calmed when Bonnie held her against her chest—perhaps because of the close and steady beating of Bonnie's heart. The child's mother had abandoned it with no apparent concern about damp winter weather, the porch beneath her infant's tender head or the rancid checkered blanket draped around her body. An unclasped diaper pin and the tiny prick marks it had clearly left on one of the baby's arms disclosed how neglected she was. Bonnie set her in the basket that had once held the twins and also Baby Wynn just three months ago and carried her into the house.

Naz was slumped on the sofa, his gaze focused on the TV screen. He didn't rise to switch the channel from the piercing sound of a station not yet signed on. He watched the vertical lines rise like the end credits of a movie.

Bonnie settled in the armchair across from him with the basket in her lap. "Folks know we care," she said, addressing his anger. "I can sho'ly think of a worser lot in life."

Naz didn't respond. His eyes stayed fixed on the TV.

"What is so wrong with helping a chile in need?"

"This is too much," he said. "This . . . is . . . too . . . damn . . . much!"

"I ain't got no control over folks droppin' their babies off."

"We turn that chile over to the law and I guarantee you this mess'll stop."

"Or maybe another baby'll die," she argued.

"Aw, hell," Naz whined. "There's a big difference 'tween a mother that abandons her chile and one that kills it."

"Maybe the only difference is me," she said quietly.

"You and Jesus," he spat. "Bonnie Wilder and Jesus Christ!"

Bonnie refused to take up the argument. Naz was angry. And when he was angry, the man was impossible to reason with. Bonnie simply carried the child into the kitchen. Naz stayed on her heels.

"We have a good life," he argued. "But all this . . . it's gittin' in the way."

"Ain't in *my* way."

He pushed aside a kitchen chair and it skidded across the linoleum. "I ain't gon' apologize fo' my feelin's," he said. "You knew who I was when we married and I ain't changed in all these years."

"Go'n 'bout yo' business, Naz Wilder! This is my concern, not yours."

"I goin' 'bout my business," he said, "and then I feel bad 'bout leavin' you alone with all of this."

"Jes' go'n, man!" She stood her guard, even if she knew the rift between them was growing. "I got plenty enough to keep me company."

"And what 'bout Dewey," Naz threw in. "My friend Dewey'll be visitin' in a few weeks."

"This chile ain't got ne'er a thing to do with yo' hunts or yo' baseball buddies. You do what you wanna do!" Bonnie reached into the cabinet for one of the six baby bottles she had purchased when the twins came. She filled a pot with water, placed it on the stove and put the bottles inside to sterilize.

"This ain't no home fo' kids," he hollered. "And these babies, they gon' keep on comin'. I jes' know it!"

Bonnie held the sleeping child. She knew he was right. But unlike Naz, she *prayed* that this would never stop.

"I ain't gon' do this no mo'," Naz quarreled. "Either we take that chile to the church," he insisted, "or we take it to the law. Your choice."

"I won't do either one," she said.

Naz kicked the bottom cabinet with his bare foot. Bonnie jumped. The baby's eyes snapped open and she began to scream.

"I don't understand," he yelled.

"It's jes' decent," she called over the crying. "That's all it is!" Bonnie set the baby in the basket.

"It might be decent," he said, slipping into his shoes by the door. "But it's also against the law."

"I don't believe that's true!"

"I told you once and I'll say it again," he attested. "You don't know what you doin' here!"

"You jes' go'n, Naz Wilder!" Bonnie snatched a set of tongs from the drawer. "Ain't got to be studyin' me or this chile."

"Hey, Wilders?" a voice called from the front porch.

Bonnie felt her heart stop at the sound of Deputy Pine's voice. Her eyes locked onto her husband's.

"Say there, Bonnie! Naz!" Pine yelled as he knocked on the wooden frame of the screen door. "Where y'all at?"

Bonnie pleaded silently with her husband. She pointed her head toward the door, beseeching him to go out and talk to Pine on the porch.

"Come on in," Naz called.

Bonnie thought about taking the baby and making a dash for the bedroom, but knew that Pine had already heard the child's crying.

"Mo'nin', all," Pine said as he walked in and removed his cap.

"Hey there, Pine," Naz said.

"Jimmy-Earl," Bonnie said, forcing a smile.

"What brings you our way this early on a Saturday?" Naz asked.

Pine slanted his head as he looked at the baby in the basket. "Ole Bailey Dial called me some time ago," he started. "Say lately he been seeing folks passing through his backyard . . . say somebody walked through first thing this mo'nin'."

"Who?" Bonnie asked.

Pine shrugged. "Say he cain't tell 'cause it be dark. Who this pretty chile?"

Bonnie never dropped her smile. Naz leaned against the refrigerator and listened to his wife's quick talking. "You 'member . . . Rita Sims, live out in Hooley?" Bonnie said.

Pine thought for a moment. "Don't believe I recall nobody like that."

"She visited Piney Grove once or twice." Bonnie plucked a

bottle from the boiling water and set it on the clothed table, then retrieved a can of milk from the fridge. "By the way, Naz jes' made a fresh pot of coffee. Let me fill you a cup."

"No, thank you," Pine replied. "Got to git back to town in a minute. This gal Rita Sims," he said, getting back to the point, "where 'bouts in Hooley she live?"

"Out there . . . by that big ole tobacco field," Bonnie said. Naz nodded at her inventive lies. "Nice lady," Bonnie went on. "Anyway, she asked me to set with her chile for the day."

"Cute lil' kitten." Pine smiled. "What's the baby's name?"

Bonnie paused. Naz pursed his lips to stop himself from smiling.

"Lucy," Naz answered.

"Pretty name fo' a pretty gal," Pine said.

"Speakin' a babies," Bonnie said. "Any more news about the chile in the creek?"

Pine straightened up. She knew that this would take his focus away from the basket. The fact that the sheriff's office didn't know any more today than they knew eight months ago was a sore spot. It made Pine, a man who took pride in his job, look weak and inept.

"We got some leads," he said defensively. "Jes' ain't panned out yet. But we ain't dropped this. We gon' find out somethin', sooner or later," he said.

Bonnie turned her back on the men as she filled a bottle with milk.

"This chile in the creek," Naz started, "s'posin' that instead of drownin' the po' lil' thing, the mama woulda dropped her chile off—say, at the sheriff station or . . . or the firehouse or . . . I don't know," he said, "maybe even with some ordinary person?"

Bonnie could feel the can of milk trembling in her hand.

"Abandonment," Pine shot back. "Mama be prosecuted."

"Least the chile be alive," Bonnie muttered.

"Wouldn't be no murder, that's true enough," Pine said, sitting in one of the kitchen chairs, "but the mama still wrong... still abandonment."

"And what 'bout that ordinary person," Naz asked. "You know, the one who took in the abandon chile? What would happen to her... or him?"

Pine rubbed the stubble on his clean face. "That kinda thing," he said hazily, "see, that got to be dealt with through the court... through lawyers and all that. A woman take in a chile like that, well, that's what they calls illegal adoption. And all kinds of things ain't right 'bout that."

Bonnie scraped a fingernail over a spot of dried egg yolk on the corner of the stove.

"I once heard of this woman," Pine continued, "she lived in the highlands, you know up there 'round Basin's Edge... she got herself into an awful scrape when she left her chile with a neighbor."

"It was *her* child," Bonnie said without turning.

"Jes' 'cause you gi' birth," Pine said, "don't mean you can do *whatever* you want. Shoo," he chuckled, "how many times have we heard a mama or daddy—they mad—say to they chile, 'Boy, I gi' you life and I can take it away too.'"

Naz laughed. "Sho'ly heard things like that."

"A mama cain't hurt a chile jes' 'cause it's hers," Pine said. "And you cain't leave a baby neither. Got to go through the courts and make it right. That woman I was jes' talkin' 'bout? Well, she come back after a couple of years to say hey and to see how the chile was doin', and they threw her butt right on in the pokey."

Bonnie felt her heart pounding.

"Take Ruby-Pearl," Pine went on.

Bonnie turned at the stove. "What 'bout Ruby-Pearl?"

"I'm sho' her and her brother did things the right way. I'm sho' she signed some papers and all." Pine tossed his head and smiled. "She crazy 'bout that nephew of hers."

"Sho' you don't want no coffee, Jimmy-Earl?" Bonnie asked.

"No, thank you," he said, rising. "Got to get back. Need to get with Bailey Dial," he said, walking toward the door. "John Brown it! I got to stop with Job Murray too while I'm over this way. Lord, that ole man! Got his tractor stolen and he 'bout to bust a vein."

"Good seein' you again," Bonnie said.

"You too," he said, then he turned back. "If y'all see any folk coming through—like what Bailey Dial done seen—let me know."

"I will," Bonnie called.

Naz showed Pine out. Moments later, the screen door slammed shut and Bonnie could hear the sound of Pine's engine and the ricochet of pebbles on the road as it pulled away. Naz wore an "I told you so" expression when he walked back in. But he never actually said the words.

"Thanks... for not tellin' it," she said to her husband.

"I think what you doin' is dangerous and crazy," he started. "But I would never, ever hurt you, Bonnie. You my wife... my heart... and I love you."

Bonnie felt the tears gathering.

"Honey," he said, lifting her chin. "We gon' keep on tryin', I promise. Tryin' to have a chile of our own, I mean."

Bonnie felt like a failure not being able to conceive. And she sensed deep inside that *she* was the one who couldn't make a baby, not Naz.

"Oh, I ain't give up," she said.

He kissed her forehead. "But, in the meantime, you got to get some help with this."

"Naz..."

"You know it's true. I don't want you to get yo'self in trouble," he said. "I'll stay behind you... I'm always behind you. But, please, just get you some help." Naz walked to the kitchen door. "I'm fixin' to mow the grass. Come on out back with me. Set out there and feed the chile."

After the twins, she had known there would be more. Bonnie'd felt it in her heart. So much so, she wanted to sit on her porch *every* night, *all* night, and wait for the babies... just like folks waited for the sweet spring vidalias that came from Georgia. She could almost accept not raising a child of her own if, every once in a while, she received one of these precious gifts. But Naz was her husband and she'd never want to lose him. Maybe she'd *have* to go to the church for help. Or perhaps... the Harvest ladies. Surely among the five other women they could find more options, someone willing to take in a child. Bonnie would still get to spend time with each baby that came her way. And Naz would feel better about it all if he thought she wasn't alone in this.

The baby girl's eyes fluttered open. Bonnie lifted her from the basket, sat in the kitchen chair and placed a warm bottle to her mouth. It all felt so good: feeding, rocking and loving. But there was no choice. She had to turn to the Ladies of the Blessed Harvest. Whether Bonnie liked it or not, she'd have to tell Tilde and those.

No tiny turkey sandwiches or deviled eggs were served at the meeting. Bonnie didn't make a pitcher of sweet tea or even a pot of coffee. On a Tuesday morning, three days after the fourth baby had arrived, she phoned the Ladies of the Blessed Harvest. Miss Idella, Tilde, Olive, Laretha and Delphine arrived within the hour. Tilde was angry at having been summoned by Bonnie, who wasn't even an officer of the Ladies of the Blessed Harvest. Naturally they were curious as to why Bonnie had convened an emergency meeting. And they also seemed surprised at the absence of food on Blackberry Corner. But even more suspicious was the presence of Thora Dean.

"I know it's our usual custom," Bonnie started, "to have food and—"

"What?" Laretha interrupted, "God ain't welcome at yo' meetin', Bonnie Wilder?"

Thora rolled her eyes.

"Ladies of the Blessed Harvest," Bonnie said, embarrassed, "let us start with thanks to our Lord."

The women rose and held hands. Bonnie said a prayer just long enough, she hoped, to make up for her lapse in judgment. She waited for all to settle down before she commenced again. During the pause, she could see Tilde contemplating the empty coffee table with pursed lips. She adjusted her pudgy hands in her lap, over and over, as if to make it known that no plate or cup rested there.

Bonnie began again, "I know this meeting is sudden—"

"Left my whites floatin' in blueing!" Olive called out.

"And today is Cal Jr.'s final game," Tilde put in. "You oughta know that, Bonnie. Yo' own husband is out there coachin' the kids!"

Thora reached up and squeezed Bonnie's hand. "Take yo' time, honey," she whispered.

Suddenly the baby began to cry in the back bedroom.

"Who baby you got back there?" Olive asked.

Thora sucked her teeth. "It's Ruby-Pearl's."

"Ruby-Pearl back there?" Laretha asked. "Wynn ain't that little. That sound to me like a newborn."

"And Ruby-Pearl ain't even come out to say hey?" Olive snipped.

"Look," Thora snapped, "this ain't easy for Bonnie. So would y'all jes' hush up so she can say her piece?"

Tilde raised a brow. Her expression clearly revealed that Thora Dean didn't belong here.

"I'm . . . not sure how to begin," Bonnie continued.

"Begin by gittin' to the point, honey-chile," Miss Idella threw in.

Bonnie clasped her hands. "Y'all . . . remember when the baby was found in the creek?"

"'Course we remember," Laretha said.

"You know something 'bout it?" asked Delphine.

"That's not what I meant to say."

"So what's all this about," Tilde asked impatiently.

"During that second meetin'," Bonnie went on, "I said that . . . maybe folks need a place to bring they babies—you know, when times get tough."

"We remember, we remember!" Tilde said.

"Well, when I said that," Bonnie stuttered, "somebody at that meetin' must've heard me, 'cause ever since that time . . . ever since that meetin'—"

"Bonnie been gettin' babies left at her do'," Thora blurted.

The ladies turned to Thora.

"What's that s'posed to mean?" Miss Idella asked.

"Young gals that cain't care fo' they kids, or *won't* care fo' 'em," Thora went on, "been leaving 'em fo' Bonnie. Sometimes in the middle of the night."

Tilde stared at Thora as if she were speaking a foreign language. "Look, I ain't got time for none of these damn games and puzzles," she said. "My children is out there on the ball field and—"

"Look at me," Thora said, standing beside Bonnie, "and hear me good! Bonnie has been gettin' babies dumped at her do'!"

"What kinda babies?" Tilde asked.

"Babies!" Thora yelled. "Like what *you* were a hundred years ago."

"Where they come from?" Miss Idella asked.

"We don't know," Thora replied. "But the mamas sho'ly think that Bonnie will find a good home fo' their chile."

"We believe," Bonnie cut in, "that one gal heard what I said at that meeting and... well, things jes' snowballed."

"You mean to tell me," Tilde started, "that a mama jes' dropped her chile here?"

"These gals think Bonnie's house is some kinda safe place," Thora said. "She got four babies over the last three months."

"Fo' babies?!!" Tilde said in shock. Delphine gasped.

Miss Idella said, "Wait, wait... hold the phone a second! Fo' gals done come to this house—"

"Three gals," Bonnie replied. "I got a set of twins."

"Mercy me," Delphine said.

"And where these babies at now?" asked Tilde.

"Ruby-Pearl took one," Thora said.

"I knew it!" Tilde exclaimed. "I knew there wadn't no damn brother! I tole y'all. Didn't I tell y'all there wadn't no brother!"

Bonnie watched the women try to absorb this news.

"Baby Wynn." Delphine smiled. "If that don't beat the band!"

"A woman live up in Hencil took in the twins," Thora said.

Miss Idella's mouth dropped open.

"What woman in Hencil?" Delphine asked.

"A friend of Ruby-Pearl's," Thora put in.

"And how y'all know she can take care a these kids?"

" 'Cause we met her ourselves," Thora said.

"And y'all jes' know a good mama from a bad mama, huh?" Tilde asked sarcastically.

Thora glared at the round woman. "We know a good *person* from a bad one," Thora replied. "Ruby-Pearl been friends with these people fo' years. She say the woman and her husband is fine folk, and that was good enough fo' us."

Tilde thrust her chin out.

"What Pine say 'bout all this?" Miss Idella asked.

"We ain't called him," Thora answered.

"Why?" Tilde questioned.

Bonnie shifted in her chair. " 'Cause he'd take the kids to the county home," she replied. "And . . . the po' things wouldn't have a chance."

"That is the truth," Miss Idella said.

"You say there was fo' babies?" Tilde said.

Bonnie laced her fingers together and set them in her lap. "That's why we decided to come to you all," she said. "I never, ever thought that I'da gotten fo' babies. And ever' last one of 'em is a blessin' to behold. I just got a lil' gal come to me a few days ago. She in the back with Ruby-Pearl and Wynn."

Delphine's face lit up. "Can we see her?"

"Jes' hold yo' horses," Thora said. "Let Bonnie finish."

"The reason that I called this meetin'," Bonnie continued, "is 'cause I done run outta places to take these babies. I run outta ideas and I couldn't think of what else to do."

"Bless yo' sweet heart," Miss Idella said.

"Why ain't you and Naz took one of these kids?" Tilde asked.

"That's Bonnie's personal business," Thora said quickly. "Let's jes' stick to the subject at hand."

"Look, I ain't in favor of no kids goin' to the county home," Tilde continued, "but we don't know nuthin' 'bout placin' no children."

"Seem to me," Miss Idella said, "that if a child need a home, we can find 'em one. That *is* what you askin' us to do, right, Bonnie?"

"Yes," Bonnie answered.

"It ain't no mo' complicated than that," Thora said.

Tilde cut her eyes at Thora. "As usual, you don't know what the hell you talkin' 'bout, Thora Dean," she snapped. "It ain't fo' us to play God."

"I 'spect not a soul in this room would *ever* mistake you fo' God," Thora shot back.

"Ah, shut yo' damn mouth!"

"You shut yo' mouth, Tilde—"

"Would you two stop it," Delphine shouted. "These is impo'ant affairs. This here is life and death business."

"And life and death should be left in *God's* hands," Tilde insisted, "not Bonnie's!"

The ladies sat in silence. Tilde's eyes had become slits. Bonnie knew they had questions. Questions she wasn't sure she could answer. After a moment the ladies had settled down, but a thick tension still loomed. Miss Idella and Delphine looked to Bonnie for more answers. Laretha seemed as resigned as Tilde. Olive appeared to be on the fence.

"What 'bout the mamas?" Laretha asked. "What y'all know 'bout them?"

"Most times we never saw the mamas," Bonnie answered. "They leave these kids and run."

"Like thieves in the night," Delphine put in.

"These been healthy babies?" Miss Idella asked.

"Looked fine to us," Thora answered.

"You a doctor too, Thora Dean?" Tilde shot back.

The room fell quiet once again. Bonnie could feel their apprehension.

"You gi' one chile to Ruby-Pearl," Tilde said, "and we know she a decent woman . . . though a lil' strange," she added. "And

Ruby-Pearl could testify that her friend is befittin', I s'pose. But we don't know who all these new mamas could be."

"But if we gi' the babies to folk we know," Delphine said, "and folks of folks we know, then we can be sho' theys good people."

Delphine and Miss Idella nodded their heads in agreement.

"Did you all ever consider," Tilde put in, "that this jes' might be against the law!"

" 'Therefore love is the fulfilling of the law'," Miss Idella said.

"What if the mamas come back fo' they kids?" Tilde asked. "And s'pose these kids get sick and need blood or—"

"S'pose, s'pose, s'pose," Miss Idella hammered. "For goodness sake, Tilde, even when kids are adopted from the county, these things can happen. Ain't nobody can do a dern thing 'bout it, even when it's legal!"

"This ain't right," Laretha said. "Don't even smell right."

"It's a different situation," Miss Idella said. "But the Lord don't give us no mo' than we can bear."

"I think it gives gals permission to abandon they kids," Tilde suggested.

"Tilde ain't wrong!" Laretha spoke up. "When my second chile, Tommy, was born," she went on, "I was nineteen, confused and tired as all git-out. I do declare," she said, raising her hand over her head, "if some lovely person like Bonnie woulda come along—*no questions asked*—and take that chile off my hands..."

"I hear you, girl," Tilde said. "Young women these days'll leave they chile with they mama, they aunties or they grandmamas. Heck, I knew one little fast girl who got herself knocked up and left her chile fo' her daddy to raise."

"If a gal gon' keep her baby, she gon' keep it," Delphine argued. "And if she gon' give it up, she gon' give it up—whether it's to the county, to her family or maybe, dear God, even to the creek!"

Bonnie watched the women bicker among themselves. She suddenly felt the enormity of the situation. The women had raised issues, some of which she hadn't even considered. "Maybe I should go to Pine," Bonnie said. "I mean, Naz say the same thing."

"'Cause he a sensible man," Tilde said, gathering her purse.

"Don't listen to her, Bonnie," Thora said.

"I know yo' heart is in the right place, Bonnie," Tilde said, "but you gon' let Thora Dean talk you right on into the jailhouse."

"She ain't gon' talk *me* into the jailhouse," Laretha said, following Tilde to the front door. Bonnie walked with them.

"I sho'ly hope you take that baby to Pine," Tilde said.

Bonnie felt her head beginning to pound. "I'm sho' I'll do that," she said. "But until then, I wanna ask that you and Laretha keep this quiet."

"My name is Bess and I'm outta this mess!" Tilda assured her.

"You and me both," Laretha added.

"Thank you," Bonnie said. "I jes' need some time to sort this all out."

"I understand," Tilde said. "This ain't no small happenin'... but you smart and you'll do the right thing." Tilde gave Bonnie a quick hug, then she and Laretha left.

Bonnie walked back into the living room, feeling as confused as she did before she invited the Harvest ladies over. She wondered if anything had been accomplished other than putting her business in the street. Miss Idella, Olive and Delphine were quiet. They seemed as perplexed about the situation as Bonnie.

"I 'spect I will take this baby to Pine," Bonnie said, falling into her chair. "I won't mention the other three kids but... Tilde is right."

Miss Idella looked at Bonnie thoughtfully. "You know what I think, honey?" she asked.

Bonnie kneaded her temples. "What?"

"I think," Miss Idella started, "that the onliest thing bigger than Tilde Monroe's mouth is her fat ass."

"Miss Idella," Bonnie gasped.

Thora laughed so hard that she nearly fell from the chair.

"Come on, now," Miss Idella said, "ever'body know it's true."

"She ain't lyin'," Olive laughed.

The older woman's expression grew serious. "All's I'm sayin', sweetie," she went on, "is that the Lord picks His helpers. He picked you, and I'm so glad you picked me. And as long as we do things from our heart, cain't much go wrong."

"I agree," Delphine chimed in.

"Me too," Olive added.

"Plus, Tilde jes' plain jealous," Miss Idella said. "Jealous 'cause these kids ain't come to her. Jealous 'cause she ain't the boss of things."

"And what about Laretha?" Bonnie asked.

The women all groaned at once. "Lil' lapdog!" Olive yelled out. "Godfrey got mo' of a mind than she do. Sniff after Tilde like the woman got roses growin' outta her butt." The ladies laughed. "I say good riddance to both!"

Thora flashed Bonnie a look that said everything would be fine.

"There's this woman I know," Delphine said. "She live down in Tucker and would do *anythin'* to get hold of one of these children."

"And my cousin Chester and his wife," Miss Idella said excitedly, "they stay in Georgia and got two kids but they'd take a chile in need. They sho'ly take in every dog and cat that come they way."

Bonnie had never seen the women this engaged. And it had to do with more than decorating cupcakes and tacking bric-a-brac on the hems of skirts. And equal to their desire to help was their need to do something important. Something big.

"We got to keep this thing quiet, ya'll," Thora said.

"How we gon' explain these babies when they come along?" Delphine asked.

"*If* any more come along," Bonnie said. "This might've jes' been a fluke . . . all fo' of 'em."

"A blessing," Miss Idella said.

"Seem to me," Olive said, "that we got to keep the whole thing outta sight."

"Not even yo' husbands can know," Thora added.

"Clebert don't notice nuthin' that don't come on that damn TV," Miss Idella said.

"Same with Wally," Olive agreed.

"And if a chile come again . . ." Bonnie started.

"*When,*" Miss Idella corrected.

"*When* they come," Bonnie said, "we gotta figure a way to move these kids."

"Quiet and fast," Thora said.

"We all live along the creek," Delphine went on. "We can use that path. Most ever'where we go gon' be 'cross the water."

"Sometimes we can take the long way down Highway 19, past Old Ginger Run, 'round where I live," Miss Idella said.

Bonnie suddenly recalled Daddy Wilbur's stories about the footpath behind Blackberry Corner. Maybe it really was part of the Underground Railroad. And, if so, perhaps it could be used again. Bonnie watched the women plan. She hadn't realized how very clever they were. In the past, their planning had to do with church socials, school projects, menus and seating at dinner parties. Bonnie's own life had been consumed with similar purposes.

"Y'all know I'm good with a needle and thread," Olive said, "so we ain't got to buy no baby clothes."

"And I could use my nursin' skills," Miss Idella put in. "Wadn't never no registered nurse but I can sho'ly check temperatures and stuff."

Bonnie suddenly felt so hopeful. Like maybe this all *could* work. At the very least she felt like she wasn't completely alone.

"And what we gon' call ourselves," Miss Idella asked.

"I'll call you Miss Idella and you call me Thora," Thora replied.

"Y'all know what I mean," she retorted. "Doin' somethin' this . . . impo'tant . . ."

"And dangerous," Olive put in. "We needs to have ourselves a name."

Bonnie flashed Thora a look that warned her not to laugh. She understood the risk these ladies were taking. Equally, she understood their need to have their own identity.

"What's wrong with keeping the Ladies of the Blessed Harvest?" Delphine asked.

"That's old," Miss Idella shot back.

"And tired!" Olive added.

"And Tilde," Thora said.

Bonnie said, "How 'bout the Ladies of the—"

"Naw . . . no *Ladies* of nuthin'!" Thora said. "Ever club in this damn town is the Ladies of this and the Ladies of that . . . Lord, them Ladies is wearing me out!"

"The men calls themselves the Brethren of Good Faith," Bonnie said. "Why don't we jes' be the Sistren or the Sisters?" Bonnie suddenly thought of her and Thora, working their way to the bottom of a bottle of blackberry wine.

"I'm gon' tell Naz how the Ladies of the Blackberry Wine been at it again," Horace had laughed.

"How 'bout the Sisters of..." Olive paused when she couldn't think of anything to complete the name.

"Sisterhood, sisterhood!" Miss Idella insisted.

"The Sisterhood of Blackberry Corner," Thora said.

The women were quiet.

Then Miss Idella said, "Well, that's right impressive!"

"Sound like we fixin' to take care some business wit' a name like that," Delphine insisted.

Bonnie could feel her body start to relax. She finally felt good about this. When Ruby-Pearl came out of the back room with the new baby in one arm and Wynn dangling from the other, it all just seemed to make sense to the ladies. Two days later, they had brought diapers to Bonnie's house, plus bottles, clothes and food that they had purchased from the change that jingled in the bottom of old purses and saved in flour tins for rainy days. The women's excitement never dimmed. It thrust them into an undertaking as clandestine as it was blessed.

PART III

NINE

Canaan Creek, 1986

"Mrs. Wilder?" The bass in his voice seemed to make the phone receiver vibrate. "Bonnie Wilder?"

"Yes."

"I'm Joseph Randall, ma'am. Augusta, my wife, wrote you a letter a few weeks back."

Bonnie sat in the seat beside the window. It had been a month since she had heard from Augusta. Bonnie had hoped that the girl had abandoned her search and moved on with her life.

"Yes," Bonnie said. "Has she . . . have the two of you had yo' baby yet?"

"She's only in the second trimester," he replied.

"I see," Bonnie said. "What can I do fo' you, young man?"

Joseph Randall sighed. In the static that crackled on the line, Bonnie could feel his frustration. She had heard it in Naz more than a few times: the frustration of trying to live with a determined woman.

"When Gussie contacted you a few weeks back . . ."

"Yes?"

"I can't tell you the . . . courage it took for her to actually call you. And she's as tenacious as most . . ." Joseph Randall sounded like a man who kept his head in books—big, brown, musty books that made no sense to most folks. "I adore my wife," he went on, "but since I first met her, back in college, there's always been a piece missing from her life. Not a large piece, and, to me, not an essential one," he quickly added, "but as the years go on, it just grows bigger and bigger. And I know it has everything to do with her mother."

"I'm sorry?"

"She's strong, Mrs. Wilder," he said. "But just like anything else, *not* knowing is worse than finding out something she might not like."

Bonnie looked out of the window toward the woods. She noticed that the blackberry bushes were bare and the bramble filled with tiny thorns.

"Did you hear me, Mrs. Wilder?" Joseph Randall asked.

"Yes."

"Ma'am, if you know anything about her birth mother, please tell her. I'd love for Gussie to be a full and confident mother to our child . . . please."

"Mr. Randall," Bonnie started, "I'm afraid that I can't help her."

"Tell her *something,*" he said. "A nice little story about a nice little lady that brought you a nice little baby girl. Just tell her something."

"I ain't in the habit of lyin', Mr. Randall."

"Then tell her the truth!" Bonnie could hear that he was beginning to lose his patience. "That's the point, ma'am. I don't have a problem with the truth and neither does Gussie."

Naz had claimed that Bonnie was selfish. He contended that taking in the babies had more to do with filling something inside of her than it did with helping the children. Maybe *not* talking to Augusta had more to do with Bonnie herself, than sparing the girl any pain.

"Have her call me," Bonnie said.

"You'll talk to her?"

"I suppose . . ."

His voice elevated. "Yes, ma'am," he said. "She'll call. And thank you, Mrs. Wilder. Thanks a lot."

TEN

Maybe it was the two glasses of wine. Or sitting on Blackberry Corner with Bonnie and Thora, giggling from twilight until the pitch-black dark. Whatever had caused it, Ruby-Pearl Yancy seemed absolutely giddy. Thora refilled her glass, then emptied the last of the blackberry wine into Bonnie's cup.

"It seems our bottle is empty, Miss Bonita," she said, struggling to lift herself from the sofa.

"I ain't gon' be fit to walk after all this," Ruby-Pearl giggled.

"Then stay the night," Thora said. "I cain't tell you how many times I fell out right here on this couch."

"And the woman woke up with cat paws all in her face," Bonnie laughed.

"In her *face,*" Ruby-Pearl said. "Guess you cain't iron them out."

The women's laughter seemed bigger than the joke. Clearly, they were feeling no pain.

"You're welcome to stay, Ruby-Pearl," Bonnie offered. "Thora sleeps here sometimes when Horace and Naz is gone."

Ruby-Pearl burst out laughing, then covered her mouth with her hand.

"Girl, let it out," Thora said, twisting open a third bottle of wine.

"I'm fixin' to wake up Wynn," Ruby-Pearl said in a loud whisper.

"He in the back room," Thora said. "And he might as well get used to it."

"Used to what?" Ruby-Pearl asked.

"Hearin' you laugh. Might even have to hear you moanin' and shoutin' once you find yo'self a man."

"Thora Dean," Ruby-Pearl squealed. "You are a caution, is all. I don't know why folks say . . . well, that you . . ."

"A bitch," Thora offered. "All stuck up and ever'thing?"

Ruby-Pearl shrugged.

"I *love* bein' stuck up," Thora insisted. "And if that's the onliest thing that separate me from these old town biddies . . . girl, I'm jes' fine with bein' stuck up as hell!"

The women's laughter rang through the silent house, so at first they didn't hear the knock at the door. Bonnie hadn't had as much to drink as Thora and Ruby-Pearl, but her legs wobbled when she went to answer.

A woman, perhaps the same age as Bonnie herself, stood behind the screen. A little girl that appeared to be about six, with two wiry plaits jutting from either side of her head, gripped the skirts of her mother's blue dress. In the woman's arms was a newborn wrapped in a white blanket.

"Miss Bonnie?" she said.

"Yes." Thora and Ruby-Pearl stood behind her.

"You prob'ly know why I'm here."

Up until now, Bonnie had only seen one of the mothers. She assumed the others were like Wynn's mama: young and frightened. This woman didn't appear to be either. "Maybe you better tell me why you're here," Bonnie said.

"Amelia..." the woman started. She clutched the baby close to her chest. "She my seventh chile..."

"Gracious, a lie," Thora said.

Both the woman and her young daughter peered over Bonnie's shoulder.

"It ain't easy," the woman went on. "And I'm 'bout to celebrate my thirty-first birthday."

Bonnie felt a twinge. She was thirty-one, just like this woman, with neither chick nor child.

"It's jes' me by myself now," the woman explained. "My husband run off when I got pregnant with Amelia and I ain't seen 'im since. And, well, Miss Bonnie, I cain't do it again. Not even one mo' time."

"Po' thing," Ruby-Pearl whispered.

"I heard 'bout you," the woman said, looking at Bonnie.

"From who?" Bonnie asked.

"She say you don't ask no questions..."

"She...?"

"Say you a nice lady who'll give a chile a chance." The woman seemed to be studying the house, taking in as much as the porch would allow.

"Who in the world is *she*?" Thora asked.

"I rather not say." The woman looked at Bonnie again. "Can you help me, ma'am?"

"Honey, are you sho' you cain't care for her?" Bonnie asked.

"I don't wanna leave her...I swear...but I don't have no mo'."

Bonnie stepped out on the porch. Ruby-Pearl and Thora remained behind the screen. "No mo' what?"

"No mo' energy, money, patience."

"No mo'," Ruby-Pearl repeated.

"Well, you come to the right house," Thora said.

"Are you absolutely sho' that you want to do this?" Bonnie asked again.

"Yes, ma'am." The woman paused. "But befo' I do . . . befo' I leave Amelia here . . ."

"Yes, honey . . . ?"

"I need to see yo' house."

Bonnie pulled her head back in surprise. "I beg yo' pardon?"

"I'm sho' you a nice lady and all, but I don't wanna leave my chile in no dirty, nasty house."

"I know that's right," Thora chuckled.

Bonnie couldn't believe the nerve of this woman. Then she considered that if she were ever driven to give her child up to a perfect stranger, she'd probably have the same concerns. Bonnie opened the screen and allowed the woman and her small daughter to enter. When they saw Thora close up, both she and the little girl stared.

"You a movie star?" the woman asked.

"Ain't you sweet," Thora said, patting her shoulder.

"Are you?" the woman persisted.

"I shoulda been," Thora answered.

Ruby-Pearl rolled her eyes.

The woman walked softly through, inspecting the room. "Don't see no baby things," she said. "Babies need things."

"I got a few stuffed toys in the other room," Bonnie said. The little girl's gaze instantly went to the back. The woman walked down the short hall and the child followed. Ruby-Pearl walked with them and looked in at Wynn sprawled across the bed.

"That yo' child?" the woman whispered.

"Mine," Ruby-Pearl replied.

The woman looked at Ruby-Pearl like she had just noticed

her for the first time. Bonnie could see the question in her expression as her eyes took in the scars on Ruby-Pearl's face. The woman stared so blatantly that Bonnie thought she'd ask about what might've happened. But after a moment, she began to examine the living room again. Her daughter trailed her like a shadow.

"Ever'thing look fine," the woman said, though she seemed to be still inspecting.

"Glad you approve," Bonnie said. "We'll do all we can to find her a good home."

"How?" the woman asked. "You jes' gon' give her to some woman?"

Bonnie was so used to girls dropping their babies then fleeing in the dead of night that this woman and her questions seemed strange . . . almost intrusive. Yet Bonnie completely understood. "There's a group of ladies that will help me care fo' yo' lil' girl," Bonnie explained.

"And we got plenty of mamas that we visit," Thora said, "and we make sho' they nice people so that this precious chile—"

"Amelia," the woman insisted. "That's her name."

"Amelia," Bonnie said.

The woman stopped at the family pictures hanging on the living room wall. She eyed the photo of Naz in his Black Crackers uniform. "I know him," she said.

"A lot of folks know him." Bonnie smiled. "He used to play for the Atlanta Black Crackers."

"Black Crackers?" the woman said. "Ain't never heard of no Black Crackers. I know 'bout some white crackers, though."

Thora laughed out. "Ain't she somethin', Bonnie?"

"That man," the woman went on, "he look jes' like this fella that live by me in Taliliga."

"That where you from?" Thora asked. "Taliliga?"

"Yes—" The woman suddenly caught herself. "Thought we weren't gonna ask no questions."

"That's my husband in the picture," Bonnie explained. "His name is Naz Wilder."

"Maybe you've seen his picture in the paper," Ruby-Pearl said to the woman.

"Naz ain't play no baseball in a hundred and twenty-two years," Thora said. "Hell, colored folks and white folks is playin' together now . . . sort of."

"Yo' man look jes' like Mr. Justice," the woman said. "Same face." Bonnie suddenly recalled the old-timer in the Big Buy. It seemed that he had called Naz a similar name. Then again, the elderly man seemed so confused that Bonnie couldn't understand what he was saying. "He and his wife, Miss Lucinda, live just a few miles from me," the woman went on.

"Naz jes' got one of them kinda looks," Bonnie said.

The woman continued to finger the knickknacks on a small shelf in front of the pictures. She suddenly stopped and pressed the baby's cheek to her own and held the child there. It was as if the reality of leaving the child finally hit her. The woman had to take a deep breath to regain her composure.

Bonnie touched her gently on the arm. "Are you certain that you won't be able to—"

"Yes, ma'am," the woman answered. Tears streamed down her thin face. "You be a good girl, Amelia," she said. "Mama only doin' this to gi' you a good life."

"Can I kiss her?" the older daughter asked.

Bonnie felt her heart breaking as the woman knelt in front of her daughter with the baby.

"Bye, Amelia," the little girl said. "You be good, now." She kissed her sister. Then the woman handed the baby to Bonnie.

"Whoever take her, Miss Bonnie," the woman started, "please

make sho' they calls her Amelia. That was my grandmama's name."

"I will," Bonnie promised. "But, honey, I gotta ask you one last time—"

"I'm sho'," the woman answered. "She'll be fine, right?"

"More than fine," Thora said as she put her arm around the woman's shoulders.

"You smell so good," the woman said to Thora as they walked to the door.

Bonnie stood with baby Amelia in her arms as the woman and her daughter walked toward the road. They got into a rusted blue Chevy parked outside the gate. Thora and Ruby-Pearl waved as the car drove away. Then they went inside and called the Sisterhood.

Miss Idella arrived on Blackberry Corner wearing a nurse's pinafore and cap, carrying her black nurse's bag. Whether Miss Idella knew a lick about nursing remained to be seen, but she certainly looked the part. The woman was the picture of calm and composure. She lifted the tiny chocolate girl wrapped in the soft white blanket. All the while Miss Idella mumbled, "What the good Lord do! What He jes' do!" Miss Idella removed the baby's clothes and diaper. She opened her bag and pushed past tongue depressors, cotton swabs, a bottle of rubbing alcohol and what looked to be a bag of lemon drops. She finally removed a stethoscope, placed the instrument around her neck, blew her warm breath on the steel end and placed it on the baby's tiny chest.

"Babies' hearts beat faster than us'n," she said. "Beat like they been runnin' a relay race."

"That's normal?"

"Oh yes," she said, pressing the sides of Amelia's neck and her stomach. "You know I ain't no doctor," she said, taking the stethoscope off, "but near as I can tell, she seem like a healthy lil' gal to me."

"What He jes' do," Bonnie repeated.

"Praise 'im," Miss Idella said.

"I'm gon' sho'ly miss lil' Amelia," Bonnie said.

"Amelia?"

"Her mama want the new parents to keep her name."

"We cain't say that fo' sho'," Miss Idella put in. "But I'll tell Olive."

Bonnie nodded.

Miss Idella took Bonnie's hand. "I guess it's time, honey."

"Maybe I oughta give Amelia one mo' bottle . . ."

"Bonnie," Miss Idella said, "it's time to wish her well."

The Sisters had decided that when a baby was passed from one to the other, each woman would offer a quick prayer before the baby went to the next. Bonnie sent her blessings, then sadly gave the blanketed child to Miss Idella.

"Olive's cousin," Miss Idella said, holding the baby to her chest, "she's already waitin' on the Manstone side of the creek. I'm takin' the chile to Olive, she'll take her to Delphine, who's gon' row her to her new mama."

"Delphine gon' row?" Bonnie asked.

"Girl, Delphine got six kids. She row that boat better than most men."

Miss Idella sensed her apprehension. "LouAnne Penny," she said. "She a nice lady. Thora and Ruby-Pearl both met her."

"Yes," Bonnie said. "They say she's lovely."

"I met her myself when Olive's daughter got married," Miss Idella added. "LouAnne and her husband already got a lil' girl. Pretty as she can be. Olive say that when she told LouAnne about this chile . . . say her lil' girl got so excited 'bout bein' a big sister that the chile wet her pants."

Bonnie laughed along with Miss Idella.

"Wish I could keep her," Miss Idella said, rocking the baby. "You don't know how much I'd like to keep this pretty lil' gal."

"Yes, I do too," Bonnie muttered.

Miss Idella kept her head down. "Maybe one day he'll change his mind."

"Ma'am?"

Miss Idella moved her whole body when she rocked the baby. "Naz a good man," she said, glancing at Bonnie. "Maybe he'll look at one of these children and decide that this is the one."

Bonnie felt ashamed that Miss Idella, or any of the women, knew the reason. But surely the older woman could read it in the pain in Bonnie's face.

"Them boys talk," she said, answering Bonnie's unspoken question. "My Clebert talk to Scooter, Scooter talk to Teddy, Teddy talk to Naz. Ever' once in a while they all jes' talk together." Miss Idella sucked her teeth. "They say us women cain't keep our mouths shut. Girl, them mens is worse than we'll ever be." She smiled tenderly. "I know you love yo' man, Bonnie Wilder. And he sho'ly is nuts fo' you. Maybe he'll change his mind."

"Maybe," Bonnie said.

Miss Idella wrapped the blanket snugly around the child. "Time to get on over to Olive. She cain't wait to see the baby . . . even if it is jes' fo' a second or two." Miss Idella left the house. Before she started for her car she glanced around the yard. "Coast is clear," she jokingly whispered.

"Yes," Bonnie answered.

"And the eagle is fixin' to fly . . ." she said.

Bonnie felt sad watching Miss Idella carry the child away. But the melancholy hardly had time to take hold, because another baby girl came the next day, and a boy two weeks later. Any nerves that the women might have felt in the beginning melted like early frost as, again and again, the Sisterhood was fired to action.

ELEVEN

Minnie Nesby kicked off her beige canvas shoes that had the back cut out of them. She sighed as she spread her bare toes and sunk back into the soft sofa cushion.

"I would tell you what a fine-lookin' place you got here," Minnie Nesby said. "But, girl, I cain't see too far in front of me without my glasses. Left 'em sittin' right at home in the chif-forobe." She laughed. "Smell good in here, though. Smell like you got a fine-lookin' place."

"Thank you . . . ma'am," Bonnie said. She titled her head toward Thora for an explanation of who the old woman was and why she was here on Blackberry Corner.

"Befo' I tell you 'bout things," Thora said, "maybe Miss Minnie want some refreshments."

"Forgive my bad manners, ma'am," Bonnie said. "Can I get you something? Sweet tea, lemonade . . . ?"

"Thora told me somethin' 'bout some blackberry wine y'all got up in here . . ."

Bonnie couldn't help but chuckle at Minnie Nesby. And

Minnie Nesby seemed to enjoy chuckling at herself. Bonnie retreated to the kitchen, quickly uncorked a bottle and set three cups beside it. The only old woman Thora ever spoke of was Mama Dean. And this *wasn't* Mama Dean—the woman was bedridden. Minnie Nesby's voice suddenly exploded in laughter, a laughter that seemed as heartfelt as it was free. When Bonnie returned to the living room she saw that the old woman's whole body was quaking from laughing so hard. Bonnie had to admit that Minnie Nesby had a rustic charm. And she looked as earthy as she sounded. A blue-black pageboy wig covered her head as unnaturally as a hat and bits of white hair peeked out from her temples and rose from her kitchen like puffs of cotton. A crocheted white shawl draped over a gray cotton blouse. And she wore pants. Most women in the Three Sisters hardly ever wore pants, especially when they went visiting.

"Me and Horace were eatin' in Mayweather's Diner jes' a while ago," Thora began. "Miss Minnie come in and ask Polly Mayweather how she can get to Blackberry Corner. She ask if there's some kinda bus that could take her here."

Bonnie poured into one of the cups and handed it to Mrs. Nesby.

"'Course, Polly point at me," Thora went on. "I look at this sweet old lady and it's gettin' late and stuff and I says, 'I'll take you there, ma'am.' I dropped Horace at the club and then we come on over."

Bonnie offered a cup to Thora.

"You know I'd love to," Thora said. "But I got to get Miss Minnie back home. She live way out in Taliliga."

"You come quite a ways, ma'am," Bonnie said. "How you get all the way to Canaan Creek?"

"Say she took the bus," Thora replied. Bonnie could tell that her friend was excited about the old woman, for now she couldn't seem to get the explanation out quick enough. Mrs. Nesby simply sipped from her cup and looked around like she wasn't even the topic of conversation.

"Naturally, I was curious 'bout what she need Blackberry Corner fo'," Thora went on. "You know me, Bonnie. I don't like to get into folks' business but . . . well, I figure it might have somethin' to do wit the babies."

"Does it?" Bonnie asked.

Thora shuffled forward in her chair. "Them twins that come to you," she said. "The ones left in yo' sewin' basket? Well, they come 'cause of Miss Minnie."

"I don't understand," Bonnie said.

"Dot is seventeen," the old woman started. She squinted her eyes to find the coaster on the table, then set her cup down. "She were the twins' mama. Seventeen and on her fo'th chile. I know it 'cause I caught all fo'."

"Caught 'em?" Bonnie asked.

"Miss Minnie is a midwife," Thora explained. "She been deliverin' babies fo' as long as we been alive. You know how we been asking ourselves where all these babies comin' from?"

"Yes . . ." Bonnie answered.

"Most of them gals had their children delivered by Miss Minnie," Thora said. "That first gal—Wynn's mama—she were at the meeting at the lodge and she went and told Miss Minnie how you take children and find 'em nice homes and all."

"I been catchin' babies fo' fifty-eight years," the old woman started. "When Carolyn told me 'bout you—"

"Carolyn is Wynn's mama," Thora cut in.

"When Carolyn called yo' name," Miss Minnie went on—"first thing I did was to fall to my knees. And, chile, I only fall to my knees fo' impo'tant things, 'cause it's pert near impossible to get back up."

Thora laughed. "I hear you talkin', girl."

The old woman's wig had slanted to the side of her head. She looked so relaxed that Bonnie dared not mention it. "Sometime a gal come to me . . . ," Miss Minnie went on, ". . . and I git 'em young as ten . . . and she be in a family way and cain't tell which end is up. Had one was 'bout to drop her daughter *and* sister at the same time." Miss Minnie shook her head sadly. "Some of these gals ain't fit to raise no children. Ain't even finished bein' raised up theyselves. After Carolyn told me 'bout you, I sent two mo' gals this way. I'm eighty-seven years old. Ain't left Taliliga in fifteen years. But I wanted to come here to meet you."

"Bless yo' soul," Bonnie said.

The old woman reached over and took Bonnie's two hands in her own. Her fingers were short and stubby and her nails as white as milk. Bonnie felt a strength in the woman that belied her eighty-seven years.

"You, my dear," she said, "are as much a part of Gawd's plan as I am." Miss Minnie looked right at Bonnie. The pupils of her warm brown eyes were surrounded by a soft blue ring. "You doin' the Lord's work, honey . . . and ain't nothin' mo' impo'tant."

"Sometimes I feel like I'm tryin' to stick my nose where it don't belong," Bonnie said.

"I know that ole story. Some peoples ain't gon' like what you doin'. Gon' be sayin' you tryin' to be what you ain't."

"If that ain't the truth," Bonnie said.

"That kinda talkity-talk," Miss Minnie said, "honey, it's all a part of it."

"I understand, but—"

"Shoulda seen me when I lost my first chile," Miss Minnie went on. She released Bonnie's hands and sat back on the sofa. "Breech baby. Had the cord wrapped 'round his neck. Couldn't grab 'im right, couldn't separate the line." Miss Minnie's hands made small circular movements as if she were still trying to turn the baby around. "After I lost that chile, I kept thinkin' that if I had mo' experience, if my hands was bigger, if my hands was smaller, if it was rainin' 'stead a cloudy, if it was Thursday 'stead of Monday..." She shook her head. "Things gon' happen. If you cain't count on nuthin' else, you can bet that things gon' happen."

"I told you, Bonnie!" Thora said. "Didn't I say that?"

Bonnie had constant doubt about taking in the babies. Like maybe she was overstepping her bounds, or as Tilde had said, "playing God." Then there was Naz. *"You and Jesus,"* he had bitterly spat. *"Bonnie Wilder and Jesus Christ!"* Bonnie brushed the tears from her cheeks. For the first time, she felt like someone really understood. She felt that maybe, just maybe, there might be a larger purpose. And Minnie Nesby reminded her of that purpose. She made Bonnie see that what she was doing might be integral to some bigger plan, even if it was one that Bonnie herself might never understand.

"One thing, though," Miss Minnie said. "Don't ever forget 'bout *you.*"

"Ma'am?"

"Don't let other folks' life always stand befo' yo' own," she warned. "Even these kids. You go out, whilst you still young, and git what *you* need."

"I got a wonderful life," Bonnie said. "I got friends and a good husband... that's all I need."

"You sho' 'bout that, sweetie?"

"Yes... yes, ma'am."

Miss Minnie shook her head doubtfully. "Ain't too many women like us no mo'. Ones that put our own needs on hold whilst we tend to other folks'. It's a good thing... it's a bad thing," she admitted. "Got me a great-granddaughter that I jes' finished raisin' up. Alice. Had her since she was three. A few years ago, my lil' Alice got herself in a bit of trouble... You know young gals and young boys..."

"That's why we talkin'," Bonnie said.

"Yes, Lord. Alice wasn't ready fo' no baby. So she gi' the chile to a preacher and his wife, live in Mississippi. Then she went on back to school. I musta raised her right, 'cause she got a heart like yo' own. Put things aside—young things—jes' to get her learnin' and also to help her Nana. Yes, ma'am," Miss Minnie said, "different breed, us." Minnie Nesby drained the wine in her cup, then licked the syrup from her dark lips. "Them some good spirits," she said, setting the glass down. "Spirits from blackberries is always a fine thing."

Bonnie poured more wine into the old woman's cup.

"Oooh, girl," she laughed. "Gon' ha' me drunk as Cooter Brown!"

"Go'n stretch out, Miss Minnie," Thora said. "You come all this way, so you might as well relax a minute."

Miss Minnie finished two more glasses of wine and still hadn't run out of stories about young girls and births, wives and husbands... or the lack thereof. Most times Bonnie found baby tales a bit painful, but Miss Minnie's accounts were told with such love that Bonnie could sit and listen for hours more.

The old woman slipped back into her loafers. "You ready to take me home, Miss Glamour Gal?" she asked Thora.

"Yes, ma'am," Thora replied.

The old woman drew her shawl back onto her shoulders and pulled herself toward the armrest of the sofa. Thora and Bonnie helped her up.

"Prob'ly won't see me no mo'," Miss Minnie said to Bonnie as they walked to the door. "Lessen you come by way a Taliliga."

"I might do that one day," Bonnie said.

"Fifteen miles east of the Main Street, out past the lil' covered bridge."

"Covered bridge?" Bonnie chuckled. "Got to be the onliest one in the state."

"Might be," Miss Minnie admitted. "The county closes it up time after time 'cause a the rains. Don't stop that old bridge from washin' away ever' so often, but that big ole piece of steel seem to make folks feel better."

Bonnie nodded.

"I'm gon' keep sendin' you my lil' precious gifts long as I can," Miss Minnie said.

"And I'm gon' take yo' lil' precious gifts," Bonnie said, " 'cause I got mo' mamas want children than ever."

Miss Minnie reached up to kiss Bonnie on the cheek. "Bless you, dahlin'."

"Bless you, ma'am," Bonnie returned.

Thora helped the old woman into her car. Moments later Bonnie could only see the red glare of taillights.

Godfrey nudged his head against her foot. This meant that he wanted Bonnie to wake and feed him. The dog prodded her face with the top of his head and she turned drowsily.

"Sit, boy," she mumbled. Hazily, Bonnie remembered that Godfrey had had table scraps of beef and rice last night. When the old hound ate people food, he was usually still full the next morning. Why was he up so early? Bonnie's head snapped up. Godfrey stood beside the bed wagging his tail. She peered over at Naz still asleep then pulled herself up quietly, took her robe and eased out of the bedroom. Before she closed the door Godfrey inched out behind her.

The dog whimpered.

"Hush, boy," she whispered as she ran excitedly through the house. The day felt like Christmas—like when Bonnie once woke in the dusky morning to the sight of a sparkling pink two-wheeler and a box with a waxy baby doll wrapped in cellophane. She could feel the joy from the tips of her toes on those Christmas mornings as she dashed into the quiet room that smelled of citrus and pine needles. Bonnie opened the front door and scanned the yard. The morning was gray, calm and quiet. Godfrey neither rushed toward the porch nor did he scratch at the door. He ran toward the kitchen.

Maybe she was wrong. Maybe he *did* just want to eat. Bonnie flicked on the kitchen light. She saw her basket, *the* basket, sitting just inside the back door. The baby that lay inside had been eased through the dog door and lay sound asleep.

Bonnie clasped her hands to calm herself, then set the basket on the kitchen table. It had only been two weeks since the Sisters had lovingly dispatched the last child and summarily put in their prayers for the next.

The baby, still asleep, pursed its small lips. The blue blanket revealed that this was probably another boy. His honey-toned skin was velvety to the touch as she brushed his cheek with the back of her finger. She wanted to wake him, hear him, smell him, but Bonnie stopped herself. This was now Sisterhood business, and she had to go through the steps that would distance her from the child. Bonnie eased her hand into the basket and felt the diaper. It was dry and smelled of fresh talcum. Then she glanced inside the basket for anything that might've been left. She found nothing. Bonnie stepped out onto the back porch and looked toward the bushes. Somehow she got the feeling that she was being watched, perhaps by the mama, who waited in a place where she couldn't be seen. Bonnie stepped off the porch, raised both arms and waved across the green. Probably to no one. But she waved just the same, and went back into the kitchen.

"What you think, Godfrey?" she asked as she stood over the sleeping child.

The dog whined at the sound of his name.

"Ain't he a handsome chile? And you done good, boy," she said, patting the top of the old hound's head. "You done real good."

She left the sleeping baby on the table and removed the bag of dog food from the cabinet under the sink. All at once, Bonnie was struck by the ordinariness of her behavior. A strange child lay sleeping on her table while she filled Godfrey's dish with food—a baby that some woman left in her charge, maybe for a day, a week or forever, now sat in her kitchen while she went about her daily routine. The child stretched his tiny limbs. His eyes opened and his gurgle turned to a piercing cry.

"Awww, lil' man," she cooed, "I know jes' what you sayin'. Sayin', 'Where am I and who is this pretty, pretty lady?'." Bonnie lifted the child. "'And where my mama at?' That what you sayin'?" The infant abruptly stopped crying and looked at Bonnie like he could understand every word. "Say, 'Where my mama? I don't see my mama!' Oh, sugar-chile," Bonnie whispered, "you with Miss Bonnie now . . . and you gon' be fine. Jes' fine."

She walked toward the sink with the child in her arms, singing "High Hopes." The child looked baffled yet pleased by Bonnie's calm and lively voice. She sang softly as she prepared yet another bottle for another baby. When Bonnie turned, Naz was standing in the doorway. He wore his pajama bottoms and no shirt.

"You make yo' calls?" he asked.

"Lord, Naz, I jes' wanna feed the chile first."

He nodded. Naz went to his wife and kissed her forehead. "I love you, Bonnie Wilder," he said.

"I love you, husband," she responded.

"And don't worry yo'self," he said. "I'll make my own breakfast this mo'nin'."

TWELVE

Naz and Scooter, Horace and Cal Monroe took turns rowing folks to the side of the creek where the fairgrounds were decorated with yellow and white banners and balloons. Halfway across the water, Bonnie could hear the harpsichord music and smell the scent of popcorn balls and barbecue pork piled on wooden skewers. Such were the sounds and scents of the Tri-County Spring Fair.

"Hold that boy down, Ruby-Pearl," Naz yelled. The muscles in his bare arms flexed as he picked up his rowing speed.

Ruby-Pearl tucked an excited Wynn into the folds of her skirt. He reached toward the edge of the boat and cried when he couldn't get loose from her grip.

"Cain't jump in the water, baby," Ruby-Pearl said. She retrieved a pacifier from her bag and stuck it in his mouth.

"Hey there, Wynn," Thora said. Her lavender scarf ballooned on the sides of her face as the boat coasted across the water. "Auntie Thora gon' take you wadin' in the creek today. How that sound?"

Wynn's eyes explored the blue sky as he sucked on his pacifier.

"What 'bout yo' hair?" Ruby-Pearl asked Thora.

"What *'bout* my hair?"

"Ain't you 'fraid it might get wet?"

"Ain't like we goin' swimmin'," Thora said. "We'll stick our toes in the water and that be the end of it."

"I might jes' have to join you," Bonnie put in. " 'Specially if the heat rise."

Bonnie enjoyed the warm breeze laden with the ripe scent of Canaan Creek. There was none so pretty as the Tri-County Spring Fair. It was the perfect time for a picnic, right before the airless summer arrived, when daisies and azaleas overwhelmed the park and before the green grass was singed brown from the hot sun. She felt so at peace today. Maybe it was the festive mood of the fair or the fact that Ruby-Pearl looked so happy. Or maybe because the Sisterhood just seemed to be working out. Bonnie recognized her blessings when they came and she gathered them up, with all reverence, like sweet blackberries plucked from the bush.

She held on to the side of the splintery wooden boat as it ripped through the water. The creek was beautiful this time of the morning. And it was never so full of life as when folks crossed the water for the fair. Times like this made Bonnie forget about the tragic event that happened almost a year ago.

"No offense, Thora," Ruby-Pearl said, "but I don't think I'm gon' let Wynn get in the water."

"Ever'body get in the water."

"Wynn is too young."

"He ain't too young, no!" Thora argued. "I been wadin' in the creek since befo' I could walk. Naz even got a swimmin' contest for the lil' kids. Ain't that right, Naz?"

"Keep me out y'all's stuff," Naz said.

"Maybe next year," Ruby-Pearl said, kissing Wynn on the top of his head.

"Lord ha' mercy," Thora argued. "You gon' smother that chile to death."

"Thora," Bonnie whispered.

Though Ruby-Pearl and the women had grown used to Thora and her mouth, her meddling occasionally still got in the way.

"I say, let the chile wade," Thora insisted. She raised her arms over her head and said, "Girl, let the lil' birdie fly."

"You fry that chicken, Ruby-Pearl?" Bonnie quickly asked.

Ruby-Pearl seemed more than happy to move on to another subject. "Jes' made wings," she replied. "Also baked a pecan pie for the contest."

"Love yo' pecan pie," Bonnie said. "And I made some navy beans and a lemon cake. Naz seasoned the short ribs."

"What you bring, Thora Dean?" Ruby-Pearl asked.

"I brung the plates, napkins and forks."

"Always was good fo' plastic," Ruby-Pearl mumbled.

"You two need to cut out that foolishness," Bonnie scolded.

"Tell *her* to cut it out," Thora said peevishly.

"I thought y'all were gettin' on fine," Naz put in. "Since yo' Sisterhood thing, I mean."

"We do okay when Thora Dean stay out my business," Ruby-Pearl said.

"I'm jes' telling the truth as I know it," Thora defended.

Naz shook his head. "Glad us men don't go through all that jibber-jabber," he said.

Thora and Ruby-Pearl moaned in unison.

"Say what you want," Naz defended, "but you ain't gon' find me and Horace or me and Scooter fightin' like two gray cats. And when Dewey come a-visitin', you won't see nuthin' but good times."

"Dewey?" Thora asked.

"Naz's baseball buddy," Bonnie put in. "He's stoppin' in tomorrow, on his way to Mobile."

"When Dewey come, there won't be nothin' but good times."

"That might be true," Thora said, "but if you ask me, you men is worse gossips than us women will ever be."

When the boat slid to a stop, Bonnie was the first one out. Naz reached for her hand, and as she leapt onto land she bumped against his chest. A naughty smile crept across her face as she felt his manhood respond to her closeness. Their sex life had declined since the morning she had tried to "heat things up." But she still found her husband desirable, and at times like this Bonnie felt his need in return.

"Hey now, baby," he whispered. "Gettin' me all bothered right here and now."

Thora and Ruby-Pearl grinned as they pretended not to notice.

"Stop that fresh talk in public," Bonnie whispered back.

He pecked her on the lips. "Might jes' ha' to take us a lil' walk in the woods later," he said.

"Watch yo'self there, Naz Wilder," she giggled.

The day felt good. Her husband felt good. The sun felt good. Naz lifted Wynn out of the boat and above his head with a big growl. The child's laughter rang out among the other children's hoops and shrieks from farther on the campground. Naz helped Ruby-Pearl out next, then reached for Thora. Bonnie wondered how her best friend would make it in her high heels, but Thora Dean always managed despite her wardrobe.

"I'm goin' back over fo' the last group," Naz said just as Horace's boat reached the bank. Bonnie waved at MaryLee and Telvin Brent as they got out with their daughter. The other couple, who Bonnie didn't know, waved just the same.

Green and white plastic windmills, and large multicolored lollipops dotted the grassy meadows ahead. Ruby-Pearl could hardly stop Wynn from squirming in her arms when he saw the blue blinking portal that said, *"Tri-County Spring Fair."*

"Go on, honey," Bonnie said. "That boy gon' bust if he don't get there."

"Hidy-hi!," MaryLee said as she passed Bonnie, her six-year-old daughter, Penny, pulling her along.

Thora nodded to the couple behind them. The woman, compact and short, smiled warmly as she held her husband's hand. His wavy hair framed a light brown face that looked as smooth as saltwater taffy.

"Pardon me," he said, "but are you Miss Wilder?"

Bonnie slowed her pace. "Yes, sir."

The wife's chest caved in relief. "So glad we found you straightaway," she said. She appeared to be a young woman, somewhere in her midtwenties.

"My name is Dorsey Porter," the husband said, extending his hand. "And this is my wife, Evelyn."

Bonnie knew where the conversation would lead. Since involving the ladies, she had been stopped in the market, at the apothecary, and gotten two unposted letters in her mailbox with names and addresses of families who wanted babies. Bonnie could spot a couple in need from a mile away. The longing in their eyes and the hope she would answer their prayers always gave them away.

"Don't mean to take up yo' time, ma'am," the husband said. "But we were hopin' to find you here. We're from Pertwell." His voice lowered when he said, "We hear that you . . . help families who want to adopt . . . ."

"Mr. Dorsey," Bonnie started.

"Porter," he corrected. "Dorsey Porter is my name."

"Mr. Porter," she went on, "this might not be the best time to discuss—"

"We know," he said. "And we apologize, truly, for the . . . the . . ."

"The po' timing," the wife put in.

"But we were sure we'd find you here at the fair," the husband went on. "A woman who live up in Hencil told us 'bout you. Didn't think it proper to jes' . . . come to yo' house," he said, "so we waited 'til we thought that we saw you cross the creek. Lady said to look fo' a tall, attractive woman with short brown hair . . . say you most prob'ly be with another lady that look . . . well, look right shiny," he said, dashing Thora a smile.

"Shiny, huh?" Thora said, trying to decide if she should be insulted.

Bonnie peered around her to see if Pine was close by. "I usually conduct this kinda business in private and—"

"Ma'am," the wife said almost desperately, "we jes' wanted to meet you and gi' you our name and address." She held out a tightly folded piece of white paper. "If you need to know anything 'bout us, we got plenty of folks who'll tell you we're hardworking and God-fearin' and that we would only treat a chile with love and kindness."

Bonnie could tell that this lady had been rehearsing her words for a while now. "One of us will contact you, by and by," Bonnie said.

The wife clasped her hands excitedly.

"And, Mr. Porter," Bonnie said, "y'all ha' yo'self a good time at the fair."

Instead of going onto the fairgrounds, the Porters walked back toward the bank. They really had come here *just* to find her. Part of Bonnie felt a bit embarrassed by her perceived authority. Another side of her knew exactly what these childless women felt like.

Harpsichord music got louder as they walked onto the fairgrounds. Soon they weaved past pastel-colored cotton candy that blew up from sugar machines and makeshift rides, like a Ferris wheel, a carousel, a fun house and, for those who dared, a small roller coaster called "the Bob Cat." Booths selling everything from tepid lemonade to homemade pot holders spread across the square.

Delphine and Miss Idella had arrived early and snagged a half dozen of the best tables, in the shade but close enough to where the kids' games were set up.

"I understand 'bout the babies club," Thora whispered to Bonnie, "but damn if I'm gon' spend *all* day settin' 'round the Sisterhood ladies."

"I promised we would all stay together," Bonnie said.

"Aw, come on now," Thora groaned.

"In fact," Bonnie went on, "we arranged what each person was gon' bring so that we would have a little bit of everything. Ruby-Pearl brought the fried chicken, Miss Idella made all the salads, Olive bringin' the burgers and hot dogs . . ."

"I get it, Bonnie, I get it!" Thora snapped. "Damn it to hell!"

"They ain't so bad," Ruby-Pearl said, still trying to control Wynn. He was restless, fussy and stretched out his whole body as he tried to squirm from her grip.

"I jes' cain't listen to them ladies today," Thora declared. Just then, Wynn let out a piercing scream. Ruby-Pearl quickly gave him his pacifier. "And I ain't gon' put up with too much of that there hollerin' neither," she said.

"Now look," Bonnie said, "*you* the one that pronounced me the president of this here club. And I say that we all sit together today. It's jes' plain neighborly."

"Hmmph," Thora grumbled. "*All* day with these ladies ain't my idea of a picnic... Hey there, Olive, Miss Idella, Delphine," Thora said, smiling wanly.

Baskets of chips and pretzels and cellophane-covered bowls of every kind of salad were set on four tables covered in white paper cloths. Miss Idella stood behind a large smoking grill.

"Y'all set yo' stuff right on over there," Delphine said. Her baggy shorts, splashed with green palm trees, nearly touched her knees. "Hey there, Ruby-Pearl," Delphine said cheerfully, "how that lil' handsome man?"

"About to bust from the excitement." Ruby-Pearl tried balancing Wynn and unpacking her picnic basket at the same time. She finally settled the boy on a blanket beside the table but he crawled toward a group of toddlers tossing a beach ball on the grass just feet away.

"Might as well take 'im to play and I'll unpack yo' things," Bonnie said. "Ain't no chile fit to sit still in all this excitement."

"Thank you, honey," Ruby-Pearl said. She picked Wynn up and carried him to the circle of children.

"Protect that chile like he come from her own womb," Delphine said, spreading plastic forks across the table.

"A lil' *too* protective if you ask me," Thora said, nibbling a grape.

"Some mamas jes' like that," Bonnie spoke up in defense of her friend. "She been through a lot and don't wanna make no mistakes."

"Ever'body make mistakes," Thora shot back. "And mamas prob'ly make the worse of 'em."

Bonnie opened Ruby-Pearl's basket and pulled out a large foil-wrapped bundle of fried chicken. She unpacked animal crackers, bottles with juice and milk, chunks of cheese and peeled apples in wax paper. A pie plate sat in the corner with a large pecan pie glistening under the glass cover. She couldn't believe that Ruby-Pearl felt confident enough to bake. Before Wynn, the woman barely came to a bake sale, let alone entered one.

While Bonnie unpacked her own basket and lay the napkins and paperware on the table, she caught sight of Kitty Wooten and Edris Collins sitting with their families. Laretha was at a table with her husband. Bonnie waved, but the woman just rolled her eyes and looked away.

"Anybody seen Tilde today?" Bonnie asked.

"Please don't talk that woman up," Delphine said.

Miss Idella looked toward the table where Laretha sat. "Maybe she ain't got here yet."

"Tilde always git to the fair early," Olive said. "She like to git on the good side of the contest judges."

"Cain't imagine Tilde on *anybody's* good side," Thora said.

Ruby-Pearl wandered back over and sat beside Bonnie. She watched Wynn just yards away with Jenna Dixon.

"I hear tell," Delphine started, "that her daughter, Natalie, got into one of them smart gal colleges up in Washington, D.C."

"But she only sixteen," Thora said.

"Tilde say the gal don't even have to go to her last year at the high school," Delphine went on. "Say she goin' straight on to that college in the fall."

"Ain't that fine," Olive said.

"Say that Natalie is gon' be staying at her sister's house in Virginia, just a few miles from the college in D.C.," Delphine added.

"Lovely," Ruby-Pearl said. "I knew it had to be something, 'cause it ain't like Tilde to miss the county fair."

"Happy, happy," Pine yelled out as he approached the table. Though he seemed light and festive, Bonnie could feel the women's tension in his presence . . . or maybe it was her own nerves that came to the surface every time she saw Pine.

Bonnie heaped her ribs onto the grill beside Miss Idella's corncobs as she eyed him. The liquid made the hot iron sizzle and the smoke rise in a fragrant cloud.

"I 'clare," he said, "whenever there's a gatherin', you ladies all seem to band together."

"Jes' like the Brethren," Miss Idella said. "Only we ain't got no guns or ammo to compare notes 'bout."

"I s'pose that's true," Pine chuckled. He straddled one of the benches and sat. "Where the husbands at?"

"Naz and Horace still down at the creek," Bonnie answered. "They're on their last trip."

"And whoever ain't got across," Thora put in, "need to row theyselves . . . or swim!"

Pine reached in one of the bowls for a pretzel.

"Can I fix you a plate?" Olive asked him.

"Sausage is ready," Miss Idella said, turning a row on the grill.

"Naw," he said. Pine's eyes glanced around the immediate area. He munched on the pretzel, then brushed crumbs from his bright red shirt. "Jes' wanted to tell you fine ladies," he started, "that y'all need to stop what you doin'."

Bonnie's head shot up. The women froze.

"Y'all think I jes' fell off the turnip truck?" he asked. No one answered. Pine's dark eyes quickly took in each woman, then he reached for another pretzel. "This a small town," he said. "Folks talk. And I listen."

"Folks like Tilde?" Thora asked.

"Never mind who said what." He focused on Bonnie. "There's an itty-bitty line here. And it be real easy for one of y'all to step over it."

Bonnie lowered her eyes.

"I know you mean well, Bonnie," he said. "But Sheriff Tucker would not understand like I do. And if he found out . . ." Pine's gaze was as sharp as a razor. "Y'all on a slippery slope," he said softly, "and I cain't tell you how many things could go wrong. You need to stop yo' lil' club, and now! Any mo' babies come, you bring 'em to me."

"But you'll carry 'em on over to the county home," Bonnie said.

"Don't you play that mess with me, woman," he warned. "You keep on with this, and not only will I take you in for illegal adoption . . . but I'll do all I can to round up every last one of them kids . . . including Wynn."

Ruby-Pearl held her stomach as if someone had punched her.

Pine stood up from the bench. Before he walked away, he said, "I don't mean to be cold 'bout this, but it ain't right."

Miss Idella slowly turned the meat. Bonnie set Wynn's bottles into the icy cooler. Olive lined up the plastic forks so that each was even with the next.

"Tilde and her big-ass mouth," Thora said. "That's why she ain't here."

Miss Idella nodded. Ruby-Pearl was close to tears.

"What now, Bonnie?" Olive asked.

Bonnie watched Wynn tossing a ball to Delphine's youngest daughter. She couldn't bring herself to look at Ruby-Pearl. "We gotta stop. Simple as that."

"Damn shame," Thora said.

"We did what we could do," Miss Idella said, "and that was fine. But I guess it's time to call it quits."

"Or . . . maybe we need to be *mo'* careful," Ruby-Pearl said.

The women were shocked.

"Ruby-Pearl . . . ?" Thora said.

"You understand what yo' sayin', Ruby-Pearl?" Bonnie asked.

"I understand that you saved my life," she said. "*Wynn* saved my life. And them there twins set Letty and Freddy's heart a pounding each and ever' day. Oh, no," Ruby-Pearl said firmly,

"I don't think that we should just stop. There's too much here, Bonnie. Too much good."

"And remember what Miss Minnie said," Thora put in. "She say that things are gonna happen."

"Pine cain't see ever'thing," Miss Idella said. "We just gotta use the creek mo' . . . use the woods and the creek."

Bonnie could see Pine watching from the reverend's table. "Why don't we get together later and talk 'bout this," she said.

"We can do that," Olive said. "But I agrees with Ruby-Pearl. We shouldn't jes' stop."

Bonnie found it amazing that these women were not dissuaded. Shaken but not dissuaded. Ruby-Pearl especially had so much to lose. They seemed to just brush off Pine's warning and switch gears. Plates were piled with good food, children were cheered to the finish line of three-legged races and wedges of cold watermelon were handed out for jobs well done. But at the edge of the ladies' laughter lurked a surreptitious delight. Tipsy from the sheer danger of it all, the women shared subversive looks throughout the day. They enjoyed the picnic and their time together as something other than mothers, wives and church members. They were sisters.

Dewey Bradshaw was the tiniest of Naz's baseball buddies. That aside, his mouth more than made up for his size. A baggy gray suit with large black buttons swallowed his tiny frame and a white Stetson sank low on his forehead. He looked like a twelve-year-old boy dressed in his father's Sunday suit. Dewey laughed loud and at the same time he clapped at his own jokes. And when he wasn't speaking, which was rare, a permanent grin seemed affixed to his face. Possibly because Dewey Bradshaw walked with his own bottle of Noah's Mill Kentucky Bourbon.

"Not for nuthin', Miss Bonnie," Dewey explained, "but folks

don't usually ha' no Noah's Mill. But Naz know me!" he yelled. "That ole boy know that Noah's Mill is my poison." His laughter roared. "And this here gal is *114.2* proof!"

"Point two?" Bonnie asked.

"Oh, yeah!" he yelled. "It's that there point two that put a nigger on his ass!"

"You crazy, Dewey," Naz laughed. "I swear 'fo' gawd, ole Dewey is a wild man!"

Naz looked like he didn't have a care in the world. He talked louder and laughed harder with Dewey around. Bonnie rarely saw her husband drink, especially before the sun went down. Today he and Dewey had been imbibing since early afternoon. Bonnie hardly understood this baseball or liquor humor but knew it would be impolite not to laugh along with them. Still, every once in a while, when she needed a break from the hilarity, she went to fetch something from the kitchen.

"Sheriff Wilder," Dewey said in the middle of another holler.

"Sheriff?" Bonnie asked.

"That's what the fellas used to call Naz's foster mama," he laughed. "Call her 'Sheriff' 'cause she wadn't afraid to stand up to nobody. Of course, the woman be drunk out her ass most of the time. Ooooo, 'scuse my mouth, Miss Bonnie." Dewey always apologized when he let loose with a cuss—which was every few minutes. "Most of the families come to the games, watch from the sideline . . . calmly," Dewey explained. "But Naz mama cuss the umpire, cuss the coach, hell, she even cuss the fans if they ain't actin' right."

"Ole Ida was something else," Naz put in.

"Sheriff?" Bonnie smiled.

"That was her name," Dewey said. He poured another two fingers of bourbon in his glass, then did the same for Naz. "Come on now, Miss Bonnie, and ha' yo'self a taste," he said, offering her the bottle.

"I'm fine, thank you," she replied.

After a sip from his glass, Dewey went on talking. "Them fellas . . . the ballplayers, they was always makin' up names fo' folks."

"And why they call you Dewey?" Bonnie asked.

He patted his chest like the answer should be obvious. " 'Cause they say I'm small like a dewdrop."

"But ole Dewey is quick as they come," Naz said.

"*Was,*" Dewey corrected. "Back in the day, boy. Back in the day." Dewey leaned into Bonnie with a devilish look on his face. A gold tooth glistened in the side of his mouth. "Say, Miss Bonnie," he almost whispered, "you gon' love what they used to call ole Naz here."

"Don't start wit' me now, boy," Naz warned. Bonnie hadn't seen her husband have this much fun in years.

"What they call 'im?" Bonnie teased.

"Ole Naz was one of them die-by-the-rules kinda guys, see," Dewey explained. "You know yo' man. Follow the rules to his grave."

"That's my baby," Bonnie said, kissing Naz on the cheek. She could almost taste the bourbon on his breath.

"Ain't let nobody get away wit' a damned thing," Dewey went on. "That's why the fellas called 'im Mr. Justice." The two men broke out laughing.

"Mr. Justice?" Bonnie chuckled.

"A sho' nuff, by-the-law kinda guy, yo' man is," Dewey went on. "Even the officials didn't catch some of the things ole 'Mr. Justice' caught. I 'member this one time—"

"Mr. Justice?" Bonnie repeated.

"He gon' bring up that old call again," Naz jumped in.

"Ole Naz was actually arguing a call *against* his own damned team!"

"You's a lie!" Naz laughed.

"You know I ain't," Dewey insisted. "You ask C. C. Baker, Wyndam, Jet Jackson—any of them guys—and they'll tell you."

Mr. Justice. Bonnie could hear the old man in the Big Buy mistaking Naz for Mr. Justice. She could still see the woman standing in her living room pointing to the photo of Naz and calling him "Mr. Justice." And now Dewey Bradshaw.

"'Scuse me," she said, rising.

"You okay there, Bonnie?" Naz asked.

"I'm fine," she said, walking toward the bathroom. "Jes' got a touch of the heartburn."

"Want I should get you some of them tablets from the medicine cabinet?" Naz asked.

"No, no," she said. "I'm gon' splash some water on my face."

Bonnie's legs felt numb as she walked into the bathroom. She turned on the tap and leaned into the sink. The possibility that the incidents were related was remote, but somehow she couldn't ignore them. She recalled when the young woman from Taliliga had mentioned the name Lucinda Justice. Bonnie took a pink hand towel that hung from the inside door with the word "Wilders" embroidered across the bottom edge. She sat on the closed toilet seat and lowered her face into her toweled hands. *"Yo' man look jes' like Mr. Justice. Same face."* Bonnie's stomach was in knots. But this was nothing, she kept repeating to herself. It was just a name—a name that confronted her, once, twice and now again.

THIRTEEN

Naz stood at the stove slicing a second helping of roast pork. He draped it across his plate, dug into the pot of lukewarm mashed potatoes and slung some on top of the sliced meat.

"Mo' potatoes?" he asked over his shoulder.

Bonnie shook her head no. She lifted a string bean onto her fork.

"Thin as a rail these days," he said, pulling his chair out and sitting down.

"Ain't had much of an appetite."

It had been a couple of weeks since Dewey Bradshaw's visit. Life had been quiet. Not a single baby had come along for almost two months. Even the mewling of a stray cat was enough to send Bonnie out to check her sewing basket and milk bins. She needed a child. Not just for the feel of young life, but to take her mind away from her silly suspicions. As many times as she had tried to push the name Justice from her mind, it edged its way back. Like a dare, it taunted her. Mainly because she had no idea how it connected to her, to Naz or to their lives.

"I'm 'bout to head on out," he said, wiping his mouth with a paper napkin.

"Where?"

"Horace's. Gon' listen to a ball game on the radio."

"How long you stayin'?"

Naz looked at her curiously. Bonnie rarely questioned him about his comings and goings. "Ever how long it take," he said, carrying his plate to the counter. He emptied the scraps into Godfrey's dish and set the plate in the sink. "You wanna come?"

She suddenly felt silly. "No."

"Thora be glad fo' yo' company."

"Got some things to do 'round here," she said. "Tell Thora I'll see her tomorrow."

Naz kissed her on the cheek. Then he left her sitting at the kitchen table.

Bonnie set the half-empty pots in the refrigerator. She washed and dried the dinner dishes and cleaned the table. She swept and mopped the floor until the pattern of orange roosters preened in the old linoleum.

"Yo' man look jes' like Mr. Justice."

The best parts of the day were the ones that required a lot of work. Bonnie had tidied the closets and even scrubbed the shed out back. But it wasn't enough. She went into her bedroom, stood at the door and looked for anything undusted, unfluffed or out of place. There was nothing. So she stripped the bed of its linen and tossed the day-old white sheets into the empty hamper. Then she stood before the fragrant linen closet. Soft green sheets this time. She unfolded the crisp cotton with one strong snap and watched it billow across the queen-sized bed—her and Naz's bed. He had carved the headboard himself from birch wood he had bought in Raleigh many years ago.

She had a good marriage. Still, she couldn't reconcile the feelings. Suspicions loomed in her mind. Bonnie sat on the side of the half-covered mattress. She had even snooped through Naz's pockets, under the guise of laundry, searching for anything that might tell her that something was wrong.

"He and his wife, Miss Lucinda, live in Taliliga."

Bonnie looked at the clock on her night table, then dialed Thora's number.

"Hey, missy!" Thora's voice was bright.

"Naz there?"

"He and Horace listenin' to the game. Hold on, sweetie, and I'll call him."

"No," Bonnie said quickly. "I jes' wanted to know if he was there."

Thora paused. "This the second time you called me like this, Bonnie," she said. "Why in the world you call and..."

Bonnie hung up the receiver. After a beat, the phone rang. She knew it was Thora, and probably spitting mad. Bonnie left it ringing and went out to the porch. She sat in her usual chair that looked down the road. This used to be the time of day she enjoyed most but now the shadows were mottled with strange forms and the trees were filled with whispers. Her mind ached with irresolution. She had thought about going to Taliliga, but realized how crazy the idea was. And where would she go? Where was this Justice house? Taliliga was half the size of Canaan Creek, but she'd still have to find the place. Aside from a few people that had visited the Piney Grove church, Bonnie didn't know many folks in Taliliga. Then she thought about Miss Minnie. An old woman who delivered more than two hundred babies would know everyone and where they lived. Bonnie tried to piece together Miss Minnie's directions. She hadn't grasped the information at the time because she never thought she'd need to go to Taliliga. Only now could she recall that the old woman lived past Main Street. She had mentioned something about a covered bridge about fifteen miles past the center of town.

Bonnie jumped when the phone rang again. She thought about letting it ring, but then rushed in to answer.

"What the hell is wrong with you!" Thora barked.

"Just... not feeling like myself today," Bonnie replied.

"Who the hell are you, then?" Thora snapped. After a beat, Thora excitedly said, "Girl, maybe you pregnant."

"I'm not pregnant."

"Well, you actin' crazy as hell! Something got to be up—"

"I have to go," Bonnie cut in.

"Why?"

"I jes' do."

"You startin' to worry me."

"I'll explain it all soon," Bonnie said.

"Explain what? Girl, what is wrong wit' you?"

"I have to go."

"Where in God's name you goin'?"

Bonnie hung up the receiver. She looked out the screen door at her yard as the afternoon slowly turned to twilight. Her arms locked across her chest as if to anchor herself in place. She couldn't go. She wouldn't go. Bonnie's arms suddenly fell to her sides. She slipped on her sweater, snatched her car keys from the table and headed out the door.

Taliliga was at least an hour from Canaan Creek—an hour straight into the bush where acres of farmland flourished with cotton, peaches and tobacco leaves the size of elephant ears.

Bonnie soon hit the outskirts of Canaan County. She drove a tree-lined path enlivened with lush spring green, then turned onto Helgar Trail, the only road that extended through all three counties. Orange and pink lines marked the sky above the dry land. God's breathtaking landscape should be enough to wipe doubt from anyone, she thought. Suddenly, Bonnie felt like a fool, on her way to find some woman named Justice for no good reason. *"Same face."* Bonnie plodded on.

Ten miles beyond the center of Taliliga, the scent of Walla Walla Sweets wafted from the onion fields that lined both sides of the road. Five miles more was a short, dilapidated bridge. Only half of the rickety wooden scaffold still bore a steel overlay. This had to be the covered bridge that Miss Minnie had mentioned. Bonnie slowed to a crawl as she crossed over, the wood moaning with the weight of her car. She took a long and thankful breath when she reached the other side.

Three miles past the bridge rested a modest cabin with a putty thatched roof. Full-sized logs made up the walls. Surrounded on two sides by willowy oaks, the house looked like it was straight out of a fairy tale.

Bonnie parked just yards away from the door. She rapped lightly, praying that this was indeed Minnie Nesby's house. There hadn't been a baby left in months, so perhaps business was slow for Miss Minnie too. Bonnie knocked again. Miss Minnie was nearly ninety, she thought, and surely it took time for her to get up from her chair.

A young, light brown woman opened the door. Her piercing dark eyes spied Bonnie from head to toe. "Ma'am?" she said.

"I'm lookin' fo' Mrs. Nesby. Does she live here?"

"You in a family way?" the young woman asked.

"No. I'm a friend."

The young woman looked Bonnie over again. Her cotton

blouse and starched tan skirts with perfect pleats must have sufficed, for the woman said, "Come in."

Bonnie entered the warm, neat house. It was filled with everything rustic and homey, which looked exactly like Minnie Nesby herself. When she sat on the overstuffed gingham couch, it felt like she'd sunk clean to the floor. A large mahogany bookshelf, containing perhaps a dozen books, held one of the oldest bibles that Bonnie had ever seen, as its soft leather cover seemed to be flaking away. The remainder of the wooden cabinet looked to be used more like a pantry. Broad jars and tall jars of every color sparkled like expensive stained glass. They were filled with beans, hominy, rice, preserves and pickled everything, including chicken feet, hogs' snouts, fish heads and giblets.

The young woman sat across from Bonnie in a pale green armchair. Bonnie could see her resemblance to Miss Minnie.

"I was hopin' that Miss Minnie could help me with a little matter," Bonnie started. "Is she resting?"

"Yes, ma'am," the girl answered. "Resting with the Lord."

"My word," Bonnie whispered. "When?"

"Just last month," the girl answered. "I'm Alice, her granddaughter."

"She tole me 'bout you," Bonnie said. "Tole me what a fine young woman you are and how proud she is of you."

"Thank you for saying." Alice wasn't a pretty girl but her attraction arrived from a calmness inside of her, a peace, which was rare for a young woman that looked to be no older than eighteen.

Bonnie shook her head sadly. "I was wondering why no babies came to us in the last couple months."

Alice leaned forward in her chair. "You're the lady?" she asked. "The one that finds homes for the babies? The one in Canaan Creek?"

"Yes."

"Nana talked 'bout you."

"Have you been to Canaan Creek, sugar?" Bonnie asked.

"Once or twice," Alice answered. "But not in a long time. Nana been there since me," she said with a smile. "Fo' fact, in the last few years, the only time she left this place was to go see you. That old woman jes' up and carried herself to Canaan Creek." Alice chuckled. "Got on the bus all by herself. She like to scare me to death." Alice's eyes filled. "My Nana...jes' as gutsy as the day is long."

Bonnie nodded respectfully.

"Mrs. Wilder," Alice said, "I know you came to see my grandmama, but is there anything I can do to help you?"

The fact that Miss Minnie was gone must've been a sign. A sign that Bonnie needn't be looking for this Justice house after all. "That's okay, sweetie," Bonnie said, rising. "I won't take up no mo' of yo' time."

"It was a pleasure, ma'am."

"Pleasure's all mine." Bonnie embraced the girl, then walked toward the door. "What's yo' plans now that yo' Nana's past?"

"I'm gon' sell the house and use the money for school," she replied. "I hope to get into Fisk...you know, in Tennessee. Then, God willing, Meharry."

"That another school?" Bonnie asked.

"A medical school, ma'am."

"A doctor?"

"I wanna do what Nana did," the girl replied. "Only I want to learn the medical way."

"Isn't that fine." Bonnie walked onto the porch. "This is such a lovely house," she said, looking at the stacked logs. "So much love. So much life. And jes' like my house," Bonnie said, looking toward the thick woods, "it's plenty isolated."

"That's why gals felt comfortable when they came here to

have their babies. Don't feel like eyes are watching them," Alice said. "Next house, Percy Evans's place, got to be five miles away. Miss Fletcher... she three or fo' miles after that, and the Justices' is ten miles past that, even."

"Justices?" Bonnie asked.

"Miss Lucinda and her daughter, Tammy."

Bonnie stood at the bottom of the porch steps. She felt the hair on her arms rise. "Where exactly do they live?" she asked.

"'Bout fifteen miles south of here, straight down 19."

"I see." Bonnie walked toward her car. "Please come see me if you need anything. I'm on Blackberry Corner."

"I know, ma'am," Alice said, waving. "And I will."

If Miss Minnie's death was a message that Bonnie should stop looking, surely this was an even louder call to continue on. Bonnie pulled back onto the road and headed south. Somehow she felt calm as she drove toward the Justice home. Perhaps this was the real sign. One that Minnie Nesby had sent herself.

Just twenty minutes later, Bonnie was standing behind high wild bushes across the road from a small house. Night was arriving quickly, but enough daylight remained to get a full view. The house looked frighteningly similar to her own on Blackberry Corner: the wraparound porch, the three rockers and even a sewing basket by the front door.

Bonnie rested her shoulder against the thick trunk of a dying oak. This was all so ridiculous, yet she couldn't walk away. Bonnie knew that if she saw this Lucinda woman, she would know immediately. But know what? She hadn't even allowed herself to say the words.

Loud squawking suddenly pierced the quiet as a hen attacked a rooster, trying to draw blood. Feathers flew and dirt kicked up in a large red cloud. Through the dust, Bonnie saw a woman come out onto the porch carrying a bucket.

"Y'all need to hush," she yelled as she splashed the unruly birds. Lucinda? Bonnie felt her heartbeat quicken. Maybe this wasn't Lucinda. And if it was, who the hell was Lucinda anyway? The woman was tall—taller than she—and while Bonnie was as slender as a blade of grass, this woman was big-boned. Her shoulders were wide, her body was solid and her ample breasts bounced under a yellow cotton dress. The woman set the bucket on the porch. She took a hankie from the pocket of her housedress and dabbed her forehead, then sat on the top step. She smoothed her dress past her calves and leaned her forearms on her knees. Bonnie had to admit there was a raw prettiness to the woman. Her eyes were large and her face, red and shiny from sweat, was as angular as the Cherokees that lived up near Gaffney. Her dark hair, in two short, neat plaits, brushed the sides of her cheeks.

Bonnie shut her eyes to get hold of her nerves. She knew she should make her presence known, but she could think of no words to even begin a conversation. This could all be nothing, she kept reminding herself. And surely she was standing in these bushes looking at a woman who didn't have a thing to do with her. Bonnie took a breath and opened her eyes. The woman now had a cigarette in her hand. That's when Bonnie *knew* this couldn't be Lucinda. That's when she was certain that this was all a stupid mistake, because Naz would never be with a smoking woman. Bonnie cursed herself for even the slightest doubt.

She started back to her car, when a hand suddenly clasped down on her wrist. It happened so quickly that Bonnie could only see the back of a wild woman dragging her from the bush. She tried to squirm from the woman's grip, but the woman turned and flashed a look that warned that she would break

Bonnie's arm. It was then that Bonnie realized that this was a child, no older than fifteen. Her hair was in one large plait that jutted from the back of her thick neck like a hog's tail. Her chest, beneath the dark T-shirt, was flat, dense and fleshy. Her thighs, in the denim pedal pushers, were like two stuffed sausages. But, young or no, the girl was determined to pull Bonnie from the bushes and never loosened her grip.

"Mama," the girl yelled. "Look a h'yere!" She pulled Bonnie out of the green.

"What the hell . . . ?" the woman called.

"She was a-watchin' you, Mama," the girl said, yanking Bonnie toward the porch.

The woman stood up on the top step. She looked at Bonnie like her daughter had dragged something foul from the woods.

"She was a-starin'," the girl said.

"This 'bout that damn census?" the mother barked.

"What?" Bonnie felt herself begin to panic. She yanked at the girl's grip and the two tugged back and forth.

"Don't wanna hear nuthin' 'bout that mess today," the woman argued. "And you oughta be ashamed of yo'self," she rebuked, "tryin' to git in folk's personal affairs."

"I'm not from the census," Bonnie yelled back. She yanked away from the daughter so hard that Bonnie stumbled backwards and stopped just short of falling. Her chest trembled as she fought her tears. She was embarrassed and scared and her wrist throbbed from where the girl had grabbed her. Bonnie tried to collect herself but her voice quivered when she said, "I . . . didn't mean to be lurkin'. I am . . . lookin' fo' the Justice house."

The daughter stepped toward Bonnie. "Why?"

"Hush up, Tammy," the woman barked.

"Are you Mrs. Justice?" Bonnie asked the woman.

"Might be! But I ain't got no time to be . . ." The woman's eyes suddenly glinted like she had figured something out—like she had placed the last piece in an intricate puzzle. Slowly she drew on her cigarette, contemplating Bonnie from head to toe. There was no threat in her observation, just intense curiosity.

"What is it, Mama?" Tammy asked.

The woman shrugged casually. "Nothin'," she said, sitting on the porch step again. "Go'n to Miss Caroline and git me that stew pot."

"You sho'?" Tammy asked.

"I'm fine."

The girl slowly walked toward the bushes again. She looked back at the porch every so often until she disappeared into the woods. Meanwhile, the woman just kept pulling on her cigarette. She hadn't taken her eyes off of Bonnie. And Bonnie allowed herself to look right back. Close up, the woman's features were even sharper and more defined. She wore no makeup but had a large mole on her left cheek, just like Marilyn Monroe. What Bonnie found odd was that the roots of her black hair were flaming red.

The woman blew a ribbon of smoke and it circled up toward the putty-patched roof. "So," she said, "you finally got here."

Bonnie felt her body shaking. "What?"

"Baby, we ain't 'bout to play no games, are we?" the woman asked. "I've known 'bout you fo' a long time. But I must say, I thought you'd a been here years ago."

"I don't know what you talkin' 'bout!"

"You know damn well what I'm talkin' 'bout."

"Are you *Lucinda Justice,* or are you not?" Bonnie asked.

"I am."

"And . . . would you mind tellin' me . . . who yo' man is?"

Lucinda flicked her cigarette butt into the dirt. The hem of her loose dress landed on her calves when she stood up. She grabbed the bucket from the top step and opened the screen door. "Come on in," she said. "Guess we got some things to say."

It seemed the longer Bonnie stayed here, the more out of sorts she became. But there *was* such a woman named Lucinda Justice, and Bonnie had to find out more. Part of her wanted to get away from this woman and this house, but at the same time, Bonnie knew she was on the edge of some precipice. Like the way Ruby-Pearl had described the subtle change in the color of a day that signaled that her life was about to change. Lucinda stepped back and allowed Bonnie to enter. She took a breath and walked into this strange place.

The Justice home was dim and cool. Even in the darkening room, she could see that the floors in the hall and living room were buffed to a shine. The air in the house smelled like a mixture of cleaning pine and potpourri, similar to Bonnie's home. She cursed herself for the comparison. But all at once the idea, the thought of Naz coming to this place seemed possible. She couldn't help but look for signs of his presence, and every testament to that presence brought nothing but pain. She saw a pair of large brown slippers by the entrance to the living room, just like Naz liked. And a coatrack draped by a man's gray flannel shirt, the kind that Naz wore on a cool morning hunt.

Bonnie longed to look into every room and closet, but resisted the urge. Instead she sat in a black vinyl easy chair and let her eyes roam. A checkered couch and end table with a crystal water glass filled with fake red petunias sat in the middle of the room. *National Geographic* magazines lay in a fan pattern across the end table. The furniture wasn't as new or as expensive as Bonnie's, but the rooms were neat and well cared for.

Without excusing herself, Lucinda went into the kitchen. Bonnie could see the back of her and could hear the clinking of glasses and ice. She noticed just the edge of a tin-topped table, like her mama used to cook on. Bonnie's eyes slowly scanned the living room, looking for anything else that might identify Naz. Baseball was his pride, but she saw none of it here. No pictures on the mantel or mitts, just rows of knick-knacks. She saw no shed as she peered out of the living room window. No shed, she thought. And no baseball trophies. Naz could never live in a house without a shed and certainly he couldn't exist without reminders of his own victories. Bonnie breathed a sigh of relief. This wasn't about Naz. This wasn't about her man.

Lucinda walked back in with two glasses of tea. She set one of the glasses in Bonnie's hands, then took a seat in a solid red armchair. Lucinda seemed perfectly calm as she sipped, then lit another cigarette. Bonnie was just about to apologize for taking up the woman's time. She was about to place her glass of tea on the coaster shaped like a South Carolina palm and go home, when Lucinda said, "I call my man Shoop. You call him Naz."

Bonnie shut her eyes. It felt like the world around her was beginning to cave. Lucinda Justice finally called him by name. "Shoop?" Bonnie said.

"Somethin' the kids made up," Lucinda said.

"Naz . . . got kids with you?"

"No," she answered. "Already had my share. And Shoop don't want no kids. No way, no how!"

Bonnie had to do something to center herself. She raised her glass to drink. The shaking in her hand caused the ice to clink repeatedly against the sides. The tea tasted sweet, but not overly sweet, and, like her own, had just a touch of lemon—never mint. This was all too much. Naz *was* here. He was in this house, with this woman.

"Shoop like the freedom of bein' wit'out kids," Lucinda

went on. Her tone was casual, as if talking to her man's wife was an everyday occurrence. "Most of mine are already grown... Desmond is nineteen, he from my first marriage; Troy is eighteen, he from the second, and Tammy is fo'teen... her daddy live in No'th Carolina."

"Three children, three daddies?" Bonnie asked.

"Babies are a blessing... however they git here."

Without much effort, Lucinda managed to put Bonnie's haughty attitude in place.

"No kids from my marriage with Shoop, though," Lucinda went on.

"Marriage?!"

"It not like yo's," Lucinda acknowledged. "You got his real name. But 'bout a year ago, we stood up in front of each other in our Sunday clothes and everything. Shoop gave me a name. Justice. Mr. and Mrs. Justice are we," she said, pulling on the cigarette.

Bonnie thought back to the day that Naz wore a suit home from a weekend trip. He said he had worshipped with Jackie Robinson. So many lies.

"I figure Justice was his mama's basket name or something," Lucinda said.

"It's what the baseball players called him," Bonnie said.

"Baseball players?"

"You don't know Naz used to play?" Bonnie asked in shock.

"Shoop tell me what I need to know. The rest is his own business."

The tears ran silently down Bonnie's cheeks. Lucinda didn't react to them. It was as if she expected this scene... or worse.

"How long?" Bonnie asked.

"We got married just this year."

"I'm not talkin' 'bout the damn marriage," Bonnie snapped.

"Need to slow yo' roll there, honey," Lucinda said. "Jes' remember, you come to *my* house."

Bonnie looked down at her hands. She couldn't believe she was actually being reprimanded by her husband's second wife. But she knew she'd have to keep her cool if she wanted to learn the whole truth.

"I met Shoop 'bout four years ago."

"Four years?" Bonnie whispered, more to herself.

"That's when I *met* him," she explained. "I tended bar at a place called Lucky's here in Taliliga. Shoop and some of his friends came through after a fishing trip."

Bonnie was humiliated at the thought that Horace Dean knew. Probably Scooter, Little Sr., maybe Jimmy-Earl Pine too. She wondered if they all laughed about it behind her back.

"It wasn't 'til a year later that he made Lucky's one of his regular stops. I guess I became a regular stop too." Lucinda leaned forward in her chair and looked directly at Bonnie. "I'm surprised you didn't come to this sooner."

"Where I'm from," Bonnie explained, "a woman believes her husband. We assume them to be honorable and true." Bonnie suddenly thought back to what Thora had told her about Horace and one of the Bell sisters. Also, Cal Monroe sitting in Mayweather's Diner, with a woman that wasn't Tilde. Naz was no better. In fact, her husband was worse. There seemed to be a whole other life for him here. She could smell him in this vinyl chair, set just the right distance from the TV. There were even slight circle stains in the wood where his sweaty tea glass sat on the end table. Bonnie always fussed with him and wiped the spot clean before it set. Obviously, Lucinda didn't mind about such things, for one circle swirled into another, like an intricate pattern in the wood.

"Why didn't you stop?" Bonnie asked her. "Why didn't you

say, 'You a married man, Naz' . . . or Shoop or whatever the hell—" Bonnie tried to stop and clear her throat but felt herself breaking down again. "Why didn't you say, 'Maybe we best not do this.' "

"Long as I know the truth," she said, "the way things really are, then I don't get down 'bout it. 'Sides, I don't need to have no man 'round me *all* the time. Shoop come 'round when I need him and leave when I'm done."

"I don't wanna hear this," Bonnie said, rising.

"Then what you come here fo'? I ain't out to hurt you no mo' than you are already," Lucinda said, "but the truth is the truth. And it ain't jes' 'bout me and Shoop layin' up."

Bonnie fled to the door.

"I love our life together," Lucinda said, following her out onto the porch. "I like having the man wit' me and I'd do anything to keep things jes' the way they are."

"You mean . . . you plan to go on wit' this?"

"Yes, ma'am," she replied. "How 'bout you?"

"How dare you," Bonnie whispered. "How dare you . . ." She ran to her car.

"I don't see why we gotta change things," Lucinda called.

" 'Cause now I know," Bonnie yelled back.

"You always knew!"

Lucinda was wrong. Everything she assumed to be true was a lie. The life she thought she had was over. And she hated Lucinda Justice. She hated her redness, her strength . . . that damn Marilyn Monroe mole. She hated that Lucinda had three babies from three daddies. For a Christian woman like herself, that meant Lucinda was a whore. But it also meant she could probably do things for Naz that Bonnie couldn't possibly imagine.

Bonnie had to steady her hands to turn on the ignition, then she stepped on the gas and sped away from this house—the

Justice house. She drove through the town of Taliliga. She drove in the dark with no idea of where she was going until somehow she found herself back at the entrance to the small covered bridge. Bonnie peered out of her window at the pond below. The bridge creaked in the wind. A half moon glistened against the water. Bonnie made it across and stopped where the water met with the dusty road. And she cried. She cried for her marriage . . . or what she thought was a marriage. She cried for the deceit, the betrayal and the lies. Lucinda was a whore, this was true. But Bonnie had to acknowledge that there was nothing that the woman could do to her marriage that Naz didn't allow. Lucinda Justice alone didn't wreck their marriage. It was Naz.

Bonnie barely made it into the house when Thora Dean's car sped through the gate. Thora threw open the car door and marched toward the house. Surely she had been calling the house all evening, worried.

"I don't know you, Bonnie Wilder!" she barked from the top of the walkway. "I don't know who you are!"

Bonnie didn't respond.

"Now that you got yo' other lil' buddies, them there Sisterhood gals," she said with envy, "you think you can treat me like a stepchild?"

Bonnie lowered herself into the rocker. She felt like someone was pressing down on her shoulders and leaning on the top of her head. She needed to sit very still or her body would crumble under the weight.

"You gon' sit there and ignore me like I ain't even here?" Thora went on. "Well, I'm through with you!"

Bonnie couldn't quite believe that this house that held so many cherished memories—her mother, her father and each and every one of the precious babies—now reminded her that the man she adored had betrayed her. Bonnie held her head in her hands.

"Honey?" Thora said, her expression softening.

Bonnie's body silently heaved.

"Oh, sweetheart." Thora knelt in front of her. "I... ain't mean to hurt yo' feelin's."

"Sorry fo' hangin' up on you," Bonnie wept.

"What is it?" Thora asked. "What happened?"

Bonnie took a used tissue from her dress pocket. "Naz," she said.

"Naz is fine. He and Horace finished listenin' to the game and then they went to the club."

"Prob'ly not," Bonnie said. "Prob'ly ain't at no damn club."

"No *damn* club," Thora said, stunned.

"He got another woman," Bonnie said.

"That's crazy."

"It's true."

Thora sat in the other porch rocker. "Not Naz."

Bonnie nodded.

Thora paused to take it in. Then she asked, "Is it one of them Bell sisters? Oh, I know it is! Prob'ly that same lil' Bessie thang that had her hooks in Horace. You know she been fawnin' after Naz fo' years."

"It's a woman live in Taliliga," Bonnie explained.

"Taliliga? Who in the world do Naz know in that godforsaken town?"

"Her name is Lucinda Justice." Bonnie felt she might cry forever. "They been carryin on fo' three years."

"Three years!"

"I went to see her and she say she won't stop."

"You went to see her?! Oh, honey-chile!"

Bonnie could feel knots tighten in her stomach. "He married her."

"What you talkin' 'bout?"

"He married me, then he married her!"

Thora stared out into the dark yard like she was trying to make sense of it. "That ain't possible, Bonnie."

"Maybe not . . . but he did."

"What kinda marriage? What kinda church—" Thora caught herself. "Wine," she said, rising. "That's what we need! Need us some wine and we need it now." She dashed into the house.

Bonnie held herself around the waist and rocked. She could feel the splinters of the chair against the hem of her skirt. Thora returned quickly with an open bottle and two cups. She threw a capful over the railing, poured two drinks and kicked off her shoes. "How you find out?"

"The woman said it herself." Then Bonnie told her best friend everything.

"I really thought Naz was one of the good ones," Thora said.

"Maybe I expected too much from him."

"Expectin' yo' husband to be true? Bonnie . . . honey, baby, that ain't too much."

"You should see her, Thora."

"A monster?"

Bonnie shook her head no. "She's . . . kinda like me." Bonnie couldn't quite figure if this was a good or bad thing. "Only she smokes."

"Hussy! Her three kids that you mentioned," Thora said, "any of 'em belong to—"

"No!"

"Baby-chile." Thora shook her head sadly. "I'm so sorry. Such a shame when it's over."

Bonnie looked at her friend. "Over?"

"It's always sad when a marriage reaches the end."

"But you forgave Horace. You didn't leave him."

Thora stared at Bonnie like she had just lost her mind. "This is different, Bonnie."

"Is it?"

"This is *damn* different," Thora pounded. "Horace carried on with that Bell trollop fo' maybe a month or two. I ain't excusin' him or nothin', but when I said something 'bout it, he ended it right away. You say Naz been goin' on fo' three years and ain't 'bout to quit."

"I don't know that," Bonnie defended. "I ain't talked to Naz yet."

"He *married* this woman, Bonnie!"

Bonnie sucked in an outburst of tears. "But he always had room enough fo' me," she cried.

"You stop it," Thora yelled. "You stop that talk!"

"He always came home with lots of love. I never felt slighted."

"I'm 'bout to slap yo' damn face in," Thora said, her eyes filled with helpless anger.

Bonnie sobbed out loud. Thora held her.

"The one thing I've always admired about you," Thora said, "is yo' dignity. Don't you dare lose it now!" Thora held her tighter. "You *know* what you gotta do, Bonnie. Gotta send that man on his way . . . he *married* another woman!"

Thora's words felt like lashes of fire against Bonnie's skin. Maybe this was why she hadn't told Thora her fears before. She knew her friend would shake her silly and tell her what a damn fool she was. And for the rest of the evening, Thora Dean did just that.

For a moment he simply stared at his suitcase sitting on the porch. At first his expression was blank. But then Bonnie saw his predicament pass over his face: the question, the possibility, then the realization. He hurried up the porch steps and into the living room. Bonnie sat on the sofa in her bedclothes.

"What the hell is that?" he asked, pointing outside.

"Yo' suitcase."

"I know it's my damn suitcase," he snapped, "but what the hell is it doin'—"

"Three years?"

Naz stood over her. "What are you talkin' 'bout?"

"Don't treat me like I'm stupid," she yelled. "Don't you dare do that, Naz Wilder!"

He pressed his eyes closed, then paused before he said, "Ain't as simple as that, Bonita."

"Don't you call me that," she yelled. "Don't speak my name!"

"Goddamn it, Bonnie," he whined.

This wasn't the response she'd expected. As if his wife had brought up some sort of inconvenience. Bonnie's growing rage gave her the confidence she needed to get her through this moment.

"I was gon' talk to you 'bout Lucinda," he said. "But . . . it ain't easy," he stuttered, "talkin' 'bout . . . another woman."

"Must be even harder talkin' 'bout another *wife*," Bonnie said.

"Ain't really no *wife*," he insisted. "Ain't nothin' but some make-believe stuff. You my *real* wife, Bonnie. You the woman I married in the church."

Bonnie couldn't believe what she was hearing. The Naz she knew would never do this. He honored her, loved her and loved their life. This Naz made no sense at all.

"Three years you've been with this woman," Bonnie said.

"You come home to me fo' three years wit' Lucinda in yo' clothes... in yo' skin," she cried. "I guess after-while, I was so used to her smell, I thought it was yo' own."

"Like I said, it ain't that simple. Come on now, Bonnie..." Naz sat beside her on the couch and took her hand. She yanked away. "We can work this out," he said softly. "You my wife..."

"Why?" she asked.

"Why what?"

"Why did you have to go to her?"

He swung his head like it wasn't attached to his body. "It started off small... you know. Jes' a woman..."

"Jes' a woman? Were there jes' other women too?"

"Lucinda the onliest one. Ain't never been no more," he swore.

"But why? Try and tell me, Naz," she yelled. "You need to tell me *something*!"

"Damn it, I don't know," he said. "I... go there to Taliliga, to Lucinda's place... and I'm jes' myself. I don't have to be nothin' I don't wanna be. I ain't got to go to church... ain't got to fix nothin'... no pressure. And she don't care 'bout no babies, mine or nobody else's."

"Is that what you feel with me, Naz? Pressure?"

"Sometimes," he admitted.

"Don't you think I feel that too?" Bonnie asked. "Don't you think Horace and... and Thora and Mrs. Reverend Duncan and every responsible person feel that way sometimes?"

"I ain't sayin' that."

"It's what you call being *grown,* Naz. It's being a *man.*" He lowered his head. "All this time," she went on, "I thought you wanted a chile with me. ''Long as it come from us' is what you said. Now it sound like you ain't never wanted no babies... yo' blood included."

"I wanted a chile 'cause *you* wanted a chile. Look," he said, "we can find a way to work this thing out."

"No."

"Come on, Bonita... we could always talk 'bout everything. Me and you is good like that." He took her hand again. This time she didn't pull away. She stared at her bare feet, cursing the fact that, even now, his touch felt good. "We've built a lot in twelve years," he said.

"This is different."

"Yes," he said, "but we can get through it."

Bonnie could feel Thora's shoe kicking her backside. She could feel the silence around them and her heart slowly filling with forgiveness.

"So, what you plan to do?" she asked.

"I'll go talk to Lucinda..."

"Talk 'bout what?" Bonnie said. "Ain't nuthin' to talk 'bout."

"Lucinda is goin' through some stuff right now..."

Bonnie's mouth dropped open. She felt so stupid. And betrayed once again.

"She ain't so... stable in the head lately," he explained. "And if I left right now—"

Bonnie yanked her hand away and stood up. "You git outta my house, Naz Wilder," she said.

"You don't understand, Bonnie," he said.

"You git the hell outta my house," she said, pulling at his arm. "You leave here and don't you *ever* come back!"

"But I love *you*! Just you. Please don't do this, Bonnie. Please..."

"Get out," she screamed.

"I ain't gon' leave you. I don't care what you say. Please, Bonnie. Let's jes' talk—"

"You go talk to yo' other wife." Bonnie pushed him from

behind over and over, inching him toward the door. Naz turned and grabbed her by her arms and shook her as if the jolts would turn her back into the wife that he knew. But the shaking only made Bonnie angrier.

"This is my house," she hollered. "My daddy left it to me, and I want you gone!"

Naz stood there, stunned. After a moment more, he turned to leave. "What 'bout the rest of my stuff—my trophies, my pictures..."

"You don't need them at Lucinda's place," she screamed. "You ain't nobody special, remember? That's what you said, right, Naz... or Shoop or Mr. Justice? What the hell *is* yo' name, man?!"

"You my Bonnie," he said, lifting his bag from the porch. "You my wife and I love you."

"Jes' leave," she yelled. "Go on to yo' other home."

Bonnie stood screaming from the porch as Naz threw his bag in the back of the pickup. He pleaded for a while but there was no more sympathy, no more thinking for Bonnie. Just anger and raw emotion. Even when Naz's truck pulled away, Bonnie was still screaming, her robe spattered with her own spit and tears. She held on to the porch railing and screamed even after Naz had gone. Bonnie yelled and cried until she had no energy, no spirit, no voice.

PART IV

FOURTEEN

Canaan Creek, 1985

Every Wednesday morning the Gray Lions charged the gates of the Old Slave Market in Charleston. With mesh sacks and shopping carts, they cruised the dusty aisles for vendors selling everything from Andouille sausages to Senegalese bangle bracelets. It had been a while since Bonnie and Thora had joined the Gray Lions for one of their shopping trips. They usually shopped at the Big Buy in town. Today, dark purple plums and multicolored peppers lured them on to take the trip with the rest of the group of mostly women mostly over sixty.

The white church bus jolted at the slightest bump in the road. A few grandkids of the Gray Lions sat in the back, their arms stretched over their heads, shouting, "Whoooooaa," each time they hit a bump.

"I wish somebody would shut them damn kids up," Thora mumbled.

Bonnie's eyes skimmed the road. I-85 was lined with billboards advertising everything from fried potato pies to fireworks. Fields of peaches spread out for miles.

"That gal still on yo' mind," asked Thora, "that Augusta?"

"Hate to drag all this nonsense out again."

Thora opened a zip-lock bag of shelled walnuts. "I'm afraid it's already dragged out." She threw a few kernels into her mouth. Thora could sense that Bonnie would go no further with this conversation, so she changed the subject. "You never did tell me," she said. "When Tally came and fixed my flat tire that evenin' . . . what in the world was he doin' at the house . . . all dressed up?"

"Mean, he ain't say?"

"The man jes' blabbed on 'bout Columbus and the history of the New World."

Bonnie smiled. "He come to see you, dear."

"Why?"

"You know he got a little thang fo' you. Had it for the last few years. I think it's right cute that he finally got the nerve to come by fo' a visit."

"Cute, huh? And what were we supposed to do when he came by?"

Bonnie knew how Thora would react, but she said it anyway. "He wanted to set with you. Maybe take you out."

"Tally Benford?"

"Yes, honey!"

"And me?" Thora sucked her teeth. "I told you I ain't interested in no damn Tally Benford!"

"You's a lie," Bonnie laughed.

"Tally don't even come to my mind."

"Lord, girl, you sound like a chile." Bonnie suddenly regretted her flippant statement. The fact that Thora turned from Tally had less to do with lack of attraction and more to do with ghosts that often came between women and men after a certain age. Bonnie understood this better than most. She hadn't looked at a man since Naz left, and that was almost thirty years ago. Just like Thora, she recognized that it was easier to stay alone, or in the company of woman friends who could only sympathize about varicose veins and hot flashes.

"Tell me somethin' . . ." Bonnie started.

"Yes?"

"And I mean tell me the Lord's honest truth . . ." Bonnie went on.

"Jes' go'n and ask yo' damn question!"

"How do you feel, *really* feel, 'bout that man?"

"I don't need to be talkin' 'bout no Tally Benford."

"Come on, now!"

Thora paused like she was actually pondering the question. "Did I mention that Horace came to me again last night?"

"You avoidin' me, Thora Dean."

"This time he was a-settin' at the foot of my bed. Had his head in his hands like he was frettin' o'er something. I say, 'What is it, honey?' He didn't answer at first. Then he looked up and say, 'Got to finish my work. And so do you, dahlin'.' He got up from the bed," Thora said thoughtfully, "and befo' he left, he say, 'See you when the sun go down.' And that was it."

"All that's fine and mighty deep, but I'm still waitin' on yo' answer."

Thora dropped the bag of walnuts into her purse. She looked up, then grimaced as if she had just swallowed a spoonful of cod-liver oil.

"Lord," Bonnie groaned, "why is the thought of wantin' a man so rueful at our age?"

"'Cause we gotta change," Thora answered. "Gotta keep our nails done and our hair straightened."

"But you always done that, honey. Always kept yo'self together, whether somebody was lookin' or not. 'Sides, Tally thinks you're beautiful. And you ain't gotta do nothin' but talk to the man."

"Goodness gracious," Thora said with disgust. "That mean I gotta say somethin' nice?"

"Jes' be yo'self," Bonnie said. "'Sides, Tally prob'ly die from shock if somethin' nice ever come out yo' mouth."

Thora fell silent for a moment. Bonnie could see her good friend thinking, planning. "Men is too much work. Too much worriment," she decided. "Don't need none of that clutterin' things up!"

"You jes' scared!"

Thora did a double take at Bonnie. "You got one helluva nerve!"

"Ain't no man knockin' on my do'."

"I'm talkin' 'bout that Augusta. You runnin' from that gal like she got the plague."

Thora had deftly relinquished the hot seat. "We ain't talkin' 'bout me, we talkin' 'bout you," Bonnie said.

"Punk!" Thora charged. "Lil' yella coward!" Thora let out a deep sigh and lay her head on Bonnie's shoulder. "We's both punks," she admitted. "But I do know this: The man upstairs, sometimes He send us things. Things we ain't expectin'. Things that make us grow and think... even at our age. And damn it to hell," she said, "maybe that's why Tally been sniffin' 'round me. Maybe he's here fo' a reason."

"Yes, dear."

"And by the same token," Thora said, slanting her eyes, "maybe Lucinda's chile come to you fo' a reason too."

"Maybe," Bonnie replied. Though clearly, Bonnie wasn't ready to face the possibility or to face Lucinda's child. She was relieved when the bus turned on East Bay Street. But Thora, being Thora, refused to let the subject die.

"This ain't jes' 'bout that gal," Thora pressed. "This 'bout yo' life too. We too old to be runnin'. This should be a time fo' us to set out on the porch, eat cantaloupe, drink lemonade and hold our heads up to the sun." Thora grasped the back of the seat in front of her and pulled herself to standing. "Think 'bout it, honey."

"Like you gon' think 'bout goin' out wit' Tally?"

Thora ignored Bonnie's words. "I'm gon' find me some nice bath salts here."

"Run, rabbit, run."

"Somethin' sweet and sexy. Yes," Thora said decidedly, "some of them lavender bubbles."

She knew that Thora would eventually spend an evening with Tally Benford, even though she was scared to death about it. And that's what Bonnie admired about her old friend. Thora had always faced her ghosts head-on. She sometimes even talked to them, abided with them. It was the *living* that gave Thora Dean the biggest problems. For Bonnie, it was the past. Maybe she wasn't as strong as she always thought she was. Perhaps, back in the day, Naz was right about her motives being more selfish than selfless. Lord, but she couldn't go back and cast doubt on any of her actions. Not now. It was too late. And much too much time had passed for that old devil called regret.

First of all, I don't want you to think that I got *any* romantic feelings for you, Tally Benford."

"Okay."

"And I don't want you assumin' that this, this so-called *date*," Thora said as if the word tasted like vinegar, "is gon' lead to anything else."

"Yes, ma'am."

"And," Thora said, pointing one coral-tipped finger, "the onliest reason I'm goin' out with you tonight is 'cause Bonnie gon' drive me crazy 'til I do."

"Fine," he said.

"Fine!" she said. "Now, let's go on in, watch this movie and then you can take me back home."

"If that's what you say."

"That's *jes'* what I say!"

Tally got out of his car, ran around and opened the car door for Thora. He wore the same suit that he wore the first time he had tried to court her. Tally looked nervous as he stood waiting for her to touch down on the sidewalk. And Thora Dean took her time. She smoothed her short wig on the nape of her neck, set her patent-leather handbag on her arm and then stepped out. She never made eye contact with Tally. Her shoes pinched her toes when she walked. Thora had always been used to the discomfort of a sexy pair of shoes, but for the last few years, LifeStride—with only a two-inch heel, roomy toes and rubber soles—had become the sexiest shoe in her closet.

Her red dress flounced around her calves when they walked to the ticket window. Bonnie had been impressed that Thora had actually bought a new dress for her date, but Thora claimed that she was looking to buy some new clothes for church anyway and that the dress had nothing *whatsoever* to do with Tally Benford.

Thora stood a few feet away from the ticket window while Tally paid. She kept her arms locked across her chest. Tally offered his hand but Thora marched into the lobby in front of him. The buttery scent of popcorn flooded the place. Doris Minton, the usher, pushed her heavy black glasses down on her nose at the sight of the two of them. She tore the tickets, and a grin cut across her face.

"Evenin', Doris," Tally said.

"Evenin' . . . you two," she smiled.

Thora flinched.

"Good movie," she said to Thora. "That there Eddie Murphy... he's a real funny fella in this film."

"Yes, he is," Tally said as he and Thora entered the theater.

Thora stopped in her tracks. "You mean you done already seen it?"

"Well... yes."

"Then why in the world you wanna see it again?"

" 'Cause you haven't. I figure it'd take five mo' years to find a movie that neither one of us ain't seen."

"You already heard the jokes, and I'm gon' be laughin' and you won't."

"I doubt you gon' even crack a smile during this date," he said.

Her eyes widened at his audacity. "Damn it to hell, Tally Benford!" she said. "I don't need this kinda talk from you!"

"Okay, I'm sorry," he said quickly. "Jes'... tryin' to make conversation, is all."

"Well, if that's gon' be yo' conversation, then you need to hush up."

"Alright, alright," he said, flashing the peace sign. Thora walked cautiously into the lit theater. The chairs felt cushy against her stockings as she inched into the row and sat. Though Thora had spent more than a few evenings at the Grove Playhouse alone, she had to admit that it was different sitting with a man. The chandeliered ceiling and grand carved pillars usually took her breath away. But tonight she felt so nervous that she couldn't even see these things. Her elbow on the padded rest brushed Tally's and gave her a tingle. Surely this couldn't be because of Tally himself. This would probably happen with anyone of the opposite sex, she reasoned. Horace had died from a heart attack almost fifteen years ago, taking her completely by surprise. One minute he was working in the garden, planting beefsteak tomatoes, and the next he was in the hospital. Horace never made it back home. Funny how, as a young woman, Thora had innocently flirted with men while she was married. But now widowed, she wouldn't even think to date. So after all these years, she concluded that she would still be nervous whether it was Tally sitting beside her or the man in the moon.

"You want some candy or pop?" he asked.

"No. When is this movie gon' start?"

"Another fifteen minutes."

"Fifteen minutes? We got to sit here fifteen minutes?"

"Ain't nothin' worse than seein' a movie after it done started," he explained. "I likes to be on time."

"There's a difference between bein' on time and showin' up yesterday."

"Oh, now, Thora," he chuckled. "You exaggeratin' and you know it!" Tally seemed unaffected by her bad attitude. "Did I tell you how pretty you look tonight?"

"Yes!"

"Smell pretty too."

"I don't need all this niceness!"

"What do you need, Thora Dean?"

"What?"

"I wanna know what you need from a man," he said gently. "What you need from me?"

"I need fo' you to take me home," she said. "'Cause you ain't s'posed to be talkin' 'bout such things!" Thora stood up. Tally pulled her back into her seat. "I'm fixin' to call the law on you, Tally," she warned.

"Why you scared of me? Scared you *jes'* might like me a little?"

She looked straight ahead at the closed velvet drapes on the large stage.

"I likes you, Thora," he said. "You my kinda woman. And I don't wanna do nothin' but be next to you and call yo' name."

"That's what *all* you men say!"

Tally laughed out. "That what you think I want? To get in yo' stuff? Lawd ha' mercy," he laughed. "I sho'ly don't want that!"

"What's wrong wit' my stuff?"

"Nothin' . . . I mean, I ain't tryin' to . . . John Brown it!" he exclaimed. "If I say something 'bout . . . yo' stuff," he said carefully, "then you wanna slap my face. And when I'm a gentleman and stay away from talkin' 'bout such private affairs, you think something's wrong. Fo' fact, yo' stuff look right good."

She had to stop herself from smiling.

"Look," he said, calming his voice, "let's jes' set here and be quiet fo' a while. Seem that if we don't talk, then we won't insult each other."

"Fine wit' me!" Thora pulled her purse onto her lap. She glanced around as more people started to file in. She couldn't wait for the lights to dim and prayed that no one that she knew would enter.

"Fixin' to get me some JuJu Beans," he said, moving to the edge of his seat.

"Go'n, then!"

"Sho' you don't want no Raisinets or Lemon Drops? I know you women like them Lemon Drops . . ."

"I don't! And stop tellin' me what I like. We don't *all* like Lemon Drops! Seem like you tryin' to turn me into yo' dead wife or something."

Tally turned to face her. "What did you say?"

"Bonnie told me how you say I remind you of yo' wife."

Tally's face dropped.

"Well, that's not who I am," she said. "I am Thora Dean."

Tally's expression had changed. The animation in his eyes

had flattened and his smile had grown sad and cold. He stood up. "I think I'm ready to take you home now."

"What?"

"Ain't no woman worth all this!"

"I never asked for this *date*!" she said. Tally started up the aisle. She followed him through the movie house, past the concession stand, a gawking Doris Minton, and out to his car. "Shoulda never come in the first damn place," she argued.

"Don't have to worry 'bout that no mo'," he said.

"Takin' me to a movie that you done already seen! What kinda date is that?"

Tally opened her door and she jumped in. They rode back in silence. Thora began to feel a twinge of remorse. Maybe she had finally crossed the line. If Tally or anyone had thrown her dead husband at her, Thora would have their head. She had always been a master at pushing folks' buttons. The more uncomfortable Thora felt in a situation, the harder she pressed. Perhaps this is why Horace Dean had been the love of her life. He let her push and push and loved her just the same. Maybe she shouldn't have mentioned Tally's dead wife. Of course, she'd never apologize. It was easier to never go out with the man again than to have to ask his forgiveness. She glanced at him, and his eyes were full of fire. Oddly, Thora found this attractive. For as long as she could remember, she was drawn to passion, displaced or no.

Tally clicked on the car radio. Kool and the Gang sang "Joanna." Thora reached over and turned it down. Tally never even looked over. He was through with her... that was for sure. But Thora Dean had achieved her goal. In less than an hour, she had managed to scare this good man out of his ever-loving mind.

The front door slammed like a clap of lightning. Bonnie turned down the sound on the TV. Why was Thora home so soon? she wondered. After the movie, she and Tally were supposed to go for dinner at the Golden Coral on Highway 10. Surely there wasn't even enough time to finish watching the film, let alone eat. When she saw Thora's face, not angry, but too nonchalant, Bonnie could see that disaster had struck.

Thora kicked off her new shoes. Her eyes darted across the television. "I was hopin' I'd get home in time to see the *Cosby Show.* You know I cain't miss that."

"Thora . . . ?"

"What you cook, Bonnie?" she said. "I 'bout starved to death."

Thora wasn't usually one to avoid confrontation. Her emotions overflowed, often to others' discomfort. Like when Horace died. Thora shouted and cried and often jumped from her chair during the reverend's eulogy. And before they closed the casket, Thora Dean draped herself across her husband's body. But those who knew her knew that this was her way of grieving.

"Thought you and Tally were supposed to go to dinner."

"We didn't."

"Honey, what happened?"

"Jes' didn't work out, that's all."

"Why?"

"I'm gon' eat," she said, heading for the kitchen.

Bonnie found her pulling pots and pans from the refrigerator. Thora stopped long enough to take off her stockings and wind an apron over her new dress. Then she slipped on her glasses, the thick black ones that only Bonnie was meant to see.

"Weren't you the one who said that we shouldn't be runnin'?" Bonnie asked. "Say we should be settin' on our porches, eatin' watermelon and holding our head up to the sun."

"I said cantaloupe! We should be eatin' cantaloupe!" Thora sliced from a small rib roast. "And you ain't done ne'er a thing 'bout that Augusta gal, so don't you say a word to me, Bonnie Wilder."

Bonnie remained silent on the subject.

Thora moved quickly through the kitchen. She set some candied yams in a pan and then some collard greens to warm.

"Why don't you jes' set yo' full plate in the microwave?" Bonnie asked.

"You know I don't like that thing, Bonnie. Gi' you cancer, sho' nuff. You 'member how Delphine started using that microwave fo' every damn thing. Even try to bake in it. And hell if that cancer ain't took her to her glory." Thora set her pan over a low flame. She wiped her hands on her apron then sat across from Bonnie at the table. "Look," she said plainly, "it jes' didn't work. Some things don't work."

"Okay," Bonnie acquiesced. "I won't mention it no mo'."

"Good. 'Cause if me and Tally started talkin'... nicely... and if I started to like him and if we were to get married—"

"Married? Lord, you cain't even have a simple date."

"Jes' listen," she ordered. "We old now, and cain't waste no time pretending!"

"Okay."

"If Tally and me like each other and if we get together... what's gon' happen to you, Bonnie?"

Bonnie felt the air leave her chest.

"I'm serious."

Bonnie was speechless. Touched and speechless. "That why you been puttin' him down? That why you been actin' like a stone fool?"

"Maybe."

"Thora..." she said. "Lord, you always did ha' the biggest heart of anybody I know."

"Stop that talk! Me and you been friends since we was eight. Buried one husband and sent the other'n on his cheatin' way. Found children, lost children, buried children. I cain't leave you now! I won't."

Bonnie hugged her old friend from behind.

"Set on down," Thora said. "You know I don't go fo' all that messy stuff."

Bonnie went to the stove and turned down the flame. She really did love Thora Dean. And she suddenly felt blessed to have had the woman in her life for so many years. "Please don't worry 'bout me, honey. I'm in good health, I have my house here and I gets loads of letters from folks. Ruby-Pearl jes' wrote us the other day from Hencil. Olive drop by ever' once in while. Come on, now. I got loads of folks. And I'll tell you something else. If you and Tally get together, that'd jes' be mo' family for me to have . . . and you'll be right there in Taliliga."

"I guess," Thora said.

Bonnie set the warm plate in front of Thora. Thora said a quick blessing and then cut her meat. "You ain't got to worry bout Tally and me, no way," Thora said. "I chased that man so far. Mercy . . . I said somethin' 'bout his dead wife."

Bonnie gasped. "No, you didn't!"

"When I aim to get rid of a soul, don't take me long."

"Tally's different, though," Bonnie said. "Even with insensitive and . . . stupid-ass remarks—"

"Did you jes' cuss me, Bonnie?"

"You deserve that one!"

"Maybe I do," Thora admitted.

"Oh, I know you do!" Bonnie confirmed. Her voice softened when she said, "But . . . I 'spect even with all yo' triflin' remarks Tally'll be back jes' the same."

FIFTEEN

Canaan Creek, 1958

Bonnie turned down the sound on the TV when she heard a car pull through the gate. She was sure it was Thora . . . again. Nearly every morning since Naz had left, the woman arrived, throwing open the window blinds, chattering about "a new day" and "other fish in the sea," all the while her gardenia-scented perfume sweetening the silent, bland rooms. Bonnie listened for the predictable sound of high heels across the porch. She heard nothing. Perhaps it was Ruby-Pearl. Though less intrusive, she had stopped by with Wynn several times. Even the other ladies from the Sisterhood had come to visit, each with a wrapped dish and a tale of love gone bad. Maybe it was Naz.

Bonnie drifted toward the window. She wanted to look out, but couldn't bear the disappointment if it wasn't. So many times over these six weeks she had regretted making him go. Then she would try to imagine living with him again—Lucinda Justice always looming at the periphery of their lives. At night, when Bonnie climbed into bed alone, she pictured him lying beside Lucinda, Naz holding Lucinda, Naz loving Lucinda. No, she thought. They could never make it work again. Naz had made a mockery of their life together and, in her heart, she didn't believe he would ever change. Still, she longed for him.

There was a light knock at the door. She cracked open the screen.

"Mo'nin', Bonnie."

"Tilde? Tilde Monroe?"

Everyone knew that Tilde had reported the Sisterhood to Pine. So what was she doing here?

The woman carried a small brown paper bag. "Hazard loaf," she said.

" 'Scuse me?"

"That's what Cal calls my spice bread, 'cause I soaks it in rum," she said, raising the bag.

"Hazard loaf?"

"Best you ever tasted. I usually bake a few this time a year and I brung you one. But you need to start soakin' it now," she said, almost as an order. "You soak it now and by August, one slice'll make you fall out drunk on the flo'."

Bonnie felt like she was missing a piece of this conversation. But somehow she sensed Tilde actually trying to reach out. Bonnie opened the door.

Before Tilde entered, she glanced back at her car. A man sat in the driver's seat.

"That Cal out there?" Bonnie asked.

"Yes'm."

"Why don't you ha' him to come in."

"By and by," Tilde said.

The last time that Tilde had come to Blackberry Corner, she had insisted that Bonnie was trying to be God. Yet, here she was again. Tilde glanced around before taking a seat on the couch.

"Not that I . . . ever go into Tangle's package sto'," she said.

Bonnie had rarely spoken with Tilde alone. How could she know the woman could drop you in the middle of a one-sided conversation.

"But they's got that dark Jamaican rum on sale," she went on. "Good for soakin' Hazard loaf." Tilde reached into the brown paper bag and pulled out a cellophane-wrapped loaf and handed it to Bonnie. Chopped walnuts were sprinkled on top. " 'Course, you can use some of that blackberry wine that Naz make—" Tilde caught herself. She had said the name.

"It's alright," Bonnie said.

"No, it ain't," Tilde said. "I know it's hard . . . losin' yo' man."

Bonnie looked down at the cake.

"Believe me, I *really* know," she said. "Cal and me—we's certainly had our troubles."

"Is there somethin' you need to say to me, Tilde?"

The woman folded the empty brown bag into a tiny square. Tilde rarely looked uncomfortable.

"I want you to know that . . . while I didn't approve of what you and this 'Sisterhood' was doin'—"

"Is that why you told Pine?"

"That's *exactly* why I told Pine! And I'm woman enough to admit that maybe I was wrong to do that."

"Well, if you come here to say you sorry, then I accept yo' apology," Bonnie said dismissively. She rose from her seat. "And I thank you kindly for the bread."

"Tilde," Cal called from the front porch, "we cain't set out here all day."

Tilde dropped her chin to her chest in frustration.

"We?" Bonnie asked. "Ain't seen nobody out there with Cal."

"I ain't got 'round to explainin' things yet," Tilde yelled to him.

"She gettin' restless," Cal called. "And I ain't 'bout to change no nappy."

Bonnie went to the door. Cal stood on the porch balancing a squirming baby and a diaper bag hanging from his shoulder. "How do," he said.

Bonnie looked from Tilde to Cal to this plump, pretty child. It finally made sense: Tilde and Natalie being gone for the last few months, Cal standing there with a baby—and more, Tilde showing up with a gift in her chubby hands and shame in her eyes.

"You gon' take her, Bonnie?" Cal asked.

Bonnie looked at Cal, then his wife.

"Natalie *did* get into college up north," Tilde started, "she really did. And she the youngest colored gal they ever had," she said proudly. "And she *was* gon' stay with my sister so she could go to school. All that's the truth. But... she got pregnant."

"Went out there and ruint herself," Cal snapped.

"She ain't ruint nothin'!" Tilde barked. "Natalie good as she can be. And she still goin' on to that school. Gon' be the youngest colored gal they ever had... so you jes' shut yo' damn mouth, Cal Monroe!"

Here was the Tilde that Bonnie knew best. The mother. The fighter. And now she truly had something to fight for.

"Bonnie," Tilde said, dropping all pretense. "I need fo' you to take this chile. Take her and find her a good home."

"What Natalie got to say?" Bonnie asked.

"She know she cain't care fo' no baby."

"And we ain't 'bout to," Cal put in. "Our baby days is done!"

"I cain't take her lessen Natalie bring her to me herself," Bonnie insisted.

"Natalie is sixteen years old," Tilde said. "She know she cain't raise no chile. But we's God-fearin' folk."

"It's still her chile."

"It's *my* chile," Tilde barked. "*I* gotta feed her, *I* gotta clothe her."

Cal adjusted the bundle in his arms. The blanket fell open and Bonnie caught a glimpse of the baby's face. She was as light as Tilde. A patch of dark brown hair sat on top of her head in a pretty ringlet.

"Fine-lookin' grandbaby," Bonnie said.

"Indeed," Tilde whispered.

Bonnie could see the shame in the woman's eyes. And it wasn't just that Natalie had taken a wrong turn, but the shame that she, Tilde Monroe, had to now make things right.

"Who's the daddy?" Bonnie asked.

"Some boy . . . live up in Hazelhurst," Cal answered.

"Do he know?"

Tilde blew from her mouth with disgust. "That boy and his family want as much to do with this chile as Natalie."

Bonnie looked into the blanket again when the baby started to fuss. "Natalie is the mama," she said. "And only Natalie can tell me so."

"But she's sixteen," Tilde pleaded. "I was sixteen when I had Natalie!" Cal cut his eyes away. Bonnie did recall how Tilde had disappeared during high school and come back to town a mama and a married lady. "And you know Natalie is smart as a whip. You know she is! Natalie say to me, 'Please, Mama . . . please take this chile to Miss Bonnie. Please ask Miss Bonnie to find her a home.' That's what she say."

"Where is she?" Bonnie asked.

"Still in Virginia," Cal answered.

"The girl had a tough delivery," Tilde went on. "Doctors say she had to rest, so she stayin' there until school start." Tilde looked right at Bonnie. "I'm sorry, Bonnie," she said. "Sorry fo' my jealousy."

"Tilde—"

"Sorry for speakin' bad of you and yo' baby club—"

"I cain't take the chile," Bonnie said plainly.

Tilde's desperation suddenly quieted. She crossed her arms over her chest and looked right at Bonnie. "If I wanted," she began, her voice tinged with sarcasm, "I coulda set this baby right outside yo' do' in the middle of the night. And you woulda never known a thing. She woulda been jes' another abandoned child and you and yo' Sisterhood gals woulda gone and sent her right on her way. But I come to you like a proper woman. Like a woman wanna be right with you and God." Tilde took the whining baby from Cal. "Don't make Natalie come here," she pleaded. "The girl ain't well and she feel sorry enough that she gotta do this in the first place."

Tilde's tiny eyes were filled with shame but also with contrition. The fact is, she *could've* left the child and run. It was bad enough that the woman had humbled herself to come here, maybe it would've been worse if Natalie had to do it herself. Bonnie looked at the child again. Just like every other baby, she needed love—positive love, and also a good family.

Bonnie accepted the baby.

"You one of God's angels," Tilde said. "And you saved my Natalie a lot of pain."

"Y'all go on now," Bonnie said.

"She gon' be somebody good, Bonnie," Tilde said. "Once Natalie get back on her feet and get her schoolin', she gon' be alright."

"You'll find the chile a good home?" Cal asked.

"I'll do my best."

"Thank you," Tilde said. She kissed the baby and then kissed

Bonnie on the cheek. "How long it take?" she asked. "How long 'til the baby be gone?"

"Sometimes a day, sometimes two or three," Bonnie said. "Depends on where the new mama live."

Tilde nodded. She looked at her granddaughter one last time. Then they were gone.

Wynn sat in the high chair at Bonnie's table, gumming a soft cookie. He watched every move that his mama made with the new baby. When Ruby-Pearl fingered the patch of curls on top of the child's head, Wynn stopped chewing. Bonnie could see him contemplating the small, gurgling creature that lay in the wicker basket.

"She look jes' like Natalie," Ruby-Pearl said.

"Who look jes' like Tilde," Bonnie added. She used a dishcloth to wipe the beads of water from the outside of a bottle, then handed it to Ruby-Pearl. Wynn flung his cookie on the floor and let out a shriek when Ruby-Pearl lifted the new baby from the basket and slipped the bottle into her mouth.

"You done had yo's already, sweetheart," Ruby-Pearl said to Wynn. "She jes' a lil' ole thing. But you *my* baby. My onliest baby." The boy was so agitated that he tried to climb out of the high chair. Bonnie carried him to the pantry, where she retrieved another animal cracker. Wynn calmed but he kept his eyes on Ruby-Pearl.

"You too good, Bonnie," Ruby-Pearl went on. "After Tilde opened her mouth to Pine, I'da made her hit the road and take her grandbaby wit' her."

"Ain't the chile's fault."

"Maybe not," Ruby-Pearl said, "but I cain't see how she could even twist her mouth to ask you to take this baby."

Ruby-Pearl pulled the bottle away and gently placed the baby over her shoulder. "You call the other Sisters?"

"Not yet. I been meaning to since yesterday, but it's so nice havin' the chile 'round."

Ruby-Pearl looked up excitedly. "You thinkin' on keepin' her?"

"Oh, no . . . heck no!"

"But Naz is gone now and—" Ruby-Pearl caught herself. "I'm sorry," she said. "Didn't mean to sound so insensitive."

"It's okay," Bonnie replied. "At least I got this lil' gal to take my mind off things . . . even if it is jes' fo' a little while." Bonnie looked at the child longingly. "I would keep her," she said, "but this is *Tilde's* grand."

"Say no more. That woman'll be in yo' business from now 'til kingdom come." Ruby-Pearl looked at her with gentle eyes. "I'll tell you this much, though, if no mo' babies come, then you gon' be Wynn's mama too. You *and* me."

"Thank you, dear."

Bonnie set Wynn back in the high chair. He banged the top of it with his spoon. "Tell me something," Bonnie asked. "When does it stop?"

"What, honey?"

"This . . . loneliness."

Ruby-Pearl's demeanor remained tranquil and patient. That's what Bonnie liked about spending afternoons with the woman. Even with Wynn fussing, their time together was always peaceful.

"With me, it lasted for years," she said. "But that was *my* choice. I decided to set there in that cold stew . . . that's what my mama used to call it. Cold stew. It wasn't until you put Wynn in my arms that I started to change. And you know what?"

Bonnie leaned against the counter as she listened.

"I wish to God that I had changed things a lot sooner."

Bonnie nodded. "You gon' think I'm crazy when I tell you this..."

"I'm sho' I won't."

"One day last week," Bonnie said, "I was hurtin' so bad that I got in my car and drove to Taliliga again."

"No."

"Oh yes I did!"

"And what did you do when you got there?"

"I never made it," she said. "I stopped right before that old covered bridge."

"Why'd you go?"

Bonnie smiled ruefully. "I wanted to ask Naz to come back home."

"Why'd you stop?"

"My pride felt a little bigger than my loneliness, I guess. I'm jes' glad that I came to my senses befo' I made a fool a myself. But I could do it again, Ruby-Pearl. This baby took my mind away from it fo' a while. But, Lord," Bonnie said, "I do miss that man."

"It ain't fo' nobody to tell you what's right or wrong." Ruby-Pearl rocked the baby. "But if Naz do come back, what kinda life would you have? Things'll never be the way they were."

"I know, but—"

"Ever' time that man leave the house, you'll be wondering. Where he goin'? Who he with? And don't let him think 'bout takin' one of his weekend hunts."

"My God," Bonnie whispered.

"I know it hurts," she said. "But, honey, it gets better. And please," Ruby-Pearl urged, "use me! Talk to me. Talk to yo' friends. Don't do what I did. Don't set in that stew fo' too long." Wynn raised his arms toward her. She lifted him out of the chair and he squirmed until she set him on the floor beside

Godfrey. "I meant to tell you," Ruby-Pearl said, her tone changing. "I decided on a birthday for Wynn."

"Decided on one?"

"We don't exactly know what day it is, remember? I thought that his official birthday should be the day that Wynn came to me. I know we'll be off by a few weeks, but August seventh sound like a good day fo' a celebration."

"That's just a couple weeks away."

"Yep, and we gon' ha' a big old party for my lil' man. What you think, baby?" she asked Wynn. The boy pulled himself up to standing as he grasped on to Godfrey's back. "Look at that big boy," Ruby-Pearl said, clapping. "And you so sweet, Godfrey," she said, stroking the dog's back.

"He seem to know how to treat these babies," Bonnie said about Godfrey. "They pull his hair, yank his tail, and he jes' wince and move on."

"And speakin' of movin' on," Ruby-Pearl said. She took her purse, then picked up her son. "When you gon' call the Sisters?"

"I'm fixin' to dial Miss Idella now."

"Oh, honey," Ruby-Pearl said sadly.

"Time jes' ain't come yet," Bonnie said.

"Or maybe it did and you gave it to me."

"Don't start that." Bonnie took the basket and set it on the dining room table.

"Miss Idella's gon' make one of her chocolate cakes for Wynn's party," Ruby-Pearl said. "One of them layer cakes that she—"

Just then, Bonnie heard a voice yelling her name from outside. Moments later, a young woman burst through the front door, her hair flying every which way and her eyes wild.

"Natalie," Bonnie said, moving toward the girl.

She wore a pair of tennis shoes, and beneath her baggy dress, Bonnie could see that her stomach was still slightly distended. "Please, Miss Bonnie," she cried, "please tell me she's still here. Tell me you haven't given Malina away."

A tall, lanky young man entered behind her and stood by the door.

"Slow down there, sweetie," Bonnie said.

"Is she here? Is my baby here?"

"Yes, yes, she's right there in the basket," Bonnie said.

Natalie dashed toward the basket so fast, Bonnie got scared for the child. But then Natalie's demeanor softened as she reached to pick up the baby. She settled in one of the dining room chairs and kissed her daughter over and over until the child began to cry.

"I don't understand," Bonnie said. "Didn't you ask yo' mama to bring the baby here?"

"No," the young man replied. "We ain't knowed nothing 'bout that."

"Tilde is jes' mean!" Natalie spat. "Mean as a snake!"

"What happened?" Bonnie asked. Ruby-Pearl sat in the armchair with Wynn in her lap. The boy sucked his pacifier, wide-eyed, as he watched the hysterical girl.

"Malina is *my* baby," Natalie said breathlessly. "And I woke up yesterday mo'nin' at my auntie's house and Malina was gone. Jes' gone! I didn't have a car or anyone to drive me from Virginia, so I called Kevin . . . he's Malina's father," she said, pointing at the young man.

"How do, ma'am," Kevin said.

"I begged him to come get me and bring me here!" Natalie stood up and grimaced from the pain.

"You okay there, sweetie?" Ruby-Pearl asked.

"I'm fine." She moved the basket to the couch and sat on the soft cushion with a sigh. "Doctor gi' me stitches and I'm still kinda sore." Natalie rocked her body from the pain, or perhaps just plain anger. "I knew Mama would bring Malina here." Natalie unbuttoned her top. She lifted the child from the basket, then quieted her with her breast. "Mama kept tellin' me, all the while I was pregnant, that Miss Bonnie could find a home fo' the chile. She said that when I give the baby up, then I could go to school. Tilde," Natalie spat, "she don't listen to no-damn-body. She didn't hear a word I had to say."

"She was . . . worried," Ruby-Pearl said.

"You know that's a lie," Natalie barked. "Tilde ain't never meant nobody no good! Not me, not my daddy, not you," she said to Ruby-Pearl. "She call you a monster-faced woman."

Ruby-Pearl didn't flinch from the insult.

"And ever'body in the Three Sisters know that she don't have *no* use for you, Miss Bonnie."

Bonnie had always been cautious of Tilde. It was hard to believe that, at Bonnie's most vulnerable, Tilde had lied. But withal, there was part of Bonnie that understood that Tilde thought she was doing the best thing for her daughter. How sad it is, though, when a mother's best involved lying, stealing and betraying her own blood.

"I know I'm only sixteen," Natalie said. "But me and Kevin . . . we want to keep Malina. From day one, we wanted to keep her."

"Tilde never tole me that Natalie was in Virginia," Kevin put in. "I showed up to see Natalie one day and she was gone. Tilde say I should forget about her *and* my chile and go'n 'bout my business."

Bonnie could tell by the young man's calloused hands and heavy brogans that he worked the fields. That alone told the whole story. Natalie was college-bound, and as far as Tilde was concerned, Kevin, a field worker, would simply hold her back.

"We're sorry to get you mixed up in this, Miss Bonnie," Natalie said, "but you know as good as me that if it ain't Tilde's way, then it ain't no way."

"What are you two gon' do?" Bonnie asked.

"We're leaving the Three Sisters," Natalie answered. "Kevin's gonna get a job when we get to where we goin'."

"What 'bout your schoolin'?" Bonnie asked.

"I'll go to school, after Malina's a little bigger." Natalie handed the baby to Kevin and buttoned her top. "They say I'm smart. I doubt that Malina'll take that away."

"Look to me like you need to rest a while," Ruby-Pearl said.

"Why don't you and Kevin have dinner with me," Bonnie suggested. "We'll set down and talk . . . you can even spend the night."

"Thank you, Miss Bonnie," Natalie said. "But I'm sho' that Tilde'll be lookin' fo' me soon enough. If you'll jes' get Malina's things, we'll be on our way."

"On yo' way where?" Ruby-Pearl asked.

"No disrespect, ma'am," Natalie said, "but when Tilde ask where we run to, you can say that you honestly don't know."

Ruby-Pearl put her arm around the girl's shoulder. Bonnie brought the baby's bag out and gave it to Natalie. "You sho' you don't wanna stay and ha' something to eat?"

"Thank you, ma'am, but no." Natalie hugged Bonnie. "I 'preciate all you done," she said.

Bonnie was worried for the girl but she also understood that Natalie and her new family needed to make their own decisions, their own way. Bonnie gave her the last twelve dollars in her purse. Ruby-Pearl gave her eight. Bonnie suddenly thought about Tilde and how angry she would be. Pine would surely ask more questions about the Sisterhood. But somehow Bonnie felt good about what she had just done. Maybe Natalie wouldn't be a scholar . . . she might not get to school at all. But the girl would get to love and raise her own child. And Tilde or no, it was her God-given right.

SIXTEEN

The wash had been drenched by the rain and dried again in the summer air. Now dark clouds hovered above the day and threatened to open up and saturate the clothes again. Bonnie knew she should take them down from the line but she couldn't muster the energy. Malina was gone only a day and the child's absence seemed to magnify the emptiness in the house.

A strong wind made the kitchen curtains rise and the back door squeak on its hinges. Bonnie peered at her laundry basket beside the door, but turned back to the morning paper. She thought about preparing breakfast but hated the idea of cooking just for one. She suddenly wondered if Naz was having breakfast right now. Did he sit with Lucinda and her daughter and eat like a family? Did Lucinda make him grits and eggs for breakfast or short ribs of beef for dinner with those tiny carrots that he liked? Bonnie pounded the kitchen table with her fist, angry for letting her mind drift there. Her man had been gone almost two months now and surely the loneliness should be letting up. Was Naz hurting as bad as she? Was he missing her as much as she missed him? Maybe he was. According to Horace, Naz had attended only one of the Brethren meetings but not any of the hunting or fishing trips. Melancholy and sadness, she thought. They were the only things that could make Naz Wilder forgo his outings.

Thunder rolled in from the woods. Bonnie wearily took her laundry basket out to the line and began plucking clothespins from over a white sheet. She snapped the sheet straight then folded it. It felt cool against her body. Bonnie pulled down a pale green tablecloth and the wind lifted it straight up toward the sky. The warm breeze felt good. There was something comforting about a gray day. Maybe because it seemed the world had slowed down a bit. And Bonnie needed the time to try and catch up. She moved to where the line had doubled around a spruce and jumped at the sight of a boy sitting just feet away. His eyes were closed and his head tilted up, allowing a curtain to skim across his face. He was about seven or eight and his dark body appeared stark against the pale linens.

"Hey there," Bonnie called.

The boy bolted to his feet. He peered nervously across the lawn, then back at Bonnie.

"Where you come from?" Bonnie asked, holding the top of the clothesline with one hand.

He didn't answer.

"What's yo' name, boy?"

"Noah," he said.

"You lost, Noah?"

"I ain't lost." His legs, scarred from old mosquito bites, looked like two brown twigs under baggy pants cut off at the thighs.

"Been pickin' blackberries in the woods?" she asked.

The child stayed focused on his feet.

"Ain't gonna talk to me, huh?" she asked. "Okay, I'll jes' talk to myself, then." The boy watched as Bonnie folded the sheets. Every once in a while Lola Flocker's kids would wander this way to pick berries in the bramble, but this boy looked too young to be one of them. Bonnie set her basket beside the boy as she piled her folded sheets in. "You know who Noah was?" she asked.

The child looked up. "My daddy," he whispered.

Bonnie smiled. "He wadn't the first." She pulled a pillowcase from the line. "Yo' mama ever tell you 'bout Noah in the bible?" she asked.

"My mama dead," he said. "But she most prob'ly tole me when I was little."

"When you was little?" She chuckled.

"Hey, boy!" a deep voice suddenly called.

Noah took off running across the back lawn. Bonnie pulled down the last sheet and could see a barrel-chested man lumbering across the grass. His hair, receding from his forehead, was matted in the back. He wore a blue flannel work shirt with the sleeves cuffed to the top of his arms. Denim jeans were caked with mud at the hem. He bowed his head respectfully when he approached Bonnie.

"How do, ma'am," he said.

"Sir," Bonnie replied.

"I'm lookin' fo' a woman . . . name is Wilder," he said.

Bonnie looked at the man cautiously. "That would be me."

"Okay," he said nervously. "Didn't know if I come to the right place. I saw that big ole brick house a few miles back. Didn't 'spect no woman lived there, though. Ain't had no womanly touches."

"I see."

"Name is Noah Bailey Sr., ma'am," he said. "This my son, Noah Bailey Jr."

"I met Mr. Man here," Bonnie said.

Senior Bailey's face was as tight and tan as a bulldog's.

"Well..." he stuttered. "My son... Noah is his name..."

Bonnie knew Noah Bailey Sr.'s type. Much like many men in the Three Sisters, he was barely educated, proud and hard-working.

"Would you like to come up on the porch and set down?" Bonnie asked.

He looked at the gray morning sky. "'Bout to come up a bad cloud," he said. Then he nodded. "Yes, ma'am, I believe that be best."

Noah Sr. carried Bonnie's laundry basket to the porch. His son ran ahead and took a seat on the top step.

"Can I get you some sweet tea?" she asked.

"Yes'm," the boy cut in.

"Noah," the man barked. "You keep yo' mouth shut, you hear me, boy?"

"Yes, sir," the boy answered.

"If I might make a suggestion," Bonnie said. "S'pose I take Junior in the house and get him a drink. Then we could talk."

The father thought for a moment. "Yes'm," he finally responded. "That be okay."

The boy's eyes opened like two searchlights when they entered the house. Bonnie watched as he took in the jars on the counter filled with flour and cornmeal, as well as the daisy-shaped magnets that dotted the refrigerator door. Bonnie pulled out a kitchen chair.

"You wanna eat something?" she asked.

He looked out toward his dad. "What you got?" he whispered.

"Got some peanut butter," she whispered back.

"Got any ham?"

Bonnie pulled her head back, surprised by his nerve. "How 'bout turkey?" she asked.

"Okay," he said.

From the refrigerator she removed the foil-wrapped carcass, cut several pieces and set them between two slices of brown bread. Noah's skinny legs wagged under the table as he leaned on his elbow and watched. Bonnie had forgotten how easy older children were. Unlike adults, she didn't feel the need to keep up a conversation. And unlike babies, her attention didn't have to be on them the whole time. She set the sandwich before him, along with a glass of cold milk. He dug in like a grown man.

"How old are you, Noah?"

"Seven," he replied.

"Big boy."

He kept on eating.

"Ain't from the Three Sisters, are ya?"

"Ma'am?"

"Ain't from 'round here?"

"We drove a long, long, long way," he replied.

"I see. And how come you aren't in school?"

"Sometimes I go to school," he said after chewing, "and sometimes I gotta pick peaches with my daddy." He suddenly looked at Bonnie with concern. "You best go talk to him, miss," he said. "He gits powerful mad when he got to wait."

"Is that right?"

"Yes'm."

"Well," Bonnie said, "I best be on my way, then."

Bonnie filled a glass with sweet tea. She took it outside and handed it to Mr. Bailey. "Thought you mighta changed yo' mind."

"Thank you, ma'am," he said, taking a gulp. He wiped his mouth with his fingertips. "My boy . . ." he started. "His mama died of rheumatic fever when he was four."

"Sorry to hear that."

"Been me and him ever since." He swirled the ice cubes in the glass. "I ain't no mama," he said. "And that's what the boy need."

Bonnie was beginning to see that some men, like Noah Bailey . . . like Naz . . . were almost afraid of children. It didn't matter if they were boys or girls. But other men were good with children. They could allow that softness it took to care for them and still be men.

"I hear you find homes for children," he said.

"Heard from who?"

"A young gal I know that used to set fo' Noah. I thought . . . maybe you could take him."

Mr. Bailey avoided Bonnie's eyes. She could feel his guilt. Still, she couldn't help but wonder how, after seven years, a man or a woman could part with their child. Then again, after receiving nine children so far, Bonnie realized that she was trying to answer for women (and now a man) through her own perceptions, her own life experience. The fact was that Bonnie had never been poor, never felt hopeless—and more, she had never been a mother.

"Haven't had no chile as old as Noah," Bonnie admitted.

"He ain't no trouble."

"It ain't that."

"Got him a fresh mouth sometimes," he said apologetically, "but I tightens that up right quick and he be jes' fine."

Bonnie worked to keep a courteous expression on her face.

"Fact is," the father went on, "I run outta patience with the boy. Ain't his fault, though. I work at that Baynard Orchard mo' than fo'teen hours a day . . ."

"Up near Columbia?"

"Yes'm," he said. "That's where we from. I comes home at night and, I swear fo' Jesus—"

"Don't swear," Bonnie said.

"Sorry, ma'am. Just that, well . . . I loses tolerance with the child. Sometime I yell at him when he don't deserve it. Sometime I go upside his head when he ain't done nothin' but breathed too hard. Noah don't need that."

"No, sir."

The father stretched his leg out to reach into the pocket of his blue jeans. He pulled out a crumpled envelope and handed it to Bonnie. "Ain't much," he said

"Mr. Bailey—"

"My boy should ha' mo'. Should ha' a place with a mama, a backyard and . . ." He looked around. "A place like this."

"How does the boy feel 'bout this?"

"I done left 'im with so many folks over the years, I 'spect he be glad to settle in one place. Noah cry 'cause he wanna go to school every day. And he dern well should! He don't need my anger. And I shouldn't be givin' him down the road 'bout things that don't concern him." Noah Bailey leaned closer to Bonnie. "The boy is a-scared a me."

"Every boy is a-scared a they daddy."

"No, ma'am," he said. "I mean . . . he *really* a-scared."

Part of Bonnie didn't want to hear the man's admission. But another part of her knew that this was why Noah Bailey was sitting across from her. This was why the child seemed so jittery.

"Coupla months ago," he explained, "I got to whuppin' on him bad. I broke two ribs and put 'im in the hospital."

"Dear, dear," Bonnie whispered.

"Wadn't the first time I lost myself like that." The man's brown eyes glinted with shame. "I ain't proud of what I did," he said. "But I ain't no mama. Ain't got that . . . that patience and kindness he need. Can you help me, ma'am?" he asked.

Bonnie looked through the screen and could see just the side of the boy, clacking his heel nervously against the chair as he ate. She thought about the children at the county home. Would it be as hard for her to find a home for Noah, an older child, as it was for Edie-Grace? Bonnie considered the families on the Sisterhood's list. They had all specified *babies,* one even going as far as requesting a girl instead of a boy. Bonnie had never turned a child away, but she had doubts as to whether she could find a home for Noah.

"You do understand," Bonnie started, "that if I find a place for Noah, you might not see him again."

"Long as he be happy," the father answered. "And safe."

Bonnie handed him back the envelope. "I cain't take yo' money, Mr. Bailey," she said. "That be against the law. But I'll try my best. Ain't never placed no big child befo'. But I'll do what I can."

He slipped the envelope back into his pocket. "How 'bout I . . . mow yo' lawn, paint yo' porch or—"

"I thank you kindly," Bonnie said. "But that might not be best."

"I understand," he said. "Noah!" he called out.

The father stood up when his son came to the kitchen door. The boy stepped outside, his upper lip lined with milk.

"I need to get on," said Mr. Bailey.

"You comin' back?" the boy asked.

"Don't think so," the father answered.

The boy's face remained expressionless. "Bye," he said.

Noah Senior stuffed his hands in his back pockets. "Miss Bonnie here, she gon' find you a mama . . . somebody good."

"Would that be okay with you, Noah?" Bonnie asked.

"Yes'm," was all the boy replied.

"You need to mind yo'self, you hear?" his father said.

"Yes, sir."

The father walked down the steps, then came back and embraced his son, landing two loud claps on the boy's back. He nodded his thanks to Bonnie. Then he left.

Noah perched on his knees in the kitchen chair. He leaned on the table and watched as Bonnie dashed vanilla extract into the bowl. The brown liquid swirled in the yellow cake batter, then settled in the center of the bowl. "Tutti Frutti" played on a small radio that sat on the counter. Noah's head moved up and down to the beat as Bonnie whipped the spoon around and around.

"This gon' be a good one," she said. "I can tell by the aroma."

"What's aroma?"

"It's what things smell like."

"I like cake aroma," he decided. "I like cookie aroma too and fried chicken aroma... don't like no hog aroma, though."

"I believe it's only called aroma when something smell good," she explained.

Noah looked confused. "What you call hog aroma, then?"

Bonnie thought for a moment. "Call it nasty," she replied.

Noah covered his mouth with his hand when he laughed. She noticed that he seemed to censor his emotions, never laughing too hard or talking too loud. The first day, the boy was so quiet that it was hard to tell a child was in the house. The second day, he had begun to loosen up and would answer Bonnie with more than one word. And now, on this third day, it seemed that Noah was finally getting comfortable. He talked more and he especially liked to ask questions... lots of questions.

"You got a mama?" he asked.

"She died when I was just a little girl."

"Like my mama?"

"I guess so . . . yes." Bonnie spooned the batter into two tin cake pans lined with waxed paper.

"What 'bout yo' daddy?" he asked. "Where yo' daddy at?"

"He passed away too," Bonnie replied. "But I was a grown woman when he died."

Noah's eyes sparked with curiousity. "So . . . you ain't got no mama and you ain't got no daddy—"

"I *don't have,*" she corrected. "Not *ain't got.*"

"And you don't have no kids," he went on.

"I told you once before that the Lord didn't bless me like that, sweetie."

"Why He ain't bless you? You do somethin' bad?"

"Sometimes women cain't have babies. Sometimes men cain't make babies. Don't mean they bad."

"So you ain't got—don't have no mama," the boy went on, "and no daddy and no kids neither." Bonnie could see his little face bunched up in thought. "That mean me and you is both orphans."

Bonnie had never heard her life laid out so simply and so sadly. "I guess we are, sugar."

"Bonnie," Thora yelled from the porch. Noah's eyes shot toward the kitchen door. Bonnie hadn't had a visitor in the two days that he'd been here. "Where you at, Bonnie?" she called.

"Kitchen!"

"Least you finally got yo' front door open," she called as she walked through the living room. "Need to get some air up in here! And, Lord, but is that the radio I hear? Mean you finally comin' back to the world? I thought we could go into town, 'cause I need to buy—" Thora stopped at the kitchen door. "Hello, lil' boy," she said. Noah didn't answer. He stared at Thora and she stared right back. "Who is this?" she asked.

"Noah," Bonnie said.

"And who is Noah?"

"A boy," Noah said.

"I can see that, Mr. Smarty Pants!"

"Who are you?" Noah asked.

Thora stood over the child with her hands on her hips. "I am Thora Dean."

Bonnie laughed. "Girl, you say that like you the president of these United States."

"Well, I ain't use to no chile askin' me who I am." She squinted at Noah. "This another'n of our foundlings?"

"We'll talk about it later, sweetheart," Bonnie said.

"Hmm," Thora said, eyeing the boy. "Ain't as tiny as the other babies."

"I ain't no baby," Noah defended. "I'm a boy."

"You a boy that ain't gon' make it to a man if you keep talkin' to me like that," Thora warned.

"Noah," Bonnie said, "don't speak to Miss Thora that way. Go'n in the back and wash the batter off yo' face, baby."

"Yes'm," he said, hurrying away.

"Fresh thing," Thora yelled. She waited until the boy was out of sight, then looked to Bonnie for answers.

"His daddy left him."

"A daddy this time," Thora said, setting her purse on the counter. "Why?"

"Why do anybody leave they chile?"

Thora plopped in the kitchen chair. "So, who is the boy's daddy? What he look like?"

Thora used her pinky to dip into the batter bowl while Bonnie told her about how Noah had arrived.

"Well, I must say that you look better than you did a couple of days ago," Thora said. "Sound better too. And, thank goodness, 'cause I was gettin' worried. Ruby-Pearl come by my house and told me about Natalie and her baby—"

"Ruby-Pearl come by *your* house?"

"We's both concerned about you, Bonnie! That much we have in common. Anyway, I thought I should leave you to yo'-self fo' a few days. That's why I ain't come by lately." She looked toward the back room when the water went on. "Also, I been dealing wit' Horace and his mama again."

It was good hearing about others' problems. Thora Dean had a knack for centering Bonnie and bringing her back to level ground.

"The woman had another stroke."

"Sorry."

"Horace sister," Thora prattled on, "they calls her Bitsy, you know . . . but I 'clare, the woman is big as this here table. Well, Bitsy don't know her ass from her elbow. So me and Horace got to go to Huntsville again, make sure his mama take the right medicine, make sho' she rest, make sho' she got something to eat."

"If I didn't know any better, Thora Dean," Bonnie said, "I would swear that you were actually worried 'bout Horace mama."

"Me?" she said defensively. "Worried 'bout Mama Dean? Puh-lease!"

"Mmm-hmm."

"It's jes' that when Horace mama is sick, *Horace* is sick. Then he make *me* sick!"

Bonnie chuckled. She had to wonder why Thora found it so hard to admit that she cared.

Thora grabbed the dishrag and wiped the flour from Bonnie's table. They heard the water turn off in the back bedroom. "You call the Sisterhood 'bout this boy?"

"Not yet."

"Keep him, Bonnie."

Bonnie looked at her old friend like she had lost her mind.

"I can see why you wouldn't keep Tilde's grand. I understand that, but . . ."

"I couldn't do that to the boy," Bonnie claimed. "First, he ain't had no mama, then he come to a house with no daddy. Anyway," she whispered to Thora, "if I took *any* chile, it would be a baby."

"You so fulla shit, Bonnie Wilder," she said.

"What?"

Thora placed both hands on top of the table. Her nails looked like ten pearls. "The onliest reason you ain't thought 'bout keeping this boy," she said, "is 'cause you waitin' on Naz to come back."

"That ain't true."

"Look, I didn't come here to argue with you, though you need *somebody* to set you straight. I come here to get you outta the house." Thora hooked her purse onto her forearm. Noah walked back in. "But obviously you got *other* things to do." She looked at Noah with pursed lips. "Hey, kid," she said. "You take care of my friend, you hear me?"

"Yes."

"Yes, what?" Thora demanded.

"Yes, Miss . . . Nora," he said.

"Thora! Thora Dean is my name. Fresh-mouth lil' monkey."

Bonnie followed her to the door. "Ruby-Pearl told me about the birthday party that she fixin' to have for Wynn," Thora said. "Say she invited all the Sisterhood ladies and they kids and grandkids and such. Ain't that gon' be fun!"

"I expect to see you there."

"You gon' bring *yo'* chile," Thora teased.

"He ain't my chile," Bonnie whispered.

Noah came outside and stood behind her on the porch.

"Boy is lookin' right comfortable here," Thora said, "and so are you. Bye-bye, baby."

Ruby-Pearl's front yard was decorated with blue and white balloons and a thin silver banner across the top of the porch that read "Happy Birthday." She had taped four red cutout letters that spelled Wynn's name.

Most of the grown guests sat in a half-dozen folding chairs that Ruby-Pearl had set up on the porch. Three snack tables held plates with potato chips, pretzels, deviled eggs and fried chicken wings. Delphine was trying to lead a game of giant step in the yard, a hopeless effort. Most of the kids were too young and were bolting out of line to run through the yard instead.

"Noah," Delphine yelled, "git them kids outta Ruby-Pearl's roses. The thorns'll tear they legs up."

Ruby-Pearl's yard looked different than it did a year ago. Then, the front doors were locked and the porch was bare. The whole area was quiet and dead. Now, red and pink tulips sprung up in flower beds on either side of the house and the porch was littered with colorful plastic balls and trucks. Ruby-Pearl drifted in and out of the house to fill the snack bowls, the Kool-Aid pitcher, and to keep watch over the chicken wings still frying on the stove. She wore shorts and a tank top on this pretty summer day—such a difference from the belted dress and the scarf that once covered her face.

"Delphine," Ruby-Pearl called before she stepped into the house. "We fixin' to sing 'Happy Birthday,' so start roundin' up the kids."

For Bonnie it was more than Wynn's party. It was *her* anniversary. About a year ago, Wynn's mama had shown up at her door and dropped the child in her arms. About a year ago, her life had changed.

Delphine gathered up her own six-year-old, Eleanor, and

Olive's four-year-old boy, Damon, and brought them back to the circle of children playing just beneath the porch. Noah shuttled Miss Idella's two grandchildren, Lula and Henry, plus Jenna Dixon's little girl, Rachel.

"Noah is a big help, ain't he?" Miss Idella asked.

"He clean his room," Bonnie said proudly, "wash dishes and even try to mow the grass."

"A lil' man already," said Olive.

The ladies of the Sisterhood had found out about Noah one at a time, for Bonnie never officially called them. Thora had told Miss Idella, and Ruby-Pearl had mentioned the boy to Olive, who told Delphine. They all thought Noah was a perfect child for Bonnie, so no one even attempted to look at the list. They knew that the longer Noah stayed, the more he filled Bonnie's heart.

"He's the sweetest boy," Bonnie said. She watched Noah yanking Miss Idella's fighting grandchildren apart. "Still a lil' on the nervous side. But he miss his daddy. Sometime he wake up at night callin' the man's name."

Miss Idella said, "I guess that's one of the things 'bout havin' an older chile. They got recollections."

"And it's sad that the boy had such a tough time," Bonnie said. She tapped her knee with the fly swatter. "But he's well trained. That boy get right up from bed and make breakfast fo' us both."

"Shut up!" Ruby-Pearl said.

"Ain't fit to eat," Bonnie laughed. "But, bless his soul, he do try." Every once in a while, Noah would glance at the porch just to make sure Bonnie was still there. "I gets the feeling that he has spent too much time alone."

"You say his father worked all hours," Olive put in. "Noah had to be his own mama and daddy."

"Always try to get him to talk 'bout Noah Sr., but he won't," Bonnie said. "Must be tough. Lovin' someone and hatin' him all at the same time."

Miss Idella bit into a chicken wing. "You gon' keep him?"

Olive fanned herself with a magazine, Thora swatted flies away from the punch bowl and Miss Idella wiped her mouth with a napkin while they waited for Bonnie's answer. She wanted Naz to come back, and she still missed her husband desperately, but she hadn't heard a word from the man since he left. Then too, after only one week, she couldn't imagine being without the boy. "I think I will keep him," she replied. At that very moment Bonnie fully gave Noah her commitment and her heart. Thora leaned over and hugged Bonnie as the women applauded. Noah and the other children looked at the adults as if they were having a party of their own.

"We're right here to help you, Bonnie, girl," Olive said.

"A boy can never have too many mamas," Miss Idella chimed in.

Just then, Ruby-Pearl emerged from the house with a three-layer chocolate birthday cake.

"Come on, babies," she called to the kids.

Wynn sat on the porch in the "birthday chair" but screamed out when the other children ran in from the yard. Olive and Delphine got them settled around the cake. Bonnie draped her arms around Noah. She felt proud, not only of him, but of herself. This party, this day, was a testament to something that she had done right . . . something she had done from her heart. For the first time in months, her tears weren't for Naz or for a broken heart but for a job well done.

Ruby-Pearl had just lit the first candle when Pine's car stopped in front of the house. He got out and stood at the bottom of the steps for a moment, witnessing the festive occasion. Most times the ladies tensed up when Pine came around, but today the celebratory mood continued as if God Himself had sanctioned this gathering.

"Hey there, Pine," Miss Idella called.

"You come jes' in time fo' cake and ice cream," Ruby-Pearl said.

"Cain't stay fo' cake." Pine stood at the bottom of the steps.

"Oh, loosen up, man," Thora said. "Miss Idella made the cake, and you know that Miss Idella got a way with a chocolate cake."

"Bonnie," he said. "I need to talk to you."

There was something about the way Pine was standing, something about the tone of his voice, his grave expression and the way he shifted the brim of his cap that suggested that something was wrong. The women must've sensed something too, for Delphine shuttled the children into the house to eat their cake. Noah stood inside the screen door.

"Maybe we should speak privately," Pine said.

"It's okay," Bonnie said. "These are my sisters."

Pine nodded. "Tilde come to me . . ." he started.

"Again?" Thora said. "That woman always tryin' to fill yo' mind wit'—"

"She say," Pine went on, "that you . . . helped Natalie run away. Say you helped her and her boyfriend—"

"I ain't *help* nobody," Bonnie said defensively. "The girl came to me lookin' fo' her chile. It was *her* chile."

"You give her money?" Pine asked.

Bonnie gripped the side of her skirt. "I give her twelve dollars."

"And I gave her eight," Ruby-Pearl put in.

Pine shut his eyes.

Ruby-Pearl asked, "What in the world is this about?"

"They been lookin' for Natalie for the past two weeks... Tilde and Cal. Tilde say she called you and you denied knowing where—"

"I *don't* know where she is," Bonnie snapped.

"Well, that boyfriend," Pine went on, "that Kevin Price... the one is the father of Natalie's chile... he finally called Tilde and say that they were in Charlotte."

"Well, there you are, then," Bonnie said dismissively.

"He said that Natalie was real sick. So sick that he had to call a doctor." Pine shifted his hat in his hands. "Natalie died at the hospital."

The women's smug expressions faded. Even Thora went quiet. The afternoon that Natalie came by sped through Bonnie's head like the movie reel rewinding in the cinema house. She knew the girl was just recovering from a difficult delivery, so did Ruby-Pearl, but neither had done anything to stop her. And Bonnie could've stopped her. She could've *insisted* the girl sit down and rest herself. She could've called a doctor. She could've called Tilde, she could've called Pine.

"You don't know what you doin' here, Bonita."

Bonnie sat on the step and lowered her face into her hands.

"This is too much... it's too damn much!"

Thora put her arms around her friend. "I know what you thinkin'," she whispered. "And this ain't yo' fault."

"Bonnie Wilder and Jesus Christ!"

Bonnie tried to stand but her legs gave out and she fell back onto the step.

"I told you to end this thing," Pine said. "I even looked the other way when I believed you would. But Tilde went to the sheriff and told him everything. Now he say I got to round up as many of yo' kids as I can find and take 'em on over to the county home."

"That's crazy," Thora yelled. "You know that ain't right, Pine!"

Miss Idella and Delphine remained quiet. They looked terrified.

"I'm sorry, Ruby-Pearl," he said.

"You mean . . . Wynn?" she cried.

He nodded.

Bonnie couldn't face Miss Idella, Olive, Delphine and especially not Ruby-Pearl, sobbing. *"Like you tryin' to play God."* But more, she couldn't look at Pine when he cuffed her. Then he placed Bonnie, a frightened Noah and a screaming Wynn in his patrol car and took them all away.

PART V

SEVENTEEN

Canaan Creek, 1985

Somehow Tally knew that they were watching him. So he leaned close to the pretty young woman in her postal uniform and the two laughed up a storm. He handed her Bonnie's mail and the girl nearly dropped it. Tally quickly put his large hands under hers to assure that it wouldn't hit the ground.

"I'll be," Bonnie said, looking from the window.

"What?" Thora called from the kitchen. She sat at the table clipping coupons from the morning paper.

"Tally," she said. "He got some woman-mailman out there."

Thora hurried through the house and stood behind Bonnie at the window. It had been more than a week since their date. Ever since, Tally had left the mail outside in the box rather than bringing it directly into the house. This morning, though, his smile was as bright as summer sky, his walk spry and confident. The young woman beside him, her hair in dozens of tiny braids, followed on Tally's heels. Her regulation white knee-socks made her look even younger than she probably was.

"Women ain't s'posed to be carryin' no big ole bag like

that," Thora said, eyeing the girl. "Mail*men* is what they called. Them bags tilt yo' womb . . . gi' you that arth-u-ritis, sho' nuff."

"Pretty lil' thing," Bonnie said.

"She alright," Thora said. "If you go fo' that type."

"Mo'nin', ladies," Tally hollered through the front screen door.

Thora hurried back to the kitchen. She flipped through the newspaper when he came in followed by Bonnie and his new apprentice.

"Morn'in', Thora," Tally said.

"Tally," she returned, without looking up.

"And who is this pretty young lady?" Bonnie asked, trying to cut the tension.

"Inez, ma'am."

"She my new student," Tally beamed. "I'm teachin' her my route."

Thora peered up from the paper.

"Why you teachin' folks yo' route?" asked Bonnie. "You goin' somewhere?"

"Not in the next year or so," he replied. "But Mackie, he the big man at the main post office in Charleston, he wanna start trainin' mo' folks for the Three Sisters. So he sends 'em to me."

"I've been sent to the best," Inez put in. Thora rolled her eyes.

"Don't think I ever seen a lady-mailman befo'," Bonnie said.

"That's 'cause there ain't s'posed to be none," Thora muttered.

The girl looked at Thora curiously.

She finally closed the morning paper. "So why's a pretty gal like you wanna do a man's work?" Thora asked.

"Isn't a man's work anymore, ma'am," she replied.

"Need to get with the times, Thora," Tally defended. "Got a woman that work for the Canaan Creek Tool and Dye. I 'clare, she drive a big ole semi all the way 'cross the state. And she even smaller than Inez here."

"You from these parts?" Bonnie asked.

"I'm from Pennsylvania," she answered. "But my husband was born here in South Carolina."

Bonnie could see Thora's body relax at the word "husband."

"I 'spect Canaan Creek must be a lot different from Pennsylvania," Bonnie said.

"Oh yes." She smiled.

"Ain't she pretty, Bonnie?" Tally said.

"She certainly is that."

"And smart too," Tally went on. Thora sucked her teeth at the old man fawning. But Bonnie could clearly see that Tally's compliments were meant more for Thora's sake. "Inez here is a college gal," Tally boasted. "Went to a big school in Pennsylvania. What's that you call it, Inez?"

"Penn State," she answered.

"There you go," he said.

"So, why a smart college gal deliverin' the mail?" Thora persisted.

"Check yo'self, Thora Dean," Tally put in.

"It's okay, Tally," Inez replied. She seemed poised and polished and well able to handle herself. "After I left school," she explained, "my husband wanted to come back south. You know, find his roots."

"Lotta folks doin' that these days," Tally said.

"We've lived in New York City for the last four years and—"

"New York City," Bonnie gasped. "Glory be, I cain't imagine what that would be like." Bonnie set both hands flat across her chest. "That big ole place," she said. "Scare the fool outta me jes' thinkin' 'bout it."

"People are people," Inez replied. "Just that some talk a little faster than others."

Thora examined Inez cautiously.

"Go'n, Inez, and gi' the ladies they mail," Tally said. "That's what a mailwoman s'posed to do."

Inez quickly separated the letters into two piles and handed one to Thora and one to Bonnie.

"You did that very well," Thora said sarcastically.

Tally's eyes lingered on Thora. When she didn't return his gaze, he said, "Let's get goin', Inez. Still got to git to Manstone."

"No breakfast this mo'nin', Tally?" Bonnie asked, following him out to the porch. Thora stood just outside the screen door.

"I'm cuttin' down," he said, patting his stomach. "Got to try to keep fit."

Inez picked up her mail sack from the bottom step.

"Best be careful with that bag, young woman," Thora said.

"See you next time, Bonnie," Tally said. Inez settled in the truck. Tally was just about to step in.

"Tally Benford?" Thora called. She stood on the top step with her arms folded. "They's got that . . . *Back to the Future* movie playin' in town," she said. "You seen it?"

His eyes narrowed. "No . . ."

"I'm gon' ask you again," she said. "You seen it?"

"Absolutely no!"

Bonnie and Inez looked puzzled by the conversation.

"I ain't seen it neither," she said. An awkward pause followed. Then she sighed deeply. "Okay," she said, "I'll go with you on Friday."

Tally scratched his head. Bonnie could see him thinking. "I'll let you know tomorrow," he said.

"You'll let me know right *now,*" she snapped.

"Well," he said, rubbing the back of his neck. "You gon' behave yo'self, Thora Dean?"

Bonnie could see her old friend struggling. But the fact was, once again Thora Dean had faced her ghosts. She stood here in the cloudless morning with her tail between her legs.

"Yes," she replied.

Tally fiddled with his mailbag unnecessarily. "Friday, you say?"

"Pick me up at seven."

"How 'bout six?"

"How 'bout seven!"

"Seven," he said.

"Fine," she said. Then she went in the house.

Tally gave Bonnie a quick wink. "A bright young woman," he said to Bonnie in a loud whisper. "It's the oldest trick in the book."

EIGHTEEN

Canaan Creek, 1958

Bits and pieces about the Sisterhood were revealed the very next day in a tiny blurb in the *Canaan Chronicle.* The heading read, *"Local Woman Arrested for Illegal Adoptions."* By the time Bonnie was released, everyone in town knew about her one-night stay in the Canaan County jail.

She sat quietly in the backseat of Horace and Thora's car while Horace drove. Horace hadn't uttered a single word since his wife had paid two hundred and thirty dollars of *his* money to get Bonnie out. But as usual, Thora more than made up for the lack of conversation.

"People been calling my house all mo'nin'," she prattled. "Mrs. Reverend Duncan, Jenna Dixon, Kitty Wooten . . . even one of the damn Bell sisters," Thora said, glaring at her husband. "Cain't believe that a Bell had the nerve to call my house . . . even if it was to ask about you, Bonnie." Horace never took his eyes off the road. "And you cain't imagine how many people are callin' you a real live hero!"

The word "hero" sounded strange to Bonnie. In fact, she

felt like she was walking around in someone else's life... like some character from a movie. Pine was an actor—maybe Brock Peters—when he led her into the stony room with two cells, a desk, a few folding chairs and what looked like a ticket window. Bonnie realized that this was the same office that she had come to with Naz for his hunting license. She recalled that the room had been warm and flooded with sunlight. But last night, the place was dim and cool. The male guard on duty, a white man named Mr. Jamison, was nearly seventy years old and wore a dark blue uniform. He had fingerprinted Bonnie by pressing her thumb onto a black inkpad and then blotting it into a small box reserved for the prints of cold criminals. Bonnie felt numb the whole time, even when Mr. Jamison had taken her picture. But oddly, while this humiliation took place, she could smell fish frying somewhere in the back of the jailhouse. This scent—this aroma—snapped her out of the distant place and made the room feel human and real. The warm and homey smell of toasted cornmeal was like when Naz would return home from a fishing trip and she would fry up his catch.

Mr. Jamison then placed her in a cell with two other women. The younger woman, Dolly King, had been arrested for holding a shotgun on her neighbor, and the other, about Bonnie's age, Precious Wilson, had stabbed her husband's mistress. Interestingly, Bonnie could relate to them both.

Mr. Jamison turned on a small TV set and angled it so the women could watch *The Ann Sothern Show.* Then the old man fed them hot fried grouper on white bread with stewed okra.

Bonnie could honestly say that her night in prison wasn't all so bad... until the lights went out. She lay on the small cot looking up at a piece of the bright moon through a high window. She thought about Natalie and cried at the idea that the girl just wanted to be a mama. She considered Ruby-Pearl and couldn't imagine the pain that the woman must be feeling, having lost yet another child. And what of Wynn? He had been separated from the only mama he ever really knew. Because of Bonnie, the child was surely frightened, surrounded by strangers. Then there was Noah. Bonnie had buried her face in the white sheets when she thought about her boy. She couldn't rid her mind of an image of him sitting on the steps of the county home waiting for her to come. But with all the people she had hurt still plaguing her, the thought that saddened Bonnie the most was how much she longed for her husband.

"Bonnie," Thora said, turning to look in the backseat of the car, "I know that you puttin' all this on yo'self. Right?"

Thora knew her well.

"Jes' you remember, though," Thora said, wagging her finger, "that if anybody is to blame over Natalie's death, it's her own mama. Tilde made that gal run out and find her baby. So you stop blamin' yo'self!"

Bonnie looked out of the window at acres of brown and barren farmland.

"I got somethin' to say," Horace put in. "Y'all might not wanna hear this, but I feel the same way Naz do. Like y'all ain't had no right to be foolin' with them children. Now, I ain't blamin' Bonnie fo' that gal's death or nuthin', but a bunch of church ladies shouldn't ha' no say 'bout who gets a baby and why."

Thora suddenly slapped Horace in the back of his head. Bonnie jumped from the loud clap against his bare skin. Horace raised his hand to return the blow but quickly pulled back.

"Don't you talk to Bonnie that way!" Thora spat. "She feel bad enough as it is wit'out yo' big-ass mouth!"

"Thora," Bonnie whispered.

"One a these days, I'm gon' lose myself, woman," Horace

shouted, "and I'm gon' slap you right back. Then you be hurtin', sho' nuff! Hurtin' bad!"

Everything was spinning out of control. Bonnie couldn't get a grip on her life. When Horace drove through the gate on Blackberry Corner, he and Thora were still squabbling.

"I ain't gon' talk to you 'bout this no mo'," Thora said, gathering her purse. "Bonnie needs me now and I'm gon' spend a night."

"Spend a night?!" Horace said. "Woman, you got a home!"

"I'm jes' fine," Bonnie cut in. "You go 'n with yo' husband."

"I ain't studyin' no Horace Dean," Thora said, sliding out of the car.

"I need some time to think," Bonnie insisted. "Some time alone."

"You ain't jes' sayin' that?"

"No, honey."

"Come on, git back in the car," Horace called.

Thora gave Bonnie a hug. "I'm gon' check on you tomorrow."

"I know you will."

"Crazy people gon' be callin' you," Thora warned. "So don't you even answer the phone."

"I won't."

"In fact, I'm gon' call Ruth on the party line," Thora said, sliding back into the car. "I'm gon' tell her not to put no calls over to Blackberry Corner . . . 'cept fo' me, that is."

"Thank you, honey."

Before they left, Thora called out, "Stop all them contrary thoughts, Bonnie. Jes' remember, it wasn't yo' fault, girl!"

The house was deafeningly quiet. And, though smack in the middle of August, it seemed more drafty than ever. Bonnie thought she had cried all she could when Naz had left. And now, three months after the fact, the tears flowed just as heavily. She walked out back and looked toward the woods. If Naz came home right now, not only would Bonnie accept his apology but she would beg his forgiveness for not accepting it sooner. She heard the phone ring, but decided to take Thora's advice and let it be. She needed to walk off the pain. Bonnie paced below the back porch, her arms folded across her chest, then started through the overgrown grass. The wind whipping through her hair felt good. She stood at the edge of the woods. The blackberries were in full bloom. She suddenly wondered if the berries would even return next season. Since Naz wasn't around to prune them she feared that the blackberries were gone for good.

"Bonnie," a voice called from the house. Ruby-Pearl was standing by the back porch. Here was a confrontation that she'd hoped not to have so soon. Bonnie knew she couldn't avoid it. She also knew that she deserved any and all of Ruby-Pearl's anger and disappointment. Bonnie made haste across the backyard.

Ruby-Pearl was wearing her Sunday clothes. A peach-colored dress was banded with a patent-leather belt. Her gray hat was brightened with tiny white flowers. "You okay, sweetie?" Ruby-Pearl asked.

"Am *I* okay?"

"Thora Dean told me that she was bringing you home today." Ruby-Pearl sat on the top step. Bonnie sat beside her. For a moment, all that could be heard was the distant sound of wind in the woods.

Bonnie fingered the pleats in her dress. "Ruby-Pearl," she started, "I didn't want you to have to feel this kinda pain again."

"I ain't made a glass!"

Bonnie was stunned. "I thought you would be angry."

"Bad things happen," she said. "Sometimes more than once. I decided to take my own advice," Ruby-Pearl went on. "I refuse to sit there with the onions and potatoes. I didn't listen to my mama the first time, but I sho' as shootin' am gon' listen this time. And I'm gon' somehow, someway, get my baby back."

"That's wonderful, Ruby-Pearl."

"Yes. But the question is . . . what *you* gon' do?"

Bonnie folded her hands in her lap. "They charged me with illegal adoption."

"And?"

"Did you jes' hear what I said?"

"Pine had to get you fo' somethin'. We all knew that. They didn't like all that baby business and they had to get you with somethin'. The sheriff jes' mad 'cause they can't find none of them babies."

"Except Wynn . . ."

"And Noah." Ruby-Pearl shook her head. "Ain't it funny that the two people caught up in this thing was the two kids that *we* took?"

"And Natalie."

"No, honey. That there is on her mama . . . not you and not me. Tilde is runnin' 'round screamin' and blamin' everybody under the sun. But she's in a lotta pain right now. She's angry, Bonnie. But I think that even she know . . . deep down inside . . . that it was her *own* doin' that harmed her chile."

"What about Wynn?" Bonnie asked. "Have you seen him?"

"Twice since they took him. I went by the county home both yesterday and today. Fo' fact, I jes' come from my visit."

Bonnie shut her eyes.

"Edie-Grace say that 'cause I'm a single lady, it's gon' be hard to adopt him. But I'm gon' keep goin' 'til they kick my butt out or 'til they let me take my baby home."

"And you will."

"She also said that I might be able to have Wynn as a foster child." Ruby-Pearl sighed anxiously. "I'll take him whatever way I can git him . . . and maybe after a while, I'll find me a husband."

Bonnie reached out and took Ruby-Pearl's hand. "You sound like you got a plan, dear."

"If I talk strong, I'll feel strong." Ruby-Pearl unhooked her belt. She let out a breath like she had been holding it the entire time. "I don't know how Thora Dean do it. Don't know how she wear these kinda dresses every day. And the shoes . . . ooooh-weee," she said, massaging the back of her leg. Ruby-Pearl didn't look up when she said, "I seen Noah at the county home."

Bonnie knew that the conversation would come to this. Somehow she didn't want to hear it. She felt guilty having given up.

"How is he?"

"They say he don't talk much. But he asked me when you were comin'."

"If you cain't get Wynn, then you know I cain't get Noah. Not only am I a single lady, but a single lady that been to jail."

"Oh, please," Ruby-Pearl said. "Ain't like you public enemy number one."

"Prob'ly best if I stay outta the chile's life altogether."

"Don't do it, Bonnie. Don't set in that stew. 'Cause if you set a week, you'll set a month. A month turn into a year . . ."

"I hear what you sayin'." Bonnie stood up on the porch.

"Go see the boy," Ruby-Pearl said. "If you ain't gon' fight fo' him, then you need to tell him good-bye. At least his daddy had the decency to do that."

"I'll see him."

"Why don't I believe you?"

Bonnie walked to the front door.

"How 'bout we go to the diner?" Ruby-Pearl asked. "Polly got smothered chicken tonight. Come on, honey, just you and me?"

"Not today," Bonnie said.

"Tomorrow, then. We'll go to the movies too."

"Maybe," Bonnie said. Though she knew she wouldn't. Bonnie didn't want to talk with anyone or see a soul. She didn't want to be jolted back to good sense or told how she should be feeling. Bonnie wanted everyone to stay away. She wanted to be left alone to sit with the onions and the potatoes.

After rapping on the locked screen for over ten minutes, Miss Idella had finally set a pot of stewed oxtails on the porch and left. Olive tucked a foil-wrapped lemon cake inside Bonnie's old newspaper and moved on. And before driving off, Delphine had yelled something about how much they all loved Bonnie.

A week since her arrest, Bonnie had kept herself apart from everyone, including the Sisterhood. The curtains remained drawn and the blinds shut. She had even locked her doors to Thora and Ruby-Pearl. Bonnie wouldn't even consider going into town to shop, for fear of running into folks. Some were calling her a hero, but the town was equally filled with others who thought that what she had done was wrong, a sin. Even Bonnie realized that her isolation, especially from her friends, was only making her sink deeper into the blues but she couldn't seem to change things. And each thought of Noah, Wynn or Natalie just buried her deeper in guilt and regret.

A quick rapping sounded on the door. Then came Thora's angry voice, "Open the damn do', Bonnie! You hear me?" Thora paused. "This the last time I'm comin' out here." Thora had said this for three days, but still she returned. "Horace and I are leaving for Huntsville this weekend. Honey, I need to see you and talk to you!"

Bonnie sat in front of the TV with the sound off. She knew

her friends were worried. She knew she was being selfish. And she also knew that it was all she could do to get up in the morning.

"Look, honey," Thora said, "I know you sad. But lockin' yo'self away ain't gon' help a bit!" She paused. "Come on, open the door! Damn it to hell!" Bonnie couldn't blame Thora for being furious, but she just didn't have the energy to hear another uplifting speech about "brighter days." "You robbin' my nerves, Bonnie Wilder! I swear, fo' God!" The woman pounded then stopped. "You go'n, then, you stubborn lil' thing! Go'n, set 'round and feel sorry fo' yo'self and see if I care!" Thora's footsteps clunked down the steps then faded.

Bonnie knew that if she let Thora in, the woman would stay and talk all day. Talk about Noah, talk about Natalie... talk about everything that she couldn't face right now. Bonnie simply wanted quiet. Quiet was nice, quiet was comforting. She rose listlessly from the sofa and turned to go into the kitchen, then jumped sky high to find Thora Dean standing right in her face.

"Girl, I'm sick of yo' mess!" Thora said.

"How in the world you get in here?"

"I crawled through that damn dog door. Tore my stockings, scraped my knee and Godfrey licked me all in my face. I must *really* love you, Bonnie." Thora eyed her from head to toe. "And look at you! Look like death on a spoon!"

"That's why I ain't let you in," Bonnie said, walking to the kitchen.

Thora followed. "You ain't the pityin' kind. So I'm wonderin' why you been layin' 'round this house and takin' the blame fo' things you ain't even done."

"Thora," Bonnie said as she made a pot of coffee, "please go home."

"You gon' hear me, first!" Thora stood at the counter right beside Bonnie. "I'm jes' as hurt by Natalie's death as anybody..."

Bonnie busied herself in the immaculate kitchen.

"And it's a shame," Thora went on. "But, honey, you ain't had a dime in that dollar."

Bonnie refused to look at Thora but she heard her words. "If I hadn't started with these babies, Natalie might still—"

"If you hadn't started these babies there might be a few mo' children floatin' in the creek... I mean, who the hell knows!"

Bonnie stood at the stove watching the coffeepot.

"And as far as Naz is concerned..." Thora went on.

Bonnie felt her head begin to throb.

"*He ain't comin' back!* You hear me? Yo' man is gone. So you need to forget him."

"Stop it," Bonnie spat.

"*You* stop it! He's gone! Naz got him another woman now."

Bonnie broke down in tears. Hearing the words out loud, point blank, was like hearing them for the first time.

"I'm sorry, but the man been gone three whole months... that's like a lifetime... and you ain't heard word one from him," Thora said. "Everybody know you done been to jail, but did yo' own husband come? No! And he didn't come 'cause he with his other woman!"

Bonnie suddenly flung a stack of pots off the stove.

"That's right," Thora said, standing beside her. "You go 'n and git mad. 'Cause that what you s'pose to do."

Bonnie threw the can of coffee grinds across the room.

"That's right, baby," Thora said.

"Oh, God!" Bonnie screamed.

"Wait jes' a second now," Thora said. "Cain't be cussin' God. You go'n and cuss that lyin' cheatin' skunk of a husband—"

"Nothin'!" Bonnie screamed. "Absolutely nothin'," Bonnie

yelled as loud as she could, then pushed the jars of rice and flour off of the counter. The clay bins burst open when they hit the floor. "Not a goddamned thing," Bonnie cried.

"Nothin' what, baby?"

"I ain't done nothin'," she cried, "nothin' but love that man!" She pitched her coffee cup and saucer onto the floor.

"Oh, honey, I know."

"And s'pose it wasn't me, Thora? After all this time, s'pose it wasn't even me?"

"Wasn't you what?"

"S'pose it was *Naz* that couldn't have no children! And I waited and stayed with that man and I coulda been married to someone else and had all these children—all these gals and boys—but I stayed wit' him! And now it's too late."

Thora led Bonnie around the debris to the kitchen table. Bonnie's feet were covered in flour.

"It ain't too late if that's what you really want," Thora said. "But you got to get on wit' things . . . you have a house to keep, friends to see—and mo' important, you already got a chile that needs you."

"No," Bonnie said, her head staring down into her lap.

"That boy loves you. Ruby-Pearl say he waits for you to come ever' day."

"That's why I cain't see him." Bonnie could feel her body rocking. "I'll never get Noah. So why I wanna get his hopes up that I'm gon' be his mama. I cain't do that to him. I rather let him stay there with Edie-Grace and have some kinda stable life."

"Stable?" Thora said. She pulled back on the harshness in her voice. "At least talk to him, Bonnie. The last thing he saw was you, his mama, being put in the sheriff's car. Lord knows what that chile must be thinking."

"I cain't see him. I jes' cain't."

Thora shook her head. "I thought you was different," she said. "Some folks saw yo' picture in the paper, read 'bout what you did with the babies and thought you was somethin' good. But takin' in them kids was easy! Putting a baby in the arms of women who wanted nothin' more . . . that was easy! But talkin' to Noah, a chile old enough to know the difference between what's fair and what ain't . . . well, that takes some doin'. And you know what, Bonnie? You ain't nuthin' but a coward!"

Thora rose and turned off the flame under the coffeepot. Bonnie sat quietly as Thora swept up the flour, the rice, and left.

Three days later, Bonnie went to the county home. She finally got the nerve, the courage, to go and get her boy. But Edie-Grace said Noah had been placed with a couple two days ago and the adoption was expected to go through. Noah was gone. Two days ago. Thora had told her to get off her ass and see her boy. But she didn't go then. Like the other bad decisions in her life, Bonnie had no one to blame but herself.

Bonnie bolted up in bed. She had been dreaming of a dozen crying babies left at her doorstep. The crying sounded so real that Bonnie thought she still heard it. There couldn't be a baby. After all that had happened, no women would have the nerve to come to Blackberry Corner. Bonnie pulled on her robe and ran down the hall. Usually, Godfrey alerted her to strangers, but the dog was nowhere to be found. She walked to the back porch. Naz sat in the rocking chair, the dog happily at his feet. He had a baby cradled in his arms. The image was so surreal on this early morning that Bonnie stood without saying a word.

"I went to a reunion game," he said. "Down there in Baton Rouge." He rocked the infant. "All the fellas were there." His face brightened. "C. C. Baker, Lyle Porter, Jet Jackson . . . all them guys. Dewey's there too. He told me to tell you hey."

Naz seemed bone tired, exactly as she felt herself. Like a person who had completely lost their way.

Without looking away from the infant, he said, "I miss you, Bonnie. Miss you bad."

She shut her eyes. God, but his voice sounded so good.

"And I didn't mean to hurt you," he said. "I swear fo' Jesus. But this baby . . . she the onliest reason I stayed."

"I don't understand," she said. "Who is this chile? Why are you here?"

"This is Lucinda's chile," he said.

"*Your* chile?"

He nodded wearily.

"You somethin' else, Naz Wilder." He was like a strange creature she couldn't quite fathom. "After three months you come back to my house with another woman's chile?" She clasped her hands to stop the pain. "Lordy, ha' mercy!"

"When I found out she was pregnant, I couldn't leave . . . I couldn't walk away."

"You stayed with the mama 'cause she was pregnant?"

"Yes."

"But why the hell are you settin' on *my* porch with Lucinda's chile?"

"She's gon'," he said.

"Where?"

Naz shrugged. "I gave her money to go. Say she always wanted to go north, so I made her leave."

"Why?"

He seemed to take an eternity before he answered. "The

reason I stayed wasn't just 'cause she was pregnant. I stayed to get the baby."

Bonnie was incredulous. "So you planned on bringing Lucinda's chile for *me* to raise?"

"I didn't exactly *plan* it, Bonnie."

"What the hell is it, then?" she said, losing patience.

"She knew I didn't want no baby wit' her. She knew it from day one."

"I heard enough."

"She knew I'd leave if she had a baby."

"What are you sayin', man?" she yelled. "Why are you tellin' me this?"

Bonnie had seen Naz in awful pain over the years. Emotional pain of having to give up his career. The physical pain of his knee, which sometimes swelled to three times its size at just the threat of rain. But this was the first time she had ever seen her husband cry. Bonnie looked at the splintered porch floor. She knew that if she looked at Naz, she might go to him.

"This . . . ain't the first time Lucinda been pregnant," he whispered.

"She got three other kids," Bonnie said. "And by *three* other daddies, I might add."

"I mean, this ain't the first time she been pregnant . . . by me."

"That's enough."

"I told her I didn't want no babies by her. I say my wife, my *real* wife, is the onliest one could carry my seed." Bonnie could hardly listen. "Then she called me one day, a few months later. I thought it was 'cause she wanted me to come see the child. But she told me that she had lost the baby and wanted me back."

"And of course you went runnin'."

"It wasn't until she got pregnant this second time that . . ."—Naz rocked the child—". . . I found out what had happened."

"Maybe you better sort this thing out with Lucinda," Bonnie said, rising. "'Cause I cain't hear no mo'."

"I stayed with her while she was pregnant this time because I thought she might hurt the chile."

Bonnie opened the screen door to go in.

"It was Lucinda," he said, his voice wavering. "It was Lucinda who left the baby in the creek."

"What?"

"That was *my* baby, Bonnie. And she told me like it was nothin'," Naz went on. "Say we ain't had to keep this one neither. Then the woman threw some ham hocks in a pot of water, cut up the greens and rinsed the rice. She was ready to jes' go'n with our lives—like a baby ain't never happened. That's why I stayed. I had to make sure this chile was safe."

Evil, Bonnie thought. Evil and crazy! Lucinda Justice, a grown woman, had killed her baby just to keep a man. And she might've killed this one too.

"Can you understand now?" he asked. "Please tell me that you understand why I had to stay."

Bonnie released the screen door and went to her husband. He held the sleeping baby and leaned against her stomach as she stood above him. Bonnie couldn't help but reach out and stroke his head.

"I want to spend my life wit' you," he said. "*You,* Bonnie Wilder. My *only* wife." He looked up at her. "And I want you to raise this chile."

He offered the baby to Bonnie.

This was Naz's child. Here was the perfect opportunity to get her husband back and have a baby too. But could she ever trust Naz again? He had lied to her for four years. And then there was Lucinda herself. Would she come around? And if she did, would Bonnie call the cops on a killer? Bonnie wondered if that evil part of Lucinda—that part that could take a human life—could it dwell inside a child? No, she thought. Babies were innocent. Bonnie believed it before and she certainly believed it now.

"It's mo'nin'," Naz said, rising from the rocker. "Brand-new day. And I promise, Bonnie, I'm gon' do ever'thing different." Again, he held out the baby for Bonnie.

"I'm sorry, but I cain't take her."

"Come on, now..."

"Ever'time I look at her I'm gon' see Lucinda Justice. You and Lucinda together. But worse... much worse... I'm gon' see a woman that drowned her own baby."

"What you sayin'?"

Bonnie suddenly hoped that she wasn't making another bad decision. After all, this was surely her last chance to have a child. "I'm saying, Naz Wilder," she went on, "that you need to take your daughter and get the hell outta my life."

"Bonnie," he said. "I know you need me and I need you too. This baby sho'ly need the both of us."

Bonnie walked into the house and locked the door behind her. She could hear his feet pace the porch, stopping every so often like he was trying to figure this out. She could hear his heavy breaths full of frustration, sorrow and confusion. Then came silence. After a while, she heard Naz's truck start. Pebbles popped against the bottom as he pulled around through the front yard and out the gate. She ran to the window and watched her husband leave. Seconds later she heard a baby crying from the back porch.

That's when Bonnie called the Sisters.

NINETEEN

Thora Dean came to say good-bye. For the last month she had been telling Bonnie that she needed to go back to Huntsville to tend to Horace's mama, but Bonnie had been so caught up in her own tragedy, she hadn't really heard her. It wasn't until Thora arrived on Blackberry Corner wearing her traveling hat, a little red pill box, that Bonnie realized that her best friend would soon be gone for Lord knew how long.

"I shouldn't be leavin' you alone like this," she said. "But if I don't go, Horace gon' ha' kittens."

"Got tend to family affairs," Bonnie said, though deep down inside she felt that Thora Dean had held her together since Naz left. "Besides, I got Ruby-Pearl, Delphine, Miss Idella . . ."

"But they ain't me! They don't tell you things like I do. They don't keep yo' lil' bony ass in line."

Horace rolled his eyes.

"You can call me from Huntsville," Bonnie said, "You can tell me 'bout myself long distance."

"I'm not kiddin' here," Thora said. "I feel bad 'bout leavin' you now."

"I'll be fine," Bonnie said.

Horace removed his cap and looked at Bonnie sheepishly. "I never did get a chance to tell you, Bonnie," he started, "but... I hate the way things wound up... with Naz, I mean."

"You and them damn Brethren," Thora argued. "Look the other way and keep each other's dirty secrets."

Horace said, "If I'da known that things were gon' turn out like they did..."

"You shoulda opened yo' mouth 'bout that Lucinda woman," Thora said bluntly.

"Maybe I better go'n back to the car," Horace mumbled.

"Need to take yo' ass *somewhere,*" Thora yelled.

Horace kissed Bonnie on the forehead. "We'll see you," he said. "I'll bring yo' gal back to you as soon as I can."

"You mean befo' I kill yo' mama?"

Horace waved his hat as he walked off.

"I cain't stay too long, sugar," Thora said.

"I know."

Thora took Bonnie's hand. "You my very best friend," she said. "Fo' fact, you the only somebody that can put up wit' me."

"You know the Sisters come to know you. Even Ruby-Pearl come to like you."

"She come to *tolerate* me. I hate to admit," Thora said, "but them women, they ain't such a bad bunch."

"They a good bunch," Bonnie added.

"I mean... they was ready to go to jail along with you if they had to. And that's sayin' a lot for a bunch of lil' ole country ladies."

Bonnie chuckled. "I never knew where this would all wind up. And although life ain't been the greatest fo' me, when I think 'bout it, things coulda been much worse."

"*That's* my Bonnie," Thora declared. "Now you startin' to sound like yo'self again. After the sheriff decided not to take yo' case no fu'ther," she nodded her head affirmatively. "I knew all this mess was finally over. But you got to keep yo' promise to Pine and Sheriff Tucker," Thora warned.

"Ain't no mo' babies comin' this way."

"Bonnie! You know I was with you all the way with helpin' these children," Thora said, "but they ain't gon' let you off so easy next time."

Horace beeped the horn.

"I got to get on, honey," Thora said, hugging Bonnie again. She held her for a while, then kissed her, leaving a print of two red lips on her cheek. "We'll be back in a few weeks," she said. "By that time Mama Dean should be back on her feet . . . or dead, one!"

"Thora!"

Thora started toward the car. She stopped in the path. "Lordy," she called out. "I almost forgot that I bought you a lil' present. Lemme get it from the car."

"You ain't had to get me no present," Bonnie called.

"You nice enough to take care of my house whilst I'm gone. Had to get you a lil' somethin'."

Thora trotted to the car and opened the back door.

Bonnie suddenly froze. For a moment she thought her eyes had deceived her at the sight of her boy Noah. He was in a little black Sunday suit with a shirt and tie. And his brown face looked so shiny and clean. So many feelings hit Bonnie, all at once. Guilt, for having left him so long, wonder at how the boy felt about her now, but mostly joy that Noah was standing just feet away, safe.

"Noah?" Bonnie said, keeping a distance. "My, my . . . look at you. How you doin', sugar?"

"Fine," he answered.

Noah seemed unsure of what he should say or do. And Bonnie felt just as nervous. She had often thought about how she'd explain things to the boy. Her explanation never seemed right.

"You didn't come," he said.

She walked to the boy and knelt in front of him, praying that she could find the words to explain.

"Why didn't you come?"

"You ever get scared 'bout things, Noah?" she asked.

"Yes'm."

"Me too. And that's how I was feelin' 'bout you. Only I didn't do the right thing. I shoulda come to you as soon as I could and talked to you and told you how I felt."

He pressed his hands in the pockets of his jacket. "Miss Ruby-Pearl, she came ever' day. I waited fo' you."

"I know," she said. "At first I got myself in a little trouble. And I thought that I prob'ly couldn't be yo' mama."

"You coulda come," he insisted.

"Yes." Bonnie reached out and stroked his face. "But when a woman that ain't yo' real mama comes along, she got to prove that she gon' be the best there is . . ."

"But you a good mama."

"You think so?"

"Yes'm."

Bonnie wanted to hug the child, but Noah seemed so hesitant and afraid. He was the same little boy that his daddy had left. Fearful, neglected, untrusting. And she couldn't blame him, only now the neglect and mistrust was her own doing. Bonnie decided to tread lightly with the boy. She would talk to him as long as it took, and she would let him ask as many questions as he needed to in order to understand. Just as she was about to stand up, Noah grabbed her around the neck and pressed his cheek against hers. He squeezed as tight as he could, and must've thought that if she couldn't move, she couldn't leave. But Bonnie never would.

"You didn't think I was gonna leave you by yo'self, did you?" Thora asked. "Girl, you do crazy things when you stay alone too long."

Suddenly, it didn't matter to Bonnie that Naz was gone or that she had spent a night in jail.

"Horace thought I had lost my mind," Thora said. "I told him I wanted to adopt a chile. He say, 'Woman, why cain't we adopt a dog instead?' When I told him that the child would live with you . . . well, that was alright with him."

"This is . . . beyond friendship," Bonnie said, embracing her best friend.

"Jes' means that you owe me. And, don't worry, I'll think of a way fo' you to pay."

Bonnie laughed, "I have no doubt you will." She walked to Horace's car. Noah stayed right on her heels. "You a good man, Horace Dean," she said, kissing him on the forehead. "I don't know how to begin to thank you."

"Jes' take care a that boy," he said. "And if you need a daddy ever' once in a while . . ." Horace pointed to his own chest. "Now, are we finished with all this stuff?" he asked. "Cain't abide too much mush. And come on, woman," he said to his wife, "we need to git gone."

"Hey, boy," Thora said, wagging a finger at Noah, "don'tcha ride that dog's back. And you make sho' Bonnie call me twice a week. Can you do that?"

"Yes'm."

"Good! Now, come gi' Auntie Thora some sugar." Noah raced to her and threw his arms around her. "Doggone it to hell, boy, you fixin' to wrench my neck!" She was about to get in the car but turned back. "See, that's why I ain't got no children," she fussed. "Kids drive me outta my mind." Horace beeped the horn. "Alright, alright, I'm comin'! And that one," she said, pointing to her husband, "he jes' as bad as them damn kids." She got in and waved out of the window until the car was gone.

"You hungry, boy?" Bonnie asked.

"Yes, ma'am," he answered.

"Come on, then. We'll get you something."

"Can we make a cake?"

"Maybe."

"Chocolate?"

"We'll see."

Bonnie held the screen door while the boy cautiously entered. He looked at the foyer and living room like it was his first time here. His shoes squeaked as they skidded across the kitchen floor. Bonnie set out the mixing bowl and spoons while Noah took the butter and eggs from the refrigerator. Clearly, the child was nervous and a bit guarded, but his presence felt so natural to Bonnie. Having him here, even right here in her kitchen, seemed to brighten the whole house. And she needed that light. She knew that this wasn't the home she had prayed for or the life she had planned. Yet her life was perfect and her prayers *had* been answered.

EPILOGUE

Canaan Creek, 1985

Augusta Randall had Naz's nose, his lips, his athletic posture and—strangely—the same long, tapered feet. But the rest of this tall, attractive woman—her red skin, her big bones, her dense Indian cheeks—were pure Lucinda Justice.

"I promised myself that I wouldn't get all sentimental when I saw you," she cried, "but . . . I guess I'm pretty emotional these days."

"*These* days," Joe Randall cut in.

Bonnie had pictured him as tall, lanky and studious-looking. She imagined that he wore little round glasses, always a jacket and tie and an expression filled with deep thought. But Joe Randall was at least a foot shorter than his wife, stocky, with a bald head and an earring. He looked like one of the Buddha statues that Bonnie had seen in the thrift shop in town.

"Girl, you 'bout ready to bust wide open," Thora said. "How long you got left?"

"Can you believe I still have two months?"

"Big as you are," Thora said, clearing the throw pillows so the woman could sit, "seem like you ready to drop any day."

"I checked on the hospitals in the area just in case," Joe said.

"Mary Immaculate is about three miles from here," Thora said, "and as I understand, their maternity is . . ."

Somehow, Bonnie didn't expect to be so struck by Augusta's looks. She knew she'd find Lucinda in the girl, because Lucinda had such distinctive coloring and a strong, craggy structure to her face. But Bonnie was astonished to see how much Augusta looked like Naz. She watched the woman as she spoke of her pregnancy and their life in New Jersey. Augusta tilted her head reflectively, much the same way that Naz did. She used her large hands expressively, just like Naz did. But it was her smile that caused Bonnie's heart to crack—Naz's smile, shy and wholly infectious. At least once a day Bonnie still thought of Naz. Most times it wasn't painful. She often remembered the early days of their marriage, the way her simple life was so fulfilled by his presence. Until she began to long for a child, he had been everything to her. Bonnie never saw Naz again after he had left his baby with her. Shortly after, one of the Brethren, Scooter, had said that Naz moved to Dayton, Ohio, to coach a minor-league baseball team. He had always wanted to do that. He had wanted to leave the Three Sisters and coach just as much as she had wanted a child. Bonnie was glad that they had both gotten what they wanted in life. Then about two years after he left, Bonnie received divorce papers. And with the last tear she would shed for Naz Wilder, she signed them and sent them on their way.

Joseph Randall skimmed the pictures on the mantel: photos of Ruby-Pearl, Bonnie and Thora in their younger days, pictures of Wynn and many more of Noah as children, teenagers and adults.

"Is this your son, Mrs. Wilder?" Joe asked as he picked up a picture of Noah and Bonnie, posing together on the bank of the creek.

"That's my Noah. He live in No'th Carolina now with his wife, Effy, and their two kids."

"Two lil' girls," Thora added. "One name is Desiree and the other'n is . . . what that tiny one's name, Bonnie?"

"Rashida."

"Lord, these young folks and they names!" Thora laughed. "But they's the cutest lil' family. And Noah's a lawyer, you know," Thora added. "He do that there civil rights law. Don't make much money, Lord knows, but Noah always had a big heart—jes' like his mama."

"Noah has been the light of my life," Bonnie said. "And he was one of the children, jes' like you," she said to Augusta.

"One of the abandoned children?" Gussie asked.

"Well, we never call 'em that," Bonnie said. "Like to call 'em our lil' precious gifts . . . but, yes, Noah did come to me that way."

"Did you take one of the children too, Thora?" Joe asked as he continued to scan the pictures.

"Hell, no! I wadn't the mama kind. But, like the other ladies, I helped out where I could."

"How many women were there?" Gussie asked.

"There were six of us ladies. Six in the Sisterhood of Blackberry Corner," Thora said sarcastically. She and Bonnie laughed.

"That's what we like to call ourselves," Bonnie explained. "Jes' this . . . identity thing, you know?"

"Yes, I know," Joe Randall put in. "At the university where I teach, every group has to have a name."

"There was me, Thora and Ruby-Pearl," Bonnie started as she counted on her fingers. " 'Bout ten years ago, Ruby-Pearl moved back up no'th to Hencil after her son, Wynn, got married."

"That was some weddin', wasn't it, Bonnie?" Thora asked.

"Prettiest I ever seen."

"And it didn't even matter," Thora prattled on, "that Wynn's fiancée—name is Cara, she a teacher jes' like y'all—was six months pregnant when she walked down the aisle and—"

"Then there was Delphine and Olive," Bonnie interrupted, "Olive still live in the Three Sisters—"

"Ain't right in the head no mo'," Thora said. "Got that Alzheimer's and once she wound up wadin' in the creek at three in the mo'nin'."

"Delphine passed some years ago," Bonnie went on, "and Miss Idella..."

"Bless her *old* heart," Thora said. "That woman lived 'til she was ninety-two."

Joe pointed to a picture at the back of the mantel. "Is that... honey, that's Naz Wilder!"

"You *know* who Naz Wilder is, young man?" Thora asked.

"Joe's quite a baseball historian," Gussie explained. "Especially when it comes to Negro League players."

He turned to Bonnie. "Naz Wilder played for the Black Crackers."

"That's right," Bonnie said.

"Wait a minute," Joe said. "Naz Wilder... You were *married* to Naz Wilder?"

"Yes," Bonnie said.

"Is he... still alive?" Joe asked.

"Far as I know," Bonnie replied. "We... divorced some years ago."

"Mrs. Wilder," Joe said, "maybe later we can we see a few more of Naz's old pictures?"

Bonnie nodded. "I 'spect we'll get 'round to talking 'bout the League and *'specially* 'bout Naz." Bonnie rose to go into the kitchen. "Maybe I oughta git us some refreshments."

"You sit and visit," Thora said. "I'll go."

Augusta was studying the pictures on the mantel with her husband. "How many babies did you get, Mrs. Wilder?" she asked.

"There were eleven, all together."

"And what number was I?"

Seeing Augusta wasn't as hard as she'd thought it would be. Yes, she was Naz. And she was certainly Lucinda. But Augusta Randall was also a living, breathing person and not the personification of a marriage gone bad. After all, the woman represented her heart's work: a child that had survived a desperate mama and a hopeless situation. It was all so personal, yet Augusta's circumstances were not very different from Wynn's, Noah's, Malina's, Amelia's or any other child's that had come her way. Thora returned with a sandwich platter and a pitcher of sweet tea that Bonnie had made earlier.

"Come set on down, Mama," Thora said to Augusta. "You and Joe both ha' yo'self somethin' to eat."

Over coleslaw and turkey sandwiches, Bonnie and Thora told Augusta Randall the story of her beginnings. At times the girl laughed and at times she wept but she seemed fascinated by every detail, every description and every bit of conversation that Bonnie and Thora could recall. Joe Randall was stunned by the entire story. When the young couple left Blackberry Corner early that evening, Augusta looked exhausted. Exhausted, content and filled with a stronger sense of herself. For Bonnie, the experience of Augusta's visit was like a circle closing. She had finally faced her ghosts just as Thora Dean had always done. Bonnie glanced at her old friend, chuckling at the *Golden Girls* on TV. There was certainly something liberating about speaking your mind, speaking your heart. Bonnie went to the phone. She had promised Noah she'd make reservations to come and visit him in North Carolina before summer's end. He and Thora Dean had been pushing her to take the trip, but Bonnie had always stayed close to home. Now, suddenly, she felt lighter, as if the world was a far bigger place than she had ever imagined. Yes. Bonnie would take the train to North Carolina. Or, better yet, maybe she'd fly.

ACKNOWLEDGMENTS

I am blessed with a wonderful family. And thank you all for staying behind me, come what may! They are: Andrew and Barbara Smith, sister Dina (verry noice!), brother Kenny, sister-in-law Sybil Sunday Smith, Patricia and all the Pattersons. Nieces and nephews Jamar, Liki, Yaro and Ulanda (and lil' Des too!), Ayana, Ralphie and their "Nooka-nooka" (Miss Anaya), Adaeze (my eye is always on you, Daz!), and my namesake, Andrea (Sunday) Smith, Carol and Yashauna and Lisa Corr, my new "cousin" (hugs and prayers). Last but not least, my son, my heart and always my inspiration, Andrew Smith Short.

I also wish to thank the guys and gals at Think Inc, especially Will duPont, Chris Wilson and Mark Sanges. Will and Chris, I'm so grateful for the wonderfully creative environment, each second I'm given to write and the bagels too! Much love to my mentor, Arthur Flowers (still in my thoughts!), Steve Moyer (you're just always there, aren't you?), Kazutoshi Kojima, Gilbert "Tookie" Lewis, James Pelton, Rod Jackman, Mr. Ken Banwart (thanks for protecting my spirit!), Teresa McMillan—the best buddy, even *before* the program, Miss Kathleen Collins (we will be old ladies together!), Danitra Easton (thanks for always tellin' it like it is!) and always and always, Miss Nora Cole, godmother to my son and god-friend to me!

Susan Kamil, my editor, you are the best! I so appreciate your clarity and your strength. Thanks to Noah Eaker, her assistant. I am also greatly appreciative of my agent, Ellen Levine, and all the folk at Trident Media Group. Thank you, Ellen, for keeping me on the path.